William Joseph Roberts

Presents:

Wyld Magick

Fantasy Short Stories of Fae, Witches, and Magical Realms

Three Ravens Publishing
Chickamauga, GA USA

William Joseph Roberts Presents: Wyld Magick by William Joseph Roberts
/Three Ravens Publishing – 1st edition, 2025

Ebook ISBN: 978-1-966507-52-9
Trade Paperback ISBN: 978-1-966507-53-6

Table of Contents

The Raven and the Crow:

The Lady of the Elms

By: Michael K. Falciani

Temuvena wiped green blood from her lips and stumbled forward, knowing to fall here at the edge of the woods was to die.

Weakened from a loss of blood, the Seraph of the Forest was cut off from her magic. The poison that coursed through her veins had neutralized her powers. Instead, she was forced to use her psyche, focusing her attention toward the center of the woodlands, praying to find one of the fae that could come to her aid. She sensed nothing, not a sentient being nearby… other than the black-hearted soul who had betrayed her.

Desperate now, the Lady of the Elms refocused, searching outside her realm for a miracle that might save her life. Her green eyes widened as Temuvena caught the essence of two entities nearby. Her heart sank when she realized they belonged to a pair of humans, *male* humans at that.

There was a sound coming from the trees behind her, and Temuvena sensed her assassin drew near. Knowing she had no other choice, one of the most powerful beings on the planet staggered forward, hoping these humans would not kill her on sight.

Two men, both dressed in the garb of hunters, sat around a campfire an hour after dawn. An iron pot sat in the middle of the fire, its contents bubbling gently. One, the taller of the two, was sitting on a log looking at the other, who was doubled over in pain, heaving his guts onto the forest floor.

"By the gods Kildare, do you have to throw up your breakfast so close to camp?" the first asked, his face turned in a frown. "We have to stay here, you know. The last thing I want is to smell your half-digested food all day."

"Zedaine," the shorter man rasped, panting with exertion. "I'm not really in the…" he paused, retching loudly once more. Once finished, he wiped his mouth with the back of his sleeve, continuing where he had left off. "Mood to listen to your griping. Keep at it and I'll…" he stopped again as his stomach heaved for a third time. Looking miserable, Kildare finished his thought, wiping at his mouth with the back of his sleeve. "Kick you into next week!"

Zedaine shook his head, having little sympathy. "I told you those mushrooms were bad, didn't I?" he quipped. "Autumn skullcaps are rustic yellow in color with spores that turn brown over time."

"They *were* yellow in color," Kildare pointed out. "The spores looked white to me. I thought it was honey fungus."

"Are you really going to argue the point?" Zedaine snapped, shaking his head. He lifted a stick and used it to stir the pot. "You're yakking all over our campsite. I'm *fairly* certain I was right."

"Alright little brother, you've made your point," Kildare offered, with a sickly wave of his hand. "Can't you just leave it alone? How long until your home remedy is finished?"

"It's done," Zedaine snorted, ceasing his stirring. He dipped a metal mug into the brew and filled it, tapping the edge against the pot's side.

"Can I drink it now?" Kildare asked. "We need to be getting on."

"Let it cool a bit," Zedaine answered, putting it on a stone next to Kildare. "I doubt we are going anywhere for a while. Even with my elixir neutralizing the toxins, you are in for a miserable twenty-four hours…"

His voice trailed off as he heard footsteps approach from the west. Zedaine tensed and placed a hand upon the hilt of his sword.

"Who's there?" he barked in challenge, standing from his place on the fallen trunk.

No answer came forth. Rather, a figure appeared from the mists in front of him. Zedaine's eyes widened in surprise. A woman, human-like in appearance, lurched toward him, reaching out for help. The tall hunter could see blood dripping from her mouth. A twist of disheveled hair cascaded behind her where it fell to the small of her back. Atop her head was an intricate circlet of woven grass and leaves.

The woman's strength gave out a half step from Zedaine and the big hunter reflexively reached out and caught her, keeping the stranger from collapsing to the ground. He noted the pale green of her skin and hair. His eyes widened, knowing with a certainty this was one of the fae.

"Kildare," Zedaine hissed, bringing the woman closer to the fire.

"Who is it?" his brother asked, failing to rise to his feet.

"One from the fae realm," Zedaine guessed, staring down at the woman's ethereal beauty. "Perhaps a dryad… or a nymph?"

"A fae?" Kildare grunted, looking up. "It can't be. We are far from the heart of the forest. It must be a traveler caught in the…"

"Are you really going to question my expertise again?" Zedaine groused. "I am the hunter; you are the warrior."

"What makes you think…"

"She has green skin and hair," Zedaine cut him off. "I'm telling you, she's from the fae realm."

Wincing against the pain in his stomach, Kildare managed to sit up straight. "I'm only telling you what I remember of old Vanni's saying," he explained. "Nymphs and dryads rarely leave their forests—when they do, it is only at night. Look around you. It's early in the morning."

"Water," they heard the woman croak, her voice barely audible.

Both men looked to the prone figure in front of them.

"Kil, pass me your skin," Zedaine ordered, laying the woman gently on the ground.

"I think she's wounded," Kildare remarked, his hand shaking, holding forth his waterskin. "She's clasping her side."

"I can see that," Zedaine replied evenly, taking the skin, placing it to the fae's lips. Carefully, he poured her a mouthful, cradling the creature's head in his lap. She managed to drink it down and opened her eyes.

"Betrayed," she whispered, her eyes unfocused. "By one of my own…" Her body was wracked with a fit of coughing before she lost consciousness. She lay there, her breaths coming in shallow gasps.

"She's delirious," Kildare snapped, grunting in pain. "Take a look at that wound."

"I will," Zedaine said, laying her head upon the ground. Moving next to her, the big hunter saw dark blood staining both sides of the creature's doeskin tunic. "There is a broken arrow protruding from the right torso." He frowned. "There is a bite mark on her left, a big one."

Zedaine frowned. "I don't understand. Neither wound hit anything vital. She'll be in pain, yes, but she's in bad shape, almost as if…"

"She's been poisoned," Kildare said, doubling over as another wave of agony struck. "Look at her: cramping, trouble drawing breath, pale skin, a sheen of sweat."

He looked pointedly at his brother. "Remind you of anyone?"

"Damn, I need to get that arrow out," Zedaine muttered.

"Careful not to nick yourself with it," Kildare warned. "I don't need you keeling over."

Zedaine nodded and glanced down at the woman's face. "This is going to hurt," he said, more to himself than the fae.

"Get on with it," Kildare said. "The longer you wait, the less her chance of survival."

"Here goes," the big hunter grunted. He drew a sharp breath and pushed what was left of the arrow through, out her back. Warm blood flowed as Zedaine saw a serrated arrowhead coated in black pitch stick out from behind her.

"That looks like Nightshade," Kildare said, wincing in pain. "Mixed with a substance I'm not familiar with… pelath root, perhaps."

He looked up at his brother. "She won't have much time." Kildare nodded toward the steaming cup of elixir. "Give it to her, before it is too late."

"Noble of you," Zedaine said, lifting the cup.

The big hunter placed the cup to the woman's lips, pouring it into her mouth one sip at a time.

"Zee," Kildare rasped, his voice carrying a note of concern.

Zedaine did not bother to look at Kildare. His brother's tone told him all he needed to know. Whirling, he looked in the direction the woman had come from.

A shadowy figure stood at the edge of the mist… a drawn bow in its hands.

"Stay down," Zedaine hissed, eyeing his own bow on the other side of the campsite.

The figure released the bowstring, and an arrow tore through the space between them. Zedaine dove to the side, narrowly avoiding the shot. In an instant, he seized his bow and nocked an arrow, preparing to shoot back.

The shadowy figure was gone.

"The arrow is in the bole of the trunk," he heard Kildare choke, his voice pained. The elder sibling was lying next to the woman, his body between her and the figure who had shot the arrow.

"I bet throwing yourself in the way hurt a bit," Zedaine sniffed, eyeing the mists.

"It didn't tickle," Kildare rasped. "Stop wasting your time here. Go after him. Hunt that bastard down."

Zedaine gave his brother a quick look of disbelief. "I need to patch her up," he argued. "Otherwise, she'll bleed to death."

"I'll do it," Kildare replied, raising himself to his knees.

"You? You can barely move."

Kildare eyed his brother pointedly. "You're right, Zedaine. You stay here and I'll chase after the killer. That's a *great* idea. When I die out there, make sure you sit around the campsite and dodge arrows the rest of the day."

A heartbeat of silence passed between them.

"Fair point," Zedaine agreed. "Don't overdo it with the elixir. More is not better. Steady sips over the next four hours should do the trick."

"Yes, mother hen, I know how to administer an antidote." Kildare grumbled, looking with concern at his brother. "Try not to get killed out there. Old Vanni used to say the fae can be… capricious."

"Just take care of yourself," Zedaine replied, setting off into the gloom. "Don't worry about me."

As he ran off, Kildare's eyes became fixed on the arrow still lodged in the bole of the tree trunk. It did not line up with Zedaine or himself. His eyes fell to the creature laying in front of him. "They shot at you, didn't they?" he whispered. "Who, in the name of the gods, are you?"

The woman shifted in pain and Kildare saw a stone the size of his thumb slip from under her tunic, where it hung on a silver chain around her neck.

"A Seraph Stone," he whispered, his eyes widening. Looking to the mists, Kildare saw no sign of his brother. "You are the Seraph of the Forest, the Lady of the Elms," he said softly to himself. His eyes widened. In front of him, close to death, was one of the most formidable creatures in the world. Kildare's heart skipped a beat.

"What kind of creature would attack you in your own realm?" he asked.

In reply, a savage roar sounded from the depths of the wood.

Zedaine considered himself an expert tracker. However, even with his advanced skill, he had trouble locating any sign of his attacker. He had heard a roar to the left when he'd first entered the forest, but that had been a quarter of an hour ago. He'd tracked the sound to an empty glade and found a single paw print. Kneeling over it, Zedaine was stunned at what he saw.

That's a dog's print, he thought. *But damn me, it must be the size of a fully grown bear. What the hell is it?*

Zedaine looked around the glade and saw another print. This time it was the tread of a human-like creature walking next to the giant wolf, leading deeper into the forest.

"Guess I'll find out," he grunted, moving to the next track.

An hour later, he stopped, frustrated with his progress. He was miles deep in the forest and more than a little annoyed. Normally, he'd have caught up to his quarry by now, but not this time. This time, it had eluded him. A few minutes ago, he'd seen the last sign of his prey. A tuft of grass pushed down on the side of a quick flowing stream. Since then, there had been nothing, not a bent limb, or a grain of earth out of place. Rarely had anything eluded him like this.

Zedaine sat down on a lichen covered boulder to consider his alternatives.

"I guess I'll have to go back," he breathed in frustration, listening to the forest around him. It was still, as though it was holding its breath.

"A mistake, you've made," said a tiny voice from behind him.

Zedaine spun around and came face-to-face with a tiny woodland creature no more than a foot tall. Six translucent wings, three on each side, flapped in unison. The rapid movement of the pale violet wings kept the creature hovering several feet off the ground.

"Hello there," the hunter said, trying to keep the surprise from his face. "Who might you be?"

A pair of full lips chittered at him from underneath a swath of dark hair. "Here to send you back, I am," the sprite announced. "But first... how came you to enter the fae realm? Know I must!"

"The fae realm?" Zedaine questioned, looking around at his surroundings. "I was following the tracks and spore of... something—an animal, I believe—with feet like a hound, but as large as a bear. I had no idea that I'd..."

The sprite's eyes widened, and she did a series of flips in front of him. "Chulin, the Grim," the sprite squeaked, hovering in front of him once more. "Passed this way he did. Searching for the Forest Mother, he is!"

"The Forest Mother?" Zedaine asked.

"Aye, faeling, the Mother of the Forest—missing is she."

The sprite cast her gaze behind her, dark eyes narrowing in fear. "They will come, and you will die. Go faeling, think it lucky I found you before the Grim."

Zedaine hesitated, casting his gaze in the same direction the sprite had. "This... Forest Mother... she wouldn't be tall like me...wearing a circlet of leaves and grass woven together like a crown?"

The sprite flew around Zedaine's head, landing on his shoulder, pointing a small, but deadly looking spear at his eye.

"Seen her, you have!" the sprite shouted. "Tell me where she is, you will, else the Circle will hear of this!"

"The Circle?" Zedaine asked, looking confused. "I don't know what you're..."

"What is amiss?" came a voice from the trees above them. Dropping toward them were more than two dozen green-skinned creatures, all but one a female. Most stood a head shorter than Zedaine. Each had a drawn bow and arrow pointed at him, and none of them looked friendly.

"Caina Lilac, get away from him!" ordered the male dryad, his eyes the shade of piercing cerulean.

"The Forest Mother, he's seen," the sprite replied, her tone defiant.

"You will not regain favor like this," a red-headed dryad warned, her voice cool.

"Tell me not what to do, Xeda," the sprite chirped back. "Answer to you, I do not!"

"You *do* answer to me," said the tallest of the dryads, as the leader of the contingent stepped forward, taking Zedaine's breath away. She had a striking countenance, with smoky colored eyes, a curvaceous figure, and a swirl of ivy colored hair.

"Mine he is, Raenen," Caina squawked back, albeit with more decorum.

"*We* will question him," the dryad leader continued. She waved her hand dismissively. "Until then, return to your post."

"Caina found him," the sprite pouted, thrusting her spear toward the speaker. "Caina will uncover the truth!"

"Begone," Raenen ordered, waving her hand in irritation. "This is a matter for the Circle."

Caina fluttered in front of the dryad and sniffed in annoyance. "The absence of our lady does not make you queen."

The sprite circled Zedaine's head once more and fluttered away.

Lowering her bow, Raenen turned to Zedaine, eyeing him closely. "You are lucky, manling," she began. "Few humans ever find the fae realm… fewer still live to tell about it."

"I've found…" he began, before she raised her hand, silencing him with a look.

"Do not speak until spoken too," she said warily. "Follow us. We will uncover the truth of your words."

"What of me?" the male dryad asked, gripping his spear tightly.

"Return to your rounds, Harker," Raenen answered, turning and striding deeper into the forest. "Report back when you discover something of value."

The male sniffed, while the rest of the dryads surrounded Zedaine.

"Did you find any other humans?" Xeda asked, moving close to Harker.

"I saw no one other than this hunter, and that was not until he crossed the stream bordering our lands," the male replied, sounding impressed.

"There is one other human out there, my brother…" Zedaine tried to say, when a look from Harker and Xeda stilled his tongue.

"You heard Raenen," the male said to Zedaine. "Go along, peacefully, mind you. I've no desire to see the Tree Matron upset." He leaned in close and dropped his voice. "Neither do you, if you take my meaning."

Zedaine snorted softly. "Women," he snickered, "they're all the same, no matter what race they…"

"Shut your face, manling," a third female snapped. She had azure eyes, and a streak of white that ran through her hair. "This will be your last warning. Speak again and I'll sew your mouth shut!"

"That's Ferra," Harker noted, turning away from his kin. "She despises humans, more than anyone I've ever known."

Narrowing his eyes, Zedaine did as he was bid, and followed the dryads deeper into the forest.

Kildare had managed to keep his stomach under control while patching up the wounds on the mystical woman as best he could. The side the arrow struck had been easy enough to cleanse, as the serrated arrow tip had missed all the vital organs. He staunched the flow of blood and stitched her flesh together with needle and thread.

The bite marks across the way had been trickier.

While the teeth had not savaged the flesh, there were two rows of piercings that ran across the skin underneath the ribcage—ample evidence of canine teeth. While messy, the wounds had ultimately scabbed over with little loss of blood. The real danger lay with what Kildare could not see. No stranger to battle, Kildare knew infection might set in. Teeth contaminated with the taint of rotting flesh offered a slow death that was often more painful than the initial wound, and no less final.

Fighting against his own cramping stomach, Kildare heated a second pot of water and soaked a clean cloth, wiping the woman's skin clear of blood. Once dried, he smeared honey upon the wounds and covered them with a bandage. Satisfied he'd done what he could for the girl, Kildare lifted a mug full of his brother's elixir and took turns, feeding first his patient, then himself.

He took a deep breath and tried to find a comfortable position in which to sit. His back to the log struck by the arrow, Kildare settled in, waiting for Zedaine to return.

His quiet did not last long.

There was a rustling at the edge of the woods. Out of the corner of his eye, Kildare caught movement among the underbrush.

"Goddammit," the warrior hissed, forcing himself to his feet, lumbering over to his own bow and quiver. A wave of nausea caused him a bout of dizziness and Kildare nearly fell over. Fighting against the need to vomit, Kildare drew an arrow and focused on fitting it to his bowstring.

"Trust Zedaine to pick a campsite next to a magical woodland realm," he muttered, his eyes searching the tree line. "Damn fae—probably grew those mushrooms just to mess with humans on purpose."

He glanced at the figure lying beside the campfire.

"You had better be worth all this trouble," he grumbled, giving the woman a withering look.

Kildare shuffled back to the stump, his eyes fixed on the edge of the forest.

A heartbeat later, he heard a growl coming from the underbrush behind him.

"Son-of-a-bitch!" he hissed, turning, knowing he was too late.

The troupe of dryads led Zedaine through the forest for more than an hour. Along the way, he saw any number of sprites and pixies whisking their way through the tangle of trees and underbrush. Bright colors and tinkling laughter followed with an abundance of curiosity. Birds and insects of a like he had never seen crawled and buzzed past him, as life teemed within the confines of the mystical woods.

The sun was close to its zenith when they entered an ancient grove of oak trees, their boughs and limbs towering above, blocking out much of the sunlight overhead. The noise of the forest faded here. Not an insect buzzed, not a worm crawled. It was as though the grove was protected; an inner sanctum against the forces of the outside world.

Inside the hallowed grounds were nine standing stones, each as tall as Zedaine. They were rough-hewn, as though cut from a rock of a like Zedaine had never seen. The face of each stone was coarse, colored a dusky gray—save for the center at shoulder height. There, carved with great care, was an etching. The big hunter recognized the nearest, a red eye spouting flames, the fae symbol for fire. Across the way, on a second stone, he made out an etching of blue, three waves stacked upon one another, the eld sign for water.

Most would not know the carvings for what they represented, however, Zedaine had trained with a mentor in years past that studied the old ways. As Zedaine's eyes searched his surroundings, he knew this was an ancient grove, steeped in both magic and antiquity.

Inside the circle of standing stones was a placid pool filled with water, still and dark.

"A Seraph Grove," Zedaine murmured, his eyes moving to the other standing stones.

"You know something of the ancients," Raenen said, sounding surprised. "It will not avail you here."

"What is this place?" Zedaine asked, unable to stay quiet any longer.

"This is the heart of the wood—the center of power here in the fae realm," the leader of the dryads answered. She turned to look at him. "It is here that we will discern the truth."

Zedaine returned her look with a shrug. "What truth is that?" he asked.

"Of what has happened to she that rules among us," Raenen replied.

The big hunter gave the dryad a frown. "I already told Caina…"

"Quiet," Ferra barked, her face hard, unforgiving. "Humans spew lies more often than the wind blows… it is what they are best at… that and murdering our kind."

The angry dryad walked up to Zedaine, staring at him, a cold hate in her eyes. "Not this time, *manling*. This time, we will hear the truth before we kill you."

"Peace, Ferra," Raenen said, stepping between them. "I will handle this."

Ferra glanced at the elder dryad, her face turned in a sneer. "Let me kill him," she begged, her voice hungry. "He is a human, how can you possibly…"

"I said, I will handle it," Raenen repeated, tapping at the base of her throat.

Ferra's gaze flicked to Zedaine and back again to her elder. "As you say—but should he be found guilty…"

"He will be yours to dispose of," Raenen promised.

Satisfied, Ferra stepped back, her face hard.

Her attention fully back on Zedaine, Raenen took a woven grass necklace from around her throat. At its base it held a thumb sized emerald fused to ivory white snowstone. Carved around the stone were markings of a like that Zedaine had never seen.

"*Aronath esse noir,*" Raenen whispered, dropping the necklace over Zedaine's head.

The emerald flashed green, and the carvings glowed white. Zedaine felt the necklace tighten around his throat.

"I'm going to ask you a question and I want you to purposely lie," Raenen said. "You need to see what will happen when you do."

"You *want* me to lie?" Zedaine asked.

"Yes."

Zedaine glanced around and saw nothing but the stone-cold faces of his dryad captors.

"Ask your question," he sniffed, knowing he had little choice in the matter.

"What is your name?" Raenen asked.

"Ferra the Goatface, bitch of the woods," Zedaine replied, smirking at the fuming dryad who'd begged to kill him.

Instantly, he felt the cord around his throat tighten, digging into the skin of his neck.

Zedaine tensed and lifted his head, hoping the adjustment would give him more space to breathe.

"That is what will happen every time you tell a lie," Raenen said, her beautiful countenance hardening with anger. "The item around your neck is a Seraph Shard, taken from the stone of our goddess. It is tuned in with the magic of Temuvena's standing stone here in the glade. Each lie you speak will tighten the chord a little bit more until it chokes the life from you. Understand?"

"You could have just told me without the example," Zedaine growled in reply, refusing to put his hand on his throat. He straightened, standing tall amongst his captors. "I am ready. Ask your questions."

Raenen shifted uncomfortably before him, as though bracing herself for the worst. "Our mother, the Lady of the Elms, did you kill her?"

"Of course not," Zedaine answered easily. "We have been working to save her life."

Every dryad eye was focused on the woven thread wrapped around the human's neck.

"That... that cannot be," Ferra gasped, looking angry. "He is lying... he has to be!"

"I'm not lying," Zedaine retorted. "If I were, wouldn't your choker of death be strangling me right now?"

"He... he must be speaking the truth," Xeda put in. "Tell me manling, how did you come to meet the Mother of the Forest?"

Zedaine eyed them all, trying to hold on to his patience. "She came to my brother and I, blooded by several wounds."

"Describe her injuries," Raenen ordered, her eyes intent upon Zedaine.

"Bite marks, the size of a bear, here," the hunter described, pointing to the bottom of his torso above the right hip. "Something bit her, though that was the lesser of the wounds."

"The greater?" Xeda asked.

Zedaine sighed. "An arrow, broken off near the tip. I had to push it through and it was coated with poison, but… it is my belief she will recover, given time."

The emerald stayed dark, a testament to his words.

"She yet lives?" Raenen gaped, her eyes wide.

"Aye," Zedaine nodded. "She was alive when I left her in my brother's care… though she is in a bad way. I would have stayed, but someone shot another arrow at her. I entered your forest looking to hunt down this would-be assassin."

The dryads of the Circle began to mutter among themselves until their discussions boiled over into arguments.

Knowing chaos was about to reign, Raenen shouted above the din.

"We can argue about what happened later," she screamed, her face resolute.

"But, Tree Matron," Xeda protested. "Someone loosed an arrow upon the Forestmother! Who? Save for this… manling and his brother, no other humans were reported in the area."

"Who told you this?" Raenen asked, looking at Xeda.

"Harker," the red-haired dryad answered.

"Harker?" Raenen said thoughtfully. "He was absent this morning, was he not?"

"Aye," Xeda confirmed. "He was out on his nightly rounds until…" her eyes widened. "You don't think…"

"Human," Xeda said, her attention back on Zedaine. "Can you describe the arrow that was loosed at you?"

"My name is Zedaine," he growled in reply. "As for your question," he dipped a hand into a pouch at his side. "I can do better than describe the arrow."

He pulled out the broken shaft that had been lodged inside the Seraph of Life.

"By the Grove," Ferra breathed, her eyes wide.

"That is a Harker shaft," Raenen said, her voice quiet.

"Impossible," Xeda gaped. "I… I have known Harker for more than a century… since his tree was no more than a sapling."

"The proof lies before us," Raenen argued. "A red cedar shaft, fitted with a serrated obsidian arrowhead…it is Harker's arrow in the human's hand."

"My name is Zedaine," the hunter reminded her shortly. "I saw hound prints the size of a bear's as well."

All the dryads glared at Xeda.

"What wolf runs at your mate's side?" Ferra questioned.

"I said hound, not…" Zedaine tried to explain, but Xeda cut him off.

"There… there must be some explanation," the dryad stammered. "Some reason that he would…"

"Enough," Raenen snapped. "There is only one thing to do."

Turning to the other dryads, Raenen issued her orders. "Sisters of the Circle, use our people. Summon the pixies and the fairies. Send word to the sprites and the nymphs. I want every tree, every flower, every root, and leaf searched until he is found. We will not rest until Harker is brought to justice."

"What of the Forest Mother?" Ferra asked.

"You and I will go to her," Raenen answered.

"I can take you," Zedaine offered.

Raenen gave him a contemptuous look.

"*Shikada don faer,*" she whispered.

The necklace on Zedaine's neck loosened, and the dryad stepped forward to remove it.

"Xeda," Raenen snapped, placing the emerald necklace over her head. "Return this… thing from whence he came."

"Tree Matron," Xeda protested. "I wish to join in the search for…"

"*You* are compromised!" Ferra shouted in anger. "Your mate stands accused!"

Silence reigned inside the grove.

"Return the human too where we found him, and await my orders here," Raenen offered. "Until this mess is sorted out and Temuvena has returned to us, *I* am in command."

The Tree Matron looked to the others. "Go… may the light of the Seraph guide your way."

The grove emptied quickly, leaving Zedaine and Xeda alone.

"Come on," Xeda hissed, her words filled with frustration.

"Let me ask you something," Zedaine said, moving next to her. "Are you blatantly stupid?"

"What?" Xeda snarled, her eyes flashing dangerously.

"Something isn't right here," he explained. "Someone knows more than they are letting on. I suspect treason."

Xeda surged forward; until her face was no more than an inch away from Zedaine's. "You talk of treason… what reason would any of my folk have for withholding any information?"

"I don't know," Zedaine admitted, "but I don't live in the fae realm. You do."

Xeda stared at him for a moment longer before skulking away. "Come on," she rasped, her voice defeated. "I have my orders. The sooner you are out of the realm of the fae, the better."

"You know I'm right," Zedaine said, falling in behind her. "Don't let your hatred of me blind you to the truth."

"Shut your mouth, manling," Xeda snarled. "Or I'll drug you and drag your carcass to the edge of the forest."

Zedaine stared at her, knowing he needed to convince Xeda to act before they reached their destination. Exhaling, he moved along behind her, scrambling to think of a way to find the true assassin.

Kildare looked at his current situation with something akin to disgust and utter disbelief. Standing over the Seraph of Nature was the biggest wolf he had ever seen. Roughly the size of a female bear, the wolf eyed the poisoned warrior warily, but did not move to attack.

More than an hour ago, the wolf had bound into the camp and Kildare had prepared to fight it until the bitter end. The wolf had ignored him, looping over, licking the face of the unconscious Seraph and stood its ground. Kildare had only watched for the first hour, waiting to see what the animal would do. Despite its protective stance, the wolf had not been hostile, though it had kept its eyes fixed upon Kildare.

When Kildare had tried to feed the Forest Mother Zedaine's remedy, the wolf had barred his way, its yellow eyes staring at him in malevolence. Three times Kildare had tried. Each time he'd been met with bared teeth and a snarl of warning.

It was frustrating to the taciturn warrior, as the Forest Mother grew ever weaker, while the poison ran unchecked, eating away at her body. Kildare had kept up his own ministrations and was feeling better, though his stomach still rolled with nausea when he moved too quickly.

The Seraph of Life whimpered in agony, the poison in her system close to killing her.

"By the gods, why is it always me stuck in these situations?" Kildare rumbled, taking up the cup of antidote once more. He moved cautiously toward the Forest Mother, his eyes never leaving those of the wolf.

The wolf bared its teeth and gave Kildare a menacing growl.

"By Dourn, you stupid creature," Kildare growled back. "Can't you see we are on the same damn side? I'm trying to save her, you overgrown pooch! I could have shot you at any time with my bow and arrows, yet have not yet done so. Get out of my way or you leave me with no other choice but to kill you, so I can save her!"

Kildare, angry now, moved closer, easing his way inside the reach of the wolf's powerful jaws. "If you bite me for this, I'm going to use your hide for a winter coat," Kildare snapped, gently lifting the woman's head off the ground. He could feel the wolf's hot breath on his neck, salivating with anticipation.

"Give me a few moments and I'll back off," Kildare continued, feeling the hair on the back of his neck rise. Gently, he fed the elixir into her mouth. The Forest Mother drank a mouthful, and then another, visibly relaxing as she did.

Kildare felt a wet nose touch his ear.

"I'm backing off," Kildare said, lifting the cup from her lips. He dared to look up and saw his face reflected back at him inside the yellow of the wolf's eyes.

"Don't you do it," Kildare warned, seeing the wolf tense.

It was too late.

The wolf leapt forward and knocked Kildare on his back, slathering his face with its hot tongue.

"Come on!" Kildare barked, simultaneously trying to keep the contents of the mug from spilling and warding off the loving administrations of the wolf.

"Just because we are friends now, there is no need for this overt display," Kildare barked, finally freeing himself from under the wolf. He wiped away the mountain of saliva now lathered on his face. "You should meet my brother," Kildare said, his sleeve now coated in wolf dribble. "He's the animal-lover between us. By the gods, Zedaine would have you fetching sticks from dawn to—"

A deep-throated roar came from inside the forest, no more than a quarter of a mile away.

"A friend of yours?" Kildare asked, as the wolf turned its head toward the sound. The Seraph's guardian snarled at the woods, and let out a series of deep barks before letting loose a challenging howl.

"I guess not," Kildare muttered, grabbing a hold of his weapons once more.

The wolf turned back toward Kildare as though trying to communicate with its eyes.

"You want to flush him into the open?" Kildare asked. "Run him past me and I'll feather the bastard."

The wolf *woofed* once and lopped off, heading for the woods.

Kildare cast his gaze down upon the Forest Mother and shook his head in disbelief. "You've got me talking to a wolf, you know. He also seems to be in charge of our strategy."

The fae creature did not stir. She lay upon the ground, resting more peacefully than before.

"Don't get up," Kildare whispered sarcastically. "I'll do everything."

He glanced at the stump Zedaine had been sitting on that morning and fought off another wave of nausea. Kildare took in a deep breath as the sickness subsided.

"I'm going to die because of a mushroom," he said bitterly. He looked up into the woods.

"I hope to the gods you are doing better than I am, little brother."

Xeda led them back the way they had come moving at a much greater pace. The sun was almost directly overhead, its warmth coating both Zedaine and the dryad in a thin layer of sweat.

"Here we are," Xeda panted, slightly out of breath. "This is where we first met. You are free to go, manling. May we never meet again."

"A moment, if you will," Zedaine said, his voice freezing Xeda in her tracks. "Please."

Xeda kept her back to Zedaine, her head down. "Why should I?" she asked, her voice harsh. "Humans know only lies and death… I see that now."

"I have not lied to you," Zedaine replied. "Nor are all humans destroyers of nature. Some are, of course, but it is a fool who thinks that an ignorant few represent the good of the many."

"What good have you wrought?" Xeda asked, spinning around. "So, you didn't kill the Seraph of Life… did you expect a reward for doing what is inherently right?"

"I ask for no reward," Zedaine answered, remaining calm. "Only a moment of your time. After that, if you wish to leave, I will not keep you."

Xeda's eyes hardened, and she crossed her arms in front of her. "Speak," she said at last, nearly spitting the word at him.

Zedaine nodded and motioned toward the east. "Not far away lies the Forest Mother. She remains in the care of my brother, Kildare."

"So?"

The big hunter drew a deep breath. "Do you not think it odd Raenen's first priority was to find Harker and bring him to justice?"

Xeda's narrowed her eyes. "Were you not listening? The Tree Matron is going after Temuvena herself. She is the most powerful among us, save the Lady of the Elms. No one is more capable of protecting our queen than Raenen."

Zedaine drew closer to the dryad, his voice soft. "Yet, it wasn't until she was pressed that Raenen offered herself to save Temuvena."

Xeda's inhaled sharply, but hesitated, thinking back to the discussion in the Seraph Grove.

"Ferra," she whispered, her gaze shifting to Zedaine. "She's the one who brought it up." Xeda's eyes grew wider still. "By the grove, she has been working closely with Harker these past few days. Sitting with him, speaking of the evils of men…"

Her voice faded as realization struck. "She sat with him while he was fletching his arrows only yesterday," she gasped. "She could have easily slipped a few into her quiver with no one knowing! By the gods, *Ferra* shot the Forest Mother. She seeks to take her place as warleader of the dryads! She will wage war upon mankind!"

Zedaine frowned. "That is…"

A deep, guttural roar sounded from close by, cutting off his words.

"That is no wolf," Zedaine muttered.

A howl answered the roar from further away.

"Chulin," Xeda said, peering easterly.

"The Grim," Zedaine nodded. "By the sound of it, he's close to my brother's camp."

A loud buzzing came from close by. Bursting from the trees, they saw an agitated sprite fluttering wildly in front of them.

"Saw it I did!" Caina squeaked in her high-pitched voice. "Come, it has!"

Zedaine glance at Xeda who looked confused.

"What are you talking about?" Xeda asked. "What has come?"

Caina's violet wings fluttered rapidly in the air. "A spirit not of this earth," the sprite answered. "Summoned by magic of the blood!"

"Blood magic?" Zedaine questioned, glancing toward Xeda.

"Harker, I saw… close he is!" Caina squeaked, fluttering behind Zedaine.

The dryad's green skin went pale. "It cannot be," she said, looking into the distance.

"East it goes, towards the Lady of the Elms!" the sprite said, thrusting her spear forward.

"Temuvena," Xeda whispered, racing forward.

"Kildare," Zedaine grunted, bolting after her.

Caina hesitated only a moment. "A demon it is," she whispered before flying higher, quickly overtaking the mismatched pair.

Kildare moved himself into a better position, standing unsteadily upon the stump Zedaine had sat upon earlier. With the open surroundings, he wanted to be at the highest vantage point possible to both increase his visibility and maximize the range of his arrows.

It had been only a few minutes since the wolf had left, but to Kildare, it seemed like hours. He felt his legs wobble underneath him and Kildare cursed under his breath.

"Come on, you furry pile of teeth, I can't stand here all day," he muttered. His eyes combed the distance as he turned his head to the side, listening for any sound that might alert him to a foreign presence.

"You are Zedaine's brother," came a voice from behind him.

Kildare turned, nearly leaping out of his skin. Blinking, he saw a dark-skinned male dryad behind him, holding onto a six-foot-long spear tipped with a rare, darksteel blade.

"That's a neat trick," Kildare said in honest admiration. "There's not many that could get the drop on me like that."

"How is she?" the dryad asked, pointed toward the Seraph on the ground.

"Stable," Kildare answered. "I've fed her my brother's elixir and patched her wounds up, the best I could, but…"

A roar echoed from close by, followed immediately by the deep-throated barking of a wolf.

"Chulin," the dryad said, leaning his spear near the fire, readying his bow.

"Is that your… pet?" Kildare asked, turning his attention back to the woods.

"The Grim is my friend," the dryad answered, moving next to Kildare. He knocked an arrow to his bow, and Kildare felt his heart skip a beat.

The dryad held the same serrated spear that had been loosed at the Forest Mother earlier that day.

"Nothing is ever easy, is it?" Kildare murmured to himself, easing one hand toward his knife.

Moments later, Zedaine burst into a clearing and came to a screeching halt.

There, lying on the forest floor, was the Tree Matron, green blood oozing from her chest.

"Raenen!" shouted Xeda, kneeling next to her kin.

"I am alright child," the elder dryad winced, struggling into a sitting position.

"What happened here?" Zedaine asked, his eyes locked on the massive paw prints on the ground.

"It was Ferra and Harker," Raenen said, unable to rise. The skin underneath her tunic was drenched with blood. "He knocked me out and cut my flesh for his dark ritual. That is when I saw him. He summoned a beast, a *Valkir,* from the depths of Iridyes. A canine spirit of earth and flame."

"A hound of hell," Zedaine muttered, wishing to be off.

"Yes," Raenen nodded. "It will feast upon the flesh of anyone it finds, including that of the Forest Mother."

"Why?" Xeda asked. "Why would he do such a thing?"

The Tree Matron shook her head sadly. "The Seraph of Life will not make war upon humanity, despite how their societies encroach upon our own. Harker and Ferra believe what they are doing is best for our people. If the Lady of the Elms will not set the fae against the uprising of mankind, they will."

"That is folly," Zedaine said, unlimbering his bow. "Most humans would side with the fae if they knew what effect their encroachment had upon your society. An attack on mankind would unite them. Instead of a few hundred farmers, the fae would have to deal with hundreds of thousands of soldiers. What chance would your people have? They would be wiped out inside a generation."

"We've no time for this," Xeda said, climbing to her feet. "Stay here Raenen. We will bring Ferra in and put an end to this idiocy."

"Close they are," came Caina's voice from ahead of them. "A battle will commence. Show you where, I can."

"Come on," Zedaine roared, sprinting forward, his bow held tightly in his hand, the sprite buzzing along ahead of him.

"Go, child," the big hunter heard Raenen say. "Do not judge your mate too harshly. He and Ferra, they know not what they do."

Nodding once, Xeda sped off after Caina and Zedaine.

From out of the forest came two figures, running along the tree line. The first, Kildare knew, was Chulin. The wolf tore out from under the trees, running for its life. Behind it came a creature steeped in fire. Standing at the size of a full-grown horse was a six-legged monstrosity borne from the depths of Kildare's worst nightmare. All sinewy muscle and bone, the hound like creature raced after the wolf, hell bent upon its destruction.

"By the Grove," Kildare heard the dryad say from his place next to him.

"Shoot him," Kildare ordered, drawing back on his string, taking aim. His knee buckled underneath him and Kildare had to hold his shot. Next to him, he heard the dryad's bow twang in release. The arrow flew true and stuck the hound on the skull, bouncing off harmlessly.

"Tough bastard," Kildare muttered, seeing that the skull was too well protected for his arrows.

"Let's see how you like this," the taciturn warrior whispered, drawing back and loosing his arrow. The oak shaft ripped through the air, striking the hound on the haunch of his rear leg. The creature slowed, and turned his attention upon Kildare and the dryad.

"Shit," Kildare swore, fitting another arrow to string.

"Cover me," the dryad shouted, lifting his spear, charging forward.

"I'm on it," Kildare shouted in reply, wetting his lips in nervous anticipation. Despite his suspicions, the dryad had given no reason for Kildare not to trust him. His stomach heaved once more, and it was all Kildare could do to keep his feet. "I just had to eat those mushrooms, didn't I?" he muttered, groaning in pain. He blinked as another figure, a female dryad, exited the woods, a long spear in her hand.

"Who in the hell is that?" he asked, drawing back on his bow as the male dryad drew even with the hound.

Kildare loosed the arrow and swore as it bounced harmlessly off the hound's shoulder. "Goddammit," he cursed, fitting another arrow to his bow.

"Anytime you want to wake up would be welcome," he snarled at the comatose Seraph.

Temuvena did not stir a muscle.

"Figures," Kildare snorted, drawing a bead upon the hound.

When Zedaine ran out of the forest, he saw several things with striking clarity. Lying on the ground in front of his campsite were the bodies of two dryads. The closer of the two was Ferra, who had blood running down her neck. The other was Harker, his spear head coated in black blood, his mouth agape in a soundless scream. Another creature, a wolf, was locked in combat with a massive hound of fire and rage.

Kildare was standing atop the tree trunk, loosing arrow after arrow at the beast, which seemed to shrug off every shot with ease.

"The spear!" Kildare shouted, seeing his brother emerge from the wood. "The black-hearted bastard can only be killed with a darksteel blade!"

Nodding, Zedaine dropped his bow and raced forward. As he ran past the still breathing Ferra, he scooped up her spear and attacked the hound from behind.

He thrust the weapon forward, driving it straight at the creature's spine. "Die, you hellion," Zedaine roared.

The tip of the spear bent to the left as it failed to scratch the skin of the fiery hound.

"What the…" Zedaine began, his eyes wide in shock.

The hound spun and snapped at Zedaine, who managed to raise the spear and keep the creature's jaws at bay. He was hurled backward, his spine slamming on the ground as the air whooshed out of his lungs. The wind knocked out of him, the big hunter struggled to draw breath. He was vaguely aware of someone dragging him away from the hound.

"Our weapons are useless," Zedaine heard Xeda say.

"Harker's… spear," the big hunter managed to gasp, remembering the dark blood on its blade.

"I'll try for it," Xeda said, leaving Zedaine on the ground next to Ferra.

The big hunter watched as the wolf battling the hound was overwhelmed by a rush of claws and teeth. Throwing Chulin aside, the hound turned its gaze to Kildare, who was staring at it defiantly.

"Come on, you overgrown puppy," Kildare was shouting. "I'll send your soul back to the shadow from whence it came!"

Zedaine struggled to his knees, trying desperately to draw breath.

Creeping up behind the hound was Xeda, easing her way toward Harker's spear.

"That's it you flaming piece of shit, have a go at me!" Kildare screamed.

Xeda inadvertently slipped on a loose stone, alerting the hound to her presence.

"No," Zedaine managed, finally able to draw breath. Fighting his way to his feet, Zedaine stood watching as Xeda raised her hands in front of her.

"Levenso gie dode!" she whispered.

A tangle of roots shot upward, snaring the hound with their growth. The hound looked down, ripping at the first root with its teeth.

Xeda made a mad dash for Harker's spear, hoping to sweep it up before the hound freed itself.

Seeing the dryads plan, the hellish spirit let out a bestial roar, the flames coating its body, flaring outward. Instantly the roots holding the hound turned to ash, and the creature caught Xeda a moment before she could reach the spear. With an angry toss of its head, the hound threw the dryad toward Zedaine. She hit the ground hard and slid, stopping a foot in front of him.

Zedaine drew his sword in a final act of defiance and stepped in front of Xeda. "You want her? You'll have to go through me," he snarled, regaining his breath.

The hound roared in response, moving forward a step at a time.

It came to a halt not three feet away.

"Come on then," Zedaine baited, knowing he was in a hopeless scenario. "Finish me!"

The hound reared back and lunged forward… only to snap its jaws in sudden irritation.

"Leave them be, you will!" a piping voice shouted from above Zedaine.

Darting from side to side, the sprite, Caina, had entered the fray.

Stabbing at the hound with her foot long spear, she managed to ward off the monster for a few heartbeats more.

"Zee!" came a shout from a voice Zedaine knew all too well.

Looking behind the hound, Zedaine saw his brother, mushroom sickness and all, had made his way over to Harker's still form and hurled the darksteel spear toward his brother with all his remaining strength.

Zedaine dropped his sword to the ground and caught the spear, reversing it in one smooth motion.

Moving with supernatural speed, the hound struck Caina, knocking the sprite to the ground.

Lunging forward, Zedaine ducked under the hound's thrashing head and thrust forward, praying his aim was true. The darksteel blade slammed into the hound's neck, drenching Zedaine in a spurt of hot blood. The visceral fluid burned at his flesh, shooting through him with tendrils of agony.

Zedaine did not let go. He drove the spear deeper, and the hound screamed, this time in pain rather than hunger. On and on it went, Zedaine's will against the hound's strength. With a last roar, the dark spirit toppled to the side, kicking all six of its legs in the throes of death.

Bone weary, Zedaine released his hold on the spear and staggered over to his brother, collapsing on the ground next to him.

The two lay there together, in pain and exhaustion.

"I threw up again," Kildare wheezed, wiping his mouth with his sleeve. "Cursed mushrooms. I'm swearing them off, forever."

"Yes, well, we are all having our little problems today, aren't we?" Zedaine replied, holding up his now smoking arms.

"That does look painful," Kildare admitted. He turned his head and made a face, sniffing at his brother. "What is that? It smells like brine water."

"I think it's the demon blood," Zedaine guessed. "I'd say it contains a high concentration of salt. The smell is terrible."

"By the gods, you are drenched in it," Kildare complained. "That blood is going to make me sick again…"

"You human scum," came a voice from the woods.

The brothers sat up at the malevolence in the voice.

Walking toward them was the Tree Matron, Raenen. In her hands was a staff, blazing with power. "Year after year, century after century, I watch as the Forest Mother lets your kind destroy our lands."

As Raenen moved closer, Zedaine struggled to his feet.

"I begged her to fight back, just a few glades a year. They won't miss them. So, a few humans will die. They breed like flies."

"Raenen," Zedaine began. "Perhaps you should…"

She lifted her staff and a ball of light shot from it, striking Zedaine in the torso, knocking the wind out of him.

"But does the Lady of the Elms listen to the words of reason?" she continued. "No. Instead, she insists on living in harmony with you creatures. Beings with a lifespan less than that of a single tree."

Raenen was close now, only a few steps away.

"You bitch," Kildare seethed, standing unsteadily.

"No, manling, I am no such thing," she retorted at Kildare. "I simply did what any good mother would do. I moved to protect my people… to keep them safe in the years to come."

"You… summoned… the hound," Zedaine rasped, trying to catch his breath. "That's why Ferra and Harker fought against it. You've acted alone."

"I met with my queen this morning at the edge of the forest, away from her center of power," Raenen nodded. "I summoned my hound, and sent it after her. She was on the brink of escape, so I shot her with one of Harker's arrows, dipped in a mixture of Nightshade and Pelath."

"I knew it," Kildare crowed.

Raenen's beautiful countenance twisted in fury.

"She would have died, my plan complete, save she ran into you two."

Raenen paused, her eyes flicking cruelly to one, then the other. "I was initially overjoyed seeing her collapse here. Two humans—sub-creatures from the vast unknown—inishing off the Seraph of Life for me." She gave them a harsh laugh. "Imagine how I could spin it to the rest of the fae realm. The perfect ending to fire their blood for war."

"You are insane," Kildare spat, reaching down to his dagger and lunging toward the matron of the trees.

With a simple thrust of her staff, Raenen struck the sickened warrior in the stomach and smashed her weapon alongside his head. Kildare crashed to the ground, groaning in agony.

"Unfortunately, you two did the decent thing and worked to save Temuvena's life," Raenen continued, without skipping a beat. "The one thing I was sure any human would do—kill a fae creature on sight—and you two faelings failed in your task."

She glanced behind them, seeing the Forest Mother lying on the ground. "I feel badly I have to sacrifice the others. I might convince Ferra to come to her senses, but Harker and Xeda… they will never go for it now, not after meeting you, Zedaine."

Raenen let out a petulant sigh. "You even managed to win over that sprite… flighty little thing. She too, will have to perish."

She focused her attention on her staff, alighting it anew. "Any last words?" she mocked. "A simple request before I send you into the beyond?"

Zedaine forced himself to stand straight and looked directly into Raenen's eyes. "Do you know what's in the brine?" he asked.

The Tree Matron frowned at him. "Brine? I've never heard of…"

"Salt," he sneered, leaping forward, his blood-caked hands grabbing hold of her staff.

Raenen fought back, trying to use her magic to attack Zedaine through the staff.

"Amil ahn Sorba!" she cried, a surge of power building.

It died, causing Zedaine no harm.

He wrenched the staff from her hands and kicked her in the stomach, sending Raenen sprawling.

"Wha—*How?*" she hissed, a stunned look on her face.

"I know that salt neutralizes fae magic," Zedaine snapped, charging toward her. The big hunter, while fast, was wounded. His attack was not as well timed as when he was hale. Raenen, a being hundreds of years old, was a veteran of many fights. She deftly sidestepped and struck Zedaine in the temple, sending him reeling. Still on his feet, Zedaine's eyes glazed over, giving Raenen all the time she needed.

Moving forward, she struck him once more and Zedaine fell to the ground.

"Stinking human," she raged, kicking him in the ribs. "You don't know when you are beaten."

Zedaine rolled to his left and climbed unsteadily to his feet. "I will defend the Forest Mother to the death. You are wrong about us humans, Tree Matron. We are not evil. Ignorant perhaps, but not the horrible creatures you make us out to be."

"You are pathetic," Raenen taunted. "Weak and cruel. The world will thank me when your kind are gone."

She raised her staff, while Zedaine looked on helplessly.

"Viser ugh Non!"

A flash of light burst between them, and Zedaine closed his eyes.

A heartbeat later, he opened them, stunned at what he saw.

Lying before him was the now unconscious form of Raenen, scorch marks smoking from her tunic.

"It seems I missed something," came a rasping, melodic voice from behind him.

Turning, Zedaine saw the now standing form of the Seraph of Life.

Wide eyed, the big hunter shook his head and let out a sigh of relief.

Less than an hour later, Harker, Xeda and Ferra escorted Raenen back to the fae realm, stripped of her magic and staff. The Grim loped along beside them, leaving the two humans and Temuvena alone.

Kildare was unconscious. They had all been fully healed by the Lady of the Elms, but the toll upon Kildare had been great. He slept, his brother keeping guard above him.

"It seems I owe you my life, Zedaine of the Forest," Temuvena said. "How can I repay you?"

Zedaine let out a deep breath and looked the Seraph in the eyes. "There is a problem with our peoples," he stated. "A distrust I had no idea existed. You and your kind are often spoken of in myth and legend. It is time for that to end."

Temuvena's eyes narrowed. "While Raenen's actions were wrong, there is much truth to what she says. Humans encroach upon our lands every year. This forest used to be five times larger. Now, we struggle to keep what we have. Who knows how much will be left in a century?"

"I understand your plight," Zedaine said. "However, you must do your part as well. Most humans have no idea you exist, or what you stand for. Give them that chance… take one into your council and get them to see what is at risk."

"You think such a thing will fix everything?" the green-eyed fae asked.

"I'm saying it is a start."

Temuvena looked at him deeply, and let out a sigh. "This goes against my better judgment," she said after a moment. "However, you are right, in one sense. There needs to be more of an understanding between our peoples. Otherwise, things will go on as they have, and war between us will be inevitable."

"Good," Zedaine smirked, letting out a breath of relief.

"Come, stay with us for the length of the next moon, after your brother is hale," Temuvena said. "I will tell my people of your imminent arrival."

"What?" Zedaine gasped, not expecting this.

"You made the request, human. You fought to save me and my people. There is no one of your kind I would trust more."

"But… I'm… I can't," he stammered.

"I will leave it to you to tell your brother," she added. "There is a village less than a day's journey away. He can wait there for your return."

The Seraph of Life made her way toward the woods, a playful smile upon her lips.

"Well… shit," Zedaine muttered, glancing at his brother. "I can't believe I'm about to say this, but right now, I wish *I'd* been the one who'd eaten those mushrooms."

A Shot in the Dark

A Nimble and Scales Mystery
By: Matthew Olaranont

The client was cool as an ice storm rolling through the front door. She sauntered in with legs for miles, peeking out the side-slit of a dress grown from maple leaves. Sultry brown eyes surveyed the room, coming to rest on the Gnome at his appropriately sized desk.

"Is this the Nimble and Scales Detective Agency?" she asked.

"It's what the sign on the door says. I'm Griffe Hardlocke, Private Eye." the Gnome introduced himself, looking her up and down, "Wouldn't wear it out. I don't know where to get a new one."

Griffe took a drag on a hand-rolled cigarette and ashed it into a tray on his diminutive desk before putting both feet up and leaning back in his chair. "And that's Urlthor Xendrax." He added, gesturing to his partner with a wave of his hand.

"A pleasure. Would you like some coffee, miss…?" Url faded in from the shadows, his figure a striking silhouette like a castle tower in a thunderstorm.

"Sylvana," she turned and saw him, "I—" she stammered a moment, irises widening, "—yes, please."

Urlthor smiled, but it came across like a laboriously arranged collection of knives.

"Mind getting one for me too, Url?" Griffe asked, as he stubbed out the butt of the cigarette in the pile formed in the ashtray. The Dragonborn nodded slowly, exhaling a cloud of smoke a shade darker than the cigarette smoke hanging in the light of the horizontal blinds.

"So what does a druid need with a couple of gumshoes like us? Bear crap in the woods? Cow jump over the moon?" Griffe said with an amicable grin.

Sylvana's eyes flashed like lightning in a bottle. She tossed two ferrous palm-sized orbs onto his desk from inside her leather satchel. The matte spheres rolled to a stop against the ashtray with a light clink.

"These," she spoke in a tone glacier cold, "were found near my part of the forest."

Griffe leaned forward over his desk, wafting the scent to himself over the orbs. "They smell like you tossed them in a campfire."

He picked them up for closer examination, their golf ball size appearing immense in his hands.

Sylvana looked about the room, "So which one—"

"I'm Scales. He's Nimble." Griffe waved the hand holding the spheres absentmindedly between himself and Urlthor.

Sylvana had a look of frustrated bemusement before Url reappeared next to her with the silence and grace of a panther on the prowl on a moonless night. He extended her a human sized cup of strong black coffee on a saucer. Moments later, he placed a smaller cup in front of Griffe. Url took his seat at his Dragonborn-sized desk, the creak of the chair punctuating the end of their pleasantries.

"Url's good people, Sylvie. A little proper sometimes, but he's not bad. Thanks, pal," Griffe said while he pulled a small silver flask from his hip pocket. The Elven-inlaid filigree caught the light of the sun in a way only Elven craftsmanship could, as he poured honey-colored liquor into the coffee.

"I tell you every time, Griffe, that stuff'll kill you some day." Url's voice rumbled over a stack of paperwork—most were final invoices from cases for the Guild a few months ago. The Gnome shrugged and sipped at the hot liquid.

"Like I was saying, Sylvie, something about these doesn't sit right with me. Why come all the way into town and hire shamuses if it's just some prank magic that comes around every now and again? These look like pretty basic catalysts, but you already know that, don't you?"

Her eyes narrowed over the rim of the coffee mug, and her stance shifted the bag behind her. A few leaves fell from the hem of her dress, the healthy green shade withering to malty brown as they came in contact with the floor. Griffe sipped his coffee and raised both eyebrows.

"I was told you were the only ones who could, and I would insist that you both need to investigate this matter." Her tone changed, more of the ice she had brought from her neck of the woods. A few more leaves fell, curling black this time once they hit the dusty hardwood. She took the ferrous spheres from Griffe, the crackle of magic arcing between them as she applied some of her own druidic influence.

The spheres went wild in response, a sort of magnetism bringing them together in a miniature orbit in her hand. Their wrought gray color morphed to a flash of indigo before the orbs launched away from each other with an explosion of magefyre and the smell of sulfur. The temperature in the room seemed to *drop* by a few degrees. Griffe attempted to remain stoic, the only outward sign of his reaction a slight shake in the cup he held. Urlthor was standing now, fist clenched around one of the smoldering iron balls in his upraised hand, a wisp of black smoke curling out. The other sphere had embedded itself into the opposite wall, a similar tendril of smoke coming from the hole it had created.

"Good catch, Url. Nice one." Griffe said after setting the coffee down. He grabbed a stepstool from next to the door and moved it underneath the hole in the wall before climbing up to inspect the damage.

"Never seen basic catalysts do *that* before." Griffe commented idly, pulling out a switchblade and picking at the sphere, prying it loose from the board it had broken. "Normally all you magic types just use these as containers—magic in, magic out—and then they're spent. None of this lightning and thunder crap."

The ferrous orb finally came loose, popping out and rolling along the floor before Griffe picked it up, the patina changing back to the matte gray of iron from the kaleidoscope of shifting indigo shades it took up from the initial charge of magic.

"I see what you mean, Sylvie, I see what you mean." He held it up close to examine the surface. Url did the same in his part of the room.

"Abyss glass." The druid spoke the words between them, affirming the reality of what they had just seen.

"Ain't none of this stuff been on this side of the Slip since the War…" Griffe said, a distinct tone of solemnity in his voice.

Url retrieved a jeweler's loupe from within his desk, and squinted through it at the comparatively miniscule orb in his hand. "This is an especially pure sample."

"What about the town guard? Did the rangers have anything to say about it?" Griffe asked.

"No. They dismissed me before I had a chance to show them what it could do. Said 'matters of the wood were King's Guard matters, not theirs.'"

"Idiots." Griffe rolled the Abyss glass around in his hand, feeling it grow warm.

"So that's why I've come to you two. The Druidic commune would be more than happy to render payment in currency or barter."

Url crossed the room and handed Griffe the other sphere.

"Find the source of this intrusion and stop it if you can," Sylvana finished.

"Well, we'll hold on to these, but our standard rate is two-hundred down and another two-hundred after—plus expenses, collected every few days. Tack on a daily *per diem*—and it's extra, if we've gotta stop some kinda invasion from the Shadowfelll." Griffe said. No sooner had he finished when a single platinum piece clattered onto the desk, jangling the cup and saucer.

"You've been paid upfront. A great danger appears to be growing near our home. I pray you find it before the rest of the world must bear the same weight."

The Druid's commune was located in the nature preserve outside the western gates of the city. Despite its location, Nimble and Scale's warrant still extended over the territory as an unincorporated area managed as a Special Administrative Region of the city's government. The two detectives caught a sharecab from their office in the city center to the street just off the western gate. The town guard waved them through and they crossed the bridge.

The preserve was a manicured forest, the smattering of oaks, elms, and maple bordering the bridge already morphing to autumnal shades whilst evergreen magical trees filled-in further into the woods.

"You got any idea which way that little Druid kibbutz is, Url?" Griffe asked, "We should probably do some interviewing." He did his best to look over the canopy from where he stood, but only saw the middle branches.

Url pointed in a direction deeper into the trees. "I see some smoke in that direction. Perhaps that is their settlement."

"Works for me. Would it kill them to put in a trail, though?" Griffe pulled his pants up by his belt and headed in the direction his friend had pointed.

They traveled over the rough terrain between the trees, stepping carefully through the underbrush in their own ways to avoid disturbing too much of the area as they passed. Url seemed to pass over the roots and dry leaves with the grace of practice, his clawed feet leaving nary a mark in their passage. Griffe, on the other hand, cut through it all at the same speed with the ease of years of experience and a touch of the Gnomish gift. The inconvenience of the woods themselves bent out of the way to give him passage.

In a short time, they reached the edge of the Druid's settlement. The design was a stark difference from the straight lines and angles of the city. All of their buildings were squat, single-story affairs that were grown out of the vines and grass of the clearing, naturally woven by their magic into functional shacks, a few of the chimneys emitting the thin bands of smoke Url had seen.

"How very… pastoral." Url said as they stepped into the open village square.

"Reminds me of how my old village used to be before the war. I had a neighbor that built his house into an enormous tree." Griffe made a hand motion to indicate the size of the tree in question.

"The ancient Dragonborn lived in a similar manner, though I believe my ancestors preferred caves. My kind did not agree with wood, for obvious reasons."

"I dunno, Url, maybe your ancestors would have enjoyed baking cookies, too."

Url chortled, and they made their way into the Druid commons. There were relatively few druids compared to the people in the city—but their makeup was just as diverse. It took little more than an affinity for magic and a call to nature to qualify for Druidic teachings, and so it was an equal smattering of races between those represented in the city.

"Where would you like to begin?" Url asked as they passed an Orcish druid holding a basket atop her head. She gave them a mean side-eye, Url's subdued kimono style top, and especially Griffe's trench coat and fedora combo standing in stark contrast to the natural fibers and homespun clothing of the locals.

"You know me, Url. Let's get some drinks." Griffe jerked a thumb at one building, a sign in common tongue labeling it as "Grimtooth's Distillery."

Url heaved a sigh. "Only for an interview."

They ducked through the woven-reed door and into the cramped interior of the distillery, a handful of barrels taller and wider than Url lining the area behind the counter.

"Oh! Welcome in, welcome in. Don't get many of you city-types here, aside from my hauler. I'm Sunlance Grimtooth, owner of this fine distillery." A human, dressed in a similar roughspun manner as the Orc from outside, looked up from something he had been working on behind the counter. The two detectives greeted him and introduced themselves.

"We're warranted investigators. A druid from hereabouts hired us to come and see about something concerning a situation you all might have been experiencing. Has anything weird happened around here recently?"

The druid looked between them a second, a thoughtful expression crossing his face before he sighed.

"Being totally honest, there might be something you two could help me with. I'll not tell you much—to not poison the well—but I need to ask you to taste some of my wares."

Griffe turned to Url with a wry smile. "See what I mean? Free samples already. I've got a good feeling about this."

"It is, as they say, all you. I am more than happy to haul you back to the office. It certainly would not be the first time."

"More for me then." Griffe said glibly.

Grimtooth returned a moment later with an unmarked bottle filled to the shoulder with a strong smelling liquor. He pulled out a pair of wooden cups from underneath the counter and began to fill one. Url placed a large, scaly hand above the other cup and shook his head. Grimtooth shrugged and set the bottle down on the counter after finishing with the first cup.

Griffe picked up the freshly poured liquor and swirled it around in the wooden vessel. Taking the natural color of the wood into account, the liquor appeared a mellow maroon that didn't seem to have any legs. Griffe gave it a tentative sniff.

"Smells pretty good," he said.

"Give it a taste." Grimtooth urged with an expectant look.

Griffe sipped it cautiously and set the liquor down with a grimace on his face. "It tastes like rainbows and unicorn farts."

Grimtooth looked like he was taken aback. "Really? This has knocked everybody on their ass when they tried it. It's far too strong now."

"It's because there's stupid fae magic crap in it." Griffe explained, "Most people don't have the stomach for it."

"And why do you?" Url asked.

"That's a long story, Url. But I've got my pride as a Gnome—"

"—And an alcoholic," Url added.

"—and an alc—*hey!* I only drink socially, and alone." Griffe retorted.

"Well, if you can drink it, do you want to take it? I bottled what was left in the cask and there's still five more bottles of this stuff."

The two detectives turned to Grimtooth, "Seriously?" They asked in unison.

"I don't think—" Url began.

"Hell, I'll take all of it. Never say no to a free drink." Griffe said. Url stopped and looked down at his diminutive partner and did nothing but sigh.

Grimtooth corked the bottle on the counter and came back with the others. Griffe took them and put them into his shoulder bag with an enormous grin.

"Anyway, what do you mean 'what was left in the cask'?"

"By the time I found it, it was half-empty." Grimtooth replied.

"Well, at least that gives us a clue about what's going on. It's rare Fae magic comes leaking into our world, or drinks our booze," Griffe said.

"Indeed," Url agreed. "Where do you keep your aging casks? We might be able to glean an idea of where this adulteration stems from."

"Oh, there's a shack just into the trees behind my shop here," Grimtooth indicated behind him, "I keep them all out there to age. Been a little spooky out back as of late, though. Noises and all."

Griffe nodded sagely. "Well, we'll go check it out. If there's anything, we'll be back with more questions."

The two detectives left the distillery storefront and went to the wood line, finding a short trail to the cask shack Grimtooth had told them about. The construction resembled the buildings from the village, naturally grown walls capped by a canopied roof. The door was unlocked, leading into the handful of casks laid out on shelves lined four deep.

Url ducked in and looked over the casks, walking all the way to the back, where one of the shelves sat empty.

"Something going on in there?" Griffe asked.

"It appears this is where your new liquor came from. I don't feel any lingering magic—but there is—" Url stopped, twisting and turning his head to take a closer look at something on the shelf.

"What? What is it?" Griffe asked from the doorway.

"There are three pieces of confetti." Url said.

It was Griffe's turn to sigh. "I'll go check." He let the door close and paced his way around to the back side of the shack, annoyed and angry at what it could mean. To his chagrin, he was right. A smattering of confetti gleamed in the dewy grass behind the shack, the multicolored speckles interspersed in a trail that led further into the deep woods.

"Hey, Url!" Griffe called, putting his hands into his trench coat's pockets.

Url showed up a few moments later, taking in the scene.

"Magic confetti?" Url asked.

"*Stupid* magic confetti crap." Griffe confirmed before walking along the trail of the sprinkled sparkles.

It was as if the forest went on forever. The trees closed in and the underbrush grew thicker as the two detectives continued after the sparse shine of confetti.

Url held out a hand in front of Griffe, stopping the Gnome in his tracks before lifting a finger to a shushing motion against his snout. Griffe nodded and followed his friend's pointing finger to a spot in the distance, noticing a small mound in the canopy's shade; rising and falling minutely.

Griffe turned away from his partner, stepping through the underbrush in a wide arc as Url mirrored him in the opposite direction. They snuck up to the little mound, now about half of Griffe's size on further inspection, and a gentle rise and fall became clear as the noises of its snoring became recognizable.

When both of them were in position, Griffe took a few steps closer to the shadowy mound and grasped the top of it. He pulled on the leafy pile and rolled over the foliage laden cover. It rolled off with a groaned complaint, revealing the pile to be a pair of pixies stacked on top of each other. The eye-watering reek of alcohol coming off both of them caused Griffe to take a few steps back and cough.

"Guess they're just sleeping it off." Griffe said. One of the Pixies rolled over and pulled a blanket of leaves over itself.

"That would explain the tainted liquor." Url said, looking around, "But there is more of the trail in that direction." he pointed, "past that unfortunate pile of vomit next to that tree."

"Hold up a second, Url. Look at this." Griffe pointed at the center of the vomit.

"If you insist."

Griffe grabbed a stick from the underbrush and poked at the pile, rolling two ferrous stones from the remains.

"What do you suppose this means?" Url asked.

"It means there's more stupid magic crap around." Griffe replied, throwing the stick off to the side.

They continued following the trail deeper into the woods. The canopy grew thicker and the natural light from above grew dimmer as the growth grew older and more wild.

Griffe closed his eyes and stopped abruptly, sniffing the air in short bursts. "You feel that, Url?"

"I feel something, but I do not know what it is."

"Kind of a lightness; maybe a bit woozy? It's—" Griffe pointed in a course tangential to where they had been walking, turning toward it before stepping away in the direction. Url followed him without question.

Around the trunk of a large tree, there was another small clearing, no larger than a few of Url's extended strides. Something that looked like an enormous shard of jagged glass floated in its center, like a broken mirror mounted to nothing hovering in the middle of the glade. The image within conveyed an unfamiliar forest, the light of an otherworldly morning shining through a hole scooped out of their reality.

"I knew it. It's the Faewyld." Griffe spat into the underbrush.

"I only know it by reputation. Do you know what it is more personally?"

"I grew up in the woods. Lived in a big tree near a natural portal to the Faewyld. I hate that place. Those Pixie fucks used to tie my shoelaces together when I was a kid." Griffe pulled out his cigarette case and lit up a smoke while they observed the rift.

"I find there aren't many places you enjoy, Griffe."

"Speaking of," Griffe said, taking a drag from his cigarette, "where are the rest of 'em? They usually show up in packs, and we've only found those two.""

"Curious."

Griffe paced around the clearing while finishing his cigarette. The opening to the Faewyld looked the same no matter what direction he viewed it from—it was the same jagged scoop that looked like it led to a stranger, older wood.

"So, what would you like to do?" Url asked when Griffe returned from his pacing. Griffe threw the butt down into the dirt and stamped it out, using the toe of his shoe to cover it in earth.

"I think we're gonna have to go for it, pal. If there's an opening here, then it smells like trouble. We signed that treaty after the War to keep them out of our hair."

"Anything I should know before we go through?"

"You're going to be dizzy at first. It's silly on the other side. Don't eat anything you didn't bring with you, and don't agree to anything if we run into anybody. Contracts are magically binding and everything's basically a contest. They love wheeling and dealing over there."

Griffe stepped forward into the clearing and felt the hair on the back of his neck stand on end. The broken hole through reality shimmered the color of forest dawn, and Griffe stepped through it. The feeling of falling and flying took hold before his forward foot crunched down on the alien loam. He took a few quick steps ahead and turned back to look at the gateway he had come through.

Url stepped through a moment later, landing on both feet as if he had just dismounted from the gymnast's bars, both arms raised for balance. He stuck his landing, but wobbled soon after. With a pause of his normal grace, Url put one foot forward and took a knee. He placed a hand on his sternum, a small belch of fire coming out before he stood.

"You alright there, buddy?" Griffe asked.

Url belched again. "Yes, I wasn't expecting it to be so disorienting."

"Yeah, you get used to it." Griffe tilted his hat up to look at his friend.

"Griffe, your eye—" Url reacted with surprise, one hand reaching out to point.

"Ugh, it's back." Griffe reached a hand up to his left eye. "The magic around here always gives it that stupid swirl. I've had it since I was a kid. Whatever, let's get going."

The Faewyld forest was ancient, old-growth trees that had probably witnessed the dawn of old gods and ancient races, gnarled roots and densely woven underbrush, a carpet of interlinked vegetation knitted on the loom of chaos. The nature of the wood on the other side was a stark contrast to the druids' manicured springtime of the city's nature preserve. The trees loomed close and tight, the abundant buzz of magic in the air humming the reasons why it had grown labyrinthine by an eon of being undisturbed.

A path opened like a curtain before them, the winding trail leading deeper into the wood while the trees around them seemed to shift closer together as guard rails. The two detectives shared a look of skepticism but followed the path all the same, nary a word between them.

"Do you have any idea as to where we might be going?" Url asked.

"Not in the slightest. That's what I hate about—" Griffe stopped midstep and spun around in place, holding up an open hand to stop Url from proceeding. Griffe closed his eyes and sniffed the air.

"You smell that, Url?" Griffe opened his eyes with a knowing look.

Url followed suit and closed his eyes, a single long inhale flowing in with the rumble of a rake over hot coals.

"Is it the smell of sulfur?" Url asked.

"Yeah. That's what I got. You have a direction on where it's coming from, from up there?"

Url tilted his head to the side and gave the air a few shallow sniffs, turning about in place to ascertain its strength.

"I do not." Url said after a time.

"Hm." Griffe said and returned to spinning and sniffing. After another handful of seconds, he stopped and pointed in a direction away from the path that was open to them.

"What do you think, Url? It's coming from over there. No forest fires here."

"It appears we have no choice but to blaze our own trail."

"Don't we always?" Griffe stepped off the path.

Griffe followed his nose, his own Gnomish nature allowing him to cut through the underbrush and looming forest. Voices called from the darkness and laughter seemed to echo through the branches as they progressed. The surrounding gloom ebbed and flowed around them like a living thing, the hazy aurora of daybreak light shifting ever present as they took step after step.

"Smoke." Url said at a volume barely above the ambient whispers.

Griffe stopped and looked back at his friend, not holding any hope at all of being able to see it above the thick canopy.

"There is a thin line of smoke above and I detect an aberrant flicker of light some distance ahead." Url pointed.

"Let's get a little closer and stay low and quiet. If there's Abyss glass involved, then who knows what else might have crawled out of the Shadowfelll."

Url nodded his assent, and Griffe slogged onward after his nose.

As they closed-in on the source of the smell, the shimmering of light came into focus as an enormous bonfire sat in the middle of a village clearing carpeted in fuchsia grass.

Griffe slowed his pace, stopping a stone's throw away from the tree line's edge, peering out along the main stretch of the village. He held up a hand to signal Url to follow him, and traced a path along the outer perimeter.

It was obvious the bonfire in the center of the village wasn't a normal fixture. Rough dirt mounds arranged in a circle with irregular branches piled in it that looked like they had been shorn from the local foliage with little care to their dryness. The fire was a fluorescent magenta, burning with the crackle of strange magic. As they circled the perimeter, a group of people kneeling in a neat row came into view, their hands bound behind their backs.

A trussed-up row of captive pixies was capped off by a larger pair of similarly bound forms; a Lizardman, who was dressed like he was ready to sail the high seas, and a squat halfling in cattle rancher regalia, his face obscured by a downward-tilted cowboy hat. Griffe stopped and took a knee, allowing Url to come up next to him and do the same, the larger detective leaning his head down to Griffe's level.

"You see what I see?" Griffe asked.

"It appears to be Rough and Tumble." Url replied, naming their rival agency, "As is the usual for these affairs, Howard Merritt and Roy Cruze have failed to solve the problem."

"They look like they've got this. Wanna go back?"

"We would have to give a refund. Not to mention this would not cease the evil machinations of the one behind this." Url pointed at a dark figure standing taller amidst a few meandering Pixies.

The Pixies milling about moved with slow, stilted gaits, performing menial tasks like they were zombies. The dark creature at the center of the event looked twice the size of the Pixies, but built in the same slight manner as the rest, with mangled gossamer wings the iridescent color of a rainy night.

The creature walked over to one of the restrained Pixies and dragged them by their hair over to the edge of the fire. It reached bare-handed into the magenta flame and withdrew an orb from within the pyre. The creature bent the Pixie's head back, forced the hostage's mouth open and shoved the sphere into the Pixie's mouth. The Pixie squirmed and flailed, struggling for a while before falling limp. The creature dropped the still form and cut the ropes binding it. A few moments later, the unconscious Pixie stood and stumbled zombie-like away from the larger creature.

Griffe gave Url a concerned look before the pair continued their circumspect journey around the village. They came up near the spot where the Lizardman and the Halfling were kneeling.

"Merritt! Psst!" Griffe whispered from the edge of the wood line, peeking his head from around the closest tree.

The Halfling in the cowboy hat turned toward him, his eyes opening wide under the felt brim.

"Hardlocke?" Merritt hissed in response and nudged the Lizardman next to him to get his attention.

The buccaneer reptilian turned and blinked sideways in surprise with his clear inner eyelid. "Urlthor, buddy!" he hissed with joy.

"I would not use that term to describe us," Url whispered so only Griffe could hear.

"What happened?" Griffe tried keeping the conversation focused.

"We were lookin' into some strangeness with the druids." Merritt replied, his bushy mustache waving in time with the words.

"We found zombie pixies and this trail of confetti that led us to this reprobate," the Lizardman added.

"How did you get captured, Roy?" Url asked the lizardman.

"We got lost in the woods following some smoke and a bunch of these Pixies jumped us," Merritt explained.

"I don't like Pixies much either, Howie. What's the skinny on that extra-large evil lookin' one?" Griffe pointed at the larger creature with frayed wings.

"Seems like he's from the Shadowfelll. Like the Pixies, but uglier," Roy replied with great solemnity.

Griffe shot a look over to Url before scanning behind and around them for any stray Pixies.

"Y'all plan on gettin' us out of here? We'd be much obliged." Merritt asked.

"Howard, the last time I untied you from something, you tried to shoot up the guild hall and got zoned for six months for drunken rioting. Gimme a minute. Gimme a minute." Griffe replied.

The Fel-Pixie came back over to the group of hostages and grabbed the last one on the end, dragging it away, kicking and screaming, to repeat the process. Griffe and Url froze stock-still while it did so, holding their breaths in the perimeter's shadow, waiting and thinking.

"We need to act soon, Griffe. We're running out of Pixies." Url said once the Fel creature had gone far enough from their whispering earshot.

"I know, I know. I think our best bet is to challenge it to something."

"Why can we not fight them?"

"This is their home turf. They'd fry us with magic before we managed to stop them. The Wilds are fickle places, Url."

"He's right, the Pixies on our side were pushovers, but here, they were like a raging storm on an unforgiving sea," Roy said.

"You can't even swim." Url retorted, "But fine. What do you suggest, Griffe?"

Griffe sat down cross-legged and took the time to think, tapping his chin in earnest.

"You got a plan brewin' pardner?" Merritt asked in an urgent whisper.

"Shaddap and let me think," Griffe muttered, eyes darting between the Fel-Pixie, the group of prisoners, and his partner. The rules of the land all hinged on bad deals and contests. There weren't any Griffe could think of that he could bring out at the drop of a hat. He rocked back and felt the bottles from earlier push up against his back.

"I think I've got it." Griffe said, slamming one fist into the other open palm. He took off his side bag and handed it to Url.

"Are you going to get us out of these ties first?" Roy asked.

"No. Now hold your horses. I'm gonna have to challenge big ugly over there, and make sure it's a contest I can win."

"How do you plan on doing that?" Merritt asked.

"Just play along. Url, don't bring those bottles out 'til I give the sign." Griffe nodded to him. Url practically disappeared, fading further back into the shadows of the wood line with an agreeing nod.

Merritt and Cruze gasped audibly as Griffe stepped out bold and strong into the main circle of the village, pointing a finger at the Fel-Pixie. "Hey, you! The Pixie from Shadowfelll! I challenge you to a contest!"

All the mind-controlled Pixies around Griffe skidded to a halt, the open challenge overriding their actions.

"What!?" The mastermind turned around, its high-pitched voice squeaking in indignation.

"You heard me, you—" Griffe paused as the dark Pixie stormed up in front of him, doing its best to loom menacingly despite being two inches shorter than Griffe. The Gnome held back a snort.

"I am Kelefer of the shaded wood, true heir of the Dark Consort! You dare challenge *me*?" Its voice was surprisingly squeaky for an evil mastermind.

"Yeah, I'm challenging you to a contest. You know how the rules work." Griffe reiterated, though the determined look on his face was offset by the sherbert-colored swirl of his affected eye.

Kelefer let out an exasperated groan. "Fine! What are your terms?"

"You. Me. Drinking contest. If I win, you let all these hostages go and you go back to the Shadowfelll and abide by the terms of the concord."

"And if I win?" Kelefer asked.

"You can keep those two over there." Griffe pointed at Merritt and Cruze.

"What?" "Hey now, that ain't right." Rough and Tumble protested.

"First one unable to continue from inebriation loses. We're drinking this stuff." Griffe snapped his fingers.

Like magic, the bottles from Grimtooth's distillery came flying in from the wood line, landing softly and rolling to a stop between Griffe and Kelefer.

Griffe picked one up and handed the bottle to his opponent for examination. The Fel-Pixie held it up to the light and grunted.

"Fine! Minions! Table and chairs!" Kelefer snapped its fingers, and the mind controlled pixies appeared from the fringes, setting up a single table in the middle of the village square with two chairs opposing each other. Two crystal shot glasses came out, and the bottles were set down. One of the controlled Pixies stumbled over and stood next to the table like a referee.

Griffe gestured toward the chair and Kelefer strode over and took its seat in a haughty strut.

"Shots!" The referee Pixie said, "One for one! First to cede loses!" The Pixie uncorked the liquor from Grimtooth's and poured each shot glass to full.

Griffe wrapped a hand around the glass in front of him and stared down Kelefer. The Pixie from Shadowfelll stared right back with harsh, unforgiving yellow eyes, grasping its own shot glass with three slender fingers.

They downed the liquor simultaneously, and Griffe slammed his glass on the table with a determined look in his eye.

Kelefer made a face at the taste of the liquor, baring tiny fangs in an open mouth snarl, "You know nothing, silly Gnome. I will drink you under this table and then, with my Pixie army, I will conquer your plane and restore glory to the Shadowfelll."

The referee poured another drink. Griffe downed it without blinking. Kelefer followed shortly after.

"Listen pal, you're not gonna touch my plane. You're not gonna win and when you go crawling back to the Shadowfelll after this, you're not going to be able to come back."

The referee poured the next. Griffe and Kelefer stared each other down with an intense hatred as they drank their next round. Griffe kept his eyes on Kelefer's drink, watching for changes. The liquor still tasted of rainbows and unicorn farts.

"You think just because you chose this potent concoction, you have a chance of stopping me?" Kelefer slammed down the next round. "I swear Gnome, you will lose. Your pitiful part of the forest will be in my hands by the end of this day."

Griffe drank the next round and stared belligerently at Kelefer. "Then keep on drinking."

The Pixie from the Shadowfelll looked shaken, a small quiver in its hand as it downed the next shot.

"Tell me, what does this stuff taste like to you?" Griffe asked, another glass imbibed to no ill effect.

"You know it tastes of the bitter fire of my eventual victory." Kelefer spat after drinking his matching shot.

"Really?" Griffe said with a smirk. "It tastes like rainbows and unicorn farts to me."

"*Wha*—?" Kelefer slammed a fist onto the table, shaking the nearly empty bottle, the sharp edge of its glare gone under a haze of drink. "You dare make fun of *me?*"

Griffe grinned at his opponent's slurring speech, coughing out the taste of Fae magic. The referee pixie poured out another round, emptying the first bottle.

"Cheers, pal. Here's to the second bottle." Griffe did a mocking toast with a mischievous grin before downing the last of the first.

Kelefer grimaced and drank his own shot, setting the glass back down with less bravado. The referee kept on pouring.

"What were you even thinking? Invade the mundane world with Pixies? None of them can hold their liquor, and neither can you. Nobody on this side of the slip drinks anything worth their weight." Griffe said as he led the way with another drink.

Kelefer was lagging, hesitating and breathing heavily, as the glass sat on its bottom lip more than a moment, before drinking it down and coughing.

"It's always the same with your kind." Kelefer glared as the referee poured another.

"Gnomes?" Griffe asked nonchalantly, tossing his shot back.

"No, *mortals*." Kelefer almost spat, "I was there in the War. My people sided with the Chiropterans to correct their injustices."

"Oh, I know. I was in the war too, pal. The Chiropterans were monsters."

"Only because of what your people did to them."

"*Ho-o-old* on there, buddy," another shot, "I was doing just fine in my neck of the forest until the Chiroptera burned down half my home. I joined up because those bat-eared monsters tore a fel-fire swath through my neighborhood and killed half the people I knew. All of that while screaming about injustice." By the end, Griffe was tapping the tip of his pointer and middle finger into the table to make his point, shaking the table they shared.

Kelefer spat at the ground to the side, the splash igniting into a sparkling rainbow gout. "We joined the war because you mortals broke your promise from the Second Age."

Griffe started laughing, "*The Second Age?!* You're holding a grudge from the Second Age? That's from my great-grandparents' time! Nobody but Elves remember the Second Age!"

Kelefer smoldered over its shot glass, the freshly poured drink refracting iridescent in the transparent crystal. "This is why I must make your kind remember your trespasses, mortal."

Kelefer drank the liquid down and slammed the glass onto the table, the mean spirited stare broken only by the side-to-side waver of the swaying of Kelefer's head.

"If anybody is regretting anything, it's going to be you, pal." Griffe downed his next drink and stared the Fel-Fae down with his one swirled eye.

The Fel-Pixie recoiled at Griffe's penetrating stare, downing the next shot and trying to return the Gnome's stare from under droopy eyelids.

"Injustice! You—you stole the pups! You stopped our trees!" Kelefer gave a drunken retort.

"Bull—" Griffe hiccupped, "—craaaap." He drew the word out in a long belch.

"You all tried sending your Fel-spawn through a gate and we kicked them back. All your stupid magic crap didn't amount to—" Griffe stopped himself and downed his shot.

Kelefer recoiled at the sudden stop before he matched him, sloppily drinking his own and falling silent in the face of his opponent.

"Unicorn fart in your drink? Rainbows stuck in your throat?" Griffe asked with a sly smile on his face, jittering, drunk eyes darting between Kelefer's eyes and hands.

"I—" Kelefer swept a drunken arm across the table, clattering both shot glasses to the ground, "I—" the Fel-Fae stumbled, both hands on the table like it was trying to stand before falling to the ground like a stone in a lake. Kelefer slammed its chin on the table on the way down, a light droning snore the only sign it was still alive.

Griffe snorted. "Serves you right, ya big bully."

"Griffe, are you alright?" Merritt asked, hands still bound.

"Don't you worry, Howie. I told you I'd come through." Griffe drunkenly pointed finger-guns in return.

"True. I've seen him drink far more than this and still be willing to fight." Url stood from the grass.

The captured pixies cheered in squeaky unison. Their mind-controlled counterparts snapped back to reality and hugged each other. One odd Pixie grabbed onto Cruze in elation. A moment later, the entranced Pixies began to retch, dry-heaving until the orbs of Abyss glass rolled out from their throats and onto the grass. Each sphere cracked and exhaled a dark inky flame, the final vestiges of the power they held broken by Griffe's victory.

"See Url?" Griffe said with pride in his voice. The Gnome stood up with a waver, grabbing the open bottle from the table and drinking another ferocious gulp.

"I told you it'd come in handy someday." He said before vomiting onto the fuchsia grass.

Trickster

By: Medron Pryde

Captain William Carter rode beneath the strange psychedelic sky, lighting the faery forest spread out around him and his traveling companions. Leroy huffed beneath him, having long since come to terms with the strange trees, ferns, and animals surrounding them. Bill was happy to have the old stud beneath him today. Leroy didn't surprise much these days.

But Bill's brain had long since overloaded on the odd colors of the faery world's daytime. He did his best to ignore them now. They were more unsettling than exotic, and he really wanted back in the real world, where he understood what colors were. You didn't *smell* colors in the real world after all. Or maybe that was a taste.

"Are we there, yet?" Bill knew the question sounded whinier than he wanted, but he just couldn't help it.

Joanna smiled from the back of the glowing faery mare that changed colors in time to the forest around them. "It's just around the foot of that hill."

Bill squinted and tried to impose some order on the faery colors around him until he saw the hill she was talking about through a break in the trees. A hill. She called that a *hill*. And he finally understood part of why he had been having so much trouble imposing order on the faery forest. He really wanted to know where she grew up because he never wanted to go to a place where the locals called a mountain that filled half the sky a *hill*.

Bill pulled in a long breath to keep from panicking.

Even Leroy's gait skipped a beat as he picked up on Bill's mood shift.

"Calm yourself," Joanna said in a tone one usually aimed towards a child worrying about night terrors. "This hill won't eat you."

Her statement was not as comforting as she may have thought. Because now hills that *did* eat people filled Bill's imagination. The mental picture of that was enough to make even a Texas Ranger tremble in his saddle.

Leroy shivered right along with him.

Joanna moved her mare in close to wrap her arms around Bill and pulled him down into her. She tucked his head under her chin and held him tight, letting him know that he wasn't alone in a strange land.

Leroy nickered in a tremulous tone. Somewhere between wondering if he should run in terror, or let the odd faery mare comfort him as well.

"Focus, William," Joanna continued in her calm tone. "Focus on staying close to me and I will brew you a cup of coffee fit to soothe your soul."

Bill followed her voice to focus on what was in front of him. Directly in front of him. Which was when he figured out where exactly Joanna had embedded his face.

Joanna breathed deep and the rise of her... lungs.... focused his mind quite nicely.

The terror of man-eating hills faded away in favor of a far more interesting rumination on the nature of faeries and their relations with men. Or perhaps one particular man. And one particular faery. Which led him to consider how such relations could work. And what this one particular faery might look like in the midst of them.

Joanna pushed him away, held him steady, and looked at him with an arched eyebrow.

That was when Bill realized his cheeks were heating up rather nicely. He was willing to bet his face was covered in one of the better blushes he had ever managed to generate.

Joanna sighed and shook her head. "You really need that coffee soon."

Bill cleared his throat and shook his head to clear his mind of the amazing mental image of Joanna in her... out of her... Bill pinched himself and felt the pain sharpen his mental control nicely. He cleared his throat again and gave her what he hoped was at least something approaching a calm smile.

"In my defense, Ma'am..."

Joanna raised her other eyebrow as his voice trailed off.

Bill coughed to gain time to consider what exactly it was safe to say, considering where his face had just been. Of course, she'd been the one to put his face there. But he doubted saying that would be helpful at the moment. So he said the next thing that came to mind.

"My Lady. A woman of your caliber... any man that didn't find you... amazing... would be a fool."

Joanna blinked. She cocked her head to the side in thought. She blinked again. Then she smiled and turned her mare to trot between two trees in the direction of the hill. The mountain.

"Come along, William," she said as her mare shone bright enough to stand out against even the undulating faery forest. "We need to get you somewhere safe before you say something you can't take back."

"I speak nothing but truth, My Lady," Bill spoke and kneed Leroy into following them.

"Joanna," the faery corrected him.

"Joanna." Bill cleared his throat again and focused on the faery sitting astride her faery mare. Yes, she had all the right curves in all the right places, as some men said it. Not Bill, of course. Bill was far too gentlemanly to say anything like that. Thinking it was another matter entirely. Just as he considered that, she moved in time with her mare in a manner most pleasing to the… eye. He let out a long breath and forced himself not to think what he was thinking.

He would have told any of his fellows they were cracked if they said he would ever be in a situation like this even a week ago. He knew how dangerous the faery were. Dangerous and fickle and always moving on whenever their business was done. Sometimes you needed the old Celtic runes only they remembered how to make, but a smart man had to keep each transaction, each debt, easily and completely payable, so all sides could walk away with a clean slate. No sane man wanted to owe a debt to the faery, and that paled in comparison to how dangerous it could be to leave a faery owing *you*.

It had all been going so smoothly until he saved her soul. Now here he was, following her on a shortcut through her home forest because he could not afford to leave her until she repaid that debt. It was enough to make a sane man go crazy.

He prayed to God Almighty that we would survive long enough to write that debt off before everything went out of control.

He was still considering all the ways that could go wrong, or very, *very* right whenever his imagination wandered back to her shapely form, when she guided them into a clearing. She came to a stop and pointed out a small mound of rocks. A signpost stood atop it emblazoned with faery runes.

"We have reached our destination," Joanna said with a nod towards the mound.

She dismounted from her multi-colored mare and pulled a tent roll off the back of her saddle. She placed it on the ground near the mound, untied the cords holding it together, and gave it three quick taps before stepping back. The tent unrolled itself to lie flat on the ground, and then unfolded itself the other way until it covered a square of ground nearly three yards on a side. A series of rapid explosions drove stakes into the ground to hold it tight, and then poles began lifting the tent up into the air.

The tent stood taller than a man in seconds, and a central pennant rose into the air to flap in the wind rolling through the faery forest.

Joanna had grabbed several small stakes from her saddlebags as the tent grew itself, and she stuck them into the ground around the tent and stone mound. Those stakes extended into the sky even faster than the tent, some quickly unfurling their own pennants, while others exploded outward at the top to become light posts. Pure white light poured out from them to drive the undulating faery lights away from the camp.

Bill watched the whole process with wide eyes. He had seen a faery camp raising a few times, but not enough to dispel the sense of wonder seeing it brought. It was enough to make a man want to have one of his own.

Joanna grabbed him by the collar and dragged him through the tent flaps. He did not resist, happily putting away the worry that a man-eating hill might track him down in her tent. No man-eating hill would dare anger a faery of her caliber after all. A comfortable warmth touched his face, and the inside of the tent spread out far beyond the dimensions of the outer wall.

This was a true faery tent. Far, far, larger on the inside than it was on the outside.

Joanna walked across the tent to a large four-poster bed and took her sword off to hang its scabbard on a bedpost. Then she aimed a wry smile at his host of weapons and waved towards a coat tree next to the tent flaps. "Hang up your weapons, William."

"Yes, My Lady," Bill said and began hanging his holsters and scabbards on the tree.

"Joanna," she corrected and grabbed a kettle off the central table to place it on the warm stove against one wall.

"Joanna," he repeated and looked at the tent walls holding the faery landscape beyond it at bay. He'd always thought those lands to be beautiful and amazing to look at, which they were. But he'd only visited them before. He understood that now. It appeared even his mind was not entirely flexible enough to handle long-term immersion in the faery world.

"My apologies, My Lady," Bill said in an even and calm voice as he looked around the interior of her calming tent. "I do believe I was not entirely in control of my faculties for a moment there."

"You need not apologize to me, William." Joanna aimed a wry smile at him and pulled a bag of coffee beans out of a drawer. "The fault was mine. I misjudged the resilience of your mind to the dangers of my world. If anyone should apologize, it is me."

Bill raised a hand to stop her. "Just hold up a moment. I'm not sure I can handle you apologizing to me because my mind is too weak to survive the faery world."

"Hat. Now." She aimed a finger at the coat tree and her eyes held his.

He let out a breath, took his cowboy hat off, and hung it on the tree as his lady ordered. A turn from the tree brought him into the double-barreled aim of her raised eyebrows and another wave towards the coat tree. He sighed and hung his duster on the tree as well. When he finally turned back to her, he felt naked as the day he was born.

Joanna smiled and pointed him towards a couch. She waited until he sat down as ordered before pouring the coffee beans into a grinder. "You are a remarkable man, William. Few men born of your world could have spent an entire day's travel in my world before showing the beginnings of the madness."

Bill winced. He shouldn't be in the position of needing her help at all.

"What are you thinking, William?"

Bill shook his head.

"Tell me, William."

Bill waved a hand towards the tent flap. "When does *that* get easier? When does your *sky* stop trying to hurt my *sanity*?"

"Never." Joanna turned the grinder and a floral aroma filled the tent. "I expect you will become more resilient in time, though. Assuming you *survive* spending time here."

Bill breathed in and out, letting the heavenly aroma calm his soul. Then he opened his eyes again and looked towards Joanna. "What happens if I don't?"

She stopped grinding, aimed a speculative eye at the coffee grounds, and shifted them back and forth to make certain they were well and properly ground. She didn't answer him until she was certain. "Then you will either need to stay out of my world or you will go quite mad."

Bill blinked. Then cleared his throat. "I'd prefer not to be quite as mad as a hatter."

"Oh, you can't help that," Joanna said with a Cheshire smile and walked over to pour the grounds into the steaming kettle. "We're all mad here."

Bill laughed at the proof that she had read that new story.

"Wonderland *has* to be a faery realm, yes?"

"Of *course* it is," Joanna answered with a twinkle in her eyes and stirred the coffee into the water. "You don't write a story *that* mad without being touched by some particularly *tricksy* fae."

"Not you, of course."

"Oh, no." Joanna winked at him. "I'm a perfectly nice faery."

"Without a tricksy bone in your body?"

"I wouldn't go that far." Joanna examined the coffee with care. "Some have dealt unfairly with me and learned that I can be most tricksy indeed."

Words popped into Bill's mind. He wondered if he truly wanted to say them in that moment, or if they were phantom wisps of his imagination. He turned the words over in his mind and decided that he wished to say them. That he *needed* to say them.

"I swear that I will never deal unfairly with you, my Lady." Bill nodded towards Joanna and her eyes widened in surprise.

"Joanna," she corrected as if in reflex.

"No," Bill said with a shake of his head, and her eyes narrowed. "Not just Joanna. *Whatever* name you claim, whatever names you answer to, in the past or in the future. Whoever you become or return to be. I swear this to *you*, My Lady. I will never deal unfairly with *you*. May your laws bind my words."

"Few men dare an oath that binding." Joanna pulled in a long breath. "It will hold you, you know."

"Until the breaking of my soul," Bill said and felt the oath settle into his bones and deeper.

Joanna dipped her head and swallowed. "I would never demand an oath like that of you."

"The oath is freely given, of my own free will."

Joanna turned away and lifted the kettle off the stove to place it on a stone in the middle of her table. She stood there for a long moment before letting out a long breath. Then she crossed the tent to pull a pair of fine coffee cups out of a small cupboard and gave him a questioning look. "The only thing you sought the day you entered my market was runes for your weapons."

"That is true," Bill said in full honesty.

Joanna placed the empty cups on the table, and raised her eyes to him again. "You considered my kind too dangerous to maintain long-term arrangements with."

"That is true," Bill said with a wry smile.

Joanna stood up tall and the faery in her shone bright and dangerous. And when she spoke, the faery forest around them trembled beneath the strength of her voice. "What have I done to make you think I was less dangerous than you imagined that day?"

Bill held his ground and his smile. "Absolutely nothing, My Lady."

Joanna blinked, and the faery faded from her face. And when she spoke, her voice had lost the faery strength as well. It even trembled. "Joanna. I gave you the name *Joanna*. *Why* can't you just call me *Joanna*?"

"You gave me your true name *first*," Bill said very carefully. "*Before* you gave me Joanna."

Joanna shook her head and began pouring the coffee into the cups. "You needed a name you could speak in public. So I gave you Joanna."

Bill sighed in frustration. "Well, maybe I want *more* than that. What can I call you in *private*? Jo?"

"No!" The faery voice boomed through the tent, and she slammed her hands atop the table hard enough to rattle the cups. The otherworldly faery stared at him, and he felt both seconds and years go by at once. Then she sighed and shook her head. The faery faded and Joanna looked out through her eyes again. "My apologies, William. I did not mean to snap at you."

Bill shook his head in response. "I should be the one apologizing this time, Joanna. I spoke too… presumptuously."

Joanna ran elegant fingers over her face and sighed again. "I demanded an answer of you. Do not apologize for doing as your lady bade you."

Then she picked up one of the cups and brought it over to Bill with a smile. "Now I promised you a coffee fit to soothe the soul, William. So drink it and be well."

Bill took the cup from her fingers, raised it to his nose, and breathed the floral aroma in. It felt… rich. He detected something honeyed and a strong citrus flavor. And was there something… woody?

Joanna came back and sat down next to him on the couch. She raised her cup towards him and smiled. "Drink up, William."

Bill did as his lady bade him do and placed the cup against his lips to take a careful sip. He detected something almost like a berry, and then just a slightly tart flavor sealed the deal. Bill leaned back into the couch, took a long sip, and his soul rejoiced at the rich and fragrant brew. He shut his eyes and felt time stop around him. Or maybe it sped ahead. He couldn't really tell. He sat still for a moment, or maybe an eternity. When he opened his eyes again, Joanna was examining him carefully over the brim of her cup.

"How are you?"

Bill let out a long breath and said the first thing that came to mind. The words of a new song from a new hymnal. "It is well with my soul."

"Good." Joanna lowered her cup to reveal a beaming smile, and her eyes twinkled at him. "Now finish your cup, William."

"Yes, My Lady," Bill whispered.

"Joanna," she corrected with an amused look.

"Joanna." He drank the rest of the cup down as his lady bade him. The smooth and rich flavor settled all the way down to fortify his soul against all attacks. She was right again. She knew exactly the right kind of coffee he needed. And sitting next to her on the couch, he realized he could sit right here for an eternity and never tire of it.

"We have business, William," she whispered into his eternity. "We have rested long enough, I think. Now it is time for us to do what we came for."

Bill opened his eyes again, sucked in a long breath, and nodded very slowly. "Lead the way, My Lady."

Her lips twitched. "Joanna."

He winked. "Joanna."

She shook her head in amusement, leaned forward, and came to her feet in a graceful motion. Then she took his empty cup and placed it on the table.

"Gear up, William."

Bill pressed himself to his feet and stepped over to the coat tree. He grabbed the duster first and slipped his arms into it. Its heavy leather weight fell onto his shoulders and he sighed. The revolver holsters came next, and he strapped them on one leg at a time, cinching them tight so they would hold in place through any fight. Then he slipped the saber scabbards and the rifle holster over his back, and the old familiar weights settled on his shoulders. He reached for the cowboy hat last, held it in his hands for a long moment, and turned his head to look at Joanna.

"My Lady?"

She stepped away from her four-poster bed and slipped her sword and scabbard onto her back with a smile. And this time when she said a name, it was not a correction.

"William?"

Bill smiled at her. "Lead the way, My Lady. I shall follow."

She smiled, strode out of her tent, and Bill followed to find her mare and Leroy waiting for them just outside the tent in a second tent that looked just the right size for a pair of horses to stand it. And their noses were wet. He glanced around quickly to see a trough full of water, and another of feed in the tent. He looked around them in search of whoever had cared for the horses and found a young tree spirit hiding behind a nearby trunk.

Bill waved a hand towards the horses and smiled. "Did you do this?"

The spirit that looked like a young girl nodded vigorously but maintained her careful distance from him.

"Thank you." Bill dug into his coin pouch, pulled out a silver coin, and tossed it towards the tree spirit.

The girl snatched it out of thin air, smiled in a delighted manner, and escaped between the trees like a breath of wind.

"You didn't need to do that," Joanna whispered.

"All debts must be paid." Bill shrugged towards her.

"Indeed." Joanna nodded in understanding. Then she glanced back to the horses and several more tree spirits looking on intently. "Her sisters will keep our horses safe. You should get your weapons."

Bill thought about protesting, but he had told her to lead the way, and he was a man of his word. So he stepped over to Leroy's side, patted the old warhorse, and pulled his old Colt Dragoons out of their saddle holsters. They slipped into the low-slung holsters on his legs where they tried to drag his trousers down. Then he grabbed his old Colt revolver rifle and slipped that into his back holster. The entire harness of scabbards and holsters set their old familiar weight on his broad shoulders.

When he turned back to Joanna, he was Captain William Carter again. Texas Ranger and hunter of otherworldly creatures and threats to mankind.

"And there he is," she whispered with a smile. "It's good to have you back, Captain."

"It's good to *be* back." Bill cleared his throat. "I owe you a debt."

"We can measure it against the debt I owe you when we return." She aimed a shining smile at him before turning to the signpost. "Now follow me."

Bill followed as ordered as she stepped out and walked around the signpost and the rock mound under it three times. She came to a stop at the end of the third circuit, raised her hands, and spoke in her faery tongue.

The veil between the worlds split open, and the Indian side of Santa Fe appeared before them. Joanna stepped out of the faery world with Bill close on her heels, and the dry desert air slapped them in the faces. But not one single person in the entire street realized that two people had just stepped out of nowhere into their midst. The veil between the worlds had a way of making otherworldly things like that fade from the memory of men. Just as most men never saw the faery world on the other side when the veil opened.

Bill now understood just how lucky they were.

Bill breathed in the dry air that seemed so strange after the long hours of wet forest air and studied the town around him. So much of it remained the same since the last time he came through decades before, and he wondered how many of the same faces he would see when he wandered down the old alleys. He wondered if they would remember him. Or if they would think him a figment of their imagination. A man who just *looked* similar to a man they had talked to all those years ago.

"William?"

Bill shook his head and smiled at his companion. "My apologies again. I got lost in the last time I was here."

Joanna nodded very slowly. "Those who live long enough often find themselves lost in the past."

"My father used to say something similar," Bill said in a wry tone.

Joanna nodded very slowly and gave him a sly smile. Then she motioned for him to follow and turned down one of the alleys running through the Indian side of Santa Fe. The worlds met here. It was the end of the Santa Fe Trail and the beginning of the heavily wooded mountains where many Indian tribes still held out. The Great American Desert his people were busy colonizing, lay tantalizingly close, while canyons and mesas filled with more Indians ruled the lands all around it. The civilized world ended at Santa Fe and the Indian world still held sway in the wild lands America had not yet tamed.

And the old magics still ruled out here. Not that they were truly superior to the new magics. But everything followed rules. They were all just different kinds of power, and power always had to be respected. Fires and forges created a new kind of power that would change the world. But faery power could improve everything. Though even the faery followed their own rules and natures. Properly otherworldly rules, of course.

And here he was, entangling himself in the affairs of the faery, far more completely than he had ever intended. His new rifle needed new runes before it could replace the old friend that had served him faithfully through many hunts over the years. But the new magic of technology made better weapons out of better metals and his old weapons were getting long in the tooth. It took faeries to make the old Celtic runes these days, and he needed to make his weapons more effective against the otherworldly enemies he faced. But that was just one excuse, and he knew it.

He walked in Joanna's wake for another reason entirely. Followed her around the Indian markets of Santa Fe as she haggled over this or that little item, herb, or mineral that she needed to make the very best runes.

A part of him tried to remind himself that he wouldn't have come here if it weren't for that. He had foes to fight in Indian Territory. No Man's Land waited for him. Kansas and Colorado. New Mexico. All the lands outside the growing railroad network needed people like him to keep the otherworldly creatures away from civilization. He needed to get back on the job, and following a faery around Indian markets in search of just the right trinket was a waste of his time and his talents. Whatever she said, she owed him. He should have just rode hard out of her market and let the chips fall where they may.

He licked his lips as they strode from one end of the Indian side of Santa Fe to the other. He scanned for enemies as Joanna haggled with merchants. He admired her gracefulness when he took a second to glance at her. She really was amazing. But she was faery. He shouldn't even be thinking about this. She didn't belong in his world. And he certainly didn't belong in hers.

But God Almighty, he wanted to.

He frowned as they approached a broken down building. The pain radiating off the structure registered, and he stopped in his tracks. The poor thing had been wounded horribly. He studied it for a moment before realizing it seemed familiar to him. He had been here before, but it looked so different now.

"Do you sense it?" Joanna asked.

"Yes."

"There is a powerful shaman nearby."

Bill blinked as he finally recognized what he was looking at. He raised a hand to point out the fallen roof. "There's supposed to be a bell tower up there."

Joanna looked at him. "You know this place?"

"I came through here back in the forties to survey this land. I remember this place."

"This is one of your churches, isn't it?" Joanna asked in a thoughtful tone.

Bill smiled. "You are looking at the San Miguel Mission. The *oldest* church in the United States."

Joanna aimed a hard look at him. "The oldest? You are certain?"

Bill nodded. "When the Spaniards came to this land, they built this church for their Indian allies. They considered it more important that their allies have a place to worship than they. They built their own chapels on the other side of the river later. This right here was their first claim to the region. Their first statement that this land belonged to God. And Spain, of course."

"Their claim is looking ragged now."

"Yes, it is."

"You know what happens when a civilization doesn't maintain a claim on their land."

"They lose it." Bill aimed a cocky smile at her. "That's why we're standing in *American* lands today."

Joanna gave him a very old look. "And here I was talking about Christendom."

Bill winced at that line of thinking. "Christendom hasn't been a united civilization in centuries. If ever."

"And yet the sun never sets on Christendom."

"That's the *British* Empire."

"*You* are British, William."

"I'm *American*, actually."

Joanna gave him a sly smile. "You can never fully escape your birth, William. No matter what name you call yourself."

"Names have power." Bill aimed a wry smile at her. "Isn't that right, Jo?"

"Joanna," she returned with a sigh.

"Joanna." He bowed his head to accept her declaration.

Joanna frowned at him for a long moment before turning to nod towards the chapel. "What did this?"

Bill followed her gaze and let out a long breath.

"I received reports of a major storm coming through here a few years back. I always meant to come take a look, but I've been busy."

"So goes the story of our lives," Joanna said. "Always thinking what we are doing right now is the most important thing in our lives."

"You won't get an argument from me on that." Bill sighed at the dilapidated church. "I really didn't realize the damage was so extensive. And I guess I just assumed that the locals fixed it."

Joanna aimed an amused eye at him. "You know what assuming makes of you and me?"

Bill chuckled at the ribald humor. "I do indeed."

"What are you going to do?"

"I'm going in there."

"To face whatever is actively desecrating the oldest church in your entire nation?"

Bill winced again. "I really don't like it when you put it that way."

"I know. There *is* a shaman out there." She aimed a pointed look out towards the edge of town and the mountains beyond it. "No telling what kind of power we are dealing with here."

"We?"

Joanna smiled at him. "I owe you my soul, William. Do you really think I would allow you to walk into danger alone?"

"Actually, I'd prefer you did." Bill grimaced and stared at the fallen church. "I don't want you doing *anything* because you owe me. I want you to... *want* to..."

He trailed off and cleared his throat.

Joanna rested a hand on his shoulder. "Then what if I said I wanted to accompany you as a friend? Would that be good, William?"

Bill turned to meet her gaze for a long moment. Then he nodded as he saw the truth in her eyes. "That would be good."

Joanna smiled. "So what do we do?"

"I go first," Bill said without hesitation and walked up to the chapel. "The chapel *should* recognize me if it has not forgotten too much. You follow me as closely as you can."

Bill smiled at her. "We don't want it thinking you are a heathen intruder."

"Perish the thought," the faery said with a wink. Then she stepped behind him and slipped up to within a hair's breadth of him. Her fae energy crackled against his own for a second. Then their energies harmonized, and the world snapped into a slightly different focus. The colors were just a little richer. The sounds sharper, and yet more pleasant. Smells became more pungent.

"Is this close enough?" she whispered, and the breath from her lips made the hair on his neck stand straight on end.

Bill licked his lips. She was the perfect height for this kind of thing.

"You're perfect," he said and started making his way through the first of the broken walls. She followed his moves with the kind of perfection one should expect of a fine faery lady, and he smiled. It took nearly a minute to find a way into the inner chapel, which looked considerably larger on the inside than it had on the outside. Not that it actually was. It wasn't a faery structure, after all. But it did a good job of copying the effect now that he was on the inside.

The chapel didn't appear as abandoned as the outer walls suggested, but it still showed the aging effects of neglect and time. And a feeling of oppression filled it. A feeling of unsanctified power radiated throughout the chapel.

Bill pulled the silver cross necklace out from under his shirt and held it out into the darkness. He poured his intent into the cross and its silvery glow came to life to bathe the church with light.

Then he spoke a few words in Latin, a command to the spirit desecrating the chapel to show itself.

A coyote in the shape of a man stepped out of the destroyed rafters with a dangerous smile on his face.

"Hello, White Man."

"Hello, trickster."

The coyote bowed in a mocking salute. "It is so good to be recognized. Now why is a White Man trespassing on my land?"

"This chapel rests on consecrated land." Bill spread his free arm out to take in the ruins. "Whatever its current condition, you have no right to be here, trickster."

"The White Man stole this land from me," the trickster snarled back. "But I reclaimed it with storm and fire! Your pitiful god has no power in my lands."

Bill cocked his head to the side. "He created *all* the lands, trickster."

"Only in the White Man tales," the trickster hissed. "But you are in *my* lands now, White Man. And in *my* lands, it is *my* tales that tell truth! Your White Man god has no power here."

Bill smiled as the cross in his hands continued to glow. "I would not be so sure of that statement if I were you."

"Haven't you heard, White Man? Your age of railroads is here! But they won't come all the way up here into the mountains. The vaunted Santa Fe Trail will die soon. This town will wither and fade on the wind. My time returns, and my ways will command the mountains again!"

"I have found a link to the shaman," Joanna whispered onto his neck. "Can you cut it?"

Joanna's movement was her answer. She stepped out of his shadow with a swift, smooth clarity of action; light glowed in her hands as she flanked the trickster spirit, and she spun in an arc to bring faery fire down behind it. Her fire illuminated a tendril of magic running from it and out through the chapel wall, most likely to the shaman that had probably summoned him. The tendril burned and faery fire flowed down it in both directions, leaving behind nothing but dead air. The fire scorched through the chapel wall in one direction, and slammed into the trickster to surround it in a sparking corona of power in the other.

Crackling power surged through the Indian trickster spirit and anger twisted its face. "Oh, you tricksy pixie sprite! You'll pay for that!"

The trickster spirit lashed out, nearly faster than Bill could track, and Joanna stumbled away as she blocked the attack with her faery fire. The spirit struck again and again, and fae energy splashed all over the inside of the chapel as she retreated.

Bill pulled his old Starr cavalry sabers out of their scabbards on his back and charged forward to attack the trickster from the rear. The silvery Celtic runes carved into the sabers by genuine faeries glowed and Bill swung his first glowing saber down towards the spirit's spine. The trickster dodged. Bill flicked the second saber in a quick distraction attack as the spirit's speed fully registered. He needed to keep it off its game, or this was going to be a very short fight.

The Indian spirit blocked the distraction saber and spun fast enough to nearly kick the other saber out of his hand. Bill stumbled back towards the center of the chapel, and the trickster turned its full attention back to Joanna. It was just in time to meet Joanna's attack. Her sword came up out of the scabbard on her back and swooped down from above in a single smooth motion, and the faery fire radiating off it cut clean through the trickster. Faery fire burned the spirit from the inside out until it simply ceased to exist.

Bill breathed a sigh of relief. They'd won.

His sabers continued to glow bright enough to bathe the chapel with light.

Joanna glanced at the sabers before meeting his gaze. They weren't done yet.

That was when the trickster spirit stepped out of the shadows behind Joanna and backhanded her into the wall. Literally. Into the wall.

The faery disappeared into the stone with a cry of shock until only her hands remained. Her faery fire died; the sword clattered to the ground, and her hands hung limp from the stone wall.

Bill knew in that instant that he was way outside his league. Nothing he had could stop the kind of spirit that could just backhand a faery into a wall. He needed help.

Bill spoke a prayer in Latin, calling on the archangel Michael to come to his aid. The silver cross necklace glowed bright as day in answer, and the Celtic cross rings on his fingers shone with a bright emerald light that filled every shadow in the chapel.

"You put on a nice light show, White Man, but it's just you and me now," the trickster said in a sing-song tone as he admired his handiwork. "Are you going to run? I like it when they run."

"Release her," Bill said in a low but determined tone and held his glowing sabers between them in a dueling stance. "Release her right now and I will let you live."

The trickster swung to Bill with a terrifying smile and chuckled. "Oh, you have no power in my lands."

"I already told you," Bill said in a calm tone. "This land is consecrated, this chapel devoted to the archangel Michael. And I can assure you that Michael is not amused at what you have done to his place."

"Michael is not here," the spirit cackled. "And I tire of this charade."

The spirit lashed out, and the full power of an Indian trickster god struck first one saber and then the other. It sent each saber sparking to the side, and it was all Bill could do to keep from dropping them altogether. But his sabers were now out of position, and Bill was a lifetime too slow to bring them back to block the spirit's next attack.

He knew it.

The trickster knew it.

The spirit's face filled with a triumphant smile, and it rushed to the attack.

That was when a feeling of power settled onto Bill's shoulders, and he wasn't alone anymore. A sword slipped into the world amidst a flash of blue lights to pierce the charging spirit's heart.

The Indian spirit shuddered as the sword's power pierced it and looked up in shock at the powerful presence standing behind Bill. "No!"

"Trespasser," the presence behind Bill spoke in a tone that reminded him of the grinding of mountain ranges.

"No!" the trickster shouted again. It tried to move, but the extended sword held it in-place like a fly pinned to a table.

Bill took a moment to flex the numb fingers barely holding onto his sabers.

"These are *my* lands!" the trickster protested. "They have *been* my lands since *long* before your paltry little religion even existed!"

"Haven't you heard?" Bill asked with a forced chuckle. He really had to do his best to keep his composure here. "The Jews were writing about Michael back before your people even learned how to build cities. You're not the first person who's desecrated a holy place under his protection. And he's really not amused."

The trickster struggled against the angel's bonds, but Michael held it fast.

Bill smiled at the spirit. "And this isn't our first rodeo."

"What are you going to do?" The spirit snarled at him. "He can't dispel me! This is *my* land!"

Bill shook the sabers again and began walking around the Indian spirit. He wasn't so certain about the truth of the spirit's statement. This *was* Michael's chapel after all, but dispelling wasn't always the best way to deal with a spirit. Dispelled spirits had a tendency to come back madder than before if you didn't really make it stick. Besides, he had a better way to deal with the spirit once and for all, now that Michael had him pinned. He aimed a glance at Michael before speaking.

"Now look here, Reynard. That's just really not going to work this time." Michael smiled.

"What? Who?" The spirit looked confused. "Who is…?"

"Reynard. *You*. Reynard," Bill said and focused all his willpower behind the image of Reynard the fox. The trickster spirit of European folklore. He held onto that image as he walked to put the spirit between him and the apparition of Michael.

"No!" the spirit screamed in anger and spun its head to face Bill. "I am—"

"*Reynard*," Bill interrupted before the spirit could say the name the Indians of this land called it. "The *trickster* spirit!"

"No!" the spirit repeated and shook its head. "I mean... yes... but... *no*!"

"I name thee *Reynard*," Bill said as he completed his circuit around the Indian spirit.

The apparition of Michael lifted his sword out of the way, but Bill felt the archangel's power still holding the Indian spirit in its place.

"No," the Indian trickster spirit recoiled from the name. "No. My name is—"

"*Reynard*," Bill tossed in as he continued walking his circuit. "Reynard the fox. The trickster spirit. You always seek to pull one over on everybody else. Isn't that right, Reynard? You want to *trick* me, *don't* you, *Reynard*?"

"No!" the trickster wailed in confusion. "I mean, *yes*! I *do* want to trick you! But, no, I'm *not* Reynard!"

Bill smiled as he got the trickster to say the name he wanted. The more often he could get the spirit to answer to that name, the more power that name would have. He raised a saber to point at Michael. Michael lowered his sword as the Indian spirit came between them and the spirit writhed in the consecrated power of Michael's chapel.

"Of *course* you're Reynard," Bill said with a smile. "Who else would you be? *Reynard*?"

"I'm..." the Indian spirit blinked in confusion as it tried to remember. "I..."

Bill finished his second circuit around the spirit and spoke a single command. "I name thee *Reynard*."

"No..." the Indian spirit wailed as it finally realized its peril and turned pleading eyes towards Bill. "Please. No. Don't take my name from me."

"I don't have a choice, *Reynard*," Bill intoned as he continued walking around the spirit.

"Please," the Indian spirit pleaded and reached pitiable hands out towards Bill. "Please. You've already taken so many lands from me. Can't you leave me *this* at least?"

"I'm sorry, *Reynard*," Bill said and took another step. "But you're hurting too many people now."

"Me? *Me*?" the Indian spirit cackled hysterically. "*Hurting* people? You *killed* my people! You drove us down trails of tears and blood! You *slaughtered* us like animals! You *erased* us from the lands we were *born* to!"

Bill met Michael's eyes as their gaze passed over the spirit. He let out a long breath and actually felt sorry for the Indian spirit. Everything it said was true. From a certain point of view. But it was a point of view Bill could not afford to give strength in this moment, so he brushed it aside and turned his attention back to the spirit.

"That's not the story here, *Reynard*. You should know that. The Indians that built this town were allies and friends."

"They were *invaders!*" the spirit hissed back. "Just like *you!*"

Bill sighed. Just one more reminder that the Indians had been slaughtering each other long before the Europeans arrived.

"Well, this time *you* are the invader."

"*No!*" the Indian spirit gasped in a pleading, angry tone and turned to meet his eyes. "*No!* This is *my* land! Can't you *see* that?"

"No," Bill said and stared deep into the spirit's eyes. "No, I can't. Because the moment I let myself see this from your point of view is the moment you gain power over me. And I can't allow that right now."

"Why? Why not?" The desperate spirit shook in Michael's grip, but it couldn't escape. "Please. I'll give you whatever you want! Just let me live and I'll do whatever you want! Gold. Women. You can have it all."

Bill took one final step to stand in front of Michael a third time and leaned in close to the coyote in the shape of a man. Desperate eyes filled his vision beyond a terrified coyote snout.

"Reynard would never imprison my friend in a stone wall," Bill said in the very coldest tone he could pull from his oldest memories.

The trickster's eyes opened wider as it realized the depths of its error. "I'll… I'll let her go… please… let me let her go for you!"

There were so many things Bill wanted to say in that moment. So many threats or promises or reasons why he could accept or not accept the spirit's desperate offer. He could go on for days about all the missed opportunities they'd had. All the ways they could have taken a different path. Worked together instead of against each other. But an Indian shaman had raised this spirit to do battle with his people and he could see the poison of hate filling its soul beneath the momentary desperation to live. The spirit *wanted* to fight the White Men. It would never hold to any agreement with him. And if he gave the spirit his words and his time right now, he would just be giving it power it could use against him when it did. That could not be allowed, so Bill shut down the pride that would have led him into a long monologue about his impending victory. He shut down the mercy that would have led him into giving it one last chance to be better. He couldn't let any of that feed the spirit. So he spoke four words for a third time with cold, determined eyes.

"I name thee *Reynard.*"

The trickster's eyes opened all the way as the proclamation hit home. It shook its head in confusion. Then a red fox darted away from Bill to quiver in a corner while looking around with furtive motions.

"Oh. Oh my. This is new," a higher-pitched voice said. "I've never been *here* before."

The trickster fox darted over to a window and looked out. "Desert!"

He sprang to another window. "Mountains!"

The trickster turned back to Bill with an eager look in his eyes. "Are these the *Rockies*?"

"Yes, Reynard," Bill said with a smile. "These are the Rockies."

"Ooohhh," the trickster said in wonder. "I've never been to the *Rockies* before, have I?"

Bill shrugged. "Some of you have. But I know the you from Connecticut, and that you has never seen the Rockies before."

"Ah." Reynard looked back out through the window with a sigh. "That makes sense. This really *is* beautiful land, you know."

"Yes, it is."

Reynard turned a sad gaze towards Bill. "I can see why the other guy didn't want to give it up."

Bill sighed and took a moment to sheath his sabers again. "I can too."

"And yet you still did it," Reynard said with a sad sigh. "Why did you do it *this* time, Bill?"

Bill waved a hand towards Joanna, still imprisoned in the chapel's stone walls.

"Oh." Reynard's nose quivered in horror. "Oh, *no*. You *know* she's not from our world. *Don't* you, Bill?"

"Yes, I do." Bill met the trickster spirit's gaze with a calm smile.

"You *know* she'll go away, right?" Reynard asked. His nose quivered with concern. "They *never* stay. They aren't like you and I, Bill. They aren't anchored to this land. They *always* go home in time."

Bill swallowed the lump in his throat. He wanted to protest. His soul cried out at the idea. But the spirit was right. Her kind *did* always leave. But by God, he didn't want that. "Will you free her? I can owe you for it."

Reynard padded over to Bill and hugged the Texas Ranger as an old friend. "*I* owe *you* a life, Bill. *Another* life. Here. Now. Tell you what. I'll free her on the house. This time. But remember that I warned you."

Bill patted the red fox's shoulder in an affectionate manner. "I'll remember, Reynard. You're a good friend to worry about me like this."

The trickster spirit's eyes opened wide. "Oh, you don't really think you can make her stay, do you?"

"Oh, no," Bill answered with a shake of his head. He chewed his lip and looked at her arms coming out of the stone. "I would never *make* her stay."

The trickster spirit followed his gaze and let out a long breath. "Oh, I see what you're doing. Tricksy, tricksy, tricksy..."

Bill spread his arms out wide in an innocent gesture. "I have no idea what you are talking about."

"Uh huh," the red fox said and scampered over to Joanna. "Keep saying that enough times. Maybe someone will believe you."

Then the trickster spirit grabbed Joanna's hands and pulled her out of the chapel wall.

The faery jerked in confusion and frowned at the little red fox patting his paws all over her clothing. "What?"

"How are you? Are you good?" the fox asked, and her confusion deepened.

"Ah… yes?"

"Is that a question or an answer?" The fox chuckled and patted her head. "Don't worry. The other guy is gone, so you don't have to worry about him throwing you into a wall again. Besides, I don't do those kinds of things. Far too messy."

Joanna cleared her throat and gave a bewildered look at Bill and the angel standing behind him. "Who…"

Her eyes turned back to the fox with a confused look. "What?"

The fox stepped back away from her and gave her a low bow.

"My Lady!" he proclaimed in a proud and triumphant tone. "I am Reynard the fox. And I am the best trickster spirit in all the lands!"

Then the red fox scampered out of the chapel and disappeared before they could say another word.

"What…" Joanna looked back and forth between the window the fox had jumped through and the angel standing behind Bill. "What just happened?"

Bill shrugged as if it was no big deal. "Oh, I just tricked an Indian trickster spirit into turning into a *European* trickster spirit."

Joanna shook her head to clear it. Then she sighed. "You make that sound so simple."

"That's because it *was* simple. Not easy. Just simple." Bill looked around the chapel and let out a long breath. A hand waved towards the angel. "I needed *him* to hold *it* in place while I got it to accept the name change."

Bill bowed towards the angel. "Thank you for answering my call, Michael. I will, of course, arrange for this chapel to be rebuilt for His glory."

The angel bowed to Bill and stepped back out of the world with a flash of blue light. It left behind a feeling of holy consecration embedded in the very walls and floors around them. A claim that this chapel was not nearly as abandoned as it looked. Not anymore.

Joanna watched the angel leave before turning her attention to Bill. "You called *him* to free *me*? I am in your debt yet again."

Bill cleared his throat. This was not going the right direction at all.

"Honestly, I should have taken care of this years ago. If I had, the local trickster spirit would not have grown so powerful. You were put at risk due to my lack of knowledge and action. You only needed saving because I dragged you into a situation of my own creation."

Joanna raised a hand to her throat and just smiled at him. "We already established that I came with you of my own free will, William. As a friend. You're not going to get out of me owing you a soul that easily."

Bill sighed and wondered what exactly he did to deserve all of this.

"Besides, I've *never* met a local spirit that could do that to me, no matter *how* powerful it had grown. There is something else going on here."

Bill sighed. She owed him for this, and there was nothing he could say to talk her out of it. He was just going to have to accept that.

"Agreed."

Joanna suddenly uttered an outraged gasp.

"What?" Bill asked in confusion.

Her hands grasped helplessly at her empty throat. "The little *thief* stole my *necklace*!"

Bill chuckled, shook his head, and patted the empty pocket in his duster. "Yeah, well, he nicked my favorite pocket watch, too."

Joanna gave him the kind of look a teacher gave a particularly stupid country yokel. "And?"

"And he's a *trickster* spirit." Bill shrugged and began making his way out of the old chapel. "Pulling one over on 'The Man' is pretty much everything he lives for."

Joanna sighed and picked up her sword and sheathed it. Then she followed him with a, "That necklace is valuable."

"Of *course* it is," Bill said and rolled his eyes heavenward. "*Everything* you have is valuable."

"Well, excuse me," Joanna said with a sniff. "But I happen to *like* nice things. And I don't like people *stealing* my nice things."

"Don't worry about it," Bill said with a mollifying hand as they stepped out into the street in front of the abandoned chapel. "We'll hunt him down later. Might as well let him enjoy his score for a bit before we take it back. He *was* nice enough to pull you out of that wall, you know. That *should* earn him a *few* hours of peace from us."

Joanna put a very unamused finger in Bill's face. "A *few* hours. Then we take it back."

Bill smiled. "And that will give us a few hours for *other* adventures!"

Joanna narrowed her eyes at him but waved a hand in a "go on" gesture.

"Well, you keep saying how much you owe me," Bill said with his best innocent expression. "And I thought you could work a bit of that off with me over the next few hours."

Joanna took a step back and aimed a very old look at him. When she spoke, her voice was as cold as a mountain river in springtime. "What exactly do you have in mind *now*, William?"

Bill acted like he didn't hear the frost in her tone, but he was pleased on the inside about where exactly *her* mind went. It meant she was thinking about it, and that could prove promising. But he shouldn't let on that *he* was thinking about that, too.

"Well, I was thinking we could go back to your tent."

Joanna crossed her arms under a pair of very nice breasts and just raised an eyebrow at him.

Bill gave her his best innocent smile. "Well, it *is* where your coffee is."

Joanna bit her lip and stared at him for a long moment. "You want me to make you another cup of coffee?"

"Actually," Bill said and aimed a far more serious look at her. "I was thinking it was time I made a cup of coffee for *you*."

Joanna blinked. "Me?"

Bill licked his lips. "I may have picked up a few tricks here and there."

"Why?"

Bill licked his lips again and let a breath out that felt far shakier than he wanted it to. His heart skipped a beat, but his soul told him he was on the right track. So he sucked a breath back in, pulled his cowboy hat from his head, and met her gaze with steady eyes.

"You've given me a name. You've given me coffee good enough to make me want to give *you* a name."

Joanna blinked again, and her eyes widened.

"But first I want to give you something physical." Bill ran his free hand through his hair. "Something tangible. Something to make you want to remember me forever."

"I can think of something physical." Joanna looked up at him through her eyelashes, and his heart skipped a beat. "Something tangible. Something to make you want to remember me forever."

Bill licked his lips. Oh, this woman was good for a man's soul. He sucked in a deep breath, felt his heart skip again, and felt words in his soul he could never take back. Words he didn't realize how much he wanted to say until the moment he was about to say them. He met her gaze and held it.

"I can brew you a cup of coffee that will make you want to stay."

Joanna blinked. She cocked her head to the side and measured him. And then she smiled at him.

"You are the first man to dare make that claim on me."

"*Want*," William said and bowed his head to her. "*Never* a claim."

"Fine words, William." Joanna looked up at him through her eyelashes for a long moment. "Can the quality of your coffee match them?"

Bill very carefully did not release a relieved breath. Instead, he jutted his elbow out towards her. "Only one way to find out, Jo."

"Joanna," she corrected in reflex.

Bill kept his arm out and aimed his very best smile at her.

Joanna sighed and shook her head. She bit her lip. Then she slipped her arm into his, pulled herself in close, and leaned her head against his shoulder.

Oh, she really was the perfect height to do that.

"Take me to my tent, William," Joanna whispered into his arm.

Bill placed his cowboy hat back on his head and did as his fine faery lady bade him.

Wings in the Dawn

By: Jesse M. Slater

"Fool girl!" the man cried, as Winifred ladled the rich venison stew onto his plate.

She had bumped his spoon, tumbling it into his lap along with plenty of the steaming hot stew. She froze.

"Just goin' to stand there, you twisted little wench?"

Winifred bent, and with a corner of her apron, picked up the iron spoon. She straightened as much as the deformity in her back would let her and tried to hand it to its owner, but he sneered.

"Are ye daft? That's fouled with rushes, probably dog muck, and All-Father knows what."

Winifred's eyes skated away. She mumbled something unintelligible, and darted to the back of her father, Jorvik's inn.

She'd never understood why so many people minded a little dirt. Winifred liked dirt. Dirt liked Winifred.

Her mother always wanted her to scrub her face and comb her hair and clean her nails… As usual, it didn't help. Before Jorvik had lit the dusk's first candle, food and ale spattered her coarse brown dress and her nails were black as ever.

Her back was hunched. Her disheveled mop of hair hung about her face, but even it couldn't hide her too-prominent ears.

Clean my spoon, she thought, disgustedly. Clean this, clean that.

Still, she ran to do it. She ignored beckoning calls from the other tables she passed. She must get the spoon back to the irate boatman and was like a horse with blinders.

At the simmering iron wash pot, she braced herself. She tried not to touch the hot pot, or the spoon more than absolutely necessary, but hot water splashed her hands and she gasped. Probably cleaner than it's ever been. Her apron corner provided some relief from the burning thing.

Before she could return it, Jorvik stopped her.

"What are you about?" her father demanded. "Half your folk cry that they hunger, or thirst!"

She tried to explain, but words rarely served her.

"Spoon!" was all that passed her lips.

She held it up, but her apron slipped from the still-hot iron. When the metal touched her flesh, she flinched, and the spoon flew. It bounced off Jorvik's jerkin and fell to the rushes again.

Jorvik, always a big man, now loomed larger still. His wild mane of yellow hair flared around his head, blue eyes sparking, and threatening to storm; Winifred averted her eyes and slid away from his glare.

Her ears began to close; she only caught snatches of his rebuke as hot shame flushed her face. "...careless... always daydreaming... pay attention... watch your sisters."

Anger spent, he laid a kindly hand across her shoulders, but it hurt like fire when he touched the deformity in her back.

"No! No! No!"

For all its faults, her young body was lithe and cat-quick as she bolted for the door. Her feet hardly slipped on the rush-strewn flagstones and she darted past the heavy-timbered door, swift as an arrow from a bow.

She wished then for her own bow, the constant companion of her forest walks. Still hanging on its peg inside, alas. She dared not linger to fetch it, not with the inn in an uproar. She ran fleet-footed across the meadow and into the wood.

As the leafy canopy closed above Winifred's head, she felt a bracing breeze on her hot face.

In the cool of the wood, peace settled over her. A weight lifted with the soft song of the brook. She could almost hear it giving her flustered spirit counsel. Einar and Dagny, the red squirrels, argued in the great oak tree. When she was very still, she could even hear the sighing breath of the titanic tree itself.

A tiny paw gripped her toe, and she struggled not to kick in reaction. Out of the leaf mold, a field mouse scrambled.

She reached into a tunic pocket, and found a rind of cheese. She offered it to her little friend. "Here, Asdr. Take to your pups. Good cheese."

"Thyra!"

Thyra Jorviksdottir spun. In the corner sat one of the regulars. He was a boatman who plied the river, taking food into the city and bringing back whatever goods the conquering Scalies felt like releasing that day.

"Thyra!" he called again. "More ale! My lads and I are dry!"

"Any more for you, and you'll all be wet," she shot back, with just enough smile to soften the barb. Her twin, Sigrid, was supposed to be minding that side, but folks mixed them so often, it wasn't worth the bother of sorting out.

Before she made it much farther in her rounds, another regular, this one on her own side, asked for a third plate of her mother's stew. That made Thyra happy, as it meant a docile guest. No one with three plates of rich venison stew under his belt was likely to be too… unruly. Even the second plate seemed to have slowed his straying hands.

Evading the swipe at her rump while she ladled was simple. Not that she minded a pat now and then, but she preferred warriors to these draymen and boatmen.

Of course, warriors were thin on the ground in these days of the Conquest. Even her father, once a proud housecarl, was now a mere innkeeper.

Jorvik Ingvarsson watched the byplay with some satisfaction.

His daughters—the twins, at least—filled his heart with pride. Tall and strong, elegant in their crisp white blouses and dark skirts, wrist thick plaits of golden hair trailed to their waists.

They had the knack of giving a man just enough flash of eye, a jest, or a quick smile to make him feel that he had gotten more than merely a plate of stew or a tankard of ale. Jorvik's inn, *The Cross and Hammer*, was one of the most prosperous on the London road. Neither the excellent ale nor Hilde's cooking were enough to set them above the rest, but the sparkle added by the twins surely did.

He'd just turned the ale-cask's tap when Ragnar, his only living son, burst through the door. He had to admire the boy. Ragnar, at sixteen summers, overtopped his father by a head and would tip the beam against a stout ox calf. Even in his haste, he bore a full cask of ale under each arm.

"Father! Father!"

"What's the matter, lad?"

"A troop of Scalies on the road!"

"Damn. You think they mean to stop here?"

"The sun is only a few fingers high. They're likely to stop somewhere soon."

By the White Christ and Thor's beard, that's all I need.

He glanced round the common, to see how the news landed. He hoped some of the guests disappearing out the doors had settled their reckonings, for the Duke's devils surely would not. He found himself holding a full tankard for an empty table and shook his head.

Moments later, he heard the clatter of the approaching column's clawed feet for himself, as they rounded onto Tor Bridge, a long bowshot from the inn.

Watching from his inn's yard, Jorvik saw the crimson banner glow as the setting sun glinted on the approaching troops' scaled red hides. Swords, shields, axes, and spears jangled. The column began to pass his gate, and Jorvik breathed a sigh of relief.

But then a booming voice called, "HALT!"

When the thunder ceased, a mounted figure approached.

Jorvik craned his neck. He guessed that even without his mount, this one would tower above the rest of the demon folk.

"Are you the innkeeper?"

"Aye, that I am. How may I serve your lordship this day?" The servile words were sulfurous in his mouth, but a man with a family did what he must. With luck, the officer alone would dine, and the rest would move off to encamp.

"You'll feed and lodge us, this night. What have you on the fire?" Then the red-scaled officer hissed, "And what… entertainments?"

"Entertainments, my lord?" Jorvik asked, though he knew exactly what soldiers wanted for entertainment.

"What about the young lovelies I see in yonder?" the captain hissed, claw pointing to the inn.

"Ah, no, your lordship. This is a respectable inn, not a low tavern or bawdy house. The young ladies your lordship refers to are my daughters, not 'entertainments', for you or your men. If your lordship requires such, then I suggest that he find an establishment more to his liking." That was bold talk from innkeeper to gentry, triply so to a demon officer.

"That won't be… necessssssary." The captain used his forked tongue and needle teeth to lend menace to the sibilances. "I'm ssssure my men will not dissssgracccce themsssselves."

Jorvik doubted that. He knew how rough even human soldiers could be; he had been one himself. There was little he could do to oppose a company of Duke William's devils, if they were bent on mischief.

"I'm gladdened to hear that, my lord," he said weakly.

"It's sssettled, then." The demon slid from his saddle, and the mount danced nervously as he passed the reins to Ragnar. "I'm Marax, Captain of this company. What are you called, landlord?"

Jorvik tried the old soldier's trick for coping with questions from nobility, or even captains and sergeants. Instead of meeting the eye directly, look slightly to one side. His eye spotted young Winifred in the meadow behind Marax. Seeming oblivious of the trouble on the road, she skipped from one stand of wildflowers to another. She crouched, peering at… what, Jorvik couldn't say. Probably fascinated by a family of field mice, he thought ruefully.

Fool girl.

With a start, he remembered the demoniac force before him.

Fool yourself.

"Jorvik, my lord," he said.

"Innkeeper Jorvik, then. After you."

Fortunately, much of the evening crowd had left without eating. It would still be a stretch to feed so many. Most of a roast ox should be left. He seated Marax, then rushed to the kitchen to warn his wife of their evening guests.

When he returned to the common room, things were already uneasy. Sigrid and Thyra rushed from table to table in a swirl of skirts, delivering ale, mead, and wine, their eyes wild. The toothy leers of the soldiery, the claws reaching to grab, all unnerved the girls.

Jorvik joined the twins, trying to get at least a drink in every talon, as soon as might be.

That's a short-term solution, at the best. The more the drink worked on them…

In a moment alone at the cask he whispered, "Remember, Thyra, Scalies are rough, but not much rougher than the bargemen and carters you cope with every night," he lied, but he had to say something heartening. "Keep your wits, chin up. Don't let them see you're afraid."

"Yes, Da," she said dutifully. he sounded no more convinced than he, though; her eyes might have been slightly less wild.

He took tankards, flagons and even drinking horns to the largest table. He shuddered to think what creature the largest horn might be from, huge and unnaturally twisted. He glanced around the trestle table, fire warming his back, as he tried to match drinker to drink. Usually his memory was faultless, but the scarlet skinned, black-eyed devils all looked the same to him. Mostly, he held up a horn or a tankard, and watched for someone to recognize it. No wonder the girls were on edge.

"Give it here!" the largest of this group growled.

"Which one, Sergeant?" he asked.

"The grolloch's horn, fool!" the creature shouted. It half stood and grabbed the huge, twisty horn.

Last drink delivered, Jorvik headed to the next table. When next he reached the casks, Sigrid was there.

"You're doing well, Sigrid, just—"

"I'm not worried about the Scalies, Da. There's hardly time for trouble, not as fast as we're running."

"Sigrid!" he hissed. "Don't let them hear that name!"

"Why? What are they going to do?"

"Anything they please, girl—and nothing we'd like. I just hope they're content with eating and drinking a week's provisions and not…" he trailed off. A lump had formed in his throat; he couldn't name his true fear, not to Sigrid, not to any of the women.

"Where's Winifred, anyway?" she asked, her favorite complaint. "Isn't she going to help in all this mess?"

Jorvik didn't answer. He didn't think that Winifred helping would be all that helpful. He set down a platter of carved meat, and was called closer to the fire.

Marax, again.

"Innkeep, there you are at last. My wine has been empty for half a candle. I appreciate your… ssssservice to the men, but I hope you can make time to fetch more?"

"Of course, my lord," Jorvik said, jerking a bow. "At once."

While he trotted after the fresh bottle, Jorvik told Ragnar in passing, "Please tell your little sister that we could use her help, if she would deign to assist us."

"Are you sure that's wise, da?"

"I'm not, but we need the help."

"I could help in the front, you know. Might be less trouble, that way."

"You're a standing temptation to trouble, son. Anyone with a chip on his shoulder wants to try you."

"And the girls aren't inviting trouble?"

"If I could fill the hall with grannies tonight, I would, boy. But what I have is us. Now, go tell your sister she's needed."

"Yes, da."

"Good lad."

When he returned to the captain's table, Jorvik drew the cork with as much flourish as he could manage.

"Ah, landlord, back at last. I could have drunk another full bottle while you were puffing after that one. I hope you'll do better. If not, it's hard to say how much future you may have." His dark, slitted goat's eyes slid to Sigrid, then back to Jorvik. "You or your house."

Jorvik's hot blood rose to choke him, but he managed to croak out, "Apologies, lordship. I have asked one more in to help. I hope your lordship will not be so disappointed in the future."

"Another, eh? As lovely as these, I hope?"

"My lord will have to judge for himself."

At that moment, Winifred herself bounded in at the door. When she saw the crowd in the common room, her smile was wiped away, and her eyes fell. Jorvik hurried over.

"Just please try and do as your sisters do. Smile, if you can—laugh, even—and move on. Fast. Don't be a deer standing for the shot. Let's just get through this, lass." He nearly clapped her on the back, but stopped himself in time.

Her brown eyes were great dark pools, as they held his for a moment, and he thought that perhaps he'd reached her this time, but then they skidded away. She looked past him, but still he thought she might say something.

Winifred never said much, and that little took tremendous effort.

Though it cost her dearly, she did force out a word. "Da…"

For a moment, he thought she would stop there, but she went on.

"Deeee—" she stopped for another breath, and began again. "Demons bad. Much… bad."

"I know it, girl. But we can't cleanse the land tonight; we just have to do our best. With luck, we'll survive."

Not if you can't keep your opinions to yourself, Jorvik.

He waited another moment, but she was looking past him, again. At what, he never knew. Shaking his head, he strode to the kitchen and grabbed another heaping platter. The dance went on; the twins serving gracefully, if nervously, and Winifred… well, doing her best, as he'd asked. He hoped her best was good enough; they danced along a cliff's edge, with a bonfire to one side and the abyss to the other.

"There you are at last!" he chanced to hear, when Sigrid's path crossed Winifred's. "Where were you when we were running all the ale in the house—"

"*Sigrid!*" he growled warningly. "She's here now. Be civil, understand?"

"Yes, Da," she said, although her whole attitude shouted 'No!'

The evening tottered along uneasily until well after sunset. Jorvik began to fear that 'all the ale in the house,' might prove prophetic. The inn was well-stocked, but the way these creatures put it away was alarming.

At last, when it was nearing midnight, the pace slackened. Hope bloomed that the ordeal might end, when disaster struck.

He was just speaking with Thyra when a sound like a whip-crack rang through the room. He spun to see Winifred standing, cheeks flushed, dark eyes blazing, and her hand still raised in a slap. The common soldier's claws still gripped her waist.

"Not… touch!" she spat.

Jorvik rushed to her, leaving his load of tankards on the nearest table. "Gentlemen," he said to the leering, scarlet scaled creature. "I mentioned it to your captain, the Lord Marax, but this is a respectable inn, not a baw—"

"You ssspeak up boldly, peasant," hissed the soldier, his needle teeth and forked tongue lending the words a serpentine sound. "I wasss only having ssssome fun. But ssshe'sss hardly got anything to grab—"

Be civil, Jorvik told himself. *Pour water on the fire, not oil.*

"All the better, then good sir," he said, nearly choking on the words. He needed to coax this creature back into its seat. He retrieved one of the brimming tankards and offered it to the creature. "Why don't you grab this instead?" He began to shepherd Winifred away.

"Sssssshe sssstruck me!" came the hiss.

The soldier would not let it drop.

"Sssssatisfaction! I demand ssssatisfaction!"

Jorvik felt a gulf yawning under his feet as he said, "What satisfaction do you require?" The words were bile, yet still he hoped to avoid the fall.

"As I sssssaid," the thing hissed, "I wassss only having a little fun…" Its goat-slitted eyes ran down Winifred's slight form. "Very little fun. We take our ssssatisfaction where we pleassse…" it said, as it reached for her again.

Jorvik struck the claw before it reached Win's slim chest. "I told you this isn't a bawdy house—" but a naked blade gleamed at his throat. The gulf yawned wider. He'd acted without thought, after treading the treacherous path so carefully all night.

He'd compounded the original crime, with no consideration for all the vile creatures drinking, carousing, and now, surrounding them.

Jorvik cursed himself. He cursed Winifred, and most of all, he cursed the foul bargain William the Bastard had made after his thrashing at Hastings. Unable to bear defeat, he brought this nightmare upon England, Normandy, Norway, and all the nations that stood against him.

The trooper's vile claw reached for Winifred once again, and Jorvik clutched the blade at his neck. It bit deeply into his palm, but better that than his throat. He made a wild grab at the thing pawing Winifred, then a commanding bellow shook the common room.

"What is this, Dargosh?" Marax asked.

"I was just—"

"Did not I give orders that you were not to disgrace the regiment?"

"Yes, Lord Captain."

Jorvik was surprised that the officer intervened. Dargosh spoke truth that the foul creatures took their satisfaction where they would.

A moment later, he saw that Marax had merely raised the stakes.

"Sit down, Dargosh. Leave this to your betters."

"Yes, Lord Captain," the trooper muttered sullenly, but sit he did.

Marax circled Winifred, looking her up and down.

"Surely, landlord, this is not your daughter also? Yours are tall and fair. This… is neither. I do not believe she can claim protection of the house under those circumstances. I judge she must be considered entertainment."

Jorvik shoved the blade away and lunged for the demon lord. In less than a foot, he was seized by many grasping claws.

A moment later, Ragnar bellowed defiance from the kitchen. From the crashing sounds, several of the demon folk had just learned how strong his son was, but his attack proved as fruitless as Jorvik's. A crash shook the inn. It could only have been Ragnar falling. Jorvik could not even turn to see if his boy were alive or dead. The twins shrieked. That told him something.

Marax, unconcerned with their attempted resistance, circled Winifred. He seemed to delight in the struggles and protests of his captives. The demoniac chief ran his clawed hand down the girl's shuddering chest.

Her dark eyes smoked, like an iron pot too long on the fire. When Marax clutched her waist and drew her in, something snapped inside the tiny girl.

Her hand darted to the folds of her skirt and emerged holding an obsidian dagger. One darting slash, and the demon captain lost an eye.

She spun behind him, his massive bulk making an effective shield for one as small as she. The dagger was held below his belt, where even his scaly hide would do little to protect him.

With tremendous pressure, Winifred forced her words out, "Tell… men… leave… family. Leave… place. L—leave this place… or be gelded."

Marax, dark-green blood streaming past his fingers, writhed in agony and indecision. The obsidian blade prodding beneath his skirt of armor decided him. "Release them!" When all stood free, he said, "Outside! We go."

Winifred stayed close, a tiny dark shadow. She never let any of the other demons get close, or behind her. As the demon and his shadow entered the courtyard, she ordered, "Cross… over… bridge."

Again, Marax conveyed the girl's orders. The rest did as their commander bid them, though with much grumbling and muttering. They stood, looking uneasy.

Jorvik knew that with the merest hint from Marax, possibly even without it, they would turn and charge back to punish his family for daring to oppose the forces of the Bastard's conquest.

"Away… march! Let not… return."

Winifred hadn't needed to be told how precarious their situation was.

"Centurion, form column! Do not halt until you reach the city barracks." When the company was marching, and the tramping feet had nearly died out, Marax asked, "Now what? You've got me alone. Going to use that little flake of stone, girl?"

"No. You go."

It was so unexpected, she was out of reach before Marax realized he'd been released.

He raked the air where she'd been, a blow that would have opened her from belly button to collarbone had his talons connected.

He looked around, and saw the whole family, bearing makeshift weapons, or in Jorvik's case, his own spear, that had rested in its place of honor above the common room fire these many years. One badly injured demon, even armed and armored as he was, stood little chance so outnumbered.

"Don't think this is over, little girl. I'll have one of your eyes for this. And oh, so much more," he hissed, but then he backed away, and fled across the bridge.

Before the sounds of his retreat faded from the boards, Hilde had rushed to Jorvik's side to bind up the wound in his palm. In the heat of the moment, he had nearly forgotten it, but when he looked down and saw the lips of the wound gaping in the moonlight, his knees would scarce hold him. His limbs shook uncontrollably.

"Where's Ragnar?" Hilde asked. "I need him to help hold, so I can get this bandaged."

The twins shared a look.

"Mother, Ragnar slew three of the demons," Thyra said finally, "but when they saw it, they killed him for it."

Hilde silently clenched her eyes, but otherwise made no answer. She shook her head, slightly, then went on briskly, "In that case, you girls will have to do. Sigrid, heat an iron and fetch it here. Thyra, any spirit we have left in the house. And a clean cloth, if it can be found. Winifred," she went on, addressing the girl who'd not moved since Marax had left. "Winifred, do you hear me?"

A mute nod was her only answer.

"You fetch the moss and spiderwebs. You know the kind."

Another nod.

When all the children—all the remaining children, Jorvik told himself, had departed on their errands, he spoke, low and quavering. "My son— my last son. And for what?"

"For Winifred. The same reason you took this wound."

"Aye, for Winifred," he muttered darkly. "Hilde, I've never spoken on this, but… tell me of Winifred. I was away much, the year of her begetting."

"You accuse me, husband?"

"That was the year of the invasion. Much evil happened. I imagined some of it might have befallen you."

"You think our daughter an evil?"

"I think her very different from all our other children. I've never asked, though. Asked what happened here…"

"After you marched off to defend us, you mean?"

Jorvik hung his head. "Yes. We beat Duke William's army, you know. Harold Godwinson, the closest England had to a king, and Harald Hardrada, king of Norway, they met at Stamford Bridge and put aside their differences. We marched together to Hastings…"

"So you've told me," she said dryly.

"It was after, when the Bastard couldn't face his defeat that he—"

"Made a pact with the devil? I know that too."

"I… never asked what happened, after those Hellspawn overran us."

"Are you asking now?" Her eyes were bright in the moonlight, steady on his.

"I suppose not," he said finally, dropping his own. "But what are we going to do? What have we already done?"

"We'll face that when it comes, if it comes," she said, serenely.

After the girls returned, his hand was bound up. The iron seared his flesh, just as his losses and shame seared his soul.

Ragnar's body, they laid on the longest trestle table.

"I watch," Winifred said, at last. "I… deserve."

Jorvik went to mutter something about what she did deserve, but he choked it off.

Whatever her faults were this night, the girl cannot help what circumstances led to her birth, no more than I can.

"Very well. Winifred will sit this night's vigil, the rest of us… we should sleep, if we can."

He turned his back on Winifred, and made his way to his own sleeping chamber. Perhaps the tangled skein would look neater in daylight.

Well before sunup, in the first blue light of day, the tramping of many feet could be heard on the bridge. Winifred burst into the chamber and shook Jorvik from his fitful doze.

She needed say nothing, for he cocked an ear, and then flew to the window.

Opening the shutter a crack, he saw the company of the night before, but this time they were merely the vanguard. Behind them trooped still more of the scaled horde, what appeared to be a full regiment of the creatures.

In the name of the White Christ and Odin's one eye, what is this?

Surely a single company was enough to ruin him, if they hadn't already. Why bring all these extras? What had the demons to fear? The inn stood alone where the river crossed the road, not even a village for a mile or more.

He thought of donning the mail hauberk, taking up the spear and linden-wood shield that hung over the fire in the common room. Those were relics of other days; what good would they do him against a regiment of Hellspawn? Four women behind him and Ragnar—his strong right hand—had been taken from him.

That thought nearly undid him, but he pushed it to one side.

In a real sense, he doubted whether his wounded right hand would serve him this day.

He flexed it, painfully. It would hold a hilt or haft, but not with much strength or dexterity. He regretted that he'd never trained more with his left.

A great hero out of the sagas might stand alone before such a horde. But what hope have I? Too stout for my mail…

In the end, he did the only thing he could do. He dressed, and went out to treat with Marax. Before that, he told Winifred to hide herself. She knew she was the spark that had set this fire alight, and ran to do his bidding.

The marching ranks of demons were even more alarming at this hour, the light from the torches they bore flaring and dying, casting their evil faces into eviler shadows, drawing the eye with their wild, chaotic jumping.

Here was Marax before him, riding another unsettled, nervous horse. It shifted and stamped and would not be still, no matter how the demon captain jerked its reins.

Yet Marax did not ride at the head of the procession.

That was another, one whom Jorvik did not know.

"My lord Marax?" Jorvik began. Hope still bloomed, if faintly, that he could somehow avert this slide into the abyss, or the fire. "Do you return

to my humble inn so soon? You and your men are welcome, so long as—
"

"Welcome?" Marax grated. "You dare prate of welcome? This is how you welcomed me last night! You and that dark wench." He jabbed a claw viciously at the new leather patch. "I've come to collect for that so-called welcome. But first," he sneered, "let me introduce the Archfiend of London, the Sorcerer-Lord, Abraxes."

It was worse than Jorvik had feared, if the Archfiend himself were involved.

It was said that although William ruled the kingdom, Abraxes ruled William.

If he had concerned himself with the *Cross and Hammer*, the outcome was certain. The whole cliff crumbled. They were falling into the abyss, and the bonfire falling atop them.

"Does the Lord Abraxes wish to sample my humble house's hospitality?" He hoped his voice hadn't quavered.

For the first time, the one named Abraxes spoke. His was a low, grating voice that carried all through the courtyard. He didn't seem to shout, or even raise his voice, yet somehow it cut through all the clatter and jangle of a well-armed regiment formed-up in a small space.

"You may produce this—alleged—daughter of yours. There are certain elements of the good captain's story which bear further… inquiry. Bring her here, at once."

"I don't know where she is, my lord," Jorvik said, with all the sincerity he could muster. After all, he hadn't seen where she had hidden herself.

"I don't believe you, Jorvik Ingvarsson." He did raise his voice then, slightly. It pierced and echoed all round the court, and probably half the county. "Cambions!"

One company, who looked slightly less demonic than the rest of the host, stepped forward.

"Cambions! Search me that inn. I want a small dark girl, and I want her brought to me. She must be alive," he said, relishing his words, "but she need not be unhurt."

If there were words in the answering bellow, Jorvik did not know them.

The company trotted to the inn, divided into parties, one for the front door, one for the back, and several to stand sentry over the windows. From the sounds they made, he could trace their progress through the building, through the life he had built with his family.

First, the crockery shattered. Iron pans clanged as they were hurled.

They must have found the larder, for a storm of smoked meats and cheeses began to pour from the windows.

Next, they were at the cellar. Casks crashed and the voices of the searchers grew louder, more boisterous.

"Would you care to tell me anything, innkeeper?" Abraxes asked. "Something that might help to guide their search?"

"My lord, I cannot tell you what I do not know."

"So be it. I say that you lie. Watch, and we shall see the truth."

The common room furniture was next; it was hurled out of the windows and door, hacked into matchwood.

As if even a girl as slim as Winifred could hide inside a table leg, Jorvik thought in disgust.

Next, the bed ticking was slashed. First the straw from the cheaper rooms, and next the few feather-beds they had, the feathers swirling from the upper windows.

She must not have been inside a mattress, either.

Still the ransack, for it could hardly be called a search, went on.

At last, the leader of the squad bellowed from a top-floor window, "Not here, my lord!"

"If the search of the blades revealed nothing, then it's time to try another tool," grated the Archfiend. "I *will* have that girl. Fire imps!"

What Jorvik had taken for torches were in truth fire imps—demon folk who blazed in fire, and were not consumed. "I tire of seeing that wretched hovel. Remove it from my sight!"

"Lord Abraxes, I can—" Sigrid began to babble.

"—tell you nothing," Jorvik said, cutting her short.

"You wish to speak, girl? Speak."

But the glares of her mother and sister had cowed Sigrid, at least for now. She hung her head, and said no more.

"So be it. Imps! Remove that pustulant sore."

The walking torches gathered up the broken furniture, and carried it back inside. Of course, the moment their flaming hands touched it, it burst alight. The building soon smoldered. The walls were of thick country rock, but the floors were timber, as was much of the bracing. And the thatch… Soon it was alight. The flames leapt high, outshining the feeble sun creeping above the horizon.

"Now speak, innkeeper. If losing your goods does not move you, what about these?" He motioned, and a squat, powerfully built demon brought Sigrid before him. "Will losing these loosen your tongue?"

"Go back to whatever hell it was that spawned you!" Jorvik burst out.

Hold your tongue, you fool, he told himself.

He shuddered, the rising rage threatened to take him over. "I cannot tell you what I do not know," he spat.

Marax and the other demons within earshot hissed at his temerity, but Abraxes himself merely sat upon his mount and gazed placidly at Jorvik.

At last he said, "No. No, innkeeper. I still do not believe you. I think that you will tell me, if I take more of your family. One, and such a one— small, ugly and addled—Marax tells me, will start to seem like the better bargain."

One part of Jorvik screamed to do it, to tell what he knew, to stop this foul demon. He did his best to quash it, but could he watch his daughters, his own daughters, be handed over to these creatures?

He could not.

He roared a battle cry, and lunged at the squat demon holding Sigrid. Surrounded by a thousand red-scaled warrior fiends, Jorvik fought.

Winifred was not far away.

She had not hidden in the inn, but had slipped outside, where she hid in the shadows, behind the low stone wall of the inn-yard.

The words she had heard buzzed in her ears, almost as loudly as the fat bumblebee which made its clumsy way between the purple thistle blossoms above her head. Their spiny stems raked at Winifred's arms, but she scarcely noticed the pain, next to what lay before her.

She might have expected such devotion from her mother, and from Thyra, always her champion.

But from Jorvik? He'd always been so distant with her. So clearly favoring the tall ones—the fair ones—the ones with his own light eyes… For him to watch his precious inn be violated and burned…

Hot tears burned down Winifred's face.

She couldn't let this go on.

When Jorvik made his mad, brave, foolish lunge, she could crouch and skulk no more.

She arose, grass and blossoms clinging to her disheveled mane.

When the thistle stems bit into her arms, she grasped them, and tore them from the earth. She darted toward the cluster of abominable creatures holding her kin, still carrying the thistle blossoms, though she knew not why.

"I here!" she cried, as loudly as she could. "No! No! No! You stop! I come!" It was more words than she had ever gotten out before without stuttering, and it seemed to have done the trick. The loathsome leader raised a hand, no more, and the struggle ceased. A large demon raised Jorvik from where he lay.

"Well, well, well," Abraxes said. "I do believe Marax, now. How could you have nourished such a viper in your bosom all this time, innkeeper?"

Viper? What viper? Winifred wondered.

"He doesn't know, Lord," her mother's voice. It was the first time she had spoken in all this.

"Doesn't know? How could he not? Isn't it plain?" Abraxes asked.

"Isn't what plain?" Jorvik asked, thickly.

"This… creature you call your daughter. She's of the Tuatha de Danann. What some in this land call 'faerie.' You can't smell her vile reek?"

"Anything you call vile, demon, I'll call fair," Hilde said.

"Fair? This?" Abraxes laughed. "I'll show you how 'fair' she is."

A twisted stave of blackened wood was suddenly in his hand. The sorcerous lord of the demons snarled, and held the crooked thing toward Winifred, who quailed as azure light streamed from its end, and engulfed her. It swirled about her, began to tear at her.

Her clumsy, thick fingers stretched, grew impossibly long and thin. From their tips tore claws.

It burns!

It swirled round her head, and her ears—always obvious even through her hair—grew longer, grew pointed. Her face, too, from her nose and chin to her very teeth, elongated and sharpened.

She screeched in agony as the deformity on her back began to shift and grow. It had always pained her, but now, fire burned through her back and shoulders until—with a ripping noise—her coarse brown dress tore asunder, and a great pair of gossamer wings erupted from her back.

Winifred looked down at herself. She didn't know what—or who—she was, but she had been unbound. Even her mind seemed to have been freed from the halter it had worn so long.

She supposed she ought to thank the Archfiend for that, at least. But how to thank him properly?

In her new hands, she still held the thistle stems.

She did not know how she did it, but she willed that they be harder, stiffer.

Flapping roots sizzled, hardened into points.

Arrows!

She cast about for a bow. Her own was kindling, no doubt, feeding the inferno.

A tiny voice called to her. From the ground, near her feet. She did not know the words, but understood its meaning.

A tiny form glowed there.

It was Asdr, the field mouse she had befriended. Yet somehow, it was also a spirit. One that belonged to this place.

It held up the tail of a snake. She could see that the snake had swallowed the head of another, and the two tails were bound in spiders' silk.

When she touched the writhing thing, it stiffened into a bow. She laid one of the thistle stem arrows across the serpentine bow, and drew.

The first arrow tore flesh from her knuckle as it passed, but still it flew true.

It struck the sorcerous demon in the throat, ending forever the foul incantation it uttered.

The next took Marax in his remaining eye.

She was just drawing the third, when the iron-mailed claw of a demon grasped her shoulder. The cold iron burned as if red hot from the forge, and she fell shrieking.

With their leaders dead or dying, as Abraxes choked on his own blood, the field became utter pandemonium.

The fiends broke ranks. They squabbled over the loot from the inn, to fight each other, and to close in, set on Jorvik's daughters.

"Back! Behind me! Put your backs to the wall!" Jorvik called to Hilde and the twins.

He saw one of the nearest demons armed with a long, bladed spear, rather than a sword. He rushed the creature and before it could swing the polearm, Jorvik dove inside its guard. A wicked elbow took the thing in the throat, and then Jorvik had the spear.

He stood, planted between his womenfolk and the onrushing foe, long haft of the weapon whirling. It was difficult for one man to fight many, unless he stood in a narrow way, where he could not be flanked.

With his wounded hand, that morning he could scarcely have even gripped a lady's dagger. In this extremity, he cared not for his wound, and the spear was as good as a quarterstaff in keeping the demons outside arm's reach, and could cut, stab, and slash, to boot.

Jorvik whirled; he darted fast stabbing, strokes, and demons died.

They were taller than men and stronger, but they trampled and impeded each other in their maddened haste to reach Thyra and Sigrid. Jorvik fought with all the desperate strength and skill he could muster, a bear defending his cubs.

But even a bear couldn't hope to last forever.

The tenth demon howled as he jerked the spear's blade from its neck, and fell atop the bodies of its brethren. It dragged Jorvik's point down with it, however, and the one behind seized the opening to dart in, and ran its sword through Jorvik's shoulder.

He bellowed as the pain lanced down his arm, but then the spear jerked free. Short-shafting it, he rammed it into his attacker's chest. He knew he couldn't last much longer. Even without the wound to weaken him, he puffed like a smith's bellows. Still, the flashing spear drank deeply of demon's blood, and Jorvik fought on.

He fought, and he bled.

He made the spear sing.

Then another check, as the fifteenth foe to feel his steel did not fall. Instead, it charged home, burying the spear-shaft in its own body, the way a dying boar might, to get at its killer.

The great overhand swing of its sword missed, but its very weight bore Jorvik to the ground beneath it.

He heard the women screaming—and those screams seared his soul—but there was nothing he could do. He lay trapped beneath the vast bulk of the dying thing. The talons of the rushing horde bit as they charged over his ragged body.

Jorvik knew he had failed; and in that stinging knowledge, he was the most wretched of men.

He could not move, could barely breathe, but he could hear.

He heard the snuffling, grunting, roaring of the horde, but he didn't hear any more from the women after that first shriek.

Then, suddenly, he did hear a shriek, but none such as a human throat could make. A wild, ululating cry arose, and if there were words within it, they were in no tongue Jorvik spoke.

Winifred was the author of that unearthly sound.

She knew not whence it came, nor what it meant, but when she saw Jorvik fight so hard, and fall as the horde overcame him, it had torn her throat.

The keening wail went on, and suddenly, her vision changed.

From the towering flames that had consumed the inn, shapes emerged.

Tongues of flame in forms of flesh—these were fire elementals, she somehow knew—and they had come to her call. Her great cry finally exhausted, she saw the creatures she had drawn forth leave the fire, and flow out into the hosts of hell. They were scarcely waist high to Winifred, and she was a short woman, but the mighty horde of scaly skinned monsters quailed before them. They drove into the mass from above and from every side. The demons lost whatever urge they possessed to stay and wreak havoc.

They ran.

Some ran north on the road, some ran south. Some ran into the river, and some crossed the meadow to the wood. Another tremendous outcry, and Winifred knew that the ones who sought escape by wood and water would nevermore trouble this earth. Awakened spirits of both places would see to the fiends' downfall.

She must see to her family.

Epilogue

"What are you?" asked Jorvik, shakily, his voice tinged with awe and fear, once he'd been pulled from the heap of dead and dying demon flesh.

"I… do not know. I am…" she paused, searching for words.

"You mentioned a question last night, Jorvik Ingvarsson," said Hilde. "Would you have it answered now?"

Jorvik looked at Winifred, saw the great changes that had been wrought, but saw too the same deep, bottomless pools of her eyes. Those eyes—darker than ebony—had not changed, and he saw the yearning written there. "You are Winifred Jorviksdottir, whatever else you may be," he said solemnly.

"I am Winifred Jorviksdottir. That is enough for now." She smiled, a sudden needle-toothed smile, and wrapped her father in a warm embrace.

It Runs in Her Veins

By: Virgo Kevonté

As the rusty shuttle van jittered up the red clay road, Priscilla reminded herself of one thing. Rumors were not to be trusted, especially ones from extended family. After all, the same aunts who vilified their ancestral town had also depicted her alma mater as "an American den of iniquities." They told her that all roads in all liberal arts buildings end at the unemployment office. They told her she'd regret graduating with a BA in social work instead of a BS in biology. And they'd been wrong on both accounts.

Despite being a day's drive from the Ghanaian coast, the September air was hot and humid. Branches scraped the windows of the van as they skirted by a wooden "*Bienvenue á Ko*" sign. French had been the official language of the region back when half of the African country had been a jewel on the French diadem. The sign was easily a century old, and from the looks of Ko, her uncle's town wasn't much more modern. Where were the paved roads and English welcome signs that even the most-humble Ghanaian villages had? Priscilla *tsk-tsk-tsk*ed each time the speeding van hiccupped from a pothole. Shook her head at the rotted fences surrounding the lots they passed, the missing planks like gapped teeth.

She didn't know what to expect from a town whose women were all *okefi*, but it wasn't this level of disrepair. If okefi were indeed forest spirits infused into earthly vessels, didn't that mean the village had a supernatural labor force at their disposal? Where, then, were the telephone poles and power lines? When the shuttle pulled up to Uncle Frank's house, the driver demanded more money.

"You didn't tell me my poor van would suffer these country roads," he said.

Priscilla pretended not to hear him as she tossed her fare into the cupholder under the hole in the dashboard where a radio should have been. She also pretended not to hear what the driver called her before speeding off angrily.

Through the dust the vehicle had just kicked up, Priscilla saw Abena, her uncle's wife, pulling faded linen off the clothesline. Obsidian coiled locks tumbled over her shoulders, their ends dyed gold.

"Auntie Abena, your hair!" Priscilla said after they'd embraced. "It looks positively regal!" But as Priscilla held her at arm's length to take her in, she noticed Abena wore the same tattered flowery blouse and apron she remembered from her childhood, along with a pair of black stilettos. Priscilla's smile cracked.

"My eyes are liars," she said, indignation curdling in her tone. "Uncle Frank is *not* having you doing laundry in stilettos."

"Why can't I?" Abena asked curiously.

Priscilla opened her mouth, but nothing came out. The truth was that the *dibia* had fashioned the okefi that were impervious to various degrees of bodily degeneration. Abena's knees would not give her back pain from decades of pushing her knees and hips forward to compensate for walking with a sharply elevated heel. She'd never develop hammertoes or ingrown toenails as Priscilla's own mother had from her career as an office secretary.

"Well, let me at least do something about that apron," Priscilla said, bringing her wallet out of her pocketbook.

Abena playfully slapped Priscilla's hand away.

"Save your charity for those who need it," Abena said, laughing. When Priscilla cocked an eyebrow, Abena gave her trademark carefree laugh. "I'm fine, niece." And then, "come, your uncle will want to see you immediately."

Abena extended an arm toward the side of the house. She led Priscilla past rows of her garden. Priscilla identified the yam plants from their verdant and tall-reaching vines, but the rest were foreign to her. Chickens *bawk-bawk*-ed as they scrambled away from them. Priscilla's eyes were not on the garden but on Abena's hands, which swayed at her sides as she walked. They had a black, almost purple, half-webbing between the fingers, her aunt's only vestige of her origins. Priscilla unzipped her pocketbook to fetch her phone for a picture, but she stopped when she remembered her phone was off. It was just as well. No one would see her webbed fingers and think the photo was real.

"Forgive the mess the chickens have made," Abena said, stepping over fresh droppings. "I still haven't finished repairing the coop."

"Why hasn't Frank done it?"

Abena laughed with ease. "Oh, I wouldn't want to pester him with something like that."

They found Frank napping on a straw mat in the courtyard behind the house. Abena knelt by his side and nudged him gently.

"*Oga*," she whispered. "Your niece Priscilla is here."

Frank's large eyes opened. He yawned, trying to blink the sluggishness away. When he saw Priscilla clearly, he smiled, slapping dirt from the bottom of his shirt.

"By the water of *Asase Yaa*," he mumbled, sitting up, slack-jawed with sleep. "My sister's daughter has come to visit me."

Though Abena looked the same as Priscilla remembered, Frank didn't. Most of his hair was gone, leaving him half a crown of gray hair. He'd grown a large pot belly, one which made him breathless as he struggled to sit up on his straw mat. Watching him reminded Priscilla of seeing male elephant seals disturbed from slumber on TV, their sloppy faces jiggling.

"I have come to give you tragic news," Abena said flatly.

"Nothing is a tragedy if it brings you to your family at last!" Frank said, livening up. "Abena, go make us some tea. Slaughter and dress a chicken. My niece has finally returned to her family's real home, and all the way from New York City in America!"

"—That's not necessary," Priscilla said curtly, with a hand up. But Abena had already disappeared behind a flowery curtain at the back of the house. Frank laid another mat behind him and patted it twice in an invitation.

"I didn't come to celebrate, Uncle Frank," Abena said. "The family sent me to tell you that your mother is dead."

Frank wept, first crying through gritted teeth as though he were fighting physical pain, then sobbing like a toddler overdue for a nap. Fidgeting awkwardly, Priscilla watched Abena rub Frank's back. Frank had never visited his mother after she'd left Ko. Never called or wrote the woman who'd birthed him, yet Priscilla had never seen a man express his emotions so honestly.

Frank remained silent as the afternoon wore on, sobbing intermittently. "Was it a heart attack?" he asked when he'd mustered enough resolve for a question. "She always did love fried food."

"A marketplace argument. The man thought grandma was okefi. He struck her several times."

"What?" Frank snapped. "That doesn't make sense—*everyone* knows okefi don't age, and they certainly can't *argue*." Frank's eyes narrowed at Priscilla. "Who did this?"

"I just know the police apprehended the man responsible," Priscilla said. As she relayed information about the man's arrest, she stood, shaking the leg that had fallen asleep, then gathering up her backpack and pocketbook.

"You're leaving?" her uncle asked. "So soon?"

"I'd never meant to stay here this long," Priscilla said with a wince. "I… only came because your sister couldn't make the trip from Accra on account of her gout. She still insists that some things should be done in person."

"The family matriarch has died," Frank said flatly. "This family needs to be together now more than ever."

Any other day, Priscilla would have apologized and bowed out graciously, but family has a way of bringing the worst things a person will ever say past their lips before they ever knew it was even a thought. Maybe it was the homemade honey wine, maybe it was the grief, or maybe the exhaustion from hours of travel in vehicles with worn shocks, but Priscilla scoffed and said what was on her mind for the first time that visit.

"Oh, *now* you care about family?"

Her uncle reeled.

"What was that?" Frank demanded. But they both knew what she'd said. The anger in his eyes swelled. "*Your* mother is the one who doesn't care about family. We all went to college, but my sisters—including your mother—never returned home. They're the reason my mother died in some strange place—"

"—And who can blame her when the men in this town prefer to marry forest spirits over real women? Imagine the emotional trauma schoolgirls suffer knowing they'll never be valued as long as they have autonomy."

In one angry breath, out it all came. All the things Priscilla had heard her aunts say. All the things they whispered over international calls when they thought she was asleep.

"I'm proud of the women in the family for leaving this place," Priscilla said. "This deal you have with this *dibia*, this sorcerer, this…" she waved the word away. "*Whatever* he is, it's *misogynistic*."

Frank shook his head. "You've been here for a couple of hours, yet you judge us." He sucked his teeth. "Typical foreigner arrogance."

"Don't call me a foreigner," Priscilla shot. "I love Aunt Abena, but if anything, I'm more from Ko than your *wife*. She's not even human."

At the mention of his wife, Frank's face hardened.

"You call us misogynistic? Can't bear your breasts in public. Your country would rather starve infants than allow breastfeeding in public. Women here have enjoyed these rights for centuries, but you lecture *me* on misogyny."

His comments were a punch to Priscilla's stomach.

"Yes," Frank hissed. "We may not have the internet, but people talk, girl."

She was angry, but even through her haze of indignation, she knew she had no response to what he was saying. Sensing he'd knocked the wind out of her sails, Frank scoffed.

"You Americans and your double standards," Frank spat. "When you were sent home from high school for spaghetti-strap shirts or too-short shorts. Do you think I lectured your mother about sending you to a school that cared more about your body than your education? No."

Priscilla was stunned at how quickly Frank had weaponized a childhood memory. Perhaps he'd had the comment holstered for years. A stinging snipe meant for her aunts when they wanted to condemn his lifestyle.

While Priscilla was still thinking of a response, Abena stuck her head out of the kitchen curtains, smiling but looking concerned.

"Is everything alright?"

"According to your husband, yes," Priscilla said. She turned to face Abena. "Thank you for *your* hospitality, Abena. *Your* wine was delicious." Priscilla slung her backpack around her. "I wish you every success in life, Abena."

And with that, Priscilla trudged out of the courtyard with the resolution of all the women in her family, a resolution to never again return to Ko.

For Frank, time did not remedy the cycles of rumination that his niece's visit had triggered. He couldn't sleep and had been drinking too much. The alcohol seemed to paint everything black and blue. That child had spoken but little during her short visit, yet everything she said had upset him terribly.

"Frank, how could you be a *misogynist?*" Nana Igo asked during Frank's visit to his house. They sat on straw mats in the older man's courtyard while the scent of fried plantains wafted from the kitchen. Nana puffed on his long pipe angrily across from Frank. "Misogynists hate women. Your mother was a woman. I ask you: did you hate your mother?"

"No," Frank said in a wounded tone.

"When my son leveled the same accusation at me, I pointed to my wives. I asked him, 'How can you say I hate women when I have more wives than you, boy?'"

At that moment, Nana's first wife entered. She wore long gold bangles that clanged against the empty saucers and cups she collected. Nana puffed indignantly, continuing to smoke as his wife gathered the rest of their rubbish. She collected their empty teacups and stained saucers, her half-webbed fingers moving with a keen deftness.

"Nana, I have a question for you," Frank said, after she'd gone. "Where are the okefi from?"

Nana blinked through the smoke. "What?"

"Your wives, my wife, okefi—the dibia makes them, but where is he from?"

No one had ever asked this question. The dibia didn't look Fanti or Ga; he was far taller than the average Ghanaian. His chin was as sharp as a cassava, and he had a bald head.

"Who cares where the dibia is from?" Nana said. "He has been supplementing Ko with wives since before the first Europeans came to West Africa."

An undisputed fact, but it did not answer Frank's question. The dibia did not wear the vibrant patterns of the Asante, nor did he speak the dialects of the Ga-Dangme. And the fact remained that he was taller than any Fanti, Grusi, or Guan that either of them had seen. The dibia was as foreign as foreign got. And if he made Abena, did that not make her a foreign good?

Nana relayed gossip from other villages while Frank pondered his relationship with his wife. What intentions lay behind those disarming honey eyes? What was she truly up to, this foreign product of this foreign man? Abena said that she was doing house chores at night, but what was she really up to when he was asleep? Perhaps Abena was scheming while he slept. Perhaps, just perhaps, nothing about her was as it seemed.

Though Frank had never been to the dibia's home, it wasn't hard to find. He simply had to find the tallest tree in the deepest part of the forests east of Ko, as he'd heard Nana say so many times. But he hadn't expected to find a wawa tree the girth of ten oaks with tall, stone doors of pumice in its base.

While he searched for some door rattle or knocker by which to summon the dibia, Abena pulled on his arm, demanding to know why he'd brought her there.

"Have I displeased you in some way, oga?" She said. "Please, tell me."

"Silence," Frank said. "The doors are moving."

The surface of the igneous doors percolated. Frank leaned closer and saw that they were bubbling, popping, and sputtering like an active tar pit. It seemed as if the stone had melted back into the bubbling lava from which it was formed. From the black ooze, a face appeared with pupilless eyes, demanding to know Frank's purpose for his visit.

"I've come to return an okefi," Frank said.

"You are not eligible for a wife exchange for another year, son of Afi," the face in the door fumed.

"I don't want an exchange," Frank said, "but rather, a return."

The face stared coldly at him and then melted back into the wall, leaving him and Abena glaring at each other. A breeze rustled the dry canopy above them as the doors' bubbling stopped.

"*Asase Yaa*! You are *returning* me?" Abena sputtered. Abena's jaw went slack. If okefi could get sick, he would have thought she was feeling nauseous. Her bottom lip quivered, but before she could shed a tear, the stone doors parted outward. From the opening, a man appeared, skeletal almost, with a purple walking staff. He was as tall as Frank remembered, his head clearing the doorway by a mere foot or so. His long, flowing jallabiya was whiter than any full moon Frank had ever seen.

"No," the dibia said. "No, no, no, no, no. I have *no* time for this human nonsense."

He paced in the doorway, ranting loudly, gesticulating so theatrically that he nearly hit the doors several times. Frank looked at Abena and then back to the frail giant before him, unsure of what to do. From what Frank had gathered from the dibia's rant, he wasn't the first man to return an okefi. Apparently, every couple of years, a Ko man would drag an okefi to him, usually accusing her of witchcraft or murder. The dibia would listen and nod, and then even make the performance of an apology.

"—And they always return," the dibia continued. "Begging for their okefi back. They've burned this forest down *twice*, leaving their incense at my door. Flies and maggots gather in the offerings they leave at my doorstep, but listen to me, son of Afi," the dibia pointed at the curved end of his walking staff at Frank. "I have indulged your kind long enough."

"I understand," Frank said. "Perhaps, if I knew your origins, I would feel more comfortable among your creations."

"You would ask of my origins? Me, the nephew of the stars, uncle to the very dirt beneath your feet?" The ensuing laugh that exploded from the dibia was somehow both thunderous and elegant. "You could not fathom where I'm from any more than a goat could understand the rising tides of the ocean."

Under those shrewd eyes, other men had felt their resolve melt into puddles at their feet, but Frank considered himself a modern man. He was college educated and multilingual, and he appreciated none of the dibia's condescension.

"Are you calling me a goat?" Frank asked.

"No," the dibia said, his tone light with acrid humor. "*Goats* do not fell a mighty tree just to nibble a leaf or two. Goats don't tax their happiness with possibilities of what could have been until their misery infects others. You're something worse than a goat—a *human*."

"Wait," Abena said. "Why are you returning me? Do I not get a say as to what I want?"

Both Frank and the dibia turned to Abena, but neither answered her. They returned their attention to each other. The dibia sighed, seeming to understand that Frank wouldn't be deterred. He walked up to Abena and snatched the arm she was rubbing.

"And what about a mate?" the dibia said, twisting Abena's forearm this way and that as he examined it. "Your species doesn't perform well without one."

"I plan to date human women," Frank answered.

"Ah, yes," the dibia said with a coy grin. "Never underestimate a man's willingness to stare down ruin for 'something new.'"

He dropped Abena's arm, frowning. "A century of life has allowed this spirit to permanently bond with this husk."

The dibia put his palm to Abena's forehead, scowling. "I can't repurpose her for anyone else. I remove the amorous spell, that's it; you'll be voiding our arrangement permanently."

"That's quite fine," Frank said. "It is past time for a change."

As the stone doors shut behind them, the dibia cursed Frank and his whole self-aggrandizing species. Humans always complained about how unpredictable life was while never giving a second thought to how often they frustrated the plans of their betters. The limestone lair expanded around the two of them as they descended the steps, steps that led to an unfathomably massive white chamber with dozens of limestone staircases going this way and that. Stalactites hung a hundred meters above them in a number and majesty that rivaled the stars themselves. Yet all the grandeur was lost on Abena, who continued to demand to see Frank.

The dibia responded, speaking only to himself. "You are of no help as long as you are under that damn spell… and this many old spirits in such a confined space is teasing fate," he muttered as he yanked Abena down the rail-less staircase. "This is not good. Not good at all."

Humans were indeed an incorrigible lot, but they were right about one thing: familiarity does breed contempt, and the kind of familiarity eternity creates could spark a quarrel that could destroy everything. Yet here he was, accepting an old spirit into the delicate ecosystem in his home. Re-introducing her into an ecosystem of spirits who each had their own separate histories, unsettled quarrels, and secret alliances. All because some man was "ready for a change."

The dibia reached the spell chamber, winded.

"Lay down on that table behind me," the dibia commanded after catching his breath. As he perused the shelves lining the wall, he grabbed some jars while only sniffing at others. When he had pinched off the ingredients he needed, he dropped them into the mortar and shoved it into Abena's chest.

"Grind everything in the bowl into a powder. Do not break that mortar or pestle. They were a gift from the goddess Olimwe herself."

As Abena ground the ingredients for the spell-removal potion, the dibia fetched a bowl of water from the aquifer that snaked its way through the spell chamber. He added it to the bowl in Abena's lap along with locust antenna fibers, a squirt of goat's blood, and two dozen other ingredients.

The dibia bade Abena to drink the mixture, and she downed the whole potion in three gulps. Then, he sat across from her and waited. Gradually, the panic disappeared from her eyes. Her breathing slowed. She had the face of someone waking from a vivid dream and realizing the last moments of her life weren't real.

"Now think of Frank, son of Afi, of Ko village. Do you love this man?"

Abena's eyes met the eyes of the dibia, eyes which had seen eons. They glimmered with knowledge, unspoken cosmic wisdom, and, as Abena also saw, a long-kept loneliness. After some time, she shook her head at the dibia's question.

"Good," the dibia said, exhaling. "Return my mortar and pestle to its shelf." As she did, he explained how Abena's untimely return threw off the spiritual balance of his lair.

"Follow me," he commanded, walking out of the chamber. He descended the stairs, gesturing as he spoke. "I have a plan to restore the spiritual balance of my home before your sisters sense that you have returned." The plan required Abena digging out the bottom of his lair day and night. With enough space, his thinking went, the more volatile spirits would never see her.

"But why must *I* labor?"

The voice was small. The dibia turned around, looked up the stairway, and recoiled at what he saw. Abena hadn't followed him, as he'd commanded. In fact, she hadn't even left the chamber's landing. She stood in the earthen archway, arms crossed, a puzzled expression on her face.

"What?" the dibia said.

"*I* am not responsible for my being here," Abena said, taking a step down to the dibia. "Why must *I* labor to solve a problem I didn't make?"

"Would you prefer to be out in the world with the humans?" the dibia asked after a scoff. "Homeless, destitute? No family, no assets, no name, no birthright?"

"I… would *prefer* to make my own decisions."

For the first time since the splitting of the supercontinent eons ago, the dibia's jaw fell open and hung there. An okefi was making a statement, one that pertained to no ends of his own but aimed to bend her environment to her *own* wishes. An okefi who had defied a direct order. The dibia's jaw tightened as he fixed his eyes on her with a gaze that could have cut through the cave's roof itself.

He could mix a hundred different potions that could cure her of her insolence, but Abena was blocking the entrance to the spell chamber. He peered over the edge of the staircase into the darkness below them. If she kicked him off the stairway, the fall wouldn't kill him, but he trembled to think of what she would do in his chamber while he ran back up the thousand or so steps to her.

"If you want to leave," the dibia said, making a sweeping gesture up the stairs that led to the uppermost floor and ultimately to the stone doors that entombed them. "By all means, please do. But when the humans come after you, just remember you left the only place that offered salvation."

Dating was not at all what Frank had expected. Somehow, electricity, a computer, and the Internet were required for what everyone swore was "the best way to date." Upon creating a profile on the dating website LoveNow, he discovered that there were no real prospects within ten miles of his house. Worse, the women didn't respond to his messages unless it was with vitriol: "What me do wit' a man the same height as my youngest born?" One woman had written in response to his profile picture. "Oo! You see dat belly? He a yam farmer or a *farmed yam*?"

The biggest shock in the weeks after his marriage's dissolution came when Frank, on his way to his favorite Internet cafe, found Abena squatting in the garden, holding the wilted stems of turnips.

"What are you doing here?" Frank grinned. He was not entirely displeased to see his ex-wife. "I thought the dibia had given you a job."

"I chose something else," Abena said. She still had trouble comfortably using the first two words of her response. For decades, the word *I* had held as much autonomy as the word *cup* or *warehouse*. "I" was always a means to someone else's end. But now "I" was no longer a constant, but rather a variable. After saying it, Abena smacked her lips to savor the aftertaste of the word.

"I chose." She repeated with a bit more confidence. She grinned shyly. Was there a stronger, more inebriating pair of words?

She smacked her lips again, then asked why the garden was dying.

"It didn't rain much while you were gone."

"Hunger has never waited for thunderstorms, Frank," Abena said, making her way to the water pump at the far end of the garden. She pumped the lever until the spout poured water into a sun-bleached plastic bucket.

Frank watched her fill the bucket. "You never did say what you're doing here."

Abena stopped pumping the water and looked at Frank. His cheeks seemed concave, his clothes flowed like the dibia's long jellabiya. He'd lost weight.

"I need a place to stay," she answered.

An old energy sparkled in Frank's eyes, energy that Abena made no space for in her thoughts.

"I think we can work out a living arrangement of sorts," Frank smiled. "Labor, cooking…" a smarmy grin spread across his face, "with other *considerations*, I think I'll let you stay here."

"*Let* me?"

"Yes," Frank said uneasily. "It's my house."

"How do you figure?" Abena asked. Her tone might have sounded accusative, but she was seemingly speaking as much to herself as to Frank. "I reroofed the thatched steeples before the last rainy season. To install a septic tank that I would never use, I dug all day. And when the shovel we borrowed from Nana Igo broke, I built my own shovel. I tarred the walls while you complained of the stench. I heaved the walkway stones fifty miles from the quarry. I wrestled the weeds out of the obstinate earth to till rows for a garden."

The same realization that had shocked the dibia now struck Frank. This okefi was not under his control, or seemingly, the dibia's for that matter.

"It's still my land," Frank said cautiously.

"—Due to paying your estate taxes with the money I earned selling *my* wares at the market."

Frank's eyes traced Abena's arms, arms that indeed had shot out like pistons as she'd hoed the ground with terrible force. Each planting season, he watched sunbaked dirt explode upward as her hoe spiked the ground with ferocious speed. He had always watched with wonder and admiration, silently praising the dibia for gifting him such a marvelous okefi. Those arms would have no trouble taking whatever Abena wanted.

"We don't have to talk about this now," Frank said, throwing his hands up. "Go inside and rest; you are home."

Once the money from Abena's trips to the market returned, the tension with Frank grew. All Abena wanted to be was fair, especially since, as she'd come to understand it, life had been so unfair to her for so long, but Frank insisted she was being the exact opposite.

"But it's a stretch to say you do ten percent of the work, Frank," Abena said after one of her trips back from the market. "So, how can you demand half the money?"

"I am not an okefi, able to hurl boulders a lake's distance," Frank said, his arms out in a humbling gesture. "But I can tell you this: that ten percent you speak of requires one hundred percent of this poor mortal's strength. So, who is really working the hardest here?"

"Still me," Abena answered.

She'd seen him work. When weeding, Frank picked from the stem instead of the root. Working the pump exhausted him almost as soon as the water hit the spout. He complained of sore muscles and a sprained back constantly. They'd tried to switch roles for a while, with Abena gardening and Frank taking their crop and wares to the market, but this was even worse. The mornings he needed to go to the market, Frank slept in, missing the morning rush. He refused to shout out prices like the other vendors. Not that it mattered—customers who did approach his table quickly grew tired of talking to a man hunched over his phone, ogling curvaceous women on LoveNow and pointing at the price signs whenever they attempted to haggle. Frank rarely remembered to bring back diesel for the generator behind the house, which meant her phone charger didn't work.

This was an insufferable problem. Abena herself had bought a secondhand touch-screen phone and was positively mesmerized by it. She was dumbstruck by the invisible force that turned the special electronic boxes into portals to any place in the world, and to any time period—even the future—predicting rain days before clouds gathered overhead.

This so-called *Internet* taught her that plants don't push water from their roots, but rather pull it upward through a vascular system that worked the same way a straw does. Abena learned that although 1,300 Earths could fit in the celestial body of Jupiter, the gas titan had no actual solid surface.

Humanity's ability to observe and access something over 300 million miles away from Earth astounded her. She only knew one individual capable of such feats, but she doubted that even the dibia's power could reach the black recesses of space. Even stranger was the inconsistency of humanity's power of observation. Humans could identify the composition of the rings of Neptune with startling accuracy, yet they consistently failed to see the humanity of those across national borders. Indeed, the same era and land that produced the astronomers who labeled every white glint in the night sky also produced thousands of slavers, brutal men who had trafficked humans from the very land in which she dwelled. These paradoxes unsettled Abena. The humans in her region, although they regarded her with a certain suspicion, seemed to tolerate her well enough, but what would happen if she chose to leave, as Frank's sisters had?

"Why are you doing all that reading?" Frank asked one day after he walked past Abena in the courtyard. She was sitting with her legs crossed and brow furrowed, a used textbook in her lap. The afternoon light that cascaded through the trees freckled her thighs with bright spots.

"Why aren't you?" Abena asked.

"You did not answer my question," Frank said, crossing his arms.

Abena returned her focus to the book in front of her. "I am searching for something."

"In an organic chemistry book?" Frank said, frowning. "Searching for what?"

"When I find out, I'll tell you," Abena said, then promptly returned to the titration graphs in her lap.

"You are lying, girl."

Abena's nose flared at the word *girl*, but she didn't respond. She'd engulfed enough tomes on human psychology to know that no answer could ever satisfy Frank.

"You're planning something, Abena, I know it."

Frank claimed he heard of it happening all the time in rich countries: ex-wives snatching houses from right under the noses of the men who had bought them, leaving the men destitute. Abena stood and walked to her room. Years of marriage taught her that it was best not to engage Frank's paranoia.

She kept out of his way in the days following, holing up in her room, which looked more like a hoarder's library than a bedroom. When Frank invited Nana Olga and other friends over, she stayed in her room and played chess on her phone.

One night, after a successful day at the market, Abena returned home to find that Frank had left the front gate ajar yet again. She clicked her tongue at her hens strutting along the roadside. After she chased them back behind the fence, she closed the gate and went inside to demand an explanation from Frank. When Abena made her way down the hallway, she froze at what she saw in the dining area. Sitting at the table were Frank, Nana, and, most surprisingly, the dibia.

"Have a seat, Abena," the dibia said.

"I prefer to stand, thank you," Abena replied. The dibia sniffed at this and rubbed his eyebrow. He still seemed unaccustomed to being declined.

"The town has given it some thought, and we think it best you return to the dibia," Nana said. "It is not natural for an okefi to be without a man to offer her direction. It is best if you return to your maker."

"Best for whom?" Abena asked.

"Why, for everyone, even you," the dibia interrupted with anxious laughter. "I mean, you haven't laughed or smiled since I removed that spell. Instead, you occupy yourself with arcane subjects and sciences. Can you honestly say you're happy like this?"

She couldn't, but she knew it was better not to debate the dibia. As crafty as he was with his tinctures and enchantments, his most devastating weapon was the one between his lips.

"I've seen the utilitarian writers lining your shelves," the dibia said, glancing down the hall that led to her bedroom. "Tell me, are you really going to push one person's compulsion over the stability, happiness, and comfort of a whole *town*? Are you really *that* selfish?"

"You let this man parade me around in stilettos when I could have been naming stars, but you call *me* selfish?" Abena snapped. "What's best for the town is what's best for me, and vice versa. Now, I've—"

"—We have tried it your way, dibia," Nana interrupted with irritation. "And I'm done being patient." He cupped his hands over his mouth and shouted for his wives. "Gifty! Mercy! Come help us, O!"

From behind the hallway, two women appeared. Judging by how tightly their fists were balled, Abena knew what Nana had meant by "help."

"I don't want to hurt either of you," Abena said, stepping as far back as the room would let her. Before she could get another word out, the two okefi charged at her as quick as leopards. Mercy dove for Abena first, her arms forward and spinning in a barrel roll, but only clutching air for her efforts. Abena evaded the second wife with a dash to the wall, and then up it. She stepped off the wall and, with hands clasped together, delivered a powerful blow across Gifty's face. Gifty crumpled in a manner so sudden that Abena had thought it a pretense. But when she didn't move, Abena panicked.

Was she dead? Abena had meant to daze her, not kill her.

Abena was kneeling to search for Gifty's pulse when Mercy jumped up behind her and enclasped her from the back. Arms trapped, Abena stomped on her foot. Mercy winced but maintained her grip.

"Dibia, now!" Nana shouted, but the dibia was already up, his hand producing something from a brown leather sack from his waist. Abena's eyes widened. She didn't know what was in the sack, but she knew it would bring illusionment, ignorance, and perhaps even death.

She drove her heel down on Mercy's foot again. Mercy howled, but her grip didn't weaken.

"Hold her," the dibia commanded. "This won't take but a second."

Abena knelt down as much as Mercy's hold would let her, and then she pushed off from the floor with everything she had.

"She's too strong!" Mercy shouted when they'd fallen to the floor.

Sensing this was their last chance to subdue Abena, everyone rushed over and pinned her legs down. Abena flailed wildly, kicking the dibia off of her. When Frank came to wrestle down a leg, she kicked him, hearing his jaw snap before he collapsed on the floor. Nana froze in his approach, his eyes locked on his unconscious friend.

"Enough of this," the dibia hissed. He stepped back, poured the contents of the sack into his hand, raised the mound of powder to his face, and blew it on everyone.

Abena awoke on a stone slab in a cave, the soft babble of running water tickling her ears. She sat up. The stern face of the dibia met her gaze from across the chamber. A bracelet no thicker than the skin of a plantain was on each arm and leg.

"Enchanted wawa wood," the dibia said, pointing at the bracelets. "To ensure you behave."

"I don't see why you're wasting your time," Abena said. "We will never want the same thing."

"Well, what I want right now is a rousing game of chess."

Abena frowned at the bracelets on her wrists. "These bracelets seem to have affected my hearing. You desire a game of chess?"

"The books in your room suggest you researched the game." He pushed a marble chess set onto a small table between them. "So, show me."

"I have nothing to prove to you or anyone."

"Perhaps," the dibia said, grinning. "But if you truly possess the intellect Frank feared, the chance of playing a worthy opponent for the first time should be irresistible." He gestured to the board. "So, please, humor me with a game."

Abena didn't move. Had the dibia just used the word *please?* Perhaps the bracelets did affect her hearing.

"How long was I unconscious?" Abena asked, her hand hovering above a pawn.

"Not long," the dibia said. Abena nodded in understanding and stamped her king's pawn firmly in the center of the board.

"Well," the dibia said, moving his own pawn forward in response. "*That's* an audacious opening."

"I've got places to be," Abena said humorlessly.

They played in silence, each making their moves almost as soon as their opponent had placed their piece.

"You've read quite a bit since your last visit here," the dibia said. "I was told you said you were searching for something in those books. Did you find what you were looking for?"

Abena moved her queen's knight to the middle of the board.

"I did."

"What was it?"

"Me," Abena said. "Or what I could be in this era. I could be an ophthalmologist, a West African philosophy professor, or a lead astronaut." She swapped one of his pawns for hers. "Or I could be an apathetic CEO or a jealous despot."

The dibia regarded this quietly as the game continued.

"And what," he asked after a moment, "do you want to be?"

"As free as you," she said. "But I think the awareness that I can be anything trumps the satisfaction of realizing any one identity or another."

"Hmm," was the response from her opponent. As the match continued, they exchanged pieces and positions, but not words. Abena found that the dibia was right, she was getting the match she'd long desired.

"Check," the dibia said. Abena reclined.

"I could move my king out of check," she said. "But we both know the most optimal result for either of us is a stalemate."

"Quite right," the dibia said with astonishment. "I'm impressed by how quickly you learned this game." He rubbed his eyes. "Under these gods, I've never seen anything like you. In all honesty, I tried to cast the mind-cleaning spell, and it failed. The sleeping spells work, but the mind spells do not. Perhaps for the better. You don't clip a hawk's wings, you free it near a thermal and enjoy the show."

"Is that what I have been to you?" Abena asked bitterly. "Mere entertainment?"

"No," he said. "You're so much more than that." He slid his hand over Abena's and looked into her eyes longingly. Abena pulled her hand away and averted her eyes from the loneliness that called to her from the dibia's deep brown eyes.

"With our sordid history, with what you have done to me, I cannot," Abena said. "And besides, is that the best you can do? I am supposedly one of a kind, yet the only role you can think of for me is wife?" Abena scoffed in a manner that could have been interpreted as almost playful. "I expected more from the great dibia."

The dibia nodded. "Then what am I to do with you?"

"Why do anything *with* me? If I am truly as special as you feel, then isn't the most logical answer that I choose for myself?"

"I cannot just let loose a forest spirit on the world of mortals," he cried. "I need time to think about this. I promise I will find a solution to this that works for both of us."

"I was hoping you would say that," Abena said. When the dibia looked at her strangely, she laughed. "You've saved me the torture of trying to find this place because I promise you," she turned to the dibia, her eyes as hard as the stone bed on which she sat. "Every fiber of my being, every modicum of intelligence I possess, will be brought to bear to bring down you and this fucking lair. So cast your spells, prepare your enchantments. I'm ready for them."

The dibia's jaw went slack. Abena laughed again, delirious with the taste of revenge.

"You think I'm a problem? Wait until I get free of these bonds and free the other spirits. Let's see what you think, then."

The dibia had stopped listening. His hands were moving around in his brown leather satchel again. They searched frantically as she ranted.

"Just imagine," Abena continued. "You return to this abysmal dungeon of dreams, and who is here waiting for you? Why, a *hundred* spirits all eager to express their gratitude for the lifetimes of indentured matrimony you put us through? A hundred vengeful spirits. A hundred *me*'s. I, personally, *cannot* wait."

Something crawling on Abena's leg woke her. She sat up, the ocean roaring in her ears. At her feet, a small crab scuttled across the shore, dodging the frothy waves. It quickened its pace as she stood.

Abena looked around. The trees in the distance had long thin leaves that were also branches. Though she'd seen coconuts at her local market, she'd never seen the trees they grew from. A strange odor lingered in the air, too. It was earthy and salty. Fermented and tangy. Though she'd never smelled it before, she knew what it was. It wasn't just the smell of the ocean; it was the scent of freedom.

Mooneyed Mandy

By: William Joseph Roberts

Frogs croaked out their mating tunes in time with the dancing lights of fireflies all around the small lake. A refreshing breeze blew across the water from the south, driving away the stifling heat of an Alabama summer. It seemed like ages since I'd seen so many stars in the sky. Even with the full moon hanging high overhead, I could make out most of the constellations I knew. Some would call it picturesque, but I called it perfect.

A man couldn't ask for a much better evening than this.

I finished baiting my hook and lobbed the chicken liver out into the dark water with all my might, careful not to fling the bait from the hook.

After setting the tension on the reel, I lit a cigar and fished a cold one from my pack. Leaning back against the ancient lakeside oak, I cut the flashlight, popped the top, and took a long swig.

It was easy to get wrapped up in the daily minutiae of life. Even as feral as I was allowed to be, working for the KCG, Krypto, Cults, and Gangs division of the United States Marshal's office. Granted, I wasn't stuck in a cubicle farm like most folks these days, but my work tended to get *freaky weird* quicker than a PTA soccer mom at a furry convention.

"Yup. This right here is the life."

I wiggled, getting comfortable against the tree, and relaxed, taking it all in.

How in the hell did I land this precious bit of downtime? I know, weird, isn't it?

It all started with Mandy signing up for a women's Beltane retreat and herbal conference over in the middle of nowhere, Alabama, at Camp McDowell, deep in the Bankhead National Forest. Since she'd complained so much about the cost of cabin rentals for the event, I suggested we could load up Jonie, my Harley-Davidson Road King Special, and make a weekend of it.

She was reluctant at first—since it was a women-only retreat—but after I told her I'd be spending most of my time down by the lake, out of sight when I wasn't cooking for her, she agreed.

So we did just that. I loaded everything we'd need for the weekend: grub, fishing gear, a tent for her, a bedroll and tarp for me. It seemed like it had been forever since we'd gone camping and had some downtime to ourselves. Even though we hadn't dated since before I'd enlisted in the Air Force, we were still the best of friends. All good in my book.

Then she showed up at my place this morning with her *luggage* in tow.

I tell you what; it wasn't easy, but I managed to get all of her gear stuffed and strapped into place before we hit the road. You tell me this; how many blankets and pillows does one woman need for a weekend camping trip? Not to mention six extra outfits.

I get that she rides that fine line between girly-girl and bad ass ole' lady, but damn. I'm all for being as minimalist as possible when on the road; camping along the roadside wherever I can find a clear spot when I get too tired to ride. It's simple. I drop my bedroll, tie off the tarp to Jonie to make a quick lean-to, and I can usually have camp set up in fifteen minutes flat.

But it just is what it is. She needed to get away from her command center and her wall of monitors at Kara-Tech as much as I needed a weekend of fishing.

She was anxious before we'd even arrived, worried that she'd miss the special Beltane Fire Ceremony kicking off the weekend. So, while she got herself signed in for the retreat, I set up camp just down the road from the facility. Even in the dark, it wouldn't be hard for her to find it since she set out several of those solar sidewalk lights around our campsite.

The main thing, though, was that this weekend was a chance for both of us to get a break from the daily routine in exchange for some much-needed downtime.

Staring up at the star scape above, I took another swig and slowly puffed on my cigar. "Yup, this is damned good."

The bell at the end of my rod started to jingle, then stopped as suddenly as it had begun. I set the beer aside, placing the cap on top of the bottle to keep the bugs out, and turned on the flashlight, focusing on the fishing pole. It bounced again, barely activating the bell.

"Hell, yeah," I said under my breath as I crept forward. "I'm gonna have me some fried catfish for breakfast. Come on, you son of a bitch. Take it already."

I watched the end of the rod with bated breath. Moments passed as I crouched there, waiting to snag the rod from the stick I'd formed to make a prop. It felt like an eternity, then it hit.

The rod doubled over, and the antique Zebco reel squealed as the fish swam downstream with its prize, fighting against the drag. I snagged the rod and yanked back with all my might, setting the treble hook before reeling in the slack.

Hitting the release, I let the line freewheel for a moment as the fish ran for cover before re-engaging the drag and really setting the hook. The line went taught once again. I leaned back, fighting the fish upstream against the current, reeling in as much of the slack as I could.

The fish fought for several more moments before turning and racing upstream toward me. Reeling like a madman, I took in as much of the line as I could, then the line completely went slack.

"Goddammit, you son of a bitch! I wanted you for breakfast!" I kicked a nearby rock into the lake, and the largest channel cat I'd ever seen exploded from the water, catching me off guard.

The monster catfish gracefully pirouetted through the air in the most beautiful arching backflip I'd ever seen before disappearing into the dark depths of the lake once again. It couldn't have been less than fifty pounds and easily over three and a half feet long from the tip of the snout to the tip of its tail.

The line jerked forward, pulling me off balance. I stumbled, slipping in the thick mud at the water's edge.

"Oh, think you're going to trick me like that? I'll show you, you son of a bitch!"

I yanked back on the rod, then reeled like my life depended on it. I could already taste those fried fillets I'd have in the morning.

We went back and forth; fight, reel, fight, reel, I slowly gained ground. Never giving an inch to the beast.

This was what it was all about: a beautiful night and one hell of a fight for the record books.

After what seemed like an eternal battle of wills, I landed the most beautiful fish I'd ever seen. Its skin glistened in the moonlight as it shimmied across the muddy shore.

Wasting no time, I grabbed my scale and tape measure to record the beast. Sixty-three pounds and almost four feet long. I pulled my phone out of my pocket to snag pictures for evidence, but as soon as I turned on the screen, it beeped twice and shut down.

"Dammit!"

It would be all right, I thought to myself. I could use Mandy's phone to take pictures when she came back from the gathering, or I could charge my phone with one of the booster packs in camp and snag the pics in the morning.

See, problem-solving at its best.

Then, the flashlight suddenly flickered before going out.

"Oh, come on! Really?"

I smacked the flashlight several times. It momentarily flashed to life before going completely dead.

"Dammit to hell. Really?" I glanced around the moonlit bank. It was dark, but not so dark that I couldn't at least fumble my way back to camp.

I gathered my gear and strapped the channel cat to the back of my pack. When I turned toward where I thought the trail had been, I caught the glimmering orange flicker of firelight in the distance at the top of the gradual slope of the hillside. Every now and then, I could hear what sounded like a drumbeat or laughter, but that made pretty good sense. The fire had to be a few hundred yards away at least, and the wind was to my back.

I thought I'd heard voices when I'd made my way down the lakeside path earlier this evening. It must be where Mandy and the others were holding their fire ceremony.

"Shit," I muttered. I didn't know of any other way back to our campsite but the way I'd come. I could go off-trail and forge my own path through the underbrush, but then I'd run an even bigger risk of walking up on a copperhead or timber rattler in the dark. I'd just have to take my chances, being as quiet as possible and pray that my guardian angel hadn't taken the night off, cause there was no way I'd spot a snake along the path, let alone in the thick Alabama underbrush.

Carefully, I made my way along the moonlit walking path, being certain to poke at anything that could be a snake with the tip of my fishing rod. I figured it was better to piss it off than step on it, especially since it was a women's retreat and I wasn't supposed to be here in the first place.

Closing the distance to where I could make out movement around the fire had to have taken over half an hour. Better slow than dead, I thought. By now, I could easily make out the sound of flutes and the rhythmic beat of drums playing out an old-world folk tune of sorts. Laughter, hoots, and hollers resounded from the clearing uphill from me once the music stopped. From this distance, I could tell the fire was more than a simple campfire. Flames licked into the sky from a bonfire any backwoods tailgate party would be proud of.

"Sounds like they're having a grand ol' time," I said, swatting at something chewing at the back of my arm. There was just enough breeze down by the water to keep the skeeters at bay, but as deep as I was into the underbrush, I was an all-you-can-eat buffet to Alabama's state bird.

The fast, heavy beat of drums echoed down the hillside, followed by a warm melodic tune of flutes to what sounded like an Irish jig I'd heard played several times over the years in Irish pubs and at highland festivals.

Humming the happy tune, I continued along the path. I hadn't taken two steps before a blood-curdling scream drowned out the music and laughter of the revelers, stopping me in my tracks.

Sprinting uphill, my feet pounded the ground as I bull-rushed through the underbrush toward the bonfire. Another horrific scream resounded through the forest, followed by a hair-raising cry for help.

This is going to go over like a lead balloon with Mandy, but I couldn't just ignore someone in distress, I thought.

Double-timing it, I reached the edge of the clearing, dropped my gear, and continued across the field amid a cacophony of curses and shouts I was sure were directed toward me. Chaos and confusion ensued as the pack of nude and nearly nude women scattered in all directions, scrambling to cover themselves.

"Braxton!"

"Less beer, more working out," I gasped between panting breaths. "Think fast, be fast. Think fast, be fast."

"Braxton Eugene Hicks!"

Fuck me. I glanced in the direction of her voice and caught a glimpse of the most beautiful sight I'd ever seen in my life. Her tawny skin glowed in the bonfire's light, accentuating every toned and conditioned line of her curvaceous body. Golden amber eyes seemed to glow with an ethereal power. She looked like some sort of goddess emerging onto the mortal plane.

"I swear to God I will cut off your nuts and shove them down your throat, Braxton Hicks!"

Okay, maybe more like a demon emerging from the fiery pits of hell would be a better way to describe her. Either way, she was luscious and sexy as hell.

"Hi, Mandy! Love you!"

"You are a dead man, Hicks!"

Another cry for help drew my attention. I veered toward it, crashing into the underbrush of the hillside on the other side of the clearing.

"Maybe later!"

My legs burned from the exertion as I continued up the light slope. I slowed as grunted words and the sound of a sobbing female caught my ear.

"I'm coming!"

"Help me!"

Something thrashed like an animal in its death throes just ahead of me amid a heavy thicket of underbrush.

"I'm almost there!" Grunting barks that reminded me of a baboon from one of those National Geographic specials answered my reply.

Dumbass!

The one fucking time I left my revolver in my saddlebag *would* be when I'd have to deal with a bear or worse in the middle of the woods.

Crashing through the thicket of bramble vine and privet, I slid to a sudden stop.

I could barely make out the shape of something short and stocky dragging the flailing girl along the ground. The figure's eyes glowed an almost electric blue in the flickering light of the distant bonfire.

The figure hissed and let out a guttural squeal like a sow in heat, then chucked something in my general direction.

I dropped to the leaf-covered ground. Luckily, its aim was for shit.

The girl let out another blood-curdling scream, and the little shit sprinted uphill like some triathlon marathon runner dragging her behind it. Feeling around under the thick leaf litter, I found a stone, stood and aimed the best I could in a dim light before I hurled the improvised weapon in the thing's direction.

The rock hit home with a loud, thud like a Louisville slugger connecting with the back of someone's skull.

If I was lucky, maybe I hit it in the back of the head and not the girl.

Either way, the thing stumbled, letting out a series of guttural grunts, or… something then sprinted away into the night, leaving the scared girl behind.

She flailed and screamed, curling up into a ball.

I hurried ahead, dropping to the ground next to her.

"It's okay, I've got you. That thing is gone," I said as gently as I could, then made a hushing sound as I gently placed my hand on her arm to calm her.

She screamed at my touch, but after hearing my voice she wrapped her arms around my neck with a superhuman death grip like she was holding on for dear life.

Pulling her close, I patted her back and continued making soothing sounds like you would for a frightened kid.

"It's okay, I've got you. You're all right now."

She continued to sob as I picked her up and began carrying her downhill. I was surprised she didn't fight me, but I wasn't a three foot tall troll dragging her out into the forest either.

And man, did I stir up one hell of a shitstorm when I emerged back into the clearing carrying the girl. Dozens of women, wrapped in whatever they could grab, were huddled around the bonfire.

You'd have thought I was the worst piece of shit known to man with the comments and slurs I overheard from the gaggle of cackling hens. No, I take that back. The worst piece of shit known to womankind. I get along with most dudes, and have been told several times over the years that I've never met a stranger, but the moment I stepped foot in that clearing carrying the half-naked young woman in my arms the pack of rabid females surrounded me like jackals on a kill.

If it weren't for Mandy, they probably would have torn me limb from limb, but she rushed over to my side as she saw me and started taking control of the situation like the most protective mamma bear I'd ever seen.

She immediately directed a couple of the girls to tend to the fire and make sure it was out or burned down well enough so it didn't start forest fires and told everyone else to gather back to the main hall as a group for safety's sake.

Grabbing a thin blanket from the ground as we walked, Mandy covered the girl the best she could, tucking it around her so it wouldn't slip off. It was a slow trek in the dark along the long, winding path through the forest back to the main camp building, but everyone was safe.

It took several minutes to get the girl calmed enough that she responded to us with more than whimpering sobs. One of the other ladies brought over a cup of chamomile tea and handed it off to Mandy, who'd sat herself behind the girl and gently rubbed her back, attempting to comfort the girl.

"It's going to be alright. Can you tell me your name?" she asked, offering the girl the steaming cup of tea.

The girl stuttered out a shaky *"Gracie"*, before taking several short sips of the drink.

"You're going to be okay, Gracie," Mandy reassured. "When you're ready, tell us what happened."

Gracie nodded slowly and took another sip of the hot tea before she started to explain.

"I'd gone off into the tree line to tinkle, but before I finished I heard something rustling about in the underbrush nearby. I tried to hurry, but before I could stand, something grabbed me by the hair and yanked me back. I fought against it, swinging blindly behind me and found arms as thick as small trees, then the thing bounced me around like a rag doll. From what I could see in the darkness, its face and beard were ghostly white, and its blue eyes seemed to glow in the dark."

Most of the other women gathered around by this point as Gracie told her story. Low murmurs and whispers passed amongst the crowd.

"Aho," a raspy voice called from the back of the crowd. "Move out of my way. Let me see the girl," barked the wizened voice.

An older woman, maybe in her late sixties, cut her way through the gathered women with a cane as gnarled and twisted as her aged hands. Slightly hunched at the shoulders, she advanced swiftly toward us.

She was dressed in vibrant flowing skirts, with colorful beads adorning her hair and pieces of native jewelry hung about her neck and wrists.

"Say that again," the old lady urged, kneeling down beside Gracie. "Tell *me* what you saw, child."

Gracie repeated herself, a little calmer and more collected this time around.

The old woman pursed her lips and let out a reflective humming sound.

"Did you hear it speak?" The old woman asked.

Gracie nodded slowly, eyes wide but fearful, as if reliving that moment all over again in her head.

"It kept repeating something over and over, but I couldn't understand what it was saying."

"Can you tell me what it sounded like?"

Gracie began silently mouthing the syllables before she spoke again. "It sounded excited and slurred, almost grunting it, but was something like, funny you high."

"Hmmmm." The old crone rocked back on her heels while crouched, more limber than I would have ever expected. She closed her eyes and tilted her head back as if in contemplation.

"Have you heard of something like this before?" I asked. The old woman shushed me in that grandmotherly way. Her numerous bracelets and bangles clinked as she shooed me with a flick of her wrist, never opening her eyes.

Several decisive grunts and nods later, the old crone opened her eyes and turned to look at the girl.

Cupping Gracie's hand in hers, she massaged the back of the girl's hand with her thumbs. "All will be well in time, my child," she said, then glared up at me, extending her hand in my direction.

"You look to be a strong warrior. Be a good boy and help an old lady to her feet."

Helping her up, she gripped my hand so tight it felt as if she could crush mine with little effort, then suddenly pulled me down to whisper in my ear as soon as she was upright again.

"I am in need of your…" she stopped and stepped back, looking me over as if appraising my value. "I need a dog soldier, but you'll have to do. Come with me," she ordered, dragging me along behind her as she pushed through the crowd.

Apparently, it wasn't a request.

Mandy rose to follow us, but the old woman waved her off. "Tend to the girl and make sure she gets back to her cabin safely."

"But…," Mandy started to say before the old woman cut her off.

"Your man will return to you soon enough, little sister." She flashed a conniving grin at Mandy, then continued leading me away toward the back doors of the hall. "I promise you, he will not be too spent for any plans you might have had for tonight." The old woman coughed through a chuckle, her arm draped through the crook of mine as we walked.

We continued out the back of the hall and down the path to one of the nearby cabins. Taking a seat on the porch, she pulled out a corn-cob pipe from an apron pocket and began stuffing it from a small pouch. She puffed, lighting the pipe, and the odd smell of spiced tobacco wafted across the porch.

"Sit, boy," she demanded, pointing toward the rustic chair across from her.

"When in Rome," I muttered, shrugged, and pulled a cigar from the breast pocket of my kutte as I sat. "So you have some idea of what that was?"

"Yes," she mumbled around the pipe between her teeth and nodded, then stared off into the dark forest surrounding us for a long moment.

"And…?"

Her teeth clacked as she bit down on the pipe stem. "Patience, young one. To rush into anything is to spell your doom."

Giving her a moment to collect her thoughts, I lit my cigar, enjoying the smooth, sweet aroma as I lightly puffed it to life.

"I believe what the young lady described was one of the Moon-Eyed people. They were defeated by my ancestors and driven out of the Blue Ridge Mountains hundreds of years ago. For them to appear here is disconcerting at the least."

"Who are you exactly?" I asked, relaxing back in the seat.

The old woman glanced back at me with a look of consternation and let out a light hum. She puffed on her pipe and nodded. "That's right. You aren't part of the women's weekend, are you? Unless you're a woman in disguise."

"No, ma'am, I am not. I was only here to fish the little lake while my friend Mandy did her thing at the gathering with the rest of you ladies."

"My English name is Brenda Lechner," she said matter-of-factly. "But most within these circles," she said, motioning to the camp, "call me Grandmother Lechner."

"Pleased to meet you, Grandmother Leckner," I said, setting up in my seat to bow slightly.

Her eyebrows rose with an inquisitive glance. "And you are?" she asked around the stem of the pipe.

"Braxton Hicks, though most folks just call me Braxton or Brax."

She let out a light giggle-snort, nearly choking on the pipe smoke. She turned back to me with a wide smile after she'd stopped coughing. "In all my years of nursing, I have never met anyone named Braxton Hicks. You do realize what that name means, don't you?"

"Yes, ma'am, unfortunately, I do. But it's the name my mother gave me because she thought it would go along well with Eugene after she heard the nurses mention it in the delivery room."

"Eugene?"

"Yes, ma'am. My father's first name."

"I see." She chuckled. "Please call me Brenda. Ma'am makes me feel old, and I'm only hitting my stride at this point in life," she said, smiling widely.

"So what do we do about these creatures? You said they were called the Moon-Eyed people? Are they people or something more… magical?"

A look of understanding my meaning painted her visage before she continued. "From the stories passed down by my elders, the moon-eyed people weren't much more than savage beasts that lived in the Appalachian Mountains well before my people arrived. There are tales of old that say they enchanted young girls away from their tribes, and that they fed on those defeated in battle."

"Do the tales mention how your ancestors dealt with the moon-eyed people back then?"

She chuckled under her breath between puffs on the pipe and nodded. "The Moon-Eyed people are said to be nocturnal, only coming out at night because they are sensitive to any light. My people tracked them to their underground lairs and drove them out with fire during the day. Supposedly, none were spared."

"Well, ain't that just lovely. What are the chances we're dealing with more than a few individuals?"

She shrugged, letting out a long sigh. "I do not know. Until now, there have been no other sightings that I know of. I suppose it's possible that a few individuals escaped and have existed in seclusion over the centuries."

"If there are any nearby caves, that's most likely where we'll find them?"

Grandmother Lechner nodded. "Yes, according to the tales, but in truth, I have no honest clue. It is only ancient stories passed down from one elder to the next."

"So, run them to ground, like a fox, and we'll find where they've been hiding." I sat there, puffing my cigar for a long moment in thought, staring off into the night. If they were a feral race, then it means they're a possible threat to anyone in the area. But then, if they hadn't been seen for hundreds of years, could they be a lost race of humans or fae that have skirted the edges of modern life by hiding in the shadows of the world like Bigfoot and other cryptids across North America? By right and writ, I had all the power of the federal government backing me to remove them from the national park, but for whatever reason, that just felt wrong, like a repeat of the Trail of Tears.

I'd have to figure out what to do with them one way or the other, because they did pose a threat to the locals. But what could I do, short of busting in and double-tapping each and every one of them I found? If… and it was a big if… If I could find where they were holed up at. For all I knew, this one was by itself and maybe even the last of its kind.

I'd have to talk to the facilities manager in the morning about caverns in the and where their entrances were. But for now, it was probably time to turn in for the night. I had a feeling tomorrow was going to be busy.

I bid Grandmother Lechner a good night and headed back to our campsite.

Mandy was already back at camp by the time I returned. I'd taken care of pitching Mandy's tent as well as setting up my roadside lean-to and bedroll under Jonie, my Harley-Davidson Road King, while Mandy was off doing girl things with the rest of the women's group. It's much easier to set things up in the daylight instead of fumbling in the dark when you don't have to.

She'd set up several of her LED lanterns around the site and was pacing back and forth in front of the tent, frantically fighting with her phone as I walked up. She smacked at her arms and legs, then let out a frustrated screech and kicked at a large root by the fire pit.

"Why won't you connect?" She scratched frantically at the back of her arm and then stuck her nose into her phone again.

Mandy, being the electronics genius that she was, must have been trying to get any signal she could on her phone. I could only imagine how the lack of signal was like an alcoholic fiending for their next drink. And when her *drug of choice* was the World Wide Web, the lack of connection had to be excruciating for her.

The only problem was that she wasn't likely to get any signal at all. The entirety of Camp McDowell sat at the bottom of a geographical bowl where cell signals were nonexistent at best.

"That isn't going to work," I said calmly as I approached the firepit.

"Finally, you're back. So why is that, Mister Wizard?"

"Geography."

She flashed a scowl in my direction, rage burning behind her golden amber eyes. "What the hell does geography have to do with anything?"

I shrugged and started stacking the twigs and small branches I'd collected earlier in the day to start a campfire. "Geography has everything to do with the lack of signal here. Camp McDowell is geographically about a hundred feet or so lower in elevation than the surrounding ridgelines. Without a nearby tower that covers the area, we're effectively cut off from the outside world without a hardline."

"Shit…" She kicked at the root again.

"Beautiful, isn't it?"

"What?"

"The silence."

She didn't respond, but her scowl had turned into one of the sternest angry glares she'd ever given me.

I smiled wide and went back to building the fire. "Nothing but us, the wind, and the critters of the forest. Kinda nice for a change."

"Braxton!"

The growl growing in her voice was all I needed to know she was nearly at her breaking point. Mandy being totally pissed off at me for the rest of the weekend was not on the top of any list, especially with the attack that happened tonight. I sat back on my heels and turned to her. "Okay, okay. What are you trying to look up?"

She crossed her arms, and her head tilted to the side with a look I knew all too well. Yup, she was really getting pissed.

"What?"

"What the hell do you think I was trying to look up? It's not like we had anything weird happen tonight."

"Like a pack of half-naked women dancing around a bonfire wasn't weird to start with," slipped out of my mouth before I could catch myself.

Mandy roared with frustration and kicked the root again before flopping herself on the ground in front of the tent.

"How am *I* supposed to do my job, so *you* can do your job if I can't access the tools that I use? Do you not understand how frustrating this is? That girl could have been hurt or, God forbid, killed, and I'm helpless to do anything that might help stop that creature."

"What makes you think it's some kind of creature?"

Her head did that weird angry tilt to the side thing again that I hated so much.

"Braxton!"

I held my hands up defensively. "No worries. It's all good," I said before turning back to starting a fire. "I've got it all under control."

"Bullshit."

"No shit." I looked up at her and flashed her my best smiling wink.

"Dammit, Braxton," she screeched and then threw a rock in my direction that went way too high and wide to count.

"You still throw like a girl."

"And maybe if you paid more attention, you'd realize *I* was one." She pulled her knees up close, wrapped her arms around them, and tucked her head before she began to sob.

Ouch, that kinda hurt.

"Listen…"

"No, you listen, Braxton Hicks," she shouted, cutting me off. "There is something out there in the woods that has the potential to hurt innocent people, and you're treating it like a joke!" She stood up, grabbed her jacket out of the tent, and started marching away from camp.

"Mandy! Where the hell are you going?"

"To find a signal and figure out what this thing is so you can kill it!"

"Mandy, stop. Please come back."

She turned and growled, then threw another rock at me. "Why, Braxton? Why should I? You keep acting like this is nothing but a joke."

"Because I know what *they* are."

"Wait? How?"

"You know that old lady I went off with?"

"Yeah…" She thought for a moment. "Grandmother Lechner. She's a Cherokee medicine woman. What did she tell you?" The tone in her voice shifted from anger to excitement.

I stood and slowly started walking towards her. "She said what the girl described sounded similar to the Cherokee tales of the

Moon-Eyed people. Her ancestors drove them out of the Appalachian Mountains hundreds of years ago."

"Wait? That name sounds familiar," she said excitedly, turning back to her phone. Several taps on the screen later, she let out another frustrated growl. "Dammit! I know I've seen mention of them before, but I can't remember what it was. I think it was something about a lost tribe of Welshmen that even predated the Vikings and the Vinland Sagas, but I can't confirm it because my phone is useless here in podunk, nothing, Alabama!"

"Don't worry about it, then," I said with a shrug, then went back to lighting the fire.

"Don't worry about it?" Mandy laughed with that sarcastic undertone I knew so well. "And how exactly am I supposed to *not* worry about it?"

I shrugged again, and then lightly blew on the infant flame. Slowly it grew, then quickly spread through the pine straw I'd lined the small pile of twigs with. "You just don't."

"Arrr! Why are you so damned incorrigible, Braxton?"

I sat back on the ground next and continued feeding the small fire larger bits of wood as it grew.

"Awww, I love you too, Mandy." I smiled up at her. She kicked another rock in my direction.

I stayed silent and leaned over to grab my backpack from Jonie. Mandy impatiently tapped her foot while I fished out a can of scum weenies, aka Vienna sausages, and popped the top.

"What exactly do you plan to do, Mister Know-it-all?"

"I think I might go for a walk in the morning." I skewered one of the gelatin-covered meat sticks with my pocket knife and popped the scum weenie into my mouth, smiling up at her as I chewed.

For the most part, Mandy was a diehard camper. It didn't matter where we went or how bad the weather got. She was usually even good with camping on the side of the road during some of these cross-country treks we'd done over the years.

Hell, for someone who looked like a glamorous girly girl, she was about as country and tough as they came. She chalked it up to all the time she'd spent hanging out with her Vietnam-era Marine grandfather.

I chalked it up to pure stubbornness.

But for whatever reason, this Moon-Eyed thing really had her spooked. Maybe it was because after all of these years of helping me with case after case, it was her first time knee-deep in the shit, so to speak.

So, to ease her paranoia, I stayed on fire watch all night, catnapping fifteen minutes here and there by the fire.

The night passed slower than a snail in molasses, and about the only thing keeping me sane was keeping the small campfire stoked so it cast enough light around the clearing to drive back the shadows.

By the time Mandy woke, the coffee was ready and breakfast was cooking. One of those 'life is good' moments, when the smell of breakfast mingled with that early morning dew and blooming honeysuckle scents.

She surprised the hell out of me with how fast she scarfed down her breakfast. I questioned if she'd even breathed while she shoveled the bacon and eggs down her gullet, then chased it with a piping hot cup o' joe, eager to get on the move to talk with the camp director.

Now, I'm one of the first people to go on about getting your ass in gear and getting shit done. But when it comes to a morning coffee and cigar, that's something that's almost sacrilegious to rush, especially considering the beautiful setting surrounding us.

It was one thing for the universe to screw with each and every vacation I'd tried to enjoy, but a man's morning coffee was as sacred as a man's bike or Ole Lady.

You just don't fuck with it.

No sooner had I downed the last swig of coffee in my tin, she was off like a shot heading up the hill toward the camp's main hall.

Luckily, we didn't have to wait long. We caught the camp director, Doug Collins, in the main hall, just sitting down with his breakfast.

He was a nice sorta dude, even though he had that odd creeper vibe about him. I never could bring myself to trust someone who wore one of those creepy smiles that you knew hid more than they let the public see, like a televangelist or used car salesman.

But, he was nice enough to oblige us and talked while he ate.

He said he'd grown up on the property, taking over the running of the camp after his parents, the previous camp directors, had retired, passing down the responsibility to him. He estimated he'd explored at least ninety percent of the property, if not more, during his lifetime, even making maps of the area in his younger years.

He went on for a while describing the ruins of old homesteads, abandoned logging equipment, and even the remains of an old whiskey still gouged full of holes from the local sheriff's axe deep in the forest. When we brought up that we were interested in any caves in the area, he described a small holler near the northeast corner of the property where a natural spring on a hill rise fed a waterfall, forming one of the nearby streams. And behind that waterfall was the entrance to a pretty extensive cave system.

He never explored the caves, but knew of other people who had over the years, mapping the subterranean corridors leading into the underworld.

The man had barely gotten the information out of his mouth when Mandy was tugging at my arm, ready to go. We thanked him, then grabbed another cup of coffee on the way out before heading back toward camp.

Mandy hurried ahead and turned to face me, trotting backwards as I walked. I'd say she looked excited, but that would have been an understatement. She beamed with excitement.

"What's your plan, Brax? How are we going to take care of this Moon-eyed person?"

"Whoa," I said, chuckling. "Hold up, now."

Her eyes narrowed, and she pursed her lips before I had gotten the words out of my mouth.

"*We,*" I emphasized, "aren't going to take care of this Moon-eyed person. I'm going to track it down and deal with it when I find it. You, on the other hand, are going to go back to enjoying your Women's Conference. Maybe you'll make a few friends for a change instead of sitting in front of those damned computers for weeks on end."

She stopped dead in her tracks, crossed her arms, and gave me that tilted-head glare again.

"What?"

"What? What do you mean, what?"

"I mean exactly that. I'm operating on almost no information. I have no idea what this creature is capable of, and *you* have absolutely zero field experience. You're an amazing researcher, Mandy. But you don't know the first thing about tracking down a critter, let alone a possibly magical critter out here in the wild."

"But, Braxton…" she started to argue.

"But nothing." I continued on down the road towards our campsite. "You have no idea about some of the things I've dealt with. Yeah, I've told you some of the stories about these gigs, but you don't *really* know the shit that I've dealt with out there."

"Braxton *Eugene* Hicks."

Fuck me. I felt bad for future youngins *if* she ever had kids, because that was one hell of a *mom voice,* and she used my middle name.

"Nope, no way in hell you're going with me." I side-stepped her and continued toward the campsite. I'd barely taken a step past her when she *sucker-punched* me with a roundhouse kick between the shoulder blades. I stumbled forward, bracing myself on my knees, and fought to catch my breath.

"What the hell was that for?" I squeaked, gasping.

"What do you think? Did you forget that I run a martial arts studio, among other things?"

"So?"

"You know, it's really annoying when your Captain Obvious brain shows up. I can handle myself, Brax. My grandfather taught me everything he knows."

I straightened, stretching the angry muscles in my back. "What the hell are you talking about?"

"My grandfather…" She let out a frustrated growl. "The Marine Recon Vi-et-nam veteran grandfather who spent five tours in-country as a tunnel rat and more?"

"You can't just kick the shit out of a ghost or any of the other supernatural critters out there. It just doesn't work like that. Hell, you of all people should know that. You're the one who feeds me all of the info on these things."

"And right now I can't feed you anything, but if you think for one second you're going to keep me from coming along, someone will have to feed you through a straw!" She shoved her finger in my face, digging the tip of a manicured fingernail into the tip of my nose. "Do not argue with me. You almost always need backup, and right now, I'm all you've got." She turned on her heel and marched away toward camp.

Dammit to hell if that woman wasn't pigheaded stubborn. But she did have a point. Having backup for no other reason than someone who could get word back to my handlers if something went sideways would be better than nothing. The gods know how many scrapes I'd been in when I didn't know if I'd come out alive or not.

"Mandy, wait!"

She stopped in her tracks, turned on her heel again, and stomped back toward me. "I don't want to hear it, Braxton," she shouted, jabbing me in the chest with her manicured acrylic nail.

"Ouch, that freaking hurts."

"Good! It'll be even worse if you don't shut your trap and get moving. We're burning daylight, dammit."

I let out a reluctant sigh and rubbed at what I assumed was a puncture wound on my chest. Those damned nails were as sharp as a bobcat's claws.

"Fine."

"Fine, what?" she growled.

"You can come. But don't do anything stupid that'll get both of us unalived."

She let out a barking laugh. "Me? You're one to talk…"

Oh, yeah. This was already turning out to be a great idea…

Before heading out, we stopped in to visit with Grandmother Lechner, and ask her a few more questions about the Moon-Eyed people.

Legend says that they like music, and especially drumming, singing, and dancing. The Cherokee legend says, *Sometimes their drums are heard in lonely places in the mountains, but it is not safe to follow it, for they do not like to be disturbed at home.*

And of course, after several hours of trekking through the backwoods of the camp into the national park, the forest rang with birdsong in time to the beat of a distant drum.

Mandy froze at the first beat she heard and turned to me, her eyes wide with surprise.

"What the hell is that?"

I shrugged and continued walking. "Sounds like drums. Nice solid beat, too. It kind of reminds me of some of the older AC/DC tracks I listened to on the ride here."

"Didn't Grandmother say that was one of the signs of the Moon-Eyed people?"

"Yup."

"Okay, so what do we do?"

"We keep trekking"

Mandy let out a frustrated growl.

"What?" I stopped and turned to look at her. "Don't growl at me."

"Shouldn't we be reporting this to someone or recording it or something?"

I just glared at her and then continued up the trail.

"Braxton."

"Exactly who are we going to report to? We have no cell signal, remember? And why would we record anything? I can barely hear it."

"To document the encounter."

"I hate to break it to you, but so far there is no encounter. At best, we probably have a couple of hippies getting high, dancing naked around a campfire, and playing drums in the backwoods."

"But what if it isn't?"

"If it isn't, then it isn't, and maybe we get to find the Moon-Eyed people."

"But if it is, we should be documenting everything we can for posterity's sake."

I let out a frustrated breath of my own and rubbed my face. "Listen. If I stopped to document every little bang, creak, or other sort of noise, I'd never get the job done. I'd be too damn busy documenting every little thing that didn't matter, and then probably get my ass jumped and eaten alive by whatever critter was waiting on me just around the bend."

"Okay, then, Mister professional. How do you normally deal with things like this?"

"I find it and deal with it," I said, shrugging before I continued on.

"Oh my god, Braxton! What the hell? You can't just wing it. You have to have a plan, dumbass."

"Dammit, Mandy. We need to find that waterfall and see if that's where they are *before dark*, mind you, and I'm willing to bet that's where the drums will lead us. If it is just a bunch of naked hippies, we might get lucky and there will be beer and tits.

Simple as that. This ain't my first rodeo, Mandy. I go with my gut, and my gut tells me to go this way. I'll deal with whatever it is when I get there. If you don't like the plan, the path back to camp is right behind you," I said, pointing back down the trail, continuing up the trail.

I knew I would pay hell later if I survived, but at this point, she was just slowing me down.

It wasn't long before I heard her growl from down the trail, so I stopped to let her catch up.

Cautiously, we continued along the trail. I wasn't too worried about one of them jumping out at us since the sun was still up, but you never know. Myth and legends are just that or complete bullshit and should be taken with a grain of salt in most cases.

The drumming continued, getting louder the farther we trekked, with the path eventually leading us to a small gorge with a waterfall running down a cliffside.

It was absolutely gorgeous, like something out of a fantasy flick. The cool mist from the waterfall drifted eerily in the air and felt amazing compared to the muggy Alabama summer heat.

The hair on the back of my neck suddenly stood on end when I realized this was the perfect place for an ambush. I half expected pixies, fairies, or something else malicious to pop out of nowhere and start harassing the shit out of me like usual.

I stopped and scanned the area, looking for any movement or sign of anything unusual. Luckily, my apprehension was nothing more than good old-fashioned paranoia, so I pressed on.

We quietly crept into the gorge, careful not to disturb any rocks that would fall into the water as we made our way towards the waterfall and the drumming.

It was rhythmic, resonating among the crumbling stone walls of the gorge and down the valley along the water's surface.

I leapt from one boulder to the next, making my way towards the wide stone ledge at the base of the waterfall.

"Braxton," Mandy shouted in a whisper. I could barely make out the sound of her voice over the roar of the falling water, but I still turned and motioned to her to be quiet, placing my index finger against my lips.

"What are we doing?"

I motioned to myself, pointing towards my eyes, then towards the waterfall. She nodded in understanding and slowly followed behind me. Taking the low route, she waded through the chilly mountain stream instead of bouncing from boulder to boulder like I had done.

Carefully, I crept up along the edge of the falls and slipped through the ice-cold sheet of water.

Sure enough, just like in any good adventure flick, there was a cavern entrance behind the falling water. The gaping maw of the opening was easily twice as tall as a man and at least forty feet wide, hidden by a stand of limestone that blocked the entrance from view.

Cold air flowing out from the opening mixed with a heavy mist was enough to drop the temperature enough that I started to involuntarily shiver.

Kneeling, I dropped my pack and rummaged through it for the pair of flashlights I'd tossed in there before leaving camp.

Mandy let out a short scream as she passed through the cold water and immediately began gasping for breath. I cupped my hand over her mouth with one hand, and the back of her head with the other.

Glaring at her was all it took, no words, nothing else. She nodded in understanding, and I handed her a flashlight, then slung the pack back over my shoulders and continued.

That's when I noticed the drumming had stopped.

Shit, I thought to myself. There went any element of surprise that we might have had.

I looked back at Mandy and let out a low growl of my own before I continued over the slick rocks into the cavern.

It quickly descended, dropping at a steep angle into the dark abyss below. The flashlights only illuminated about thirty or forty feet ahead of us.

That was the last time I bought cheap flashlights from the big-box store. Cheap Chinese crap, man.

Boulders and loose rubble littered the bottom of the cavern. Footing absolutely sucked, so I went slow, making sure I could catch Mandy if she slipped.

You could tell somebody had been through here recently just by the scuff marks on the rocks and the disturbance of sediment along the path.

A hundred yards down the slope, the path began to narrow and level out. Small rivulets of water trickled down the walls, collecting along the edges of the cavern before flowing deeper into the earth as two tiny underground streams. I panned the light upward, discovering a massive cathedral of rock formations above us. Light glistened on the damp limestone and calcite surfaces.

"That is so beautiful," Mandy mumbled, stopping beside me.

I nodded in agreement and leaned over to whisper in her ear. "You still like cave diving?"

She stepped back and nodded.

"Then we might have to come back here to explore a bit after we square away these Moon-Eyed shenanigans."

Mandy smiled up at me and leaned in for a side hug. "Deal." The sweet smell of her perfume filled my nostrils and assaulted my senses, fueling a flurry of memories that pulled me away from reality.

It had been years since we'd officially dated, and you'd think that any sign of affection would be nothing since we were still best friends, but I'll be damned if this woman didn't have some sort of demonic hold on my heart and soul. There were times I missed waking up beside her, but the scales of balance always turned things against me.

I reciprocated the lean and wrapped an arm around her, pulling her in close.

The sound of a tumbling stone echoed through the cavern, breaking the silence and ruining the moment.

Mandy froze and sucked in a short breath of surprise. Every muscle in her body seemed to tense as hard as stone.

I panned my light down the path and spotted a movement of light. Two blazing red orbs wavered about in the distance, reflecting like the eyes of a deer in the headlights and then quickly disappeared deeper into the darkness.

Mandy's breathing suddenly sounded shaky, shallow, and forced as she tried to form words. "W…w…what was that?"

She had a fair question, and I honestly wasn't sure. The fact that they reflected the light from our flashlights meant there was a good chance the thing was a living thing, but it wasn't necessarily an indicator of anything supernatural.

What that living thing was, was anyone's guess. It could have been anything from a cougar, bear, wild dog, maybe even one of the moon-eyed people or a wild forest elf, even. Been there, done that already.

The fact that it's most likely something living, means if it comes down to it, I can make it bleed and it can die.

Reaching behind my back, I drew my Smith & Wesson .357 Magnum, and continued ahead. There wasn't any way I'd have left it behind this time, knowing I was hunting something unknown.

It didn't take us long before we started seeing signs of habitation. Whoever had been living here had been here a long time and seemed to be a bit of a pack rat. Scattered bits of clothing, tools, kids' toys, ect., ranging from modern to antique, littered the space.

We continued into a large open chamber. Something skittered ahead of us on the wet stone, then let out a yelp as it sounded like someone had fallen into a pile of junk.

Before I could spot what was moving, something let out a throaty growl and then slammed into me, biting down hard on my left leg.

Off balance and struggling to stay upright, I backhanded the thing with the butt of the revolver. The blow landed, and whatever it was felt hairy and solid. Fat lotta good it did me, because *it* doubled down on its bite; throwing itself into the act like a starving dependapotamus on rib night at the Chuck and Shuck outside of Seymour Johnson Air Force Base.

Grabbing a handful of hair on the back of the thing's head, I pulled it away from my leg.

"Sorry, sweetheart, I'm not into furries," I said, then let out my own roaring growl.

Frantically, I pistol-whipped the creature over and over again on what you'd assume was the side of its head before kicking it away.

It winced, growled, then scrambled away, back into the darkness. I rapidly fired several shots in the direction I heard it run off, hoping I'd at least slow whatever it was down.

Mandy screamed, dropping to the floor. The .357 magnum slugs ricocheted several times off the walls of the chamber, sending sparks into the air before plinking into a pool of water somewhere near the back of the space.

I picked up my flashlight and turned its beam in the direction the thing had fled. There among the abandoned refuse was a small figure in ratty, filth-caked rags. It let out a growling hiss, covering its eyes with its hands when the light hit it.

"Mandy, are you okay?" I asked, keeping my attention on the grubby little cave troll.

"Do you think I'm fucking okay?"

"Are you hurt?"

"No," she excitedly replied, panting.

The individual was short, maybe four feet tall at best, and as broad across the shoulders as I was. He sported a long white beard and hair that was matted in several places, but was otherwise a wild mess. He honestly looked like the homeless, bat-shit crazy uncle of the dwarves from The Lord of the Rings.

Pasty white skin shone through where the grime had been smeared and knocked away by my blows; small red rivulets trickled down the side of the guy's face.

Apparently, I had done some damage after all.

The little man let out a keening wail, then scrambled to get behind the remains of a rotten canvas tarp that hung from the cave wall, mumbling something under his breath.

"Keep your light on him and don't take your eyes off," I said over my shoulder to Mandy as I panned the light around the chamber. The last thing I needed was to get ambushed by another one of these crusty dudes hiding in a dark corner.

Nothing else moved in the cavern; only the sound of the dwarf's whimpering and the slow trickling echo of water filled the space.

I panned the light down to check out the damage to my leg. The force of the bite still hurt, but luckily my jeans hadn't torn and there weren't any bloodstains to be found. Other than a little bit of pain, and what I expected to be one hell of a bruise in the morning, I was no worse for wear.

The dwarf repeatedly mumbled something under his breath that I couldn't make out.

Mandy sucked in a sharp breath and took a step forward. "Brax…"

I looked up and turned my flashlight back at the dwarf. It was still more or less hidden behind the tarp, so I turned the light toward Mandy and quickly scanned her for injuries.

"What's wrong? Are you hit?"

"No…," she said softly, kneeling on the damp stone floor.

"Then what is it?"

She crept closer, staying low on her knees.

"What he's saying, sounds familiar. Unalii," she said in a gentle tone, but loud enough to be heard over his mumbling.

"Unalii?" the dwarf parroted and slowly, ever so cautiously, peeked around the edge of the tarp, shielding his eyes from the light.

I moved the beam lower towards the floor so we could still see him, but hopefully he wouldn't be as blinded.

Mandy nodded and smiled at him. "Unalii." Taking off her pack, she rummaged around for a moment before producing a bright yellow banana she'd stolen from the camp chow hall for a trail snack.

"Unalii," she said again, holding the banana out to him.

Concern, fear, and indecision painted his face all at once before he stepped out from behind the tarp and forward toward Mandy.

Instinct kicked in, and I raised the revolver, aiming for center mass.

"Braxton Hicks," Mandy hissed. "Put it down. Can't you see he's just hungry and scared?"

I shifted my footing, looked down at her and then back up at the dwarf. "What was it you said to him? Unalii? What does that mean?"

She turned back and looked up at me, smiling-wide, like she'd just cracked some sort of high-level security code.

"It's Cherokee for friend." Sliding forward, she handed the dwarf the banana and then took several steps back.

He sniffed it like a hound on the trail, muttered something I couldn't even begin to comprehend and devoured the banana, peel and all.

"So you can talk to him?"

"No, not really."

"Then how did you know it was Cherokee?"

"I sorta took classes for a few years when I was running around up at Red Clay. One of the grandmothers took an interest in teaching me and helped me to learn as much as I could in the short time we had before she passed away."

"But you don't know enough to understand everything he's saying?"

Mandy let out a giggle. "Not even close. It's similar enough that I can understand, and speak some that he understands, but I think he's using an older dialect."

"Then how do we tell him to move on and leave the girls alone?"

"We need Grandmother Lechner's help. She speaks Cherokee fluently, so there's a better chance she can understand him."

"Sounds like as good a plan as any," I said, dropping my pack to the ground.

"What are you doing?"

Rummaging around in my pack, I pulled out what snacks I had with me, along with a bottle of sweet tea, and sat them out in front of the dwarf, keeping a few strips of jerky for myself before handing the grub over to him.

I held up a piece of jerky, then bit into it, motioning toward the bag I'd tossed in his direction.

Eagerly, he dug into the dried meat and indulged himself.

"Go back to camp and find Grandmother. Do whatever it takes to bring her here. I have a feeling we will never get him out of this cave to meet her, so she has to come to him."

"What are you going to do in the meantime?"

I retrieved a cigar from the breast pocket of my kutte, and struck a light. The dwarf flinched and stared at the lighter flame.

"I'm going to make a new friend."

Elfshot

By Pete Aldin

A reminiscence of William Edward Duigan, being a true and accurate account of the happenings near Hawkesbury, in the Colony of New South Wales, upon the eighteenth day of January in the year of our Lord 1856

Our poor, ailing milk-cow Lisbeth lay on her side in our high paddock, the cleared field that ringed the hilltop in the direct center of our holding. Her 'bed' was a wide and natural ledge in the hillside. All thirty-three of her sister animals had gathered at the lowest point of the field, calves and mothers sequestered against the fence behind the dam we'd dug to capture water from the stream on the other side of that fence. I'd been a mere boy during that digging, all of three years old, but eager to cart dirt, to help. This was back when our cattle had numbered but three, when both Da and Ma were naught but former convicts, struggling hard to make an honest living. Now, mere days after my fourteenth birthday, they were seen as respectable members of local society, a fact they treasured among their best accomplishments, along with raising a son destined to study the sciences.

On this day, the day that the old woman looked over our unwell beast, I was fourteen, broad-shouldered, and with a broad and curious mind that stood me in good stead to study those very sciences in future. I watched her keenly. She was dressed all in patches of cloth. Wool. Linen. Silk. Stitched together into blouse and skirts and gloves, covering all aspects of her skin except that creased and drooping face of hers. My parents did not know her name. To them, and to the population of farmers, traders, convicts and artisans throughout the Hawkesbury district along the Glendale River, she was known only as the old woman. (Though some called her witch, it must be said). Despite the fierce heat of this January late-morning, she had gathered her hair beneath a woolen bonnet. And she kept on muttering the same string of nonsense words as she worked: "Reveal thissen, small spear, if thee be 'ere within."

As she muttered her nonsense, she moved around and around Lisbeth with one gloved hand scratching at her own pointy chin, and the other feeling the animal: along her ribs, under her jaw, the length of her tail, udder, fly-ridden ears.

Once in a while, Lisbeth would let out a quiet and short-lived lowing at the old woman's ministrations, before lapsing again into silent misery. By way of contrast, the woman cooed and hummed in lively fashion as if she had pigeons and bees inside her all at once.

It was my mother who had invited her. Not my father. Whenever her back was turned, Da would mimic her squint-eyed face and bow his back and nudge me with an elbow, making me bite down on the laughter that threatened to spill from my mouth. By the time she had completed that circuit around the ailing animal, Da would be standing straight and respectful again as if he had never made sport of her. It seemed to me each time that he could have mocked her with impunity since she never so much as glanced our way. In point of fact, since the moment my Ma had pressed coin into the woman's hand's and bade her precede the manfolk up the hill, the woman had not once acknowledged us.

Da's discourteous impersonations were doubtless to take his mind off the heat and the boredom. Despite his constant good-humor, he had never borne colonial summers well. He was not born to it as I was. Originating in County Cork, a vivid world of green mystery to me, six months by ship had brought him to the sunburned brown and greys of the Colonies, and each summer and autumn here served him with five months of misery. Marooned once his sentence was served, without money for a passage home, he found himself in love with another freed convict. A plot of land and grant of money from the government allowed them to start their farm. And then came a child. Unlike his parents in so many ways. Born to love the heat and the washed-out colors. Me.

This was the subject of my thoughts as the woman commenced her thirteenth circuit around Lisbeth. Shaking myself from reverie, I drew breath to ask what on earth her odd behavior was intended to achieve. My Da's hand applied a brief and warning pressure upon my arm. His small grimace and shake of the head was enough to discourage inquiry. I felt of course that my inquiry was warranted and justifiable. Yet I loved my Da, so just as the cow had lapsed back into silent misery, so did I (although I itched with impatience and boredom).

I should have had more compassion for the beast. As a young man, however, I was selfish. Just as my father was sensitive and patient.

So sensitive was he toward my situation that he began another interpretation of the woman hoping to provide a modicum of amusement. Once again, I forced back a snicker.

Then the old woman raised her voice.

"I'm aware o' thy antics," she said, her back fully to us. "Thou be makin' skit o' me."

Since she too had come to these lands as a convict, it had not surprised me that she be English. However, her words were flavored by an accent and dialect I had not heard before.

Caught in his transgression, my father turned a chagrined face toward me, his mouth forming a wide O of surprise.

The woman continued, "Just as I'm aware o' t'fella behind thee both."

Da and I exchanged a frown and turned.

Sure enough, a man stood a few yards behind and downhill of us.

Trooper Enwright.

How he'd passed across the brown and brittle grass without alerting either of us to his presence was as much a mystery as the old woman's awareness of shenanigans happening behind her back. Enwright was known locally as a big bastard. (I do hope the reader will pardon my language). To be precise, Enwright was a tall man and wide. He carried a short sabre on one hip and a revolver on the other. The latter weapon was something of a novelty at the time and my attention was instantly drawn to it. Despite the rarity and cost of revolver bullets, the trooper had something of a reputation for using them liberally, sometimes upon wildlife and sometimes upon Natives.

"Good morning," Trooper Enwright said to my Da. Me, he ignored.

He took off his dark blue cap revealing greying hair so limp with sweat that the breeze could not shift it.

Peering past him and squinting against the sun, I made out his two horses near the copse of wattle trees on the other side of the creek. His tracker Gunung was distinguishable standing with them, a musket slung on his back as he watered the animals.

The tracker was a Native, though native to lands far south of Hawkesbury and near the colony of Melbourne. Enwright, it was said, had 'imported' Gunung from there, so that he had a tracker who bore no local sympathies.

Through the morning glare, I also perceived three more shapes pressed into a crouch behind the horses. Natives, like Gunung. But also not like Gunung. I could not see the chains that held them, preventing their flight back across our property and into the forests but chains there would be. The thought of them shackled like convicts made me sick to my stomach.

"Top of this good morn' to you too, Mr. Enwright," Da responded. "You've walked a long way up this hill, sir. We could have come down to speak with you."

"No bother, Duigan. After six hours spent on a horse, a little walk has helped stretch my legs." His eyes shifted to the old woman. "Trouble with your animals?"

"Oh, just this one." Da took a small step sideways, blocking the trooper's view, discouraging further examination of either the cow or her arcane physician. "And how can I be of help to you, sir?"

Enwright leaned left, still interested in the woman, but he came to business smartly enough. "My tracker's horse has thrown a shoe. Probably the rider's fault and not the animal, though I can't work out how he caused it. Always buggering up something, these Blacks. No matter. I was told some years back you're a competent smith? I need a new shoe…"

Da rubbed at the stubble across his throat and scrunched his face in thought. "Well, sir. Hm. You see, it takes some time to fire up the forge. And this is fair hot weather to be smithing. I could send Will here into town for a farrier and a loan horse."

"Damn it, man," spat the Trooper, his cursing unmindful of either me or the woman uphill of us. His face was red with more than just the sun. "It'll take the boy days to get there and back. I want to be gone by tomorrow. I'll pay you fairly. Gunung will be walking the whole way, since the wretched savage caused this predicament. But the horse is my personal property and I'll not see her lamed wandering this godless wasteland when there's a perfectly capable smith who can see to her wellbeing."

Da was already making reassuring gestures long before Enwright completed his ranting. "Not to worry, not to worry. I shall get to it right now, sir. If you'll follow me back, we'll take a look at the damage done and see if we can re-smelt that shoe."

He moved down the hill and Enwright followed. "And my own boots need some retacking, if your wife has time to see to that."

"Yes, sir."

"Also I'll need food for my tracker and me too," the trooper said. "I'll pay you."

"Of course, sir, of course, we'll find something in the larder for you. Something for those prisoners of yours too."

"No food for those bloody wretches! Bugger them!"

Enwright's swearing caused my Da to glance back toward me in embarrassment and I turned my face up toward a passing cloud, pretending I had not heard. When I looked back, they were several yards further on and neither man was talking.

"No food for his prisoners," I said and shook my head in disgust. I tried a little bad language of my own: "What a big bastard he truly is."

A tugging at my sleeve startled me and I swung around.

The woman.

I had forgotten her presence, if that can be believed. Her gaze rested, not upon my eyes as one would expect, but upon my chest. It was as if she could not raise that gaze any higher, or as if there were something inside me she could see.

In her youngish voice, the old woman said, "Elfshot."

Having never heard such a word before, and being unfamiliar with her accent, my mind made sense of her sounds by thinking she had asked me, "'Ave shot?"

"Er, no," I stammered. "No shot here. My Da's gun is down in the house." I wondered did she want us to put Lisbeth out of her misery.

She startled me again by striking my chest with the back of her hand, and none too lightly. I staggered, taking three or four steps to find my balance on the hillside.

"Not musket shot, fool lad," she said with mouth twisted up so that her stained and rotted teeth were visible. She pronounced her word (as it turned out, her diagnosis) more carefully this time. "Elf-shot. Elf."

I frowned, not knowing what she meant. Elf seemed but one more strange word in the mouth of a woman who knew many.

"May be I can I fix it," she continued. One gnarl-knuckled thumb and forefinger ground together as she held them to my face. "Hast tha more brass tha can give?"

By way of reply, my frown deepened.

"Fagh!" she spat when it was clear I wasn't following her meaning. She brushed by me and waddled downhill, leaning on the polished gumtree branch she used for a cane. "Owt to be gained talkin' wi' fool lads. I'll tell ee Mam." She paused a moment to get her balance before raising her stick to the sky and proclaiming a loud string of completely unintelligible words. From the bottom of the slope, the two white-skinned men turned back to regard her curiously. Enwright made some joke about her, and climbed the fence laughing loudly.

My Da, I noted, did not laugh.

I returned to the relative cool of our homestead after an hour of chores about the farm, having eaten the rough lunch of biscuits and dried river fish my Ma had packed for me in the morning. Closing the door fast behind me to keep out windborne dust and heat and flies, I doffed my cloth cap and mopped my forehead with it. In the dimness within, and with my sight still white from the sun's glare, Ma was a soft blur at the table. From her movement, the scent of butter, and the soft smacking and squelching sounds, I could tell she was kneading dough. That seemed a fine activity to me for, being a young man, I was ever hungry, a bottomless pit for food of any kind, but especially bread.

Blinking in the gloom (Ma had only a single candle to work by and the shutters were drawn against the summer day) I made certain that the old woman was absent before venturing a question.

"What did she tell you?"

Ma sniffed. She said, "She has an answer to the problem of our cow."

"And it is?"

"None of her concern, now. Have you cleared the brushwood from the western fence line?"

"Yes, Mam. But…"

"And the fallen tree from upcreek?"

"Did that yesterday. The woman said to me something like elf and shot. She speaks like a magpie, so I've no idea what she meant."

"Now, now, young rascal. I'll not have you speaking of her like that." The words were stern, but the tone was light.

I grinned, happy to get away with the insult. "Well, then, did you understand her?"

Another sniff. Another smacking of dough on board—I could see it this time, my vision adjusting. Eventually she said, "I did."

My impatience was back, but because of my great affection for my Ma, I stowed it away deep and asked as lightly as I could, "Can you please tell me, then?"

"I've told your Da and that's all that matters. Now, clean those hands and you can help me here."

I made no move toward the wash basin, remaining with my back against the door. It was warmed with the sunshine from the other side. "And what did Da say?"

"Never you mind. Wash your hands."

I took three steps toward the wash basin, then stopped to rest those hands that so concerned her on the back of a chair. I tried again, "What is elfshot?"

This time the dough was flung to the board with a loud thud. "You've nothing better to do than pester me with this?"

I grinned again. "Nope."

Her scowl melted as suddenly as it had arrived. "Rascal," she whispered and plunged her fingers into the blob of dough, busying herself. "Very well. I suppose you should know about such things, being of Irish blood after all. Let's only hope your mind is more open on the subject than your dear father's. It seems our woman believes that the cow was hurt by… by the little folk."

It was my mother's turn to say things I couldn't understand. "Little people? Who are they?"

She sighed, wiped her fingers on her apron and sat upon a stool. "Pour me a water will you?" When I had done, and passed it to her, she said, "There's a good lad. Well, then. Your father and I grew up in Ireland where he was an educated man and I an educated woman. Not that this made us any richer with the English being the way they are. Poverty and restriction forced us both into acts that we regretted in more ways than just the punishment. Any way. You know the story of our deportation here. What you don't know is much of the lore of our homeland. Both of our families produced good Catholics, as I hope we have produced in you, son."

She fixed me with a stern look until I said something pious that I don't remember now.

Satisfied she went on. "But whereas his family rejected all of the old ways and the old stories out of hand, mine did not. Many a time, my Maimeó, my grandmother, would regale me with tales of old, and with ancient remedies for all sorts of ills. A frequent subject of our conversations were the little people. I was fascinated by them. In the old days before Christianity came, you see, before the British came too, our people believed they lived side by side with another people."

"Like we do here with the Blacks," I chimed in.

She cocked her head and rubbed dough on her chin as she thought about that. "Similar. But not the same. No, actually, not the same at all. Those poor souls."

Ma kept a small nativity figurine on the mantle. She faced briefly toward the Holy Family while crossing herself. I wasn't sure if she did it with the Enwright's wretched captives in mind or because there was something she feared that had to do with the story she was telling me. "The little folk I'm telling you of are the ones we also called fae. The English in some parts— like where she hails from—called them *ælfe*. Elves."

She sighed and drank from her cup, wiped at her mouth. Keeping my silence, I waited until she was ready. There was a gravity about her mood that fascinated me as much as the subject matter.

"The fae, the elves, are not something I particularly believe in. I mean, I did at one time. As a child. But I grew out of that belief. And upon my confirmation, well, I renounced such things. Much to my parents' relief, and my Maimeó's irritation. And fae were something I gave not a thought to when I called on the old woman. But when I saw the state of young Lisbeth, well, my grandmother had uncanny ways for curing everything from a bad cough to a chicken's inability to lay. Except for that dreadful, dreadful accent she has, our old woman reminds me very much of my Maimeó. And it's her belief that the elves, the little folk, are behind Lisbeth's ills."

I scratched at my cheek a while as Ma emptied her cup in small sips. When she set it by the bread board, I said, "What do they look like?"

She stood with a little groan as she stretched her back then flexed her hands. "As their name suggests, they're little and they're folk." She smiled and picked up the dough. "So I'm told."

"But—"

"I'll tell you what, my son. The one with all the answers is the one who truly believes in the creatures. Why don't you go take her a cup of water and see if she'll fill that fine young mind of yours with more knowledge?"

I frowned a moment, thinking she wanted me to go all the way to the river, then along the local valley, past the township and finally to the hut the old woman lived in. Then it made sense to me. "Oh, she's still on our farm? Why?"

Ma shrugged and slammed the dough down on the board. "Looking for herbs she thinks might give our Lisbeth a fighting chance at recovery. Take her an apple, too. Make her more inclined to answer you."

I glanced at the triangle of apples piled beside the Holy Family on the mantelpiece. Reluctantly I took one. Our last three apples for the season and I'd been hoping that Ma would bake them one of these nights. Taking one meant dividing two between three people: not the kind of mathematical problem I enjoyed.

Trudging to the door, I paused with a hand on the knob as my Ma spoke one more time.

"Maybe take that back to her too. That's what she says she pulled from within Lisbeth's leg." I followed her outstretched arm to the rocking chair by the door. A small rock sat in the middle of the cushion. I picked it up with the hand that held no apple, opened the door and ducked outside, in my haste slamming the door and provoking a cry of annoyance from Ma.

"Sorry!" I called.

I stepped from the veranda into full sunlight. Flies swarmed me but accustomed to them, I let them roam my face and buzz about my ears.

To my left and two hundred yards away, wattle trees and a few young gums marked the line of the creek. The prisoners were visible there, slumped together in the shade. Near them, Gunung had a small campfire going and I thought he had a billy on, making tea.

To my left and from the other side of our small barn where Da had his smithy, there came the clank and bang of iron on iron.

A kookaburra cackled from somewhere along the creek.

Up on the hill, Lisbeth was vaguely distinguishable as a brown blotch of different hue to the other browns around her.

The woman was not in sight, but I would find her. By the angle of the sun, the time was around one o'clock, which allowed me plenty of daylight in which to search for her. I had forgotten a mug from inside, but figured she could drink direct from the creek if she was thirsty. Just like the unfortunate Blacks had done. She was getting one of my apples, and she'd already cheated (or so I believed) my Ma out of one or more coins.

I held the stone she had brought my Ma up close to my face. It was half the length of my thumb, sparkling from tiny crystalline fragments scattered throughout, perfectly symmetrical, sharply pointed and smoothly polished. I grunted in surprise as I recognized the shape from English story books.

Very strange, I thought.

It strongly resembled an arrowhead.

I searched inside all the folds of land in our property, the dales and the scattered copses of trees and the struggling apple orchard. I even looked around the backside of that hill and out into the bush we hadn't cleared. No sign of the old woman.

None, that is, until I returned back around the hill and toward the creek. I found her squatting there in imitation of Gunung. The captives seemed to pay her no attention, their focus uniformly upon the dirt and twigs before them. When I saw her, I stopped in amazement, wondering how she could have evaded me on such open, sparsely-vegetated land and circled back to the wattle copse. And why on earth was she consorting with Enwright's Tracker? Better to keep her distance from anything that belonged to Enwright.

I drew nearer around the hill and saw that she had a pot she must have borrowed from Ma on the fire going on the fire. Gunung's billy was sitting in the dirt and he was sipping from a tin mug, watching her. Approaching the fence and I could hear that the Tracker was talking.

"Yeah, that's good, missus," he said as I reached the other side of the creek from them. "My mob down south, they use that stuff too, eh."

The woman nodded and stirred and said nothing in reply. Gunung chattered on about the medicinal properties of different bush plants while I navigated my way across the fence and down one creek bank, across the sluggish and shallow flow of water, and up the other side. I smelled unpleasantness, a sour stench like wet clothing left sitting too long.

When he noticed me, Gunung fell silent and dipped his head, concentrating on his tea.

I said, "Mr. Gunung, no need to stop talking on my account."

"Allgood, mister," he returned, his eyes downcast like those of the captives. "I been talkin' too much anyhow."

"My Ma said to bring you this," I said and offered the old woman the apple. Whatever she was brewing smelled so much the worse for being nearer to it, though the breeze blew it and the smoke toward the captives. The concoction looked like a broth containing leaves of some sort.

She took the apple and inspected it with a wry smile forming. "Thirty-one year ago, I were sent here for thievin' such as this. Now thee be givin' it me. Ee, but life's a funny thing."

Surprising me yet again, she tossed it to Gunung. The tracker, while appearing not pay no attention, snatched it deftly from the air.

"Quarter that," she told him. "Share it wi' thy kinfolk."

Gunung pulled his short-bladed knife from a sheath on his belt and set about complying.

I took opportunity to sneak a glance toward his 'kinfolk' as she had called them: two skinny men and one skinny woman, all completely naked but for the hobbling shackles on their ankles. Immediately embarrassed and ashamed I snatched my gaze away. Ma would not approve of me seeing any woman exposed.

But though I made my eyes busy inspecting nearby blooms of wattle so starkly yellow against this sun-washed landscape, the impression of all three captives remained clear upon my mind. The contrast of deep brown flesh against the rust-brown and dirty grey of their shackles. Their downcast eyes though large and sad, it must be said, so very beautiful with long thick eyelashes. Softly featured faces and kind. One man, I had noticed, had bled from a forehead wound and it was now dried and attracting flies.

"What's that stuff?" I asked, trying to distract myself from their plight.

The old woman grunted and picked up her stick. She used it to lever herself upright, waving off my offer of assistance. "Grab thee that branch there and take t'pot from t'fire."

As I moved to obey her, she shuffled close to Gunung. She spoke to him then, in labored strains of what I thought of as normal English. "These three prisoners might not speak your family's language, son. But they share many things in common with you. From far south of here, you might be. They are yet your people. And you are strong, son. They need you." She startled him with a single and gentle stroke to his beardless cheek by the back of her hand. When he stared up at her frankly, breaking the taboos that many of the Natives shared about locking gazes, she said sternly, "And you do not need white men."

She had me follow her up that hill once more. The pot was heavy; my arms ached with its weight and with the awkward way I had to hold the branch under its handle. It reeked worse the longer I carried it. I had thought it broth, but it had thickened now like porridge. Like paste. When finally I was able to put it down close to Lisbeth (but far enough that she would not accidently kick it over), I gasped with relief and swung my arms about to loosen them. I fell to massaging my forearms as the old woman made busy.

She slipped off her gloves, revealing pale and much-scarred skin loose over the bones within it. She drew her wooden stirring spoon from a fold in her clothing, dipped it in the potion, sniffed it, touched it to her lips, grimaced. "Too hot yet."

The spoon dropped into the pot and the woman eased herself down on the lip of Lisbeth's resting shelf.

While I still maneuvered my joints and muscles to ease their pain, I checked on Lisbeth (who lay still on her side). One eye turned up to me; a tear leaked from it. Her ribs rose and fell with a breath.

"Close enough to death, lad," called the old woman. "Needs to drink but can't bring hersen to walk to t'dam."

"You said she was elfshot."

"Aye."

"Well… I mean…"

She shushed me then, slashing her walking stick at me through the air. I fell silent. Her head twisted toward the top of the hill and then her body followed as much as age would allow it. A few seconds later, she whispered, "Thou hear it?"

I frowned, concentrating. Did she mean the hiss of wind of grass, the buzz of the passing bee, the faint birdsong from down in the wattles?

"Not those things," she hissed. Her seeming knowledge of my thoughts caused me to flinch. She stabbed the stick toward a point forty feet up the slope. "That."

But I heard nothing. Nothing save the things I have already mentioned here.

"Lad, at thy age, thou should still have the ear."

"For what?" I asked in a quiet voice, for though I could not hear what she did, I was convinced by her manner there was something indeed to be heard.

"There," she said and pointed the stick again. "That little knoll wi' t'slightly greener grass."

"What about it?"

"It's where they live."

I gawped. "The…" I dropped my own voice to a whisper. "The little folk?"

"Aye."

I strained my eyes, seeing nothing but the knoll as she had called it, a lump of soil and grass, like the dozen or more similar lumps of soil and grass across the face of this hill. Nor did I hear what she heard.

"What are they singing?" I asked.

She faced forwards, but listened a while longer. "They're askin' why they were brought here so far from their home. And when finally they found a quiet place, why did 'you' follow and disturb them."

"Who's 'you'? Who followed them?"

"Thee, fool lad. Thy family."

"Oh. They sang that? They sing English?"

She shook her head. "Gaelic."

"You speak Gaelic?"

"I understand it."

"Well, what do they mean we followed them and disturbed them?"

"Fagh! I can't ask them, lad. If I give sign that I see or hear them, they'll tell me nowt and likely shut their mouths. Which means thou should stop starin' their way too."

"Can you see them?"

"No."

"Oh. But you hear them."

"Thy curiosity gives me hope for thee. Never lose it, lad." She stretched out to pluck at grass, sniff it and crush it between her wrinkled fingers, allowing the breeze to carry away the remains. "Here be my best guesses on the matter. I'm guessin' they got here early in the piece. Perhaps that god-be-damnin'-it first fleet, perhaps later. They're very cross at bein' brought here. But they found a nice quiet place to settle out here until thee and thine came along. Until thy croft expanded and thy cows procreated and wandered up this hill and—" Here she poked her stick at a dried cow pat "—and shat liberally upon the very landscape where the elves like to play." She paused to knock dung from her stick.

"Play? Are they children then?" I came over to crouch beside her.

"Smartest question thee asked thus far." She reached up and patted my hand with some warmth. But clarify, she did not.

I thought I would try my hand at coarse language again. "How the hell did they get here though?"

Rather than reprimanding me for the swearing, she shrugged. "That I'd love to ken, lad," she replied. "Surely, I would. Perhaps they were investigatin' a ship that stopped at an Irish port. Perhaps they became interested in a rum keg, drank a little and slept t'journey."

We sat a while, her cocking an ear uphill, me trying in vain to hear it too. Eventually, she shook herself and gestured to the pot.

Reading her intention, I roused myself and went to lift the spoon. I carried it to her bearing a glob of the paste.

"Thee won't try it?" she asked.

I stared back aghast, uncertain as to how to decline without causing offence.

She cackled and took the spoon, stuck her tongue into the middle of the paste. "Fine, fine." She handed it back while she got herself upright. Then she dipped spoon into pot and withdrew a larger portion of the muck therein. "Carry t'pot here, lad."

I followed her to Lisbeth's hindquarters.

She tipped the muck onto a wound I couldn't see. In an official tone, she began thus: "Whether it were the ēse's pain or the shot of the ælfe or a wounding by hægtessan, then now, dear beast, I will help thee." As she spread it around the wounded area, stroking Lisbeth's belly with her free hand, she intoned, "This for thee as remedy for the pain of ēse." The spoon dipped again to the kettle and she spread more brew onto Lisbeth's thigh in an even larger circle. The cow did not complain or startle. "This for thee as remedy for the shot of ælfe." A final time, the spoon returned to the pot and she repeated her action, saying, "This for thee as remedy for the wounding by hægtessan." She indicated for me put down the kettle and she dropped the spoon into it. Her clean hand moved to Lisbeth's head to pet her gently. "This will help thee. Run thou around this mountain top. Run around the fields. Move free. Live long. Be healthy. May the Lord help thee."

The rite complete, the old woman stooped to wipe the leftover paste from her fingers. "Thou and thine be lucky the elves wanted only to hurt thy cow and not kill her outright. However, best be thou appease the little sods. Get thee some cream or buttermilk and leave it up by t'mound there." She indicated the knoll. "All will be well by morn, lad. Mark my words." Her clean hand thumped me none to gently in the gut. "And make sure thou never ever stop listenin'."

With that, she departed our hill and our property, leaving me staring after her with a heavy, stinking kettle to clean and so very many questions in my mind.

My parents allowed me to sleep outside that night with the cow.

I wanted to observe Lisbeth's recovery, if recovery there would be. And also, it must be admitted, I wanted to see if the night's quiet would break with snatches of the little folk's song. Perhaps they would make an appearance at the dish of buttermilk I'd left by the knoll.

The lump of earth the old woman had identified as their home was three feet high and not much broader. Up close, there was no sign of its habitation by tiny people nor by non-arcane animals like wombats. Just a heap of dirt. And for the moment, the buttermilk was serving no one besides the local population of flies and black ants.

There was always the very good chance, I thought, that the old woman was a trickster, offering falsehoods and false hopes in exchange for an apple and a pair of shillings.

As the sun set, Enwright sat by Gunung's fire. To my disgust—and my Ma's, I am certain—he drank steadily from a brown bottle he had pulled from his saddle bags, singing bawdy ditties. His boots were off and occasionally he would take one up to inspect the sole as if he didn't trust my mother's working. Meanwhile, his captives huddled together. Gunung was nowhere to be seen, but Enwright seemed untroubled by this; I guessed the man was collecting local food. The Natives always seemed to find things to eat where we white fellas saw nothing but trees and grasses.

With my Da's help, I set two small campfires into the hillside. Though the night was warm, there'd be cooler hours before dawn. Also there were snakes to keep away, though I rarely encountered them in the open nor up hills. After Da brought me supper, he topped up the buttermilk—to humor my Ma and me, he said—then he sat a while, entertaining me with tales of Enwright's fussiness over the horse's shoe and with news the Trooper had mentioned of the wider world. Eventually, Da retired for the night. I cracked sticks from the pile of kindling, or used them to tap rhythms against the water pot I'd kept in case the campfires spread to the grass. I hummed hymns I learned in Mass and songs of Ireland my Ma had taught me. A huge owl startled me as it flapped past in the dark. I lay on my back and counted stars. I fell asleep.

Sound woke me. An eerie intonation, carried by several voices. Upon the air I tasted Lisbeth's animal-stink and the campfires' smoke. The irregular surface of the hillside poked my spine and ribs in discomforting ways. Blinking gummy eyes, I sat up to seek the source of that compelling music.

The fae? I wondered. The elves?

But, no. The chanting came from the creek, from the deep shadow beneath the wattles.

The captives were singing.

I had not heard Natives sing before. It was, I must report, mesmerizing. I confess that I could well have sat there the rest of that night listening to it. However, mere moments after it had awoken me, their vocalizing was cut off sharply by a shout from Enwright. His drunken, uncouth mutterings followed for several seconds before the wattle grove lapsed again into silence.

And that was when I heard the other sound. The kind of bass-toned fluttering I might make by running a stick along fence palings. Bardi moths made such noise, whenever those huge insects came into our house attracted by light.

I turned my head ever so slightly toward the fire and my gaze caught upon Lisbeth's great eyes staring back at me. She was standing. She seemed calm. In fact, she seemed well. But she was not the source of that fluttering sound.

What I saw next—I will never know: was it a dream, was it a trick of poor light and sleepy eyes, or did I see what my mind and memory still insist I saw?

The furiously beating wings did not belong to moths.

The beings hovered in a cluster right between the campfires. There were seven of them and their tiny faces had set their gazes on the wattle grove below us. Each had a body no longer than any of my fingers. And they wore clothing of sorts, its design reminiscent of nothing I had seen before or have seen since. I blinked my eyes to focus better, squinting: yes, they appeared as if they'd been enraptured by the recent Native music as I had been. I wonder now: were they hoping for its return?

And in the humming of their wings, I now heard more music, chords. And beneath it, ever so faintly, I heard singing. Their mouths moved in unison.

One of them (a female) noticed me noticing them. She flew immediately out from among her kin, a scowl defiling the innocence formerly upon her features. She said a single word I didn't know, and flew directly into my face to strike me on the nose.

I awoke later.

Dawn was a smudge in the east. One of my fires had burned out and the other was coals. I added kindling, then logs, wrapped my blanket about my shoulders and sat beside it while the fire caught.

Lisbeth was gone. A moment after I realised this, I thought I could make her out down among her herd by the fence. This made me smile.

Remembering, I searched the air around me for signs of the little folk and strained my hearing for the sound of wings. Using a stick from the fire as a torch, I went up to check the mound the woman said was theirs. It appeared as quiet and unremarkable as it had earlier. The dish of buttermilk was empty, but other creatures might have lapped that up. My only proofs of the elves' existence in that moment were: one shaky memory; the healing of our cow; and the sharp stone the old woman had given my Ma.

More than a little despondent, I returned to the campfire and lay by it, returning to a sleep troubled with dreams.

In the morning, Trooper Enwright was dead.

He lay flat on his back, head on his saddlebag, blanket pulled up to his nose.

His horses, his man and his captives were gone. And never were they seen again.

Stories persist from this event, even today. Perhaps you, Dear Reader, have heard them?

Some believe that Gunung rebelled and murdered his master in his sleep, hit him with a rock, or stabbed him in the heart. Then he followed the other Blacks into the night, carrying away the white man's goods. Those who believe this take no stock in the facts: his horses and their saddles were taken, but the rest of his goods remained, including his revolver; no wound was found on Enwright's head, no stab wound on his body and there was no indication around his neck of stranglement.

"Then," others claim, "he was smothered." And yet the ground around him was undisturbed as would be expected in a struggle, since no man would accept suffocation without a fight.

Others say that Gunung poisoned Enwright's tea. But that belies the common knowledge that Enwright (fearful of such treatment from the Blacks he so despised) always had his Tracker drink from the same billy a full half hour before he would touch it himself.

Of course these stories persist. Because it is only now that I inform the world of the truth, of what I found on (or rather in) the Trooper's body.

Under pretense of checking him for snake bite, I did what I had seen the old woman do with Lisbeth: I ran my hands along the exposed areas of the man's skin. Until my hand caught upon a lump, so small I almost missed it. Something inorganic and tiny protruded from the flesh, just below the collar of his shirt and along the triangular muscle of his shoulder. Between my fingernails, I seized it. Tugging brought it loose. I turned it over in my hand. Not much larger than a splinter someone might get by bumping against a fence: but this was stone. The size of the moon on my smallest finger's nail.

And perfectly shaped.

Like an arrowhead.

An Autumn's Farewell

By: Chuck Greystone

Cass shut the rental car door and looked up at the fluffy cloud shaped like a rabbit passing in front of the sun and her belly twisted with anger. She couldn't believe she was standing here; a place she swore she would never return. She angrily gritted her teeth at the betrayals of the people who populated the ranks of the Faire's performers. She took the carefully wrapped packages and supplies out of the trunk and headed for the main gates while breathing deeply and wishing her mother hadn't bought into these people's lies.

A woman waved from the distance while walking toward her. She had met this old hag of a woman at the wake earlier that week. Cass arrived at the locked fence first and looked to her left at the massive twisted tree that held a faded sign that read: *Knight's Bridge–This way!* With an arrow pointing toward the Faire. The woman smiled as she approached Cass.

"Cressida Calendula Mckonkey. Welcome back," the old woman said, unlocking the chain and pulling aside the rusted fencing.

Cass hated when people knew her real name. She vacantly thanked the woman and stepped through the gate into the seasonally abandoned fairgrounds.

The woman escorted Cass down the dirt and stone path and over the footbridges toward the main entrance. She went on about necessary repairs, security concerns, & unreliable attendance. Cass wasn't really listening to the woman's mounting problems. She realized the woman had asked her a question and stumbled for a second and apologized.

"I asked what it's like being an architect?" She repeated, then under her breath, "destroy any green spaces for a condominium?"

"My firm actually focuses on rehabbing existing spaces for community centers and…" Cass began defensively and then felt the weight of the package in her hands and stopped abruptly. "I apologize Mrs.…,"

"Orchid," the groundskeeper replied.

"Mrs. Orchid."

"Just Orchid, dear. No Mrs.. We don't like those types of… prefixes here," she said, disgusted at the word. "Names have power. Mister and Missus… those are demeaning. They rob us of individuality and try to make us part of a structured society. Puts us in little boxes. We prefer prefixes of empowerment, not prefixes of subjection…" The woman went on, but Cass had heard these types of speeches from her mother's mouth over a hundred times and she didn't care to hear it from someone she barely knew.

"Orchid, I'm just here to say goodbye," Cass cut her off awkwardly. The elder woman stopped walking and looked at Cass with a judgmentally raised eyebrow and clicked her tongue behind her teeth, making a tsk-tsk noise.

"Oh, dear, you have been gone too long. There are no goodbyes. It's this way" Orchid began her trek up the hill, toward the massive stone arch at the main gate. She pulled the heavy wooden door just wide enough for them to pass through. Cass then took a few steps in front of her as she continued talking about the new plans to ID people at the gate and give them a wrist band if they wanted to buy mead or wine.

"I can make it on my own," Cass interrupted. "It's been a while, but I know the way." Cass proceeded up the hill alone, leaving Orchid standing somewhat dumbfounded near the main gate of the Larksborough Renaissance Faire Grounds.

Orchid loudly called after her, asking if she wanted help or needed any supplies, to which Cass hollered back no thanks as she passed the sword cemented into a large rock just up the hill from the main gate. Cresida couldn't help remembering unsuccessfully trying to yank that sword out of the stone as a child.

The Fairgrounds were desolate and quiet. The autumn wind occasionally spun fallen leaves across the ground, like they were dancing. Cass had been here when it had been relatively empty before. Quiet spring mornings before the Faire was open to the public and there were only vendors sleepily setting up.

Walking up the hill alone in the beginning of November was eerie. Many of the permanent buildings that would open up like flowers during the festival, with hanging banners and costumes, were tightly closed and boarded up. Food stalls were vacant of the normal sounds and smells of delicious fair-food being prepared. Stages that were normally full of magician's props, acrobats equipment, or musical instruments, were barren. The only noises were the birdsong echoing and the squirrels chasing each other through the fallen leaves.

Cass couldn't help smiling as the squirrels circled each other around a tree trunk. There were signs that larger animals had retaken the side of the mountain since the Faire-season had ended. She had to avoid stepping in the scat as she went up the mountainside.

The Faire had been closed for many months, but there were still signs of recent human visitors. She passed the Venetian Chapel that the Faire rented for pictures or weddings, even in the off-season. The outdoor chapel came complete with faux Italian marble altar, columns, and statues. The remnants of dying floral arrangements that had most recently been attached to the arbors told her someone had gotten married here within the last month.

She remembered sitting inside that chapel late one night her last year at the Faire with an older boy. His name was Cyrus, he had beautifully severe cheekbones, and he played guitar. She shook off the memory and stomped away in anger.

Further up the hill, she saw some trash bags that had been torn up by animals with scattered debris and balls of used gaffers tape. This told Cass that a film crew had obviously been there too and neglected to take all their trash with them.

Her boots crushed the colorful leaves as she walked uphill, avoiding fallen branches and shaded patches of mushroom growth. The animals that had been living in the abandoned fairground must be near, though, hiding.

Cass could feel eyes watching her from all around. Several birds took flight from a tree hanging over one of the food stalls and made her jump. She took a deep breath and looked around her.

No one.

She swore when she began walking again she saw something in front of her for a moment.

Nothing.

She thought she heard voices behind the corn on the cob on a stick stand and she called out 'hello' as she approached it slowly. Cass swore she heard giggling, but when she looked behind the counter, no one was there.

She knew that coming back to this place would bring back ghosts from her past, and she steeled her nerves and continued toward the plateau. When she passed the Haunted Dungeon, she saw a movement in the window. She was terrified, and began picturing that the displays inside depicting medieval torture chambers had come to life.

She wanted to drop the basket of supplies and run for the rental car parked outside the fairgrounds.

Instead, something inside her compelled her to walk quickly forward and knock on the window. She stood resolutely, with her free hand placed firmly on her hip, and waited. The window creaked open slowly and an old man's bearded face popped through the window.

"Can I help you?" he said politely through a cough.

"No," Cass said, confused for a moment. "I mean. Are you following me?" Cass demanded.

The white whiskered man raised an eyebrow the same way that Orchid had. He looked to the left and the right out of the window and then back at Cass.

"Is someone following you dear?" He asked, leaning forward. He was impeccably dressed with a vest, bowtie, and tweed jacket. The picture of this professorial man leaning through the rusted window frame of this crumbling concrete castle was strange. "Your Hazel's daughter, aren't you? You're Cressida?" He smiled.

"It's Cass," she said, frustrated.

"I'm so sorry about your mother. Sorry I was unable to attend her wake," he said, sympathetically. "I heard you were going to honor her wishes yourself." He said tilting his head, assessing her for a moment. "That is very good of you."

Earlier that week at her mother's wake, Cass had met many of her mother's friends from the Faire. They each took turns expressing sympathy and then made her feel guilty for not taking after her mother. She was continually pressured to invest herself in the path. She waited for his expression of shared grief to turn to blaming her for leaving her mom, but it never did. His kind eyes were full of warmth. Cass thanked him. She wanted to ask him why he was sitting in the window of the Dungeon Museum in November, but, instead; she asked how he knew her mother.

"Your mother was a special woman. She had the type of selflessness most people don't anymore. My family and I were lost; homeless, some years ago. She helped us all find a place to live."

Cass was surprised to hear such a well-dressed man was ever homeless and then she felt guilty for making assumptions.

"I've never met someone so in touch with the path," he said, and she expected him to try to convert her, like the others had. "She was truly connected to the Mother." When he said 'the Mother' a glimmer shined across his eyes.

Cass felt a breeze cross her skin, but she heard no wind in the trees. This momentary disconnect snapped Cass back to her task, and she thanked the man and bade him goodbye. He called after her, asking if she needed any help with her mother's ritual and she said no, and continued on.

Cass was breathing heavily when she reached the top of the hill, and stopped to remove her jacket. It was a cool day, but the sun on her back was too much after the climb. She looked back down the uneven rocky paths of the Renaissance Faire and wondered how they got away with operating the place without accessibility complaints.

She pulled her phone out of her pocket to check the time. There was no service. She couldn't help but roll her eyes at the isolation of this place her mother called her refuge. She folded the jacket over her arm and picked up the package and headed toward the Pishogue Path.

This footpath had a disguised entrance behind two large trees and was out of bounds to people who visited the Larksborough Renn Faire as mere guests. It was only for the performers who lived here for ten weekends a year.

There was a road that went up the rear-side of the mountain, to the camp above the fairgrounds. Orchid had informed Cass before her arrival that the bridge was out, making the winding road up the rear side of the mountain impassable. The Pishogue Path led toward the camp of six cabins, that were more like shacks, and many clearings for tents, camper vans and pickups that people would sleep in the rear.

Cass thought back to laying in one of the rusty pickup beds, looking up at the stars, and sitting up to see Gavin the Conjurer arguing with her mom in the camp. He'd taken some supplies she had just gotten for new sales the next day and thrown them into a fire pit.

Cass shook off the memory as she came to the end of the path and looked at that now cold fire pit in the center of the divine circle. She could see remnants of the people who populated these campgrounds every spring leading up to the summer solstice. The center of the wooded area had a large fire pit where the artisans, brewers, cooks, actors, musicians, and soothsayers who stayed at the Faire for the two and a half months would drink and dance together and sometimes perform rituals to the old gods late into the night.

A swell of memories came back to Cass from her childhood and, for a moment, it was difficult for Cass to hold on to her grudge.

She walked into the clearing around the firepit at the center of the camp and set down her coat and her packages. She immediately went to work collecting wood from the forest floor around her and tossing them into the center of the well-used pit.

She hadn't made a fire in a decade. The last time was at a high school party, and the other kids made fun of her for making the bonfire so efficiently and called her Cowboy Cressida. Making the fire was as easy as if she had made one yesterday. She collected twigs and dried leaves to use as kindling in the center of larger pieces and lit the whole assembly.

She wiped her brow and went for a sip of water before realizing it was the wrong bottle. She couldn't drink from that one. It was for the ritual. Cressida tried not to roll her eyes at the thought of performing these rites in this strange place. She was going to do it no matter how silly it seemed out of respect for her mother.

Hazel Asphodel Binns-Mckonkey had died three weeks ago, and she had very specific requests for her daughter upon her death. Cass's mother had prepared everything to the last detail. She had planned her own funeral up to this last ritual she wanted her daughter to do.

Cass resented that her mother wanted her to return to the Faire she had not visited in over twelve years and walk down the Pishogue Path, to the divine circle of wish and prayer, to perform her last rite and spread her ashes on the ritual funeral pyre.

As she stoked the fire, Cass looked around the clearing. The firepit was surrounded by makeshift seats of stones and log benches. Cass could picture the seats filled with the usual band of misfits singing into the evenings, after the Faire closed.

Beyond the seats and surrounding the whole glen was a small mock-Stonehenge edging the forest. Some of the structures were genuine monolithic pieces of stone that had been placed there long before the opening of the Larksborough Renaissance Faire. The circle had been completed with some large tree branches, two-by-fours, a few discarded mannequins, and the hood of an old junker.

For a moment Cass swore she heard giggling behind her in the woods, but she told herself it must be the echoes from the now cracking fire.

Cass scooted one of the benches close enough to the fire to burn the items for her mother's ritual.

She saw a few loose pages from a coloring book in the dirt and she thought about the times she had spent around this fire as a child coloring and listening to folk songs. Those years had been wonderful in the eyes of a child, but Cass now knew she should have been in school like a normal kid.

Since before she could remember, her mother had taken her to this refuge in the woods. Her mother had called it an escape from the oppressive modern world. Her mother sold handmade beaded necklaces and bracelets. She would also braid flowers into people's hair and charged extra to perform bonding rituals. She would take a lock from two people's hair and braid them together in an intricate pattern with special threads that were meant to bond them in friendship or as lovers.

When Cass was young, she would get the attention of passersby while dancing with ribbons in front of her mom's stand. As she got older, she helped braid the necklaces or hair. Eventually, she would help take the money and make change. She had learned enough about the bonding braids and had braided her own hair together with Cyrus'. It didn't seem to work when she caught him with one of the glassblower's daughters.

Cass stopped coming to the Faire with her mother after that year. She found other activities to occupy her weekends when she was in high school. Other kids her age made fun of the weirdos at the Ren Faire, and she shyly agreed, never telling them her mother spent every weekend there.

She never told her mother about the boy who broke her heart or the creepy way that Ansura, one of the sword dancers, would watch her while sharpening her blades. She never told her mother she was embarrassed by her hobbies.

College was thirteen hours away, by car, and she fell in love with the city and only came for the occasional visit. Her mother always tried to sway her to return with her to the Faire.

In recent years, her mother would send her pictures of little girls whose hair she had braided, and ask Cass to help Instapost it, for likes. Cass would help her tech-illiterate mother by posting the pics for her under the handle 'Gypsywishes'. A Romanian friend had told Cass the term was derogatory, but Cass's mother had insisted that was what she wanted to be called.

She talked to her mom once a week, so she never felt she was being a bad daughter. Standing here now, she realized exactly how much time she had lost. How much time she had selfishly given away.

When she came home to organize her mom's funeral, she met Orchid, the groundskeeper, and another woman from the Renaissance Faire, who was named Blanche Cartwright. Cass had listened to the woman talk about her mother's final days, and wanted to slap the woman who claimed to have helped Hazel in her final days, but Cass blamed them all for her mother's death.

Her mother left a long list of strange requests that culminated in this ritual that would return her to the refuge she loved most. This final request had herbs, powders and liquids that had to be burned with the ashes and strange poetic phrases that had to be spoken aloud and they had to be done by Cressida alone in the woods.

Cass looked at her phone, which still had no service, and saw that it was almost noon.

She thought the ritual was ridiculous.

It was foolish.

She was embarrassed to do it.

No one would know if she didn't actually do it, right?

She would know.

She already felt guilty enough for abandoning her mom. For not helping her more during the last years of her life.

She respectfully sat before the fire and awkwardly began chanting the invocation. She didn't whisper it to herself, but out loud, trying to mean the words, for her mother's sake. Taking out the ceremonial dagger that had been left for her, she poured the first vial of oil on it, and then the bottle of rose extract.

She moved onto the chant and put the dagger into her mother's ashes. Then she ran the dagger through the flames and asked the spirits to find the lost soul.

She moved her hands in the forms drawn on the paper. Not dramatically, but accurately. She dumped the ashes into the flames, along with several packets of herbs. She then wiped the blade of the knife with a handkerchief and added that to the flames.

Finally, she took two bottles of liquid and dumped them into the flames, and watched as green steam rose into the sky.

She felt better as she finished the ritual. She felt glad she could do this one thing for her mother.

Cass breathed in the air around her that now had a sweet smell coming from the fire. She sat on the ground and poked at the coals with a stick. This took Cass back to being a little girl learning to carve a sharp point in a stick that could be used for marshmallows or stabbing boys.

She yawned a deep breath and swore for a second she saw the faces of several children watching her from the other side of the fire.

She leapt to her feet and her head felt woozy. This was more than standing up too fast. The woods were spinning around her…

Reaching for her coat and phone and car keys, she fell to her knees, hearing voices. She reached for the knife. She felt the sting of the campfire smoke in her eyes and they began to water. Cass could only smell the herbs in the fire as her vision blurred, and she passed out on the ground.

Cass dreamed of her mother passing through a cloud of green mist.

Hazel was young and healthy at first. Then she quickly aged.

They were together at her mother's small kitchen table, arguing.

Cass remembered this argument, but it wasn't in person in real life. It had been the same argument over texts, phone calls, and video chats.

She begged her mother to go back to the doctor. Begged her to get into the hospital. Screamed at her to begin the Chemo. Her mother calmly said she was trying some more holistic methods. Her mother told her that Blanche and Hyacinthe and the others were helping her find some alternate paths to clear her body of the problems caused by the modern day.

Cass would grit her teeth and give dozens of reasons why these methods were fruitless. She pleaded and begged. They both cried. Her mom would say with a pure serenity if these methods didn't work that she accepted her time in this world was at an end, and it was her time to return to the Mother.

The green mist enveloped her mother, and Cass cried and wished her mother had never met the freaks at the Faire who had convinced her not to avoid modern medicine. Cass ran through the mist, looking for her mother. She couldn't find her. She couldn't find anything.

When Cass woke, she felt acutely aware something was wrong, but her heart was strangely not beating fast.

She looked around.

Somehow already it was night.

Where were her phone and coat? They were gone.

The fire was somehow still going strong, and flames were dancing wildly. It took a few seconds for her to realize the flames were dancing.

She saw small humanoid bodies in the flames, made of flames. They were balletically leaping and twirling and dancing. Some were rhythmically gyrating. She blinked her eyes and rubbed at them unsuccessfully.

Then she saw small faces across the flames on the other side of the pit. Each of these small beings wore green and brown tunics and had hair that looked like the bark of a tree. They pointed at her and moved to the sides of the firepit. These tiny, innocent, and beautiful creatures tilted their heads at her in wonder. Each had a basket of berries or leaves they were carrying to the fireside.

They were speaking some lovely druidic language she couldn't comprehend. Cass understood body language and knew they were arguing.

One nymph with a small nose, bright lavender eyes and freckles looked at her kindly, almost defensively, while the others were moving toward her with aggression. She tried to talk, but felt no words. The faces of the beautiful nymphs twisted and contorted. They snarled at her with animal eyes, and their idyllic teeth became jagged fangs.

She bumped through the bench, and realizing she should have tripped, fell to the ground. Searching for a stick or anything to defend herself, a chilling fear washed over her, and she suddenly felt cold as death, as she saw her own body leaned unceremoniously against one of the stone pillars.

Was she dead?

She tried to stand, but this new reality affected her ability to function. Her connection lost with the earth and floated helplessly above it. She drifted upward, and the tiny creatures laughed at her, except the one with the lavender eyes who ran forward and leapt up, grabbing her foot.

They tried to drag her back to her body. Cass had no autonomy. She couldn't control her movement through space.

She could feel the call of her body. The closer she got to her physical form, the more sensation returned. She could smell the fire and feel the moist cold earth beneath her. She could hear the chanting of the small nymphs, who had mostly returned to what they were doing.

Unfortunately, a few of them were pestering the small helpful creature with the lavender eyes. They jumped her, pulling her down away from Cass's foot. This caused Cass to jettison up into the air as if someone released a stretched elastic band.

As Cass felt her consciousness float up into the trees she became aware of the landscape in a way she never had before. The Stonehenge-like structure around the firepit was part of a larger pattern. There were smaller but evenly placed boulders making concentric circles out into the woods. Somehow the stones seemed to have a pulse, a heartbeat.

She saw movement in the woods of creatures large and small coming toward the meeting place. Cass would have felt blessed to see the odd tableau before her if her own body wasn't lying at the edge of it. She had been able to feel herself breathing when she got close. She must still be alive and she must get back!

She tried to move toward her body on her own but she hopelessly floated higher away. Suddenly, an unnatural wind sent her spinning far away from the divine circle and down the hillside. She was terrified as she drifted back toward earth.

The entire fairground was thrumming now. There seemed to be dark music coming from everywhere, emanating from the ground itself. There were crowds of creatures in the moonlight.

The first thing that caught Cass' attention was all the lights moving around. There were tiny pixies flitting around in every direction and every color. They seemed to glow from their insides and danced through the air zipping between trees and clouds.

She descended into the darkened forest near the tournament stadium and observed a collection of a dozen hooded figures who were chanting around candles and stones that had been placed to resemble the zodiac.

Cass tried to hear what they were saying, but helplessly floated away. She bumped into a tree that stopped her, and she felt it and was able to steady herself. She learned how to step forward. The sensation of moving was different. She couldn't think about taking a step, but instead had to feel where she wanted to be. There was no room for indecisiveness.

Lumbering through the trees beside her were some large and gangly golems that looked like they might crumble apart. She had to desire to be out of the way quickly, worrying they might crush her. She was not sure if she could be crushed, but didn't want to find out.

She moved past the animal yards, where she saw strange rabbit-like creatures that had six limbs racing in circles and wrestling with each other playfully. Beyond that there was a wishing well that during the festival season had a woman painted from head to toe as if she were a marble statue and she performed as the living fountain. In her place now was living water. These elemental creatures jumped into the air and danced with each other the way the creatures of fire had done back up at the divine circle. The water creatures would merge together and separate in beautifully symbiotic performance.

Cass felt an itch a hundred yards behind her and she floated toward a small grove of trees where she saw a long and lithe cat clawing at a tree. She could feel the tree's discomfort as its claws sunk into the wood.

"Please stop," she said, and the catlike being looked at her and narrowed its eyes. She realized that the cat's face was flat and almost human. It smiled and a disturbing shimmer ran down its body. It skittered around the tree and up to a higher branch crouching and staring at her.

"Where in all of Odin's sight did you come from?" The creature said in a language that Cass didn't recognize.

Somehow, the intentionality of its words pushed the meaning into her consciousness. She gestured to the circle of wish and prayer atop the hill.

"Oh dearest child. You need to get back up there don't you?" It said, "Well, I will be happy to help you." It skippered quickly down to a lower branch closer to her and seemed to taste the air with a flickering tongue similar to a snake. "All you need to do is make a promise to owe me a favor?" It said smiling and blinking at her.

"What kind of favor?" Cass thought.

"Not to worry about that now of all things true yes true. You need to return back up there is my correct assumption?" The Cat said hungrily and Cass suddenly felt a twinge of nervousness.

"I'll be fine," Cass thought as she floated away purposefully "Stop scratching the trees, they don't like it," she repeated.

The catlike creature appeared on the tree in front of her and watched her maliciously. Every time she thought it was behind her it was in front of her again.

She saw a crowd ahead of her and floated toward the Rose and Crown stage. There were a dozen children sitting on the benches facing the stage while two other children danced about. She realized quickly that, despite their size, these were not children. They had goat legs and horns but the torsos of humans.

These were mythical Satyrs.

The two onstage were arguing in some type of Greek she didn't understand. The audience members chortled at the jokes she was not able to comprehend.

Her interest in the performance brought her closer and closer to the stage. She was entranced in their production and after a time found herself laughing at the jokes on stage. She never understood the words they spoke but began to comprehend the feeling well enough to understand that they were two men vying for the affections of the same woman. Each character was arrogantly sure the object of their desire would pick them.

It took Cass a long time to realize that one of the two performers was the man she had seen in the window of the Dungeon museum. No longer in his tweed jacket and bowtie, replaced by flowing robes of a Grecian poet.

When the show ended they bowed and the audience clapped and cheered. The audience departed and headed up the hillside. The performer Cass didn't know was collecting hats and scarves off the stage into a carpetbag when they turned and looked directly at her.

"Sebastian. I firmly believe we have another lost psyche." said the taller of the two Satyrs.

The shorter and older of the two who she recognized came forward to the edge of the stage and rummaged in the carpet bag for a moment. He produced a long jagged stick and pointed it toward Cass. She immediately felt herself being drawn closer to the stage.

"This one is fresh, not wandering long," said the one known as Sebastian who was speaking something like Greek but Cass could feel the context. "Tell us, Cass. How did you like our show?" he said smiling.

Cass felt herself saying that she loved the show. She wasn't sure if she was talking or not but he seemed to hear her.

The older Satyur breathed in her praise like oxygen. He told her she was very lucky to see their shows on a special night. Very few humans were even allowed to see them. The younger satyr complained in the corner that no humans should see their productions. They were the destroyers of the greenlands. Humans were a poison to Nature. Then he trotted to Sebastian's side and asked her how long she had been dead?

"I'm not. I don't think I am. My body is up the hill" she told him.

Sebastian scratched at the white and gray hairs on his chin and came close to her. He sniffed the air and looked at her suspiciously.

"Aphrodite's gift! You didn't promise anything to that miscreant did you?!" He asked.

Cass looked around her and felt the eyes of the strange cat on her.

Sebastian spun toward the roof over the stage and yelled "BEGONE!"

And the Catlike trickster clawed the air in front of it, and hissed, before it disappeared

"Casius, can you make sure to reinforce the binding on that winsome spirit?" He asked the other Satyr who begrudgingly agreed.

For the first time Cass wondered what she had burned in the fire. Did it cause her to have hallucinations? Was she having a bad trip in the forest? Was this all some type of mid autumn nightmare?

Sebastian reached out a hand to her and she suddenly felt connected to all the plants around her. She felt the pull of the tiniest particles of water in the dry autumn ground being pulled into the roots of the briar. She could feel the feathers adjusting for flight on the owl who spotted a rodent amongst the leaves. She felt the call of the circle down the Pishogue path at the top of the hill.

"Hazel was a great benefactor helping protect our refuge here. Her contributions will be greatly missed."

There was a knowing sadness in the Satyrs eyes. Cass wondered what he meant by their refuge. She never even tried to speak her questions allowed but he seemed to hear her thoughts.

"Well, yes my dear. The green is constantly shrinking. The hidden places of power and ritual in the forests of the world have been bulldozed and cemented over. We have found a few places to ensure we can keep some doorways between our world and yours. We can come here to do the work we need."

She wondered what work they had to do and he responded again.

"Well, tonight we are planting seeds here in the theaters. It is good to plant some things in the fall so they can germinate and flower in the springtime." This time he didn't wait for her question. "We were planting humor. Laughter. We want to help ensure that when Stanley the Stupendous or Edrik the Informal comes back in the spring to perform their illusions that the audience has a wonderful time. A good flowering humor can help their spirits and those patrons return and ensure the survival of this refugee. Between ourselves, no developers will build within miles of the fairgrounds because of the automobile traffic two months in a calendar year... we sometimes ensure the traffic remains bad." he laughed uproariously.

The two Satyrs hopped from the stage and began walking up the hill. Cass floated alongside them. She wondered exactly how well Sebastain knew her mother and he heard these thoughts as well and answered and they passed some of the games stands and the stall for the tarot readings.

"Your mother knew us. She could see us, not every mortal can. But those who are gifted with an open spirit are welcome to dance with the forest folk."

Light began to intensify from the distant top of the hill where the bonfire was growing.

"We are all proud your mother wanted to rest here and welcome her to cross over to the evergreen"

After passing some of the dark and empty stalls where leathered goods, chain mail, and corsets hung during the faire season the old Satyr had to sit. The winding paths were beautiful even with all the foliage covering the ground and the moonlight creeping through the fingers of the trees. They could feel the rhythm of the dance and drum beats echoing through the roots in the ground.

"I need a rest" Sebastian said as he took a seat across from the Queen's hedge maze. "My legs are not as spry as they once were. I will rest. Casius will see you the rest of the way?" He said with labored breath and handed the younger satyr the wand he had been carrying.

Casius took the stick and continued up the hill past all the same things Cass had passed earlier. Now she saw little fae beings moving around playfully. Even the patches of mushroom growth seemed to be telling each other stories. The thrum of the earthly music from the divine circle changed and Casius became agitated.

"Great, we are going to miss the consecration!" he said disappointedly.

"What Consecration?" Cass thought directly, not even pretending to speak anymore but willing her thoughts forward.

"The burning of your mother's fleshly body, of course. That is the final step. Humans can't cross the veil into our world during their lives. But with the right ritual a door can open for them after the end, so they can go there to… retire," he said awkwardly.

Cass couldn't get her thoughts straight.

"But I already did that. She was cremated, and I performed a ritual with her ashes this afternoon." Cass said confusedly. Now she recognized the chanting that echoed through the forest, it was the same chanting she had done that earlier that day.

"But your body is still up there?" asked the younger Satyr. He looked up at her nervously. "Oh. No, no, no, no! So don't freak out" Casius said, and Cass realized that he might be younger than she thought. "So, the nymphs who are dancing and chanting up at the circle. Well, to them humans all look alike. And you and your mother definitely smell alike. They must think that your body is hers and they think they are preparing her for the ritual."

If Cass had access to lungs or a heart they would have been pounding. The air around her began to whirl violently sending the leaves coating the ground spinning into the air. Sebastian had begun the trek again and was approaching them from around the corner. He had also realized what was happening and urgently followed. He was waving to them and coughing.

"You must return to your body at once child. The window of opportunity is swiftly closing!" His cough became more violent. "Take the roots, it is the fastest way."

At first the sentence confused Cass and she thought the Greek they were speaking didn't translate to feelings. She quickly realized he was speaking English, like he had earlier that day. She could feel the pull. She felt a pulse in the roots beneath her. She gave into the sensation.

Suddenly, she was inside the roots speeding through the bodies of the trees. Cass was aware of a million sensations she never dreamed of experiencing.

She jumped from tree to tree and cruised through the ground between roots and through the air between branches. When she entered a particularly large old tree, she let her soul fill the space from its roots to its tips, and for a moment thought that if they did burn her body this wouldn't be a bad way to spend the rest of her life. The view from here was stunning.

Then she remembered her dog Franklin Beezleton and knew she had to get back to him before making a decision like that, and lept into a shrub nearby, and continued her journey.

Suddenly, she jumped into a tree that was already crowded. This tree was moving up the hill, walking! This tree already had its own soul occupying it, it was a dryad. She felt perverse and embarrassed having jumped into someone else's body and quickly lept to the next and zipped along the roots.

Eventually, she found her way to the trees encircling the fire pit and she saw, as she had feared, her own body raised on a platform next to the fire. There were beautiful flowers all around her and a shroud had been draped over her. There were the same ceremonial herbs and twigs and oils she had used that afternoon. She saw how beautiful she looked and felt guilty for not finding a way to bring her mother's body here to do this for her.

With a force of will she leapt down from the tree and into her own body.

Blackness.

Her eyes were closed. How does a human open their eyes again?

Oh no. choking.

How does a human breath?

The experience of floating freely had made her forget how to do some of the things she needed for survival.

She opened her eyes and took in a massive breath. With great effort she swung her dead legs off the edge of the board; pins and needles shot through her body. It was excruciating and still magnificent to feel her body again.

She pulled the shrouds from her face and let them fall into the dirt.

As she slowly stood up, her blurry vision adjusted and she saw hundreds of creatures around her. There were creatures she had always known; like squirrels, owls and wolves. There were creatures she had seen during this night like Satyrs, and the fiery elementals in the pit, and the little nymphs. Beings made of trees and flowers that bent around the clearing giving offerings. There were old gaunt golems that stood sentry and tiny flitting pixies that emanate their own lights.

Deep down Cass recognized that she may have met some of these creatures when she was young but had written the memories off as the delusions of childhood. The whole scene was surreal and filled with horror, beauty, & magic.

Cass realized they had all stopped and were staring at her. One of the little fae creatures pointed at her and began cursing at her in the strange druidic language she had heard before. Somehow, her mind was opened the way she had heard Sebastian by feeling his meaning and she could understand the being.

"This witch had broken our law bonds, and we need to punish her!" the little angry sprite said. The kind lavender-eyed nymph came to her defense.

"She didn't mean to do it! Besides! As I have been yelling all night! She is not dead! And this is Hazel's blood-kin!"

The crowd murmured in many different tongues. Many of the creatures rolled their eyes at such a mundane thing as the difference between alive and dead.

All of the voices silenced quickly as two shadows emerged from behind the Stonehenge replica monoliths. These long thin cloaked figures had hoods that covered their faces. Each was followed by a short humanoid with pointed ears and long tattered hair. Behind them came a few others including Sebastian who was short of breath, limping, and smiling at her.

"Is it true you are the blood-kin of our dearly departed Hazel?" one of the voices whispered beneath the cloak.

"Yes," said Cass proudly. "I am her daughter."

"Yet you have not visited this sanctuary in many years?"

"No. That was a mistake, " she said honestly. She couldn't see their eyes beneath their cloaks but she could feel them watching her inside and out.

"Is it true she had the divine sight?" the second of the hooded figures asked.

"Yes, my liege," Sebastian said enthusiastically. "And she green-walked"

"Without training?" they asked, surprised.

"Yes, lord Hyacinth." Sebastian explained "We told her to take the trees to return to her body once we discovered the confusion, and she was away!" She looked around and made a type of eye contact with the Dryad she had mistakenly entered and awkwardly looked away.

"Then, I see no reason to punish her," Lord Hyacinth said deviously. "If she is prepared to take the oath.

"What Oath?" Cass asked.

"The Oath to the forest and the green-folk," Lord Hyacinth said.

"The Oath to protect the magical creatures before you," the other hooded figure said.

"The same Oath your mother took," Sebastian added kindly.

"I want to see all of you protected and safe," Cass began hesitantly. "I'm not sure how I can help. I'm willing to learn." Then she saw the strange catlike creature with the humanoid face on top of one of the Stonehenge Esque monoliths and she got nervous. "But I'm not here to take an Oath today. I'm here to say goodbye to my mother and that is my purpose here."

One of the hooded figures looked up at the cat creature and it disappeared as it winked at Cass. The Second hooded figure pointed to the fiery altar she had been laying on and said that the ritual would continue.

Cass stood between Sebastian and Casius as the crowd of creatures began the uproarious party. They danced and swayed to the beat of drums. The chant became a song that created shapes in the smoke that resemble the patterns she had made with her hands that afternoon.

Cass realized that as much as she tried to honor her mother by speaking the rituals that she didn't truly believe the incantation. The belief and force of will was what mattered in these moments. She also realized that her mother never relied on her alone to see her to the otherside, but knew that her friends and found family in this place would finish what she started even if she had departed unaware.

Eventually, the shapes in the smoke took form. Cass saw hands and feet. She saw her mothers torso and eventually her face surrounded by her braided hair. A tear fell down Cass's cheek and she wanted to go to her mother. As she stepped forward toward the fire Sebastian took her hand. She looked down at the kind old satyr.

"You do not have to take the oath, Cass. We know you are a good person at heart. Just do what you can for us Green-folk, that would be a beautiful way to honor her," he said.

Cass thought about all the times she had her mom talking about Green-Folk and how Cass had dismissed her comments as people who lived in sustainable communes. Cass never realized what she had meant. She had wanted to keep the blinders on.

"Are you going to be alright Cass?" Sebastian asked.

"You can call me Cressida," She said, smiling down at him. She then joined in the chant.

The flames created dancing shadows that bounced around the glen and slowly the smoke body of her mother raised out of the fire.

Across from them there was a shimmer between two of the monoliths in the henge circle. The smoke body of her mother moved across the space and through the shimmer.

For just a moment, Cass thought she saw her mother's eyes open and a smile spread across her thin lips.

In a flash many of the creatures around her lept though the shimmer to the other side, obscuring her view of her mother. Sebastian told her that her eyes were not meant for their world, not yet.

By the time she looked back the shimmer disappeared and all she saw was the flickering shadows dancing on the forest around her.

Cass realized she was starving. Fortunately for her, Satyrs were amazing bakers, and had baskets of pastries they enjoyed together while watching the fire beings dance in the pit. There was gyrating that Cass thought she had seen in clubs when she was younger.

For the first time in years Cass had her hair braided. The little lavender-eyed nymph braided her hair the way her mother used to do it when she was young. Other creatures went to rest or do different activities, but Cass stayed and watched the fire. It slowly dwindled to embers and ash and she laid down on the bench watching it until she fell asleep.

When she awoke, the morning dew covered her in a curious way. She was dry from head to toe, except on her eyelids. She felt as though she had been gently kissed on her eyes.

She looked at the now cold fire pit. Mist covered the glen. She felt her jacket and found her car keys and phone. She clicked her phone to see what time it was but it was dead.

She thought about everything she had seen the night before and did not for a second wonder if it was all a dream. She could feel the roots in the earth pulling at water in the dry autumn soil. She could hear the bird singing to each other and she knew what they were saying. She could feel the other creatures too, the ones who sought refuge in the mystical places of the world. The ones who knew that the only way to hide the entrances to other realms and protect the true green spaces was to have them wear a disguise of what they were pretending to be over top of what they actually were.

She heard a voice over her shoulder.

"Are you ready to go my dear?" Sebastian asked.

She turned and smiled at him. He was once again wearing his tweed jacket and bow tie but his Satyr legs were on full display. She walked slowly at his pace as he escorted her through the mist-filled grounds of the Larksborough Renaissance faire.

"Will you be going back home?" He asked her as they walked.

"Yes, but first I need to go back to my mom's house. She wanted most of her things to go to various charities and groups. I had already separated out the photos I wanted to keep, but I think I would like to keep several more of her books. I want to learn her craft. So maybe I can come up here to braid hair next spring" She said proudly.

"That sounds like a wonderful plan," said Sebastian.

"It's far, but I'll work something out. I will be back here. I promise." Cass said.

"Cresida, Promises are a serious thing to Green-folk..." Sebastian warned.

"My mother always said you want promises to be like bridges, we don't want the ones we rely on to be weak and flimsy." She said firmly.

"As I said, your mother was a good woman." Sebastian said and bade her goodbye, not wanting to walk all the way back up the mountain.

Cass passed all the stages, stalls and the dueling grounds. Finally she walked back by the sword in the stone at the base of the hill and Cass saw Orchid the groundskeeper waiting for her by the entrance.

"I'd have expected you to have left yesterday," she said dismissively, while raking leaves off the path.

Cass smiled and looked at her with a wrinkled brow and tilted her head to see past the glamor.

"If you expect so little of humans then you won't be able to count on them for much help, will you Lord Hyacinth?" Cass said, and then bowed respectfully. Cass then passed the Lord High Fairy, "I will see you in a few months, not sure what the future holds, but this spring 'Gypsywhishes' will be in its usual place, between the corset couture and the Drunken Sailor pub, and we will be hashtag granting wishes, hashtag braiding fates, hashtag bonding braids, and of course this year we will be accepting cash and a variety of digital payment options."

The Groundskeeper looked stunned from beyond the gate.

Orchid heard Cass call back, "I'll be in touch about getting the bridge leading to the camp fixed before the season. And if Gavin the Conjuror is still coming around I'd like a word with him!"

Cass bounced confidently down the pathway and pushed aside the rusty old fence and headed back to her rental car.

She felt the grass and weeds around her and the wildflowers sleeping under the soil waiting to bloom in April. There was something awake in her that connected her to the living things around her, and she wanted to nurture it and let the connection grow.

She saw a cloud cover the sun and looked up. She could tell it was the trickster who had taken the shape of a cat the night before. She smiled up at the cloud, knowing she would have to keep an eye on this one. She was sure that her mom had its name somewhere in her journals.

As she drove back toward her mom's house she was elated knowing that her relationship with her mom was not done. She might be gone, but she would still be teaching her and helping her.

Her mother always talked about the cycle of the year. Autumn might lead to winter, but that would transition right back into spring. Cass smiled and a tear rolled down her cheek as she thought that this coming spring would be transformative.

The End

The Magical Creeping Jenny

By: E. D. Edwards

All afternoon my neighbor sat in a lawn chair with his handgun resting on his knee, performing his merciless reconnaissance of the undeveloped flood zone that bordered the back of our neighborhood. I could see him from my kitchen window. The black suit and turtleneck Darren wore and the martini he sipped hinted at his secret agent fantasies. I was busy in my craft room when I heard the shot discharge, echoing wickedly from next door. I rushed outside, worried I'd find a deer in the last, panicked throes of life. All I saw was Darren in his shooting stance, legs apart, one hand gripping the gun, the other hand supporting his aim, and his gun still pointing into the woods as if he'd just fired on a terrorist.

"I nicked him," Darren growled jubilantly, swaggering as he slipped his gun into his sleek, chest-mounted holster, and ran his fingers through gray, thinning hair.

"I wish you wouldn't discharge your guns in the neighborhood, Darren," I complained. This was my habitual objection. "Take your weapon to your gun club to shoot it."

"You should be thanking me, Hannah. That deer won't be jumping more fences to get at your nasty garden tomatoes."

The man glared at my vegetable garden with open disgust.

He was a proud carnivore.

Deer loved suburban gardens, which was one reason why the neighbors had fences separating their carefully landscaped yards from the undeveloped wilderness behind us. The deer still jumped fences as high as six-feet just to nibble prized landscaping. Rabbits and chipmunks dug holes underneath these fences to venture from their woodland homes into delicious suburban territory, the land of exotic bulbs, delicate flowers, and tender, carefully mowed grasses. My yard seemed to be the biggest magnet, but even yards without vegetable gardens were ripe for destructive plunder.

Bordering the back of our suburban neighborhood, were several miles of creek, bog, woods, and ravines combining to make an uncultivated area officially classified as a floodplain. My neighbors had a love-hate relationship with that bit of boggy woodland. This acreage was zoned so it couldn't be developed, which was good. An ugly big box store wouldn't be built on that land to spoil views from a terrace, deck, or patio. And the visions of that feral woodland were enchanting.

The hate part was that as the city grew and developers encroached on other forested areas, the most determined and aggressive wildlife tended to relocate to that soggy wilderness behind our homes. Ravenous deer, insatiable rabbits, rancorous woodchucks, poisonous cottonmouth snakes, and noisily belligerent fish-crows all had homes in those woods. The insects could be particularly wicked, especially the mosquitoes and the fierce, invisible, stinging flies, sometimes called 'no-see-ums,' which continually fed on my welt-ridden skin. But my love for this protected greenway dwarfed any annoyances about losing vegetables, fruits, or flowers to thieving wildlife or enduring itchy skin because biting flies routinely ignored my Vitamin B deterrent. I enjoyed putting on my gumboots and meandering through those boggy woods so much that I had a cute gate built into my little section of ivy-covered chain-link fence, giving me direct access to the marshy wilderness. My favorite wanderings created narrow footpaths through the woods toward the creek, ravines, and ancient oaks.

"There's movement in the brush," my neighbor suddenly hissed. He squinted his eyes toward the woods, zipped his gun from his body holster, and popped off another round.

"It's dangerous to be firing into those woods, Darren. You could hit someone," I scolded. "This neighborhood isn't the appropriate place for your target practice."

"I'm exercising my Second Amendment rights, Hannah," he declared as he reloaded. "And anyone fool enough to wander around back there, Madam, deserves the painful lesson she might learn if she got shot."

"*I* hike around back there."

"Case in point. You wanna go hiking? Hike the mall with all the other elderly ladies." Darren thought he was cleverly insulting. The man was a minimum of two decades older than me, but considered that a forty-year-old spinster was barely worth his sarcastic courtesies. "When the deer get bold," he arrogantly continued, "I will do some culling and if you get shot, well, madam, you've been warned."

My neighbor Darren and I barely get along.

Darren had been marinading in his casino and cocktail party illusions since this neighborhood was developed in the early 1990s. I moved in eight years ago and added elaborate, raised bed gardens with mulched pathways in my backyard. Darren already had a carefully cultivated lawn of Zoysia grass around his patio where he sipped his martinis, admired his symmetrical planters of mature roses, and fantasized that he really was an international political and corporate virtuoso.

He was a retired accountant.

Darren certainly didn't admire the fanciful, farmhouse style I brought to the community.

The neighborhood hadn't maintained a homeowner's association that forced a formally identical aesthetic on everyone, but I was an obvious interloper on the boring, middle-class panache that predominated here. I introduced colorful whirly-gigs, birdhouses, hummingbird feeders, toad huts, solar-lights, birdbaths, wind chimes, and garden signs into my backyard. The generous employee discount at the lawn and garden store where I worked, helped finance my adorable outdoor whimsy.

My yard was a defiantly quirky wonderland that Darren loathed.

Perhaps highest on the list of Darren's active disgust was my Creeping Jenny. To be fair, it was an invasive plant. Especially in damp areas. Its wildly prolific stem-rooting encouraged the Jenny to spread rapidly. But I loved it. Seven years ago, the Creeping Jenny fell from my hanging baskets to take root in the ground below, slithering into the pathways between raised beds. I thought it made a pretty groundcover, crawling across the mulch. It was especially lovely in spring, when the tiny, yellow, cup-shaped flowers were in bloom. As a member of the loosestrife family, the Creeping Jenny was thought to increase serenity and reduce conflict, but my Creeping Jenny became the source of constant arguments with Darren, who objected to the entire view at the back of my house.

Darren could have put up a privacy fence and solved his problem, but he had obviously spent a small fortune back in the 90s on his four-foot tall, black ironwork fencing that surrounded his yard with a distinctive, upper-class New Orleans vibe. Too bad for him, Darren could see both over and through the black lace into the colorful paradise of my yard, where Creeping Jenny covered my pathways, and inched its way from my yard into his. The poisons Darren sprayed on the perimeter of his property killed his Zoysia, but not my Jenny.

My neighbors on the other side had a solid, eight-foot wooden fence. I rarely saw or heard them. They didn't object to my wind chimes or my Creeping Jenny, which perhaps hadn't crawled through their denser fencing.

The only fencing I had was the bit separating my yard from the flood zone. The Creeping Jenny slithered through my ivy-covered chain-link to mingle with mosses and wild grasses on the other side. Because of its rounded, coin-shaped leaves on long vines, the plant was sometimes called moneywort, two-pence herb, or two-penny grass. Despite its golden richness and coin-shaped leaves, my neighbor saw no value in my Creeping Jenny.

Darren considered it the worst of weeds.

A backyard is a relatively private spot. Neither my Creeping Jenny nor my fanciful garden décor was displayed in the front of my house. Except for the slight deviation of a tasteful, concrete, unicorn-shaped lawn ornament the size of a child's rocking horse near my entryway, my front yard was as mundane and respectable as the rest of the neighborhood. My fanciful indulgences were hidden inside and behind the house and shouldn't have been Darren's concern except for his overwhelming paranoia that the corrupting influence of my Creeping Jenny slithered through the porous lacing of his fence and infected his Zoysia.

And, of course, my fairytale aesthetic disturbed his sophisticated, yacht-club ideals.

"Grow up, Hannah. You are too old to keep acting like a fool," he snarled at me.

Darren took aim at an especially robust patch of Jenny on the path where I stood and unloaded the remainder of his clip into the ground. Bits of vines, leaves, dirt, and mulch exploded in the air inches from my foot.

I marched into the house and called 9-1-1.

It wouldn't be the first time I'd made this call.

When Darren complained to the police that he had the right to protect his home from intruders—whether they were humans, animals, or invasive plants—the police were sympathetic to Darren's point of view. Darren also told them how he considered my flamboyant yard décor to be heretical, pointing to my witchy garden sign declaring that "magic grows here." Ultimately, the police told Darren that he could stand his ground in his own yard, but they mildly warned him to avoid firing his gun into mine. Then they left without taking any action.

The status quo remained.

It was hotter than normal that spring and the biting insects were doubly vicious. I began burning handfuls of Jenny in my barbeque. Smoke from burning this plant was once believed to keep away insects and vermin. I hoped it would discourage the mosquitoes and biting flies.

Darren hired a company to spray a poisonous gas over his property, which likely killed the pollinating bees in my yard, too. Neither the smoke from the Jenny, or Darren's poisonous gas discouraged the biting flies.

Darren continued to shoot at the wildlife—which wasn't deterred in the least—and I continued to risk the occasional stroll through the quirky gate at the back of my yard, into the uncultivated woods beyond.

After a particularly heavy spring rain, the ravines had filled with cascading waters and the creek swelled to the size of a small lake. The damp woodland kept me enthralled.

Today, I had gotten as far as the first boggy ravine and the exposed roots of an ancient oak, when I saw the little cup sitting on some moss. The cup had been molded from red clay and was about the size and shape of half a quail's egg, with odd, diminutive, rune-like designs etched into the surface near the rim.

It seemed like the lost mug from a strange little play set. The cup had been hard-baked or kiln-fired because when I picked it up by the delicate handle, I saw it held cloudy water.

Someone had been having a tea party.

There weren't many children in our neighborhood and none I was aware of who played in these woods. All the children I knew had lives tightly scheduled around school, sports, and extracurricular lessons.

I had dipped my fingers into the water in the cup, when an invisible stinging fly suddenly smacked the side of my face, near my left eye. I yelped, dropped the cup, and rubbed the offended area with damp fingers, blinking rapidly. For a moment I felt dizzy, but the area next to my eye where I'd been stung seemed strangely and immediately improved.

I collected and pocketed the cup before beginning my hike back home.

In hindsight, I suppose I should have taken Darren's warning more seriously.

He did shoot me.

I was still a distance from the house when I heard the shot and felt the bullet scorching past my head, grazing my left cheek and ear. I don't think Darren realized it was me he'd shot. Surely, he wouldn't have left me lying in the woods if he knew he'd hit a neighbor and not a deer. I collapsed backward, grabbing my wounded head and ear as I fell.

I don't remember if I screamed or not.

When I woke, I was lying on my back in the mud, the left side of my face pulsing, my wrists and ankles trussed and staked to the soggy ground with thin ropes made from braided vines.

When my head finally cleared, I realized I was the prisoner of tiny, Lilliputian-sized people, no more than two-feet-tall. I could see them, but only with my left eye.

I heard them, too. High-pitched chirping voices argued in an old-timey, weirdly accented English; arguing about whether I should have been secured with my feet pointing north or east, and how many and what type of knots should have been tied at my wrists versus my ankles.

Between all the odd, archaic words, and their accent. it was nearly impossible to follow along. It was clearly a bitter debate, though, with plenty of angry name-calling. The little people referred to me as 'the giant fustilugs', and insulted each other with words like 'dalco' and 'saddle goose.'

"Who *or what* are you?" I asked from my place on the ground. Maybe the blow to the head was making me hallucinate. Or maybe Darren really had shot me, and my mind was distracting me with grumpy Ren Faire Punch and Judy caricatures, as I bled out.

"The giant fustilugs can perceive and hark us," one of them shouted angrily.

"Tha thoughtless, lazy quisby hath done this. The lady wast careless enow to leaveth sacr'd water f'or the giant fustilugs," an ancient, wrinkled creature shouted. "Or't wast *intentional?*"

He seemed to be angry with a tiny woman in a gauzy gown, her arms bound in front of her and a gag in her mouth. A blindfold over her eyes wrapped around her head, flattening the long curls of her green hair. He slapped her, and she moaned into her gag.

"This dalcop hath truly earned her execution, My King," another little creature shouted. "Not only didst she deceive thee and conspire to run away, she hath committed treason with the giant fustilugs, leaving hallow'd water for the giant to discov'r."

They began arguing again: what type of execution they should use on a giant fustilugs; who should die first, me or the tiny woman they called Mothblossom; and what should be done with such a large and stinking carcass as mine would be.

When I sat up, easily pulling the stakes from the soggy ground, their quarrels became screeches.

Their archers unleashed a furious volley of their tiny arrows at me; each of the needle-sharp projectiles disappearing on-impact. These arrows; they were the invisible stinging flies from my garden.

In self-defense, I swept my left arm, knocking the closest swath of archers to the ground. Grabbing one of them by the suspenders of his grassy pants, lifting him high in the air. They had me outnumbered, but I had an impressive advantage in size and strength. Their restraints couldn't hold me, but their stinging arrows were painful.

When I whacked half-a-dozen or more of them over like bowling pins, the ancient, wrinkled creature screeched with authority.

"Hold thy fire!"

The onslaught of arrows stopped.

"Unhand our soldi'r," the ancient, little man demanded. He wore a fancy robe made of ivy leaves, and sported a crown fashioned from braided vines. Between his attire and the warriors heeded his frosty command, I guessed he was their leader.

We eyed each other for a moment, though I was careful to keep the squirming archer between me and the other soldiers.

The old man leaned against the knobby wooden staff in his hand. He was an ugly thing, bald with bulbous warts across his gray-green face, and ears like a bat's wings. Woolly chest hair poked from the open neck of the long tunic he wore, which was intricately woven from bits of colorful foliage. He was barefoot and his feet were exceptionally large compared to his body.

"Why should I release your soldier?" I asked him. "If I release your soldier, your archers might fire on me again."

"Thou hark and und'rstand us, Giant Fustilugs?

"I am called Hannah. Who are you?"

"I am Bubonum Rex, King of the Western Hobs." He glared haughtily at me. "Thy great, destructive size and appetites pose a threat to mine people. And now, because of Mothblossom, the trait'r princess and our defiant queen, thou see and hark us." The wizened little man turned to glare at his smaller prisoner. "Mothblossom's father shall wot the lady's betrayal and her carelessness with hallow'd water."

The angry little man seemed most offended that I was able to have any conversation with him at all. It appeared that Mothblossom's negligence, leaving a cup of hallowed water where I could find and touch it, had upset a centuries-old disconnection that kept a giant fustilug like me magically unaware of Hobs; who successfully thieved gardens and garbage cans undetected.

Rubbing my eye with their hallowed water allowed that eye to see them. Similarly, by rubbing my wounded ear with my damp fingers meant I could hear them, too. It also meant that my wounded ear was improving. Apparently, their special water was also a medicine.

The little monarch continued to rage while I sat stupefied, trying to comprehend my situation.

From what I could gather, Bubonum Rex had sentenced his bride to die for her defiance, negligence, and infidelity. I also understood that Mothblossom hadn't been eager to marry the old king, but didn't have much say in the matter. Even with her arms bound, a gag in her mouth, and a blindfold over her eyes, contempt for the wrinkled king radiated from her. She snorted beneath her gag and mumbled something rudely indiscernible.

"Thee shall p'rish, Traitor," the tiny monarch growled at her.

"Stop, please. I think we should negotiate," I announced, interrupting the king as he walloped Mothblossom across the legs and bottom with his staff, grunting with the exertion. "Would you consider diplomacy, your majesty?"

I didn't know much about the Hobs of folklore. All I knew was that Hobs were supposed to be ugly, hairy little men who misplaced household items, caused mischief, and occasionally did a domestic chore. But these creatures standing around me weren't domesticated. They weren't particularly ugly or hairy either, though a few had beards and long hair. The only obviously woolly, ugly, and wrinkled one among them was their king, and his head was bald.

Bubonum Rex was a despicable little creature, yet his subjects seemed to admire their king's spiteful displays of authority. They cheered when he thumped Mothblossom. They shouted approval when he insulted her family or denigrated and threatened anyone he perceived as an enemy, which included several Hob factions who lived in a wooded area across the interstate. And, of course, he insulted me. He paused his beating of Mothblossom to make a proud speech, reminding his soldiers of their history and his exalted role as their leader. It seemed like an inappropriate moment for speeches. My arm grew tired as I continued to dangle one of his soldiers in the air, but his subjects didn't seem to notice his impropriety or the illogical ramblings so disconnected from our current situation. I did learn a few things from his posturing. Apparently, a deep political rift among Hobs had caused Bubonum Rex to migrate with his subjects across the interstate to this floodplain, risking the big trucks and speeding cars that hit some of them before his people reached this promised land. Many had died in the exodus.

I imagined driving the interstate and experiencing a palpable little collision or bump, looking out the car window, but seeing neither pothole nor roadkill on the highway.

Bubonum Rex obviously liked to hear himself talk, spouting all manner of irrelevant things, some of which were nonsense, others which were outright lies, and most of it pure hogwash. According to the king, Mothblossom enticed me into Hob territory and formed a conspiracy with me to betray their people. My neighbor's habit of randomly firing his gun into dense foliage had wounded one of them. The threat was that if Darren could perceive the Hobs when he aimed his gun, the Hobs were surely doomed. Darren would have more accuracy killing the targets he could see. And Hob murder was supposedly the giant's goal.

"Mothblossom hath lur'd the giant mistress onto Hob estates by transf'rming the col'r of the mud and feeding h'r walnuts," he declared, "wh're on the lady did kiss the giant fustilugs who swallow'd h'r hallow'd wat'r."

He offered no motive for why Mothblossom would betray her people so brutally.

It was challenging to deal with Bubonum Rex. He was crazy and difficult to understand, but with a lot of flattery for his 'obvious' virility and bravery, I eventually managed to set forward terms for a truce. A prisoner exchange, Mothblossom for the dangling soldier I still held by his galluses.

Bubonum Rex wasn't too happy with a prisoner exchange. He was eager to execute the "distemperate daw" who had so recently become his wife but stood accused of illicit relations with soldiers she seduced.

Ultimately, he agreed to release Mothblossom to me as a slave, which was not the relationship I intended.

I wasn't sure what I intended.

I just couldn't stomach the thought of her execution or continued abuse.

I swore on my life to keep their secrets and in an additional show of goodwill, I promised to leave a weekly tribute from my garden in a basket outside the chain-link gate to my backyard. The king promised that his people would not fire their stinging arrows at me unless I traipsed too close to his estates beyond the creek.

"Prisoner exchange," I announced as I picked up Mothblossom and simultaneously lowered and released the Hob soldier.

I took the gag from Mothblossom's mouth, liberating hair that grew in tight tangles of greenish whorls. I gently raised the blindfold from eyes the color of blooming clematis. Her bat-wing ears were small and delicate. She had flawless skin the color of bleached buttercups. Her long neck held an oval-shaped head tilted upward at a proud angle. The threats of her execution had not panicked Mothblossom.

I broke the bonds around her arms.

"Am I thy s'rvant?" she asked. She showed no fear. In fact, she looked at me with the arrogance of a born aristocrat.

"We'll discuss our relationship when we get home," I whispered to her.

I stood up, closed my left eye, and the little people disappeared. I opened it again and gazed down on the king and his company of archers.

"I'm taking Mothblossom to my home now," I told Bubonum Rex. "You can look for my tribute outside the gate tomorrow at dusk."

"Sayeth mine own secret at thy p'ril and valorous riddance to the both of thee," he spat.

I gently held Mothblossom under my arm as if she was a favorite lap dog and began the muddy hike home.

When I reached my yard, I was able to take Mothblossom directly into the house without any interference from my neighbor. Darren wouldn't have been able to see the little Hob, but I was glad he wasn't doing backyard surveillance.

It's not like I could confront him about my wounded ear, anyway, because it seemed to be miraculously healed. Darren's bullet had skinned across my cheek and ear, but brushing the wound with fingers still damp with hallowed water had been an effective cure. The only clues that I'd been shot were the splotches of dry blood on my clothes. The mud caked down my back was stronger evidence of the awful morning I'd had.

After we were inside the house and I set Mothblossom down on the coffee table, I realized that a gown made of cobwebs and insect wings wasn't a durable outfit. It had disintegrated where I'd touched her.

Mothblossom was tattered, disheveled, and likely upset, though her dignity wouldn't let her show it. She was haughty and graceful.

A good bit taller than a fashion doll; she had a triangular-shaped body, with narrow shoulders, tiny bosoms, and a torso that developed toward substantially broader hips. Her legs were disproportionately long, but shapely, with feet the size of my thumbs. The creamy yellow color of her skin was different from the greenish-gray skin tones of her fellow Hobs.

She was lovely.

"First things first, you are not my slave or servant. You are free to go or stay."

"I has't nay home," she sorrowfully replied. "I am disown'd. What shall I make of mine freedom? Though I stand unshackled, naught hath naught for value." Her proud bearing crumpled, and she whimpered. Her purple eyes swelled and her little round shoulders shook.

"Please don't cry," I told her. "I know you've had a rough day. So have I. But you're safe here. I won't hurt you. You'll decide your circumstances when you're ready. For now, this can be your home."

I changed my muddy clothes, set her on my shoulder, and walked around my house, showing her how I lived.

Mothblossom was fascinated. My house must have seemed like a titan's palace to her. The kitchen might have been daunting at first, but she loved my colorful craft room.

She seemed to instinctively understand my sewing machine, and fawned over my bins of beads, spools of ribbons, and art supplies. She became really excited when I showed her my boxes of fabric scraps. Given the tattered state of her cobweb gown, I offered to make her an outfit.

After selecting the scraps she liked best, she eagerly ripped the remains of her cobweb gown from her body, waltzing gracefully across my craft table, delighting in the freedom that had worried her to tears a short time ago.

It wasn't too long before I'd finished sewing and she put on the little patchwork tunic and the pair of loose trousers that gathered at her waist with a ribbon tie.

"This outfit won't be as soft as cobwebs," I told her, "but it's practical, more colorful, and you look adorable in it."

When I let her see herself in my hand mirror, she gave me a look of pure gratitude, clapping her hands.

"These art bett'r robes f'r c'rtain." She seemed happy.

I fed her carrot slices, a shredded lettuce leaf, salad croutons, and apple juice, which she seemed to enjoy. I made myself a salad, too. We ate in the kitchen, me at the table next to the window with Mothblossom sitting cross-legged in the windowsill.

I had clothed her and fed her, but I wasn't sure what should happen next.

"What would you like to do, Mothblossom?" I asked.

"I desire to be reborn. Grant me the name of a free soul."

I glanced out the window to my colorful backyard, considering the tussock moth that might have been her namesake and wondering about this free soul she wanted to become. I noticed my Creeping Jenny blooming flamboyantly across the yard. Mothblossom's skin was pale in comparison. What she had most in common with the flower was her unwillingness to be defeated even when trod upon.

"How about Jenny?" I replied. "It's the name of that vibrant flower."

"Doth thee admireth this floweth'r?" she asked, also looking out the window.

"Without a doubt."

She became Jenny, a buoyant part of my household. She crept into my heart and took root.

I had saved her little cup and, on the following morning, found it miraculously refilled. After I wiped my right eye and right ear with this water, I could clearly see Jenny with both eyes and hear her with both ears.

She suggested I drink it, which I did. It tasted awful but left me feeling invigorated. Every morning the cup magically refilled, and I drank it like a daily tonic.

I kept the little cup on the kitchen windowsill, where it seemed to offer the promise for wishes I didn't know I had.

I didn't know I wanted a little Hob, playing in my birdbath, dancing in my houseplants, and watching movies on my cellphone. I didn't know I wanted to design clothes for her or hear about her adventures.

But here she was.

She wasn't my daughter, my pupil, my roommate, my house pet, or my doll, yet I taught her, made clothes for her, fed her, scolded her, and petted her. She wasn't quite a friend, either. We didn't exchange secrets. She told me about her frustrations, but I had no worthwhile stories to share.

But I listened.

She told me that Bubonum Rex was more than nine hundred years old, that many of his soldiers were his sons, that he'd outlived all his wives, and that he'd personally risked the interstate to visit her father and belittled himself with toadying and gifts to coerce her father into allowing Mothblossom to become his wife. He'd brought her back across the interstate to the floodplain, which Bubonum Rex considered his estates. She didn't tell me about ordinary life among the Hob, but she did tell me how much she hated Bubonum Rex. She hated his arbitrary rules and capricious demands. She hated their wedding. She hated the way he took credit for anything beneficial and blamed others for misfortunes and disasters. She hated that he was so ugly and so old.

"And how old are you?" I asked her.

"Twenty-one," she laughed merrily.

"Twenty-one years? That makes you almost half my age. Or do you mean twenty-one decades? Twenty-one days? Twenty-one centuries?"

She laughed again, but refused to clarify.

She was Jenny now, a free Hob. Within a month, Jenny had replaced her quaint speech with more current jargon, adding expressions she invented. She willingly and easily adapted, but never surrendered. She didn't change anything she didn't want to.

For a little Hob, she could make a tremendous mess.

She microwaved a stainless-steel fork, causing sparks and a fire that damaged my microwave. I forbid her to use my appliances—an edict she ignored. She dropped a can of soda that sprayed a messy fountain when she opened it and promptly decided that all the cans of soda in my refrigerator needed to be vigorously shaken so that "tensions" in carbonated water could find their joyful release.

She created her own superstitions.

She spilled potato chips on the floor and walked across them because she enjoyed the way they crunched under her feet. She emptied coffee grounds on my countertop and played in them as if they were the sands of a dark beach. She frolicked among the button jars, making a mess of my craft room. She made tangled wads in the chains of my costume jewelry.

Jenny took ownership of my house and yard, moving through the dog door a previous owner had installed in my kitchen. She was aggressive, unrestrained, and as unsettling as a stubborn weed but too enchanting to ever consider pulling.

When I realized that the clothes I created for her were as invisible to other people as a cobweb gown was, I took her to work with me, rather than leave her at home to make mischief.

She enjoyed herself at the lawn and garden store.

My fellow coworkers were startled when garden flags suddenly fluttered without the help of a breeze, ornaments levitated, and wind chimes made eerie music. After she took it upon herself to reorganize seed packets, my boss joked that the place had become haunted.

I was the only possible witness as Jenny pulled down her trousers and urinated in the dirt of a potted plant, only to hop from pot to pot to finish her business in what seemed a vulgar display, wagging her bottom as she sprinkled. Her behavior shocked the unacknowledged prude in me and I gasped.

One of my coworkers looked at me quizzically.

"Are you okay, Hannah?" he asked, staring in the direction of what had startled me and seeing only a row of potted plants that merely appeared vibrant and healthy, nothing at all to gasp about. He straightened his garden store apron and gazed back at me with a lifted eyebrow.

"I'm fine," I muttered.

Jenny tugged her trousers up and fabricated a complicated knot with the ties. "Don't get in a priggish snit, Hannah," she said. "I'm only sharing the benefits of hallowed water with these root-bound vegetables." She curtsied with an ironic grin. "You're welcome."

"Hallowed water," I growled at her when my coworker was out of earshot. "I've been drinking *Hob piss* every morning?" I asked, feeling nauseated and outraged.

"It's done you a world of good, Hannah. My body is a factory for superior health."

Maybe Jenny told the truth, but it sounded like conceit. Upon learning that the special water was urine, I decided to replace my morning routine of drinking it with taking a daily vitamin. I moved her toilet from the kitchen windowsill to the bathroom.

Having Jenny in my house and garden forced me to the realization that I was both squeamish and prudish. Despite my embrace of liberal causes and fantasy aesthetics, my core was tight-laced into a near-Victorian sense of decorum.

How strange.

For most of my life, I'd assumed I was a free-spirit. I was a backyard environmentalist, a conscientious recycler, an upcycling crafter, a believer in alternative medicines, a pacifist, and a generally tolerant person, yet Jenny daily shocked me.

She was Hob royalty, and yet she might prance about the house naked. In her opinion, the mission of clothes was foremost a decoration and secondly protection for the skin, or for warmth, never for modesty.

She was self-indulgent, shirking any chores I assigned her. Instead, she took long, luxury bubble baths in my kitchen sink, where she shamelessly pleasured herself.

She was haughty and entitled, never cleaning up any of the messes she made. Because she was Hob royalty, she acted as if everything belonged to her, from the beads in my craft room to the seeds at my garden store.

Though I gave her a tiny, commemorative souvenir spoon to eat with, her table manners bordered on the barbaric. And her appetites were exotic.

She didn't listen to my objections about bugs in the kitchen, insisting on catching, cooking, and eating them. No matter how adventurous I thought my culinary spirit was, I couldn't stomach the thought of eating palmetto bugs seethed in salt and wild garlic and it upset me to find the severed legs of cockroaches scattered across my kitchen countertops.

Jenny also said whatever she thought, even if it was hurtful. She didn't lie, and she wasn't generally mean-spirited, but Jenny never softened her opinions. On the occasions when she hurt my feelings, she shrugged and said she wasn't a sentimental sort.

"It isn't in my nature to flatter anyone or be affectionate, Hannah. I'm sorry if my bluntness disturbs you."

And she admitted to me that Bubonum Rex's accusations of infidelity were true. She had seduced more than one of the sons of her ugly king.

Marital fidelity was not something she honored.

Perhaps the most unsettling thing Jenny did was to torment my neighbor. It was also dangerous because, when she pinched Darren with invisible fingers as he was shooting his pistol at squirrels in the floodplain, he sometimes wildly swung the gun and used his free hand to slap at the biting insect he couldn't see.

More than once he made impact, knocking Jenny sideways, so that she limped home with swelling bruises the color of ripening pumpkins, and a deeply offended dignity. As much as I didn't like the idea of touching Hob urine, I would need to spread hallowed water across her wounds.

And yet for all the times she bristled my spine, I loved her.

She was fierce, proud, smart, and beautiful.

And she cared about her people.

Once a week, from early spring throughout a hot summer, she helped me prepare a garden harvest as my tribute, sometimes supplemented with curb market finds. She told me what she thought her people needed most, encouraged my generosity, and watched as I carried the basket, placing it outside my gate just as I'd promised the Hob king I would. The following day, the basket would be empty.

"Hunting and gathering has been displaced for border patrol," Jenny explained. "Bubonum Rex fears that Hobs from aggressive factions will hazard the giant road to invade the paradise of his estates."

I kept my promises to Bubonum Rex. His secrets were safe. His people were fed. And his queen was cared for, whether he liked it or not.

"Bubonum Rex is dead," the ragged soldier told us when we discovered him sleeping in the empty tribute basket with his broken bow and scattered arrows. The little man had been beaten. He was bleeding and was obviously distraught. Without Bubonum Rex to tell them what to do, their society had disintegrated into a warring muddle.

"Brother against brother. Every Hob for himself. We know Mothblossom hath told our secret and now we are all doomed," he ranted, bleary-eyed and woeful.

The little man had taken it upon himself to plead with us to stop the murders, though some among them felt it was traitorous to even speak with us, and had thrashed him for this effort. Others thought his mission should be the slaughter of Mothblossom rather than arbitration and kicked him for disagreeing. Some of his fellows had wished him success in negotiations with the giant fustilugs, but pummeled him for this endeavor, anyway.

One characteristic of the Hob seemed an inability to come to any consensus.

The little man's name was Webwort. From the adoring way he looked at her, I deduced that he'd been one of Jenny's illicit lovers in her Mothblossom days. He'd come on a heroic—and what his fellow Hobs thought was a doomed—mission to stop the crimes against them.

The lie they believed was that I had betrayed their secret and shared hallowed water with Darren, who'd had a more accurate aim in recent days, wounding two archers with his gun and killing another before he'd managed to fatally wound their king.

Webwort was one of the few Hobs who didn't believe that Jenny was a traitor. He'd ventured here to warn her that a squad of Hob assassins was preparing to come for her, if they could quit bickering long enough to enact the plan.

The assassins also wanted to murder Darren and then kill me before the "monstrous folk" could achieve the genocide of the Hob race—which they insisted was the goal of the giant fustilugs.

I swore that I had kept their secrets and had upheld all parts of the negotiations between me and Bubonum Rex, including the weekly delivery of a grocery tribute, and protested that I was in no way responsible for Darren's behavior.

The problem was that Bubonum Rex had himself given voice to the lies before he died. The little king was certain that I must have betrayed the Hobs. Darren's bullets would not have had such accuracy otherwise.

Jenny was incensed.

"Something must be done, Hannah," she declared. "We need to turn our assassins into our allies. Your neighbor must pay for his crimes, and the Hobs must be reunited."

"Those are admirable goals, Jenny," I told her with a touch of sarcasm. "What are your methods to achieve them? What are the timely, effective, and measurable tactics?"

I didn't expect her to have a plan, but she did. As much as her haughtiness, her near-vulgarity, and her hedonism annoyed me, I admired how she took command of the situation. Jenny pronounced herself Queen of the Hobs. She argued that she had been the wife of Bubonum Rex and she had never been divorced or executed. She convinced Webwort of her argument. He went down on one knee and pledged himself to her service.

Obviously, the little man deeply admired Jenny. I noticed the ragged little man was still bleeding from the beating his fellows had given him.

"Webwort needs to produce hallowed water and cure himself."

"Webwort can't make hallowed water," Jenny laughed. "Hallowed water is for me to make." Whereon she explained that the body of the rare female Hob produced this curative.

"If that's the case, how could Bubonum Rex call for your execution?" It astounded me that the Hob king would so blithely destroy such a precious resource.

"I insulted him." She shrugged, as if that was reason enough.

"So, now you are a queen with one subject," I remarked. "What next?"

"The Hobs still come for your weekly tribute, Hannah. We shall set a snare and capture them. I will show them the truth that Darren does not see them. I will allow them to go after him with their arrows, until he is sufficiently punished. I will reunite the Hobs as their queen, but I need to look like a queen, Hannah. Not like a jester."

She had a point. The clothes I made for her from scraps of colorful fabrics were fun but perhaps too comical to inspire allegiance. One thing

I had learned about the Hobs was that they were more about appearance than substance. Not that Jenny didn't have substance. She was smart, but she also needed to look like a queen. So, I offered to help with the packaging of a royal. It was too late to pretend I was an impartial outsider.

I was about to meddle in Hob destiny.

I went to the craft store and bought a yard of a silver, cotton-blend fabric that had a nice drape and shimmer to it. I made Jenny a flowing tunic with tighter fitting trousers that buttoned at the waist. I made a cape that swirled impressively. I upcycled a bit of old costume jewelry to create a breastplate that I hoped would protect her heart from assassins' arrows. And because Webwort was looking ragged, I used leftover fabric to make a silver tunic for him with black trousers and a matching cape made from one of my old black tee-shirts.

Unlike his father, Webwort had a good figure, broad shoulders, a narrow waist, nicely muscled thighs, and shapely calves. With his wounds healed, his body washed, his beard combed, and outfitted in the clothes I made him, Webwort seemed a valiant fellow. He was so handsome that Jenny decided to make him her official consort.

He stammered, went down on one knee, and accepted the role with bowed head.

Now that she was properly outfitted for authority with a loyal consort at her side, the next step was to capture the Hobs who came for their weekly tribute.

Webwort explained that the Hobs who gathered the tribute might also be the assassins on a mission of murder. One assassination plan had been to wait until after the next tribute to attack, because after their mission was accomplished, I would be a corpse and there would be no more tributes at the gate.

The Hobs had waited to kill me because they enjoyed their easy groceries.

There were twelve soldiers we managed to capture with bird netting.

Webwort scampered around, confiscating their bows, while the confused Hobs wailed, cursed, and thrashed around. One at a time, I lifted them from under the net, and, with Webwort's help, I secured their hands and feet with rubber bands, then carried them in my wheelbarrow to my backyard. I sat them in a bunch near my birdbath to wait for Jenny's speech.

I was sure these little soldiers wouldn't listen to her. They were too busy muttering insults and curses at both me and Webwort. Yet, the moment she marched in front of them, looking like a miniature Saint Joan of Arc, they hushed.

She swirled her cape in a dramatic show and declared that I had maintained all my promises to Bubonum Rex. She vowed that the Hob would take their revenge on the large fustilugs known as Darren. She explained that Darren could not see or hear them, but he could hear the rustling of bushes and scuffling of leaves from their movements when they came close to his yard and that was what directed his better aim, not our betrayal. Finally, she made her argument that she was their rightful queen and had their best interests at heart. She countered every argument any of them yelled at her with reason uttered in a powerful voice, the powerful voice being the operative bit, because reason didn't always convince the Hobs.

I noticed that she'd reverted to Hob dialect in this speech.

Ultimately, she got all twelve archers to kneel before her and swear their loyalty.

I was impressed.

She was magical.

We waited for the late afternoon when my neighbor was likely to emerge with his handgun and martini to perform his reconnaissance on the flood zone.

In the meantime, I tried to show goodwill by feeding the Hob archers bananas and peanut butter on crackers, foods the little soldiers had never eaten but enjoyed, just as Jenny predicted they would.

When Darren finally appeared on his back patio, martini in-hand and gun in his holster, Jenny rearmed her archers. Darren's reactions made it obvious he couldn't hear Jenny's instructions or see the Hobs taking position against his fence with their arrows aimed through openings in the black iron lace. Darren did glance in my direction for a muttered insult, as he took his gun from its holster. Darren had settled into his lawn chair with his focus on the enchanted wilderness of our floodplain when Jenny commanded her archers to draw their bows and take aim.

I worried about Darren's reaction when invisible Hobs fired upon him. Maybe he would run indoors and call the pest management company to come spray their poisons across his property again. I didn't know what he might do, but I was unprepared for his fierce howling when Hob arrows hit him. Twelve arrows found their mark almost simultaneously. Darren dropped his martini, and the glass broke on his stone patio. With his newly freed hand, Darren began slapping his own face and body. He stood up, turned in the direction of my yard, and accused me of unleashing venomous, invisible wasps onto his property.

"What have you done, Hannah? Is this an example of your old lady spite?" he screeched.

Jenny ordered her archers to reload, take aim, and fire again.

I suffered a weird combination of remorse, dread, and gleeful revenge as I watched the second barrage of Hob arrows hit my neighbor. Darren screamed and staggered over the broken glass under his boots.

I keenly remembered what it felt like to be the target of so many little arrows. It was painful, but certainly not as painful as Darren's reactions seemed to indicate. But then I remembered. When I was targeted, I'd already had a bit of protection from Jenny's hallowed water. The pain was likely worse for him.

I tried my best to feel sad for Darren, but couldn't. Perhaps I was as vengeful as I was prudish and squeamish. I wasn't firing any arrows at my neighbor, but neither was I suggesting that Hob soldiers should turn the other cheek. It was disappointing to recognize my total lack of compassion for my suffering neighbor.

My delight in his agony wasn't the reaction of a pacifist. Or a very nice person.

Webwort climbed Darren's ironwork fence as the archers reloaded. I wasn't sure what the little man had in mind, but he looked like a tiny superhero with his black cape flowing behind him as he jumped from Darren's fence to land in my neighbor's Zoysia grass.

Darren stared at me. I wondered if he could hear the thump of Webwort's landing.

"Hannah. What are you doing?" he roared at me.

"Nothing." I shrugged, showing empty, open hands.

"You evil witch. You've trained the invisible wasps in some sort of wicked circus trick. Wasps instead of fleas, Hannah?" He snarled and lifted his arm to aim his pistol at me.

"Are you going to shoot me, Darren?"

This had gone too far.

"Yes. I believe I will shoot you. A man has the right to stand his ground, Madam."

"I haven't put a single toe on your property."

"Your wasps have invaded my space!" he shouted, depressing the trigger.

In that moment, Webwort jumped up, grabbed Darren's arm, and pulled it down, so that Darren shot himself in the foot. He yelled as the bullet pierced his boot.

"Take cover, Webwort," Jenny commanded, before she ordered her archers to fire on Darren again. Darren shrieked. He lifted his arm to aim at me, but Webwort caused him to shoot a second round in his boot.

I calmly took my cellphone from my pocket and dialed 9-1-1.

"I believe my neighbor may be experiencing mental health challenges," I told the policeman who interviewed me. "But to be fair, the biting flies have been awful this year."

Darren had been carried away on a stretcher, loaded into an ambulance, and was now on his way to receive hospital care. The policeman was still taking my statement.

"He must have walked into a swarm of something," the police officer told me, looking up from his little notebook. "The man had welts across his face and arms. His face was all punctured and swollen. There were bites under his clothes." He frowned at me. "I notice the bugs don't seem to have bothered you."

"Vitamin B," I briskly told the man, "Vitamin B and oil of lemon eucalyptus tincture rubbed on the skin will discourage the bugs." I smiled at him. "I dabble in home remedies."

"I see," the man grunted, but of course he didn't see. He glanced around my backyard, but the policeman couldn't perceive the group of archers standing behind their lovely queen or Webwort with his chest out, looking very dashing. The policeman did frown at my "magic grows here" yard sign. "Do you consider yourself a witch, Miss—" he stammered and glanced at his notes, searching for my name.

"Hannah," I quickly told him. "No. I don't consider myself a witch."

"Your neighbor does. He believes you are responsible for sending the bugs into his yard."

"Like I said, Darren may be experiencing mental health issues, but of course, that would be for a professional to determine. I am concerned that he is allowed to keep a gun, especially given his wild ideas about me."

The police officer nodded but made no comment. The interview was over.

"That was exciting," Jenny remarked after the police were gone. "Timely, effective, and measurable. Doth thou regard that we've solved our problem, Hannah?"

"For now, maybe. I can't say if it's a permanent solution. What will you do next, Jenny?"

"Tis Mothblossom now, Hannah. I'm not a free Hob anymore. I have responsibilities. I have a nation to reunite and govern. Treaties to make among Hob factions. I'm not an independent soul. I am a queen."

I watched as she assembled her archers and explained that they were going home to locate their fellows and once again become a united people with a single, honorable resolve. I discussed the tribute with Mothblossom, suggesting that the basket should be left deeper into the woods than my gate. A healthier distance from Darren's yard would make it less likely for him to hear any rustlings. I couldn't be confident that the police would confiscate his gun.

"A weekly tribute isn't necessary, Hannah," she told me. "As much as I appreciate thy kindness, I don't crave mine people to become dependent on thee. Yet, I won't object to an occasional gift," she said. "An *occasional* gift. Nay charity. Peace 'twixt us shall ne'r be dependent on thy generosity, Hannah. Thou art not a target for mine archers."

I opened the back gate for them.

"I would wish you good luck, Mothblossom, but I suppose a person with skill and motivation makes her own luck."

"I appreciate thy good wishes, Hannah. Should'st I comprehend how to experience love, I sincerely believe I'd love thee. Thou are a principled individual," she said.

I stood at the gate, watching the Hobs disappear into the wilderness of the floodplain.

Was I a principled individual? Did she even know what it meant to be principled?

Yes, I decided, maybe she did.

As the sky began to blush with the beginnings of sunset, I returned to my yard. The Creeping Jenny seemed to straighten from where Hobs and police officers had trampled it. It was buoying to see such resilience.

Of course, I couldn't know what would happen when Darren came home from the hospital with his dark suspicions, itchy welts, and wounded foot, but I considered that if I had been able to make a truce with Bubonum Rex, managed to live with the continual disruption of a destructively entitled Hob, and befriend a burgeoning queen, I should be able to negotiate with one surly neighbor. If diplomacy failed, I would bite the bullet (pun intended), build my own solid wood privacy fence between our yards, and put to test the truth behind that old proverb regarding good fences making good neighbors.

People Of The Trees

By Faith Hunter

"**C**ome," she whispered. "My visions are ended." Her voice was a croak, weakened by age, by the years of calling her people together, and by the smoke and fire that was the center of their tribe.

Wood smoke and fire meant life, and it was ever and always with them: the smoke of cooking fires, the smoke of preserving meat, the fire that warmed their circles, trapped in the thatch, the smoke of cleansing and purification, and the smoke of the *gatherings* as the flames leaped high.

And after the ceremonial burning, the wood ash would be carefully collected, mixed with fat and pigments and stored in folded bits of hide until needed. For ceremony, the images of hunting and the images of the womb would be painted upon their bodies. The ash of wood from fallen limbs would cover them. Everything in all their long tribal lives had been twined with the trees and the wood and the fire, smoke, and ash of their burning.

After so many years, the smoke had darkened her brown skin. And after these last visions, the dreams of the Vision Moon—the terrible images of loss—she was hoarse, her voice rough, dry, and weak. Her body feeble. The leaves of her head dry and crackled and brown. The vision—the *seeings*—had lasted long, and she had cried out her body's moisture.

Vision Moon had been hard this winter season, but it was the prophecy that had broken Old Mother of Winter Trees. Had broken her voice as she screamed and grieved.

She had hoped to survive until the First Gather of the new year, the solstice and that first mating moon, when her great-great-great granddaughter would be born, when her favorite great-great-granddaughter would choose her first man from among the clanless Hunters. She had hoped to pass her staff to the woman of its choosing at Spring's First Gather festival. Old Mother of Winter Trees had hoped so many things. Desperately, fervently hoped for another cycle, another gather.

Most importantly, she had hoped to deliver a different vision of the coming years from the one she had been given. But it was not to be.

She tried again to call, but instead, coughed, the sound a wet rumble in her chest. A horrible tearing pain. She rolled to her side and hacked deeply, a racking spasm. She spat out the contents blocking her lungs and there was blood in the gobbet. The visions were true. *Sun and Moon*, she thought, *the visions are true*. The coughing fit left her exhausted. She lay in her bear furs, trembling, but breathing easier, regaining her strength. Outside, winter sleet whispered on the thatch above her. It shushed and sang against the stone walls of the Womb Circle where she lay. The cold had come early and brought with it much ice, just as her summer visions had foretold.

When a measure of strength had returned, Old Mother slid her long bony fingers from the warm furs and found the small stone. It was her singing stone, and was perfectly fitted to her hand. With it, she tapped three times on the calling Stone of the Winter Solstice on the circle's back wall. The clear tones each tap made upon contact would call her women to her.

Moments later, a thread of cold air swirled through the smoke as the outer-hide-cover slid aside, allowing two women to crawl into the curving Womb Passage and across the ancient staffs embedded in the clay floor. The Womb Passage was the symbol of mating and birthing and death. Each time they crawled through the curving narrow passage, their fingers and knees on the wood staffs of the previous Old Mothers, it was a reminder of their ways. It was a reminder of who they were and what they were.

The outer hide closed against the winter air. Then the inner-hide-cover opened, and the air shivered with cold, the low flames of the Womb Circle dancing with the delight of mating and joy, of life and death, of the hunt and feasting, of the turning of the seasons. Except now, with the visions overlaying their future, all Old Mother could see was death and destruction.

With the proper ceremony of the Vision Moon, her great-granddaughter, Summer Blossoms, said, "Old Mother of Winter Trees, we attend you. Old Mother and Staff Bearer of the Women of the Womb, we attend you. Old Mother of All the Tribes, we attend you. Speak and we will listen."

Her words carrying the weight of decades and many Vision Moons, Old Mother gave the ceremonial reply, "My visions are ended. You may feed the Womb fire and give me to drink."

Summer Blossoms and Rippling Stream set aside their burdens, difficult to carry through the entrance, on hands and knees. Silently, they added dry twigs, broken limbs, and dried herbs to the fire, where it crackled and its fragrant smoke rose. Old Mother of all the tribes coughed and hacked, her body as desiccated from the days of fasting as the herbs that blazed high. She accepted the water offered by the two who served her, though she dribbled most of it onto the ground, as she was too weak to raise her head.

When they sat back on their heels, Old Mother continued with the formal words of the visions. "The Vision Moon has spoken its wisdom to me. My vision is true."

"Yes, Old Mother of Winter Trees," the two women said softly, together.

"You will call all the Women of the Womb in all the tribes to meet here before the next full moon. They must hear the visions. They must know the future."

The eyes of the two went wide and shocked. The leaves that grew from their scalps rustled; the vines that twined from their fingertips quivered. A winter calling had never been done, at least not in their lifetimes.

Only once, in her own.

She said, "You will send word for all the Old Mothers of all the tribes, all who lift toddlers, all with babes at the breast, all who are with child, all young who are newly bled, yes all the Women of the Womb. And you will call all the women who war and hunt, who trade and weave, who make baskets and who fish among the men. All the women of every tribe will come here, now." She raised her head and met the eyes of the two women. "It is time. My staff must be passed. A new Staff Bearer of the Women must be chosen by the next full moon. I will not last until the Spring Gathering. The Earth and my tree call for my bones."

"Surely you will not go to your tree before the First Gather," Rippling Stream whispered in horror. "I will place offerings of honey in the roots of your tree. It will be satisfied and not call for you."

Old Mother laughed. It was a harsh sound, composed of fear and grief more so than amusement. "Call the women. Call all of them. The Vision Moon has spoken."

Summer Blossoms, who had always been wise and full of understanding, knelt beside her, touched her face and hissed softly. She lifted Old Mother upright and Rippling Stream handed her a wood cup carried among their burdens. Summer Blossoms held the cup to her lips. "Warm willow bark tea," she said, "with honey. This will help with fever and give you healing."

"I will need bone broth as well," Old Mother said when the cup was empty. "My vision has driven strength from me."

"We will bring it," Rippling Stream said. "We have frozen bones stacked and waiting for need."

"What can be so terrible that it drives strength from the bones of the Old Mother of all the tribes of women?" Summer Blossoms asked her, easing her back to her furs.

"The killers of trees are coming."

Both women sucked breaths of distress. Their leaves rustled and twined and grew as if it was summer. The flowers that gave Summer Blossoms her name budded upon her scalp.

"How would anything live without the trees?" Rippling Stream asked.

"The invaders will cut them down," Old Mother said, the words like ashes in her mouth.

"We will fight," Summer Blossoms said, slamming her hand flat upon the clay floor, making it an oath. "We will put aside our birthing and join in battle with the men. We will war and battle and kill them all. We will feed their blood to the earth and save the trees."

"Yes," Old Mother said. "You will fight. And for a time, you will win. But the years will be few when the shores are safe. The time will come when you will die and you will go to your trees and the invaders will leave none alive on these islands of the west. The invaders will do as I have seen. And the trees will all be cut down."

"This is a thing most foul," Rippling Spring said, her out-of-season leaves quivering as if in childbirth, with great fear and stress. "We will not let it come to pass."

"You must be ready," Old Mother said. "They will come soon. And they will come forever. They will *farm*."

"I choose a new name," her great-granddaughter said. She spat upon the clay floor and placed her palms flat upon it in oath-taking. "I put aside mating and birthing. I will no longer be called Summer Blossoms. The name of my vow shall forever be Warrior Woman of Blood and Battle. I will be called Warrior Woman."

Beneath her palms, the ground erupted with the vines and rootlets and wrapped around her, sealing the vow. A single thorn pierced her flesh, the trees taking her blood.

Rippling Spring copied her gesture, spitting, palms to the earth, speaking her own vow, "My vow name shall be Woman Who Left Her Children's Children to Make War. I will be called 'Make War'." The vines took her at her word.

It was done. The first of the visions of change had begun.

Old Mother smiled, but it was bitterness of wormwood upon her tongue. "Call all the women, from the Old Women and the Staff Bearers, to the youngest who have their moon cycles, all the women of each tribe. Call them to gather at the Womb Circle. Call them before the fullness of the Cold Wolf Howls Moon."

Warrior Woman of Blood and Battle lifted her once more and held a second cup to her lips. "Drink." Her voice went harsh. "All shall be as you have said. Except we shall not lose the trees."

"And you shall not go to your tree," said Woman Who Left Her Children's Children to Make War.

Old Mother of Winter Trees had known they would choose war. As the two women lay her frail body back onto the hides and furs and covered her, tears trickled down her creased, furrowed face and dripped slowly into the bed.

The Speaker of Hunters—called Killer of Lion—emerged from the Men's Circle after the Vision Moon and led the men to hunt. Though he had only one eye that viewed the world, and one eye that viewed the darkness of the blind, he was the best leader of the hunters and warriors in many spans of hands. Perhaps since the three floods.

His visions had been things of horror. Battle. War. Blood. Plague. Death. And the new enemy, a tribe with white skin and strange eyes and rounded ears. And hair upon their heads like beasts instead of vines and leaves.

He had braided his vines out of the way for the hunt, but… there was much pain in his heart. The Vision Moon had been… nightmares of horror.

When Killer of Lion returned later that day, he placed gifts at the entrance to the Womb Passage: the liver of a hart and its long-bones still with meat and fat and marrow. It was a prized gift, and the first steps of a request to speak to the ancient crone who led the Women of the Womb.

He left the gifts without words, without meeting the eyes of the women who attended Old Mother of Winter Trees. His one-eyed gaze was hard upon the ground, his shoulders rounded with the weight of his visions. His body was heavy, as though his youth had left him as he returned to his circle.

Behind him, he heard one of the women Hunters speaking to the Women of the Womb who served the Old Mother. "The Speaker's spirit is full of grief from his visions, some deep pain he has not shared with us on the hunt."

A familiar voice said, "Old Mother of Winter Trees has called all the Women of the Womb from all the tribes to gather."

At the reply, his steps faltered and stopped.

She spoke of invaders and war," the woman said. It was Summer Blossoms, once his mate.

"Has she asked to parley with the Speaker?"

"Not yet. She is unwell."

With a gesture, Killer of Lion gestured his men to follow, and dropped to his knees. He crawled through the straight tunnel path and entered into the Men's Circle.

Invaders and war.

His visions had been true.

That night, Old Mother heard murmurs from the men's circle, where the walls touched. The Speaker and his closest councilors were gathered there, and though she heard no words, the tones were dire. She knew her women had shared her own warnings, and could only presume that the Speaker's Vision Moon had portended ominous warnings, similar to hers. The leaves on the tips of her fingers sprouted, dark as mid-summer, before they browned and crinkled into winter brown.

Her women attended her, and brought draught after draught of herbed decoctions, bone broth, and added mushrooms and onions when her cough worsened.

Dreams of blood and battle raged within her, guided by herbs and mushrooms. She woke fevered, her mind thoughts running with blood and the sound of battle cries. Her skin burned. Leaves and vines sprouted from her as her fever rose in the night. The women added her own leaves and theirs to the broths, and added the bone and flesh from the hunters' offerings, feeding them to Old Mother. Three days passed in a haze of pain and fever, and the terror of war dreams.

On the fourth day, she began to improve, finding strength enough to relieve herself without help and to cleanse her own body. Her cough subsided, and her breath came easier. She asked her women, "Did you send for the Women of the Womb?"

"Yes, Old Mother of the Trees, Staff Bearer of the Women of the Womb. Your words have gone out." But the woman's tone did not bode well for the responses the runners had received. It was winter. Only Brings

Stone Tribe traveled in winter. All the others traveled only in the solstices of the warmer seasons. Yet, they would come. This she knew. The Old Women would think on her words, consider her many years, and decide they needed to be present in case it was time for Old Mother to go to her tree. They would not miss a chance to move up in the hierarchy of the women, the opportunity to gain power.

"Has the Speaker of the Hunters and Warriors asked leave to parley with the women?" she asked the young girl who tended her fire.

"Yes, Old Mother. Do you have a reply?"

"Tell him to call his Hunters and Warriors."

The young woman went silent, positioning a larger limb across the fire. When she had the broken end to her satisfaction, she risked a look up into the eyes of the Old Mother. "He has already sent word, Old Mother. He sent runners while you lay ill and we tended you."

"Ahhh. His visions…"

"Yes, Old Mother. His visions were of darkness and evil upon the land."

The new moon came, dark as death, and with it a bone-freezing cold and deep snow. It blanketed the earth, rested on the branches of the trees of the people, falling so hard and fast that it coated even the sharply pitched thatch of Old Mother's circle. It lay across the entire land like the hide of the pink-eyed white deer.

But inside the Circle of the Womb, the fire and smoke kept her warm. She talked with her closest advisors, blessed the few babes born out of season, and instructed the young women in the preparation of hides and the methods of making into clothing.

Against the back wall of her Womb Circle, she heard the Speaker teaching the young men how to knap spear heads, ax heads, and tools for skinning animals for the tribe. Later, she heard him and his oldest advisors as they instructed the mated hunter men on the proper ways to make thatch roofs, and how to create rope and tie knots. How to fish with nets. He taught the women Hunters as well, and guided them in their own ceremonies.

Days passed. The earth stayed cold. Sleet and freezing rain coated the snow, hardening into a thick crust, freezing creeks and ponds and bringing death. Fevers were caught by the young. Babies died. Old men and women died and went to their trees.

Her own fever had passed, and her water ran clear again. But she did not rescind her calling for the Women of the Wombs from all the tribes. Old Mother knew her visions were true. She *knew*...

The day after the new moon, she woke to the tickling of small vines curling around her fingers. It was the earth speaking, warning of the arrival of the first of the tribes, the women coming early to take the best circles, closest to the Womb Circle, closest to the top of the hill. Voices came to her from outside her circle, and her women brought new telling her who had arrived and how they had come.

"The snow came to their knees," Woman Who Left Her Children's Children to Make War, told her, "but though the way was long and hard, Wolf Tribe arrived first, as always. The Staff Bearer of Wolf Tribe is a young woman, strong in her loins, and though she carries a child within her, she ran with the fleetest of her women."

"Wolf Tribe has always been the fastest," Old Mother agreed. "What color are her leaves?"

"The evergreen of the Holly Tree."

"This is auspicious." Old Mother wondered if the Staff would choose such a strong woman to take her staff. "Who else?"

"The Women of the Womb of Autumn Harvest of Gourds."

"A much longer journey and hard travel with babes at breast," Woman Who Left Her Children's Children to Make War said. "Old Wolf Mother and young Gourd Mother wait outside the passage with their women. May they enter?"

"Yes. But their staffs must remain outside."

"But you are well now," Make War said, shocked. "So their staffs will not contaminate—"

"I have spoken," her voice snapped out, the sound of falling stones in the tone.

"Yes Old Mother," Make War said.

Leaving their staffs in the cold, the women entered and sat at her fire. They gossiped about travel and their women, and bragged about the skills of their tribes. "We shared the weight and the nursing of the young, forcing the men to carry the trade goods," Old Wolf Mother said. "They grumbled until I told them to be silent or I would cut out their foolish tongues."

"She would do it too," Autumn's daughter said.

"Summer Blossoms," Autumn Harvest of Gourds said, later, her tone sly. "It is whispered that you have changed your name. Has your womb gone dry at such an early age?"

"My Moons are still with me," her great granddaughter said. "There is no secret. I am Warrior Woman of Blood and Battle. You will know why soon enough."

"Go away," Old Mother said, her bony hand waving them out. "I tire."

Silenced, the leaders of the two tribes crawled out through the Womb Passage. Old Mother felt well enough to twist wool into threads and knot them for swaddling clothes. She ate and drank and her body passed both solids and fluids. Her joints moved with less pain. Her breath came easier. The Earth had granted her enough days to fulfill the visions.

In midafternoon, Make War crawled through the curving passage, Warrior Woman behind her. Make War said, "Salt Tribe has arrived in their hide canoes. They will have salt and fish to trade."

Warrior Woman added, "Salt Tribes' warriors sailed to the east land and brought back prisoners and trade items. One such prisoner has red hair and eyes the color of a cloudless summer sky."

Old Mother closed her dark eyes upon hearing the words. Though she knew she did not speak the truth, she said, "There is no such human."

"There is. I saw her with my own eyes," Make War said. "She is tall and limber, taller than the tallest man here, and her ears are round and small." Make War touched her own pointed ears. "Her ears are very ugly. Salt Tribe is bringing her with them. They are calling her Sky Eyes. The men are all besotted."

"Men are easily besotted," her great granddaughter said, her tone wry.

Sky Eyes… Old Mother's tears beaded and fell, leaving salt to dry upon her face. Salt Tribe had taken the first step upon the path that must be trod. The path of the visions. "This prisoner is not to be brought to the Womb Circle," she stated.

"She will enter no circle," Warrior Woman said. "She has painted her white skin blue and she must be tied at night to keep her from running away."

The visions showed a sky-eyes in the circle, making magic, suckling a child. "She will enter a circle with one of the tribes. There is safety in the circle," Old Mother said. "Unclaimed by a circle, the men might take her. But she may never enter here." Old Mother spat twice upon the ground and slapped her palms upon the spittle. "This is now Law of the Womb." Old Mother felt some of the burden shift from her shoulders into the earth. Vines rose and twined through her fingers and up her arms.

"This is now Law of the Womb," the women said together.

Make War said, "Sky-eyes fights with the staff Salt Tribe gave her. She fights with great strength and speed for one so large."

"Her daughter will lead a tribe one day," Old Mother said. The daughter of Sky-Eyes will be a great warrior. But not Sky-Eyes herself.

"Tell me of the other tribes."

"Tribe of the South Sea is a day's travel away. They sent runners to say they bring shellfish."

"Weaves Baskets and Cloth Tribe travels with Makes Beads and Dries Fruit Tribe. Eagle Tribe and Hunts Harts Tribe travel with Fishes the East Sea Tribe."

"Good," Old Mother said. "It is auspicious that the northern tribes travel together."

"Why?" Makes War asked.

"Their alliance will give us more time. Before the Farmers kill all our trees." Old Mother ripped the vines from her hands and wrists and threw them on the fire, along with drops of her blood.

The hunters and warriors who were mated into a tribe, and whose women were already gathered, assembled in the Men's Circle. The unmated men arrived together just after dusk, nearly a hundred strong, the elders among them bringing much dried meat and the hides of aurochs and tales of battle against a herd of the savage horned beasts. The younger ones came looking for mates out of season.

The Speaker, Killer of Lion, let them talk, but his white eye looked into the darkness, seeing the truth of his visions even through the pain of the blindness of one eye.

He stood and said, "Be warned. Your mating urges and actions could result in you being turned over the Women of the Womb. No man wants to be turned over to the gathering of the women."

From the shadows, a female laughed. It was the laughter of one who had changed from the way of the womb to the way of the hunter. "If you wish to keep your balls, stay away from the Old Mother of the Salt Tribe. She will take them and eat them."

The other women of the hunt laughed with her.

Dusk came, and the land wrapped vines about the ankles of Ole Mother of Winter Trees, warning her that the tribes were gathering out of season. She peeled them away and sent soothing peace into the earth through her palms. *Sleep. It is winter. It is not yet your time,* she told it. But the vines did not wither and withdraw. They lay upon the clay floor, their presence a warning of great danger.

A young woman, unmated, and nearly giddy with excitement at the presence of the unmated men, sat before her and tended her fire.

"Speak, Beautiful Flowers. I attend you," Old Mother said. But the words spoken by Beautiful Flowers said were not the ones she expected.

"The hunters of Hart Tribe, Works Flint Tribe, and Weaves Wool Tribe have put aside their weapons and their staffs of war and have made peace with Salt Tribe, Weaves Baskets and Cloth Tribe, and Makes Beads and Dries Fruit Tribe. Eagle Tribe, Hunts Harts Tribe, and Fishes the East Sea Tribe have sent their warriors to make peace as well."

"Why?" Old Mother asked. "They fight for the joy of killing and death. Why make peace?" Though she knew. She knew from her visions, visions that had clearly been shared by Killer of Lion. The Earth had given them wisdom, and warnings, and though Killer of Lion was young, he was wise and was forging alliances among the tribes.

Beautiful Flowers said, "The Speaker of the Hunters has seen in his visions a cave with a sleeping bear and her cubs. Together they go beneath the earth, into the eternal dark. Those who survive will bring out fat and meat and the furs of the bears."

"Even though it is not yet Cave Bear Hunt Moon?"

"Even so," the girl said. "We will have bear fat and thick fur and we will dance upon the Earth."

They would not dance. Old Mother knew this. But she said nothing as her vines crawled around her ankles and her legs and up across her body.

Later, after the sun fell behind the western sea and the night was blanketed with clouds, her fire cast shadows on the stones of the Womb Circle. Smoke clung against the thatch in a dark cloud. Her eyes were growing weak with age, but she could still feel the wool knots she made on small sticks for the length of swaddling. This would protect her last great-great-great-great-granddaughter. The girl would be born in spring and she would eventually become the last Old Mother of the Womb Circle. Her visions had told her this.

When the last of the knots were tied, she broke the sticks away and smoothed the soft cloth. She opened the small bag of ground hematite and began to rub the red pigment into the knots. When she was born this spring, this child would be named Woman of the Blood War.

A different girl, this one wearing the regalia of the Salt Tribe, entered and added sticks to her fire. Old Mother said, "Who are you?"

"At my first moon cycle, I chose the name She Who Walks in Water."

"It is a good name. Walks in Water, tell me of the day and the early night."

"Brings Stone Tribe is pulling three massive stones over the ice, to be placed at the spring gather. They sent runners to request help to pull the stones, that they might arrive in time for the gather. Two hands of the youngest hunter women from Salt Tribe and Wolf Tribe go to help."

"Salt Tribe and Wolf Tribe work together. This is a good omen."

"Yes, Old Mother of the Womb Circle."

Later, Old Mother felt the vibration of running feet, followed by the softer vibrations of a woman crawling through the curving entrance. Breathless, before she even entered the inner door, She Who Walks in Water said, "The staff bearer of Trades with the East brings items to trade, and news of attack. A white-skinned tribe on boats made of trees raided their shores. All were killed, except for a woman and two men. They are prisoners, but they have not been questioned. It is said that they do not speak words we understand. One of them has eyes like Sky-Eyes. One has eyes the color of the fir trees in winter, deep green. Is this part of the visions of the Old Mother?"

"Old Mother of the Womb Circle," she corrected gently, "has no words to say."

Time passed. Old Mother slept. Woke. With her singing stone, she summoned wood for fire and food and bone broth and the willow broth that kept the pain in her joints at bay. Outside, she heard a young woman's voice grumble, "This gather is foolish. Women should be in their circles giving birth, making shoes from the hides of the autumn hunt, treating the sick and dying. The tribes never travel in the dark days after the winter solstice, and never during the moons of ice and snow."

"Shhhh."

A third voice hissed, "No one alive now has seen a passing of the staff. Old Mother of Winter Trees is the last one of her years. Her visions foretell disaster. We must be prepared."

Old Mother of Winter Trees agreed with all she heard. Her visions had been true.

Killer of Lion entered the cave, a torch held aloft. He looked to every corner, memorizing every rock and every dripping water source. The talks of this cave were few, shared only during drought, as there was much water and no place to shelter that was not wet. He stopped and sniffed. The scent of bear was strong on the air, a bear he had never smelled before. The scent was healthy and full of fat and meat. The scent of bear milk. The scent of birth. The cubs would be small. Their hides would not tan well. He could call off the hunt. But the bonding of the men, one-to-one, outside of tribe, would benefit the coming war.

He gestured into the dark. "There is a female bear with three cubs ahead. And to the left, there is a male bear, sleeping. Mated men of Salt Tribe and Gourd Tribe will go first. Keep to the center. The unmated men will move to the left, led by the mated hunters of the other tribes. All shall be silent until the death strike is made. Spears held ready."

Killer of Lion led the way into the dark, his one good eye, watching everything, knowing that if the torches died, he would have to lead them out in the darkness.

Old Mother of Winter Trees was waked by Warrior Woman of Blood and Battle. Gently, her great granddaughter helped her to drink. Helped her to pass water through her body. The woman in the midst of change, cleaned Old Mother of Winter Trees, using a decoction made from strong plants, then rubbed soothing fats scented with flowers and herbs into her dry flesh.

Old Mother said nothing, waiting, knowing something important was to occur. It was too soon for the gathering she had called, as there were still three nights before the full moon, but her great granddaughter was not yet ready to speak.

When Old Mother was clean and fed, Warrior Woman of Blood and Battle said, "Killer of Lion has brought back the fat and blood and meat and bones and hide of the sleeping great bear and three cubs that his Vision Moon foretold. The unmated men have brought back a second bear, a male who was sleeping in the cave. But Killer of Lion is troubled."

Old Mother studied the child of her line. Warrior Woman of Blood and Battle had shared the mating circle with the Speaker of Hunters for five years. Together they had three children, though none at the breast, and all running with the other young ones in mock-battle, mock-hunting, mock-gathering, learning the ways of the older ones. "Is your mate troubled because you have changed your name?"

Her great granddaughter did not answer that question, but her mouth was hard and her jaw firm. Her voice was devoid of inflection, stating only fact, in the words of ceremony, when she said, "He has requested to enter the Womb Passage into the circle of Old Mother of Winter Trees."

The firelight danced across the dark features of Warrior Woman of Blood and Battle. She was sitting back on her heels, like the men of war, knees spread, a breechclout around her hips and covering her womb entrance. She wore a stone knife sheathed at one hip. Though Warrior Woman had not entered her new vows, Old Mother knew that a battle ax lay atop the pile of furs she had left at the inner door.

Warrior Woman of Blood and Battle had painted herself in the marks of the hunter and warrior, with bloodstone-hematite pigmented bear-claw marks across both cheeks and her upper breasts. The three rolling waves of the great flood were marked in blue at both temples and on her upper chest below the notch at her neck. She had pierced her nose with the sharpened rib bone of a small seabird, a drop of blood still on the bone to indicate the freshness of the piercing. Woven in her hair were the bird's white and gray feathers. Her areolas and nipples had been painted with chalk and animal fat to indicate that they would no longer give suckle to young. She had painted her hands with ocher and hematite and symbols of the hunt had been tattooed upon her shoulders, pricked with sharp stone and pigments rubbed into the wounds. Her pointed ears were pierced with the bones of fish and birds and had been hung with white feathers that were stained with her own blood. The blood of ceremony.

Old Mother of the Womb Circle should have noticed when her great granddaughter left the Circle of the Womb and moved into the Circle of the Hunters and Warriors, and she had not. Days and nights had passed since the vow of her change. The Woman of the Womb known as Summer Blossoms had been purified and brought into the Circle of the Hunters and Warriors. She had passed the rigors of the testing. She looked fierce. She *was* fierce.

Pride welled at the sight of this warrior, but such pride could wait, as could her own questions about the changes wrought by her daughter's change. More important for now—a male wished to enter her circle. *A male*. This had happened only once in the oral tales and his ending had been a bad one.

Old Mother thought on this. According to the oldest teachings, Killer of Lion was the Speaker of the Men and Women Who Hunted and Made War. He was also Bearer of the Hunting Staff. His hunters guarded the entrance passage to the Men's Circle. He taught the ways of the hunt, of battle and war, the ways of killing to the young. He punished the young men who brought shame upon themselves.

Killer of Lion was male. Passage into the Womb Circle was dangerous to men. Evil would befall him and much evil had already befallen Killer of Lion. In an autumn raid in his twelfth year, a defender of an enemy tribe— Weaves Baskets Tribe—had hit him with a battle ax. His men had avenged him, but he was deeply damaged by the blow and had slept for many days. Even his mother, a woman of great knowledge and medicinal lore, could not save the vision in his eye. Now one eye looked into the world of the people, brown as the earth, seeing much. The other eye was white and looked into the spirit world, seeing the darkness to come.

Though only thirty summers of age, his vision into both worlds had made him wise. If Killer of Lion asked to enter the Passage of the Womb, despite the known danger, he must have important news, strong reasons, great need, and much strength.

This had not been in her visions, for a man to crawl through the curved entrance of the Womb Circle. There was more than the strength of Killer of Lion, more than his need, to be considered in such a decision.

Had the Speaker simply forced his way in, Old Mother would have accepted his passage and allowed the evil to fall upon him, but if she allowed *this* man passage and evil came upon him, there would be repercussions in the world of the spirits and in the world of the tribe. His two-eyes told her this.

Even as she considered, there was much evil coming. Killer of Lion was important in his own right. He was the son of the Staff Bearer of the Salt Tribe. Staff Bearer of Salt was an important woman among many tribes, as her tribe alone had kept alive the making of boats and rafts after the floods. War with the Salt Tribe would damage their ability to fight the coming war. The Old Mother of Salt was prideful and rash. She might declare war between tribes.

Most important to her own heart, Killer of Lion was the former mate of Warrior Woman of Blood and Battle. She had given up childbearing. If her former mate entered the Womb Passage, he would live with an evil that might prevent him from offering his seed to any woman. And her great granddaughter would grieve this.

So many things to consider in this seemingly simple request.

She asked, "Does Killer of Lion understand the danger that such a passage may bring upon him?"

"He does. He brings gifts and many questions," Warrior Woman said.

Old Mother looked upon the child of her line. "You have lain with him. You have told him of my visions?"

"No, Old Mother," she said, scowling in the flickering light of the flames and the dark of the winter circle. "When I chose my new name and told him I would bear no more daughters, he left me. We are mated no more." Her voice went bitter as wormwood, but resolute. "If he survives entering the Womb Passage, he will place himself among the unmated men at the First Mating Moon in the spring's First Gather. At Fish Famine Moon, in the language of the women, at Trout Salmon Moon in the Hunters' language, he will offer a different woman his trout and salmon and the seed that gives daughters."

It was certain by her words, that Warrior Woman had told him she would lie with him no more. Had she then expected that his love would be enough to keep him close to her and living in her circle? Old Mother sniffed the air. From her face, hard like stone, and the pungent smell of her anger, yes. Her great granddaughter was seldom so foolish.

Killer of Lion was a man of great responsibility and power. Yet, he was still young, too young to be satisfied without mating. Old Mother had known this, and if her great granddaughter had told her of her plans before her oath, Old Mother would have warned her. But she had sworn to the Earth, upon the clay floor of the holy circle, and painted her intention upon her body without seeking counsel. Her life had changed because of this. It was too late to undo the action. The visions would be true unto themselves, even if her daughter went to war.

"Ahhh," Old Mother said at last. "Your sorrow is my sorrow."

"Tell him his request is being considered. But first send runners to the Salt Tribe where they camp, to the Staff Bearer of the Salt Women. You will not go yourself. Is this understood?"

Warrior Woman nodded reluctantly.

"Tell the Staff Bearer that her son has requested entrance to the Womb Passage. Tell her the passage will take place after full dark has fallen this night. If she wishes to counsel against this passage, she must send her marker and her staff with one who will speak, or come herself to counsel him against this danger."

"It shall be as you have spoken, Old Mother of Winter Trees." Her granddaughter fed the fire from dry fallen wood gathered among the trees, made sure the opening in the thatch for the smoke to escape was free of sleet and snow, and departed through the Womb Passage.

As the sun began to set, the cold grew. Winds howled. Sleet and ice fell and froze solid. Old Mother of Winter Trees waited.

Before sunset, Warrior Woman of Blood and Battle stood with two other women, guarding the Passage of the Womb Circle, facing to the west, as witnesses to the setting sun. The torn flesh of her wrists and ankles burned and cracked as she shifted and moved. The pain was a sharp reminder that soon—when the First Gather was called—she would no longer be counted among the women. At the gather, she would move her possessions from the Womb Circle into the Hunter's and the Warrior's Circle.

She flexed her fists as the sun set, bringing blood to the surface of her skin as the wounds cracked.

The night after her vow, she had walked deep into the forest to sleep beneath her tree. Like the earth, the trees had whispered of coming danger, and she woke with vines around her and thorns pressing into the flesh of her wrists and ankles. Her decision to join the hunters and warriors had been approved by the earth. Her decision to hunt and battle the Killers of Trees had been good.

She had torn the vines free and taken them back to her fire. Placing them on a pile of fresh picked fir needles, she had burned the vines and the fir, mixed the ashes with her own menstrual blood, and added ground minerals of the earth. She had pressed the mixture into the wounds to stain and mark them forever.

Her heart was heavy at the thought of her children being cared for by others, and broken at the knowledge that her decision had separated her forever from her mate. But she had placed her hands against the Earth and the earth had spoken of the great danger and deep change, as deadly to them all as the three waves of the floods that had destroyed the world. And the trees had sealed her vow.

Now she stood, marked and tattooed and hurting, with the women at the entrance of the womb chamber, among the daughters of the Staff bearers, selected women from each of the tribes. They knew of her choice.

They knew of Make War's choice. They feared what the changes might mean, though no one had asked them about what they had learned.

The Women of the Womb who guarded Old Mother now stood a little apart from her, accepting her vow, as they did with Make War. The two who had heard the words of prophecy were with them, yet they stood all alone.

Motion caught her eye. The Staff Bearer of Salt Tribe had left her campsite and was striding up the royal road that ran to the wall joining the Hunter's Circle and the Womb Circle. Silence fell across the hilltop as she climbed. The nighttime preparations at each family circle halted, all eyes watching. Warrior Woman of Blood and Battle followed the Staff Bearer of Salt Tribe to the boundary of the women's court, at the place where the two circles touched.

The Staff Bearer of Salt Tribe stepped through the narrow outer opening into the men's circle.

The men guarding there stepped aside, shock on their faces at the presence of a woman on their side of the hill.

Bare branches of the hawthorn trees shivered as the Earth reacted to the shock. No staff Bearer had stepped into the men's circle in many years. Warrior Woman stopped outside the men's circle, viewing through the narrow opening.

The Staff Bearer of Salt Tribe stopped at the inner Entrance Passage of the Men's Circle and called out to her son, "Killer of Lion! Attend the mother of your birth!"

Warrior Woman's leaves and flowers stirred in shock. It was a command of a mother to a son, such as was given to a child who had not yet gone to the Hunter's Circles, but still suckled from the breast or toddled along behind. Such a demand was an insult. Such an insult was the first step to the disunion of mother and child.

The leader of the Salt Tribe waited at the entrance passage to the men's ceremonial circle, a passage which was long and straight, symbolizing the man's part of mating. There were tears upon her face. She *knew* she was causing a great pain. Warrior Woman did not interfere. She slammed her staff upon the frozen ground three times and called out, "Warrior Woman of Blood and Battle is witness!"

Two of the men attending outside the Men's Circle slammed their staff ends upon the ground three times and called out their witness. They joined her near the outer entrance, though inside the circle, one to either side.

Time passed. Deeper darkness fell. Wind blustered from the northwest, cold, and clouds in the sky covered the stars and the moon. Three men crawled from the Hunter's Entrance Passage and stood to the right. They were armed and tattooed and painted with the pigments of war. When Killer of Lion stood upright at the doorway, meeting the eyes of his once mate, before he strode to his mother. He had dressed in his regalia, with feathers piercing his long pointed ears and a slender bone through the hole in his nose. And he had taken time to mark his blind eye, a black streak of ash and fat across his face from brow to jaw.

Staff Bearer of Salt Tribe opened her hand and took a breath. He barely closed his eyes before she blew a palmful of chalk at him. It hit him in the face. He blinked it away from his eyes and focused on the woman who birthed him.

"You have asked a foolish thing of the Old Mother of Winter Trees. The tribe of your birth shall not bear the cost," she said. "You seek what is not yours to seek. You are disowned. Your curse shall not fall upon me or upon mine. It shall not fall upon your tribe, nor your sisters nor your daughters. If the night devourers your root and it lays limp in your hand, the fault of it will not rest upon the woman who birthed you, nor will it touch the Salt Tribe. It will rest on your brow and be yours alone."

"Should the curse fall upon me, my mother, I accept its weight. I have seven healthy daughters with three mothers, two of them part of Salt Tribe. They are yours. If my root fails me, I shall pass the Staff of Speaker to another. My news is urgent, as urgent as that of the Mother's. It should not have waited for you to come. My Vision Quest Moon was…" he stopped. Slashed his hand across the air between them. "Your message has been delivered. I am no longer your son. The daughter born by the woman now called Warrior Woman, shall remain with the tribe of her mother. My future daughters will not dwell in Salt Tribe."

His mother gave a single jut of her chin. "So it shall be." Staff Bearer of Salt Tribe turned away from her son. Her head was high, but her face was drawn down with grief and fear.

Warrior Woman leaped back to give her passage, back into the land of the women. She met her former mate's eyes. *What had he asked of his mother, of his tribe?*

Killer of Lion held her gaze and his eyes were rimmed with tears that pooled in the white chalk. "I will speak to Old Mother now," he said. "Tell the Old Mother of the Womb Circle that I await her attendance." He walked to her, where she stood to the side of the entrance wall. Softer, he added, for her alone, "Should my root fail, I will not lay claim upon you to care for me."

The heart of Warrior Woman of Blood and Battle clenched in her chest. He still loved her. His vow protected her from what he saw as onerous duty. She took three breaths before she calmed enough to say, "No. When

I take my Hunter's vows, I will care for my Speaker, who was once my mate, should evil befall him. Come. You must bathe away the dust of the curse of the Salt Tribe before you enter and leave the Womb Passage. Before you are born again."

"You honor me," he said, his tone saying much more.

Warrior Woman set the single torch in the crevice created by three smaller stones that were used as holders, pulled her battle ax, and knelt on a rock that extended over the springhead's pool. Her toes, knees, and one hand were stable on the flat stone, even with the ice coating it. "Yes," she said, gently. "I honor you."

She reared back and slashed the stone ax down onto the ice, grunting with effort as the surface shattered. For this task, she had bound her breasts against the milk and the cold, but the movement and the recoil of the ax brought back the pain of the first few days. It brought home her decision, and the warnings of great danger she had felt from the Earth and from her tree.

She reared back again and hit the ice. And again. The crack she had made widened and broke through to the water beneath. The pool she had chosen was where the women came to bathe after their winter moon cycles; when the earth warmed with spring, the ice cleared here first, and even in winter, the ice was thin here, for reasons only the Earth knew.

The location was private and the pool beneath was deep. And yes, to be brought here was an honor. Only a few men had ever been privileged to see this place. Fewer still had received the honor of being allowed to bathe here. Quickly, she widened the hole, tossing chunks of ice onto the shore. When it was wide enough to allow the Speaker to immerse himself with safety, she placed her staff across the hole and stepped back. "You will wash both hands first. Then hold onto the staff and step into the hole and beneath the surface of the water until it is over your head. Hold your breath. The Water of the Earth will steal it and your strength if she can. I, she who has named herself Warrior Woman of Blood and Battle, will watch over you and draw you out should your strength fail."

"You have always been a Warrior Woman," he said softly. "When you claimed the name in truth and painted your breasts, my spirit departed from me. Should the Holy Water of the Earth claim me tonight, I could not grieve more."

She raised her face to him in shock. His good eye was hidden in the darkness, his white eye glowing in the torchlight. The edge of his jaw was strong and hard beneath his long, viny beard. His scent came to her on the air, man and smoke and the blood of the hunt. She said, "I will not let the Waters of the Earth take you under, Killer of Lion."

The faint light caught his scarred face as he smiled, revealing a broken tooth from a recent battle. Quickly, he dropped his furs and stripped his garments from his shoulders. He removed the winter boots she had made for him. Untied his breechclout and placed it within the warm fur. Naked, he stood before her. He knelt and washed his hands, the water splashing, sharp and tinkling. He did not look at her when he spoke. "From the first time I beheld you, you have had my heart, Warrior Woman."

She struggled to find breath beneath the tears that gathered at the sight of Killer of Lion on his knees on the ice. Flakes of snow landed, sprinkling across his brown back, the very color of the hide he used as a breechclout. His arms were strong and his thighs lean, his chest and back muscled and tattooed with both the Hunt and the Visions of the Speaker. He was not a tall man, nor beautiful to look upon to most, but he was fast when he chased after prey, and wise in the ways of the hunt and in battle. Tears dripped down her cheeks, hot where they trailed on her skin until the cold air stole the warmth and left her flesh icy. "And you mine, Killer of Lion. My heart is yours for as long as I might live."

"My vision showed much," he said, his back to her, his voice faint on the night air.

"I hear the words of Killer of Lion," she whispered. Promising to say nothing of his words, she continued, "and I keep the words of the Speaker of the Hunt tight in my breast."

"I saw battle. We will fight together, make war together, side by side, against the pale-skinned ones from the east. And you shall be my Beloved Warrior Woman, who shall take my place when I fall in battle." With the words, he stepped over the edge of the ice and dropped into the hole. At the last moment, his hands caught the staff and broke his plunge.

Killer of Lion breathed deeply of the night air. Though he was still shivering from his bath in the women's pool, he once again removed his clothes, because a man did not enter into the Passage of the Womb Circle clothed, no more than he came forth clothed. Few men had been born again, passing twice from the womb into the world. If he survived, he would carry the horror and the honor for all of his remaining days. With a final breath, he dropped to his knees and lifted the hide flap, crawling into the darkness. The hide dropped into place behind him, leaving him in blackness, dark as a cave, cramped tight, sitting on his heels, his knees drawn up, his head bumping the stone roof of the passage. His flesh sweated yet was icy cold. Fear settled into his bowels.

The passage was tight. His shoulders would be scored by the stone while making this passage. He felt to the sides, and his fingers encountered rocks, deeply etched with swirls.

The waves of the floods. Reverently, he traced them as he crawled slowly forward, the floor unexpectedly uneven and rough. He reached down to feel… thin wood buried in clay. His fingers traced the wood, all rounded and worn, all about the same size. At one end, he felt a sharp edge. He realized the wood flooring was made of staffs. All the staffs of the women were brought here when their trees claimed them. He knew that, but… he and the other men had assumed they were burned in the fires of winter. Not placed on the floor of the Womb Passage.

He was resting on the power of… of all the women who had gone to their trees.

His body reacted, flashing with shock that quickly became the fear-dread-panic of the grave, of death, of the end of all. His flesh went cold and slick and damp. His breath came fast and too short in the blackness of the passage of his second birth.

But he did not die. Eyes straining, seeing nothing, he crawled forward, his hands and knees flat on the staffs, his shoulders touching to either side, as the passage narrowed and curved. Ahead, he made out a faint red glow. He reached to the redness and his fingers met the suppleness of hide, a hide so pale, so thin that light was showing through it. It was so supple that it moved with the slightest breeze.

Killer of Lion knew this hide. It was the hide of the pink-eyed white deer, the White Hart he had killed in his first season as a Hunter. Such deer were rare, and portended both change and rebirth. He had presented the entire deer at the entrance of the Womb Passage to honor the Old Mother who led all the tribes. He had never known what Old Mother of Winter Trees had done with his gift.

She had hung it here. In the women's most sacred place.

There was an inevitability in finding this hide here, in this place, at this time. An assurance. His heart steadied. His breath blew deep and slow. He pushed aside the hide and crawled into the warmth of the Womb Circle.

At dawn, Killer of Lion crawled out of the Womb Circle and crossed to the opening in the wall. He was sweat-streaked and his leaves were dead; small vines hung limp and parched from his fingertips and his lower body. As he crossed from the outer wall of the Women's Circle into the Hunter's outer wall, he collapsed into the arms of his Hunters. They doused him with fresh icy water and dusted his body with chalk, turning him white all over, to drive away the dangerous spirits of women. They carried him into the Men's Circle, where they fed him and painted his body with their hands dipped in powdered red pigment mixed with the fat of the bear. They wrapped him in the largest segment of the hide of the lion he had killed as a youth. They built the fire high. Around his body, they placed the bones of the man who had struck him and had given him his vision eye. They brought in drums made from the skins of small animals and they began to beat their drums to drive away the power of the spirit of the women.

Killer of Lion drank much water to restore his leaves and vines, and thanked his men for their service. Then he fell into an unnatural sleep, where he dreamed of tight passages and the fragmented visions of the future.

When he woke from the strange sleep, he sat up and drank and washed his hands and his face. He spat upon the ground and placed his palms upon the spit on the clay floor and whispered to his men, "I will no longer be called Killer of Lion. I am now Sees into Darkness."

They murmured in the dark. The circle was packed with men, bearing witness to his words and deeds, so he added to his vow. "I have seen much foulness that the pale-skinned men will bring. I have seen my own visions and heard the visions of the Old Mother of Winter Trees. Those who come to make war against us shall be known as *Farmers* and *City Builders*. And they will cut down our trees and destroy the Earth."

There was much grumbling and anger from the men.

His voice grew stronger. Loudly, he said, "The full moon begins the time of change. All who gather to hear the Visions of the Womb and the Visions of the Hunters shall no more make war against each other. "From this day forth, there will be war only against the white-skinned invaders. Swear it upon the earth. Swear it upon your tree, each of you. Swear, or be cast from the mating circles forever. "

Most of the men instantly swore. Over time passed and the enormity of what the Speaker demanded of them sank in, all but one so swore. In anger, Fishes Whale with Spear left the men's circle through the straight entrance. Fishes Whale with Spear had been a childhood friend. The visions of Sees in Darkness had told him some men would leave the circle and band together, to raid and make trouble, but there was nothing he could do to stop that from happening. Not until the day he tracked them down and killed them with his own hand.

Sees in Darkness looked out over his men. "Bring meat and broth and dried fruit. We will feast, for the last of the tribes are to gather soon, and we must share the visions of the change with them as well."

At dawn on the fullness of Cold Wolf Howls Moon, Old Mother of Winter Trees woke with a cough that shook her body. Bloody gobbets collected in the moss brought by her women to cleanse her. At her command, they built up the fire and washed her body with various decoctions of strong herbs, some with wormwood, some with mint. They fed her strong infusions of willow bark and others made with dried berries and rosehips.

The full moon would rise after nightfall and set before dawn. She asked of the Earth that she would live that long, though she knew the Earth would not allow her to stay in her body much longer. Her tree called. She felt the ache of it in her bones, in her joints, in her spine and her belly. It *called...* Her time was near. This time, she would not revive from illness. According to the visions she had shared with Killer of Lion, now known forevermore as Sees into Darkness, she would be taken before the end of the three days of the full moon.

She asked of her women, "Does Sees into Darkness still live?"

"He still lives and his root is strong," Make War said.

Old Mother took this as a good omen. She said, "Tonight, my staff will choose the next Old Mother."

They murmured, various tones threaded through their words like knots in wool: excitement, fear, worry, pride, hope, and some sounding of sly covetousness.

From her own memories, she gave them instructions. The women went out into the snow and dragged in dead trees, gathered fallen leaves, and cut fresh fir branches to create potent smoke for fires. They placed them below the Speakers' bench at the west joining of the outer walls. Outside, she heard the sounds of the Hunters, men and women both, as they dug into the earth to find the firepit there. The circle had been buried when the staff of the former Old Mother chose her, many hands of years in the past. No one alive knew of its existence but her.

They exclaimed loudly with the discovery of each of the stones, of the waves and the animals and the images carved into the largest stones at the base. When the pit was cleared, they too gathered wood for fires.

Then all went to their ceremonial pools for cleansing.

Though snow lay upon the ground, they adorned themselves in their tribal regalia as if at the First Gather of the Spring Solstice, and added many furs and hides and things of beauty. Energy rose from the gathered. Vines and leaves pushed through the frozen ground as the trees and the forest responded to their massed power.

At dusk Old Mother made her way through the narrow, curving Passage of the Womb. It took all of her strength to crawl across the staffs of time buried in the clay of the Passage. This was the final time she would leave her circle, in nine hands and six fingers of years.

Her women had rubbed her body with rendered fat cooked with mint leaves, and drawn symbols of war and trees across her body in chalk and hematite powder, in the dark shades of stones and plants. She was dressed in wool and hides. Lengths of hide thongs tied with bones and stones and shells and clay beads adorned her neck, her wrists, her knees and ankles. Her shoes were made of warmest lamb skin, the wool against her flesh, the tanned hide against the cold. Her delicately pointed ears were hung with the feathers of the blackbird and the vulture; more of the feathers were twined into her braided hair. A bone of the eagle pierced through the hole in her nose. She wore all her finest clothing, including the small leather bag around her neck, the bag made by her own hands to be given to the staff's chosen one, the next Old Mother.

Exhausted, she crawled into the night and let her women lift her, to carry her outside the outer walls. They placed her atop the side flat stone in the sheltered spot between the men's outer circle wall and the women's, the one place with a clear view down the low hill, so that all the gathered could see her. In front of her were three singing stones and the stone firepit, the pile of dry wood and other flammable material stacked within it. Her women placed heated rounded river stones from her own fire all about her, and wrapped her in more furs from the Womb Circle. They added furs from every clan, and every tribe until she was swathed in the skins of animals. Yet, even with the extra warmth, she felt the cold of winter. Soon, before dawn, she would be within her tree and she would be cold no longer. Her heart beat unevenly, booming and fluttering. Her breath blew pale clouds into the dark of night.

Sees into Darkness took his place beside her and his men wrapped him within his own skins and furs, and then stepped away. Silent, together, the Speaker and the Old Mother sat, facing away from the rising moon.

The scent of smoke, salt, old snow and ice, bear fat, dried fish and shellfish cooked in ocean water, and the scent of the gathered—the blood of Moon Times from the women, and the scent of bear blood from the Hunters, was a ripe miasma on the air. Old Mother breathed the wind. It was fresh, from the unpassable ocean to the west.

She looked up, and saw that the clouds had blown away. The brightest of the night's stars were visible, and more would have been, had her eyesight not lost the sharpness of her youth. She let her eyes drift down.

The hillside was full of silent people sitting around their tribal fires, the men on her right, on their side of the hill, the women on her left, all looking up at her, and toward the place where the Cold Wolf Howls Moon would rise behind her, in the east, full and majestic. The women sat with their kindred by birth, each tribe with its own fire. The mated sat closer to a woman's tribe, but seated outside of it. The unmated men and hunters sat in loser groups, close enough to try and catch the eye of a woman.

A baby wailed, shushed by its mother. Some of the Elders coughed. Old Mother of Winter Trees took a sip of the sweet and potent berry juice, boiled from dried berries and water with honey.

All the darkest shades of blue spread across the rare, cloudless sky. True night fell, and it grew colder, darker. All the people were staring in the direction of the moonrise, waiting for it to appear on the far horizon. A shout went up. The first glimmer of the moon's fullness could be seen behind her, in the distance. Sees into Darkness raised one arm and brought it down on his drum, the head tanned from the last piece of the skin of the lion he had killed, the lion that had given him his Hunter-name.

Again and again, three times in all, his drum boomed out into the silence. On the fourth downstroke, the men and hunters began to beat to their drums in time with his, slow and steady, the sound rising and falling like a wave in three beats and three beats and three beats, over and over as the silver orb of the moon lifted from the far hillside.

Smoke from the tribal fires swirled slowly up the hill and away as each tribe and clan fire was covered with fir boughs. Darkness, except from the moonlight on the hard-frozen snow, covered the Earth everywhere as the curve of the moon rose and the drums beat in harmony.

As the drums sounded, small lights appeared on the women's side of the hill. Glowing, held aloft in fire-hardened clay or cupped in frozen wood bowls, fires began to move through the night and up the hill. The fires had been transported overland from every tribe, carried by each Old Mother. Now, she or her designated one climbed the hill to the firepit at the conjoined circles where Old Mother of Winter Trees and Sees into Darkness sat.

Salt Tribe's Old Mother reached the hilltop first. She bent and began to feed her fire to the kindling of the Womb Circle firepit. Old Mothers from other tribes followed: One hand of the tribes of the People of the Trees. Two hands. More. The fires caught and blazed, creating both flames and glowing embers. The Old Mothers or their designated ones all sat around the pit in a circle before the fire, ringing the fire they had built together, from their own tribal and clan fires.

When the fires from each tribe had been added to the burning, Sees into Darkness set aside his drum, the rhythm continued by the men. He stood and walked to the Womb Circle firepit. He extended an unlit torch, its end smeared with animal fat and resin from trees. The torch lit, blazing from the women's circle. He carried it to the wood of the hunter's unlit firepit and placed the flaming torch within it.

This was a simple firepit, one not deep, never buried, not lined with huge stones, but a traveler's firepit, lined with whatever stones were nearby, as the Hunters and Warriors made when they were far from their tribes. It was a fitting firepit, as was the firepit of the Women of the Womb, fitting for them. Different. Side by side.

Sees into Darkness returned to his side of the hill as the branches ignited. The fire whooshed high. Sees into Darkness retook his place as Speaker of the Hunters, sitting beside Old Mother, again leading the drummers, beating his own drum. Strong strokes, deep and rhythmic. The drumming echoed down the hill, and all the way to the great waters.

The important men and women of the Hunters, those attached to the tribes by mating and children and three from among the unmated, took their places around their circle.

Old Mother watched the Staff Bearers as they watched the rising full moon. The moment the bottommost part of the fullness rose above the far horizon, they each dropped their heads in a bow. She raised her calling stone and brought it down on one of the three singing stones. One tone for each drumbeat, the three tones singing, calling into the night, into the moonlight. The drumming stopped, the last traces disappearing as she hit the singing stones again. And again. Three and three and three strong tones, echoing across the moonlit snow. The song sang out, fast and fast. The Women began to beat their own stones, the tones clear and sharp and calling to the trees.

Around the hillside the trees shivered, hearing the calling, their bare branches clacking. The silver orb rose higher, full and glowing. The Earth went bright, reflecting the moonlight from the snow. Power from the gathered, from the singing stones, from the drums, from the hearts and wombs of the People of the Trees rose, bright as the moonlight.

The trees shivered in expectation.

The moment the moon was full in the sky, Old Mother's stones went silent. Her arm ached. Her fingers felt frozen. She pulled them into the furs and wrapped them around a heated stone for warmth.

The voice of Old Mother was weak, and so she had arranged for one of her granddaughters, Wise with Herbs, to repeat her words. The encircling tribal Old Mothers were to be witnesses that she spoke true when she called out the vision of the Old Mother of Winter Trees.

Her granddaughter introduced the words. "The Vision Moon has passed. Old Mother of Winter Trees, Old Mother and Staff Bearer of the Women of the Womb, Old Mother of All the Tribes, we have gathered. We attend you."

Old Mother spoke, and Wise with Herbs repeated her words. "The Vision Moon gave unto me evil visions, dire and dangerous. Killer of Lion, now called Sees in Darkness, received the same visions. We sat together within the Womb Circle and shared the evil tidings."

"Old Mother of Winter Trees, we attend you," the gathered women said.

"Tonight Sees into Darkness and Old Mother of Winter Trees," she tapped her chest, "will reveal these tidings to all the People of the Trees. Then I will pass my staff to whomever it will choose, for my tree calls to me. I will go to my tree this night."

Rumblings of discontent and grief rolled across the land like the waves of the floods after Wise with Herbs spoke her words. The whisperings of sorrow and anger subsided only when Old Mother lifted her staff high in command for silence.

Old Mother spoke in halting statements, her voice pausing, allowing her granddaughter to carry the burden of shouting her visions. Wise with Herbs was no longer young, but her voice was strong, and always had been.

She called out, "Old Mother of Winter Trees speaks her vision. Soon strangers will come from the east. Some will be pale-skinned ones. Some will be darker, as are we. Many will have sky eyes that shine like the summer sky. Eyes that are the color of flax flowers. Colors of moss and leaves.

Many will have hair like animals, hair that is the yellow of furze and gorse flowers. Hair the red of autumn leaves and clover flowers. Their ears will all be rounded. Their stature will be taller than the People, and strong.

"They will kill for our land, sending many to our trees. They will bring death and war and plagues. When they have killed many of us, they will *kill our trees.*"

The rumblings rose in wails. The men clacked their teeth. The women bared their breasts to the cold wind in horror. When the grief settled, Old Mother continued. Her daughter's voice carried the dire tidings from the hilltop to the four corners of the cardinal road, to all the People of the Trees, repeated by those with the best hearing, so that all, even the near deaf, would hear the visions of the Old Mother of Winter Trees.

"They will be called *Farmers.* They will cut down our trees and plant *Crops.* They have already forgotten the ways of the Gathering and the Hunt. They will kill our people and destroy our way of life. They will try to convince us that the way of the Farmer and the Man-seed is better than the Way of the Womb."

The wailing rose on the icy air. But Old Mother's eyes were still sharp enough to note that some of the men shifted, thinking that perhaps it was time for such a change. Sees into Darkness had warned her that some of the men would do so.

Her strength waning, Old Mother spoke again when the wailing softened. "It will take long, many hands of years. The People of the Trees will fight and we will die, and we will lose this battle. They will make war. They will kill all the Hunters. They will maim the young boys and force them to *farm.*"

The men who had shown desire for change shifted again, not happy with the words of the seer.

"When the Farmers defeat us, after each battle, they will violate the women and the children."

The screams this time lasted long. Long and long. Wailing and grief and fear and horror. When silence again blanketed the land like ice, Old Mother said, "They will desecrate and cut the Earth and plant few kinds of seed for fewer and fewer crops. They will plant no hawthorn trees. No oak. No nut trees. No trees of any kind. And the way of the People of the Trees will die."

More wailing caught on the wind, swirling with the smoke of the gather. Grief and anguish and moaning.

Old Mother of Winter Trees whispered more tidings, and Wise with Herbs spoke into the silence that followed. "From their visions, Sees into Darkness and Old Mother of Winter Trees have this wisdom and these commands. Each tribe will capture *all* of the women the *Farmers* send to *Farm* and to War. If a young *Farmer* man survives battle, his seed will be given to any Woman willing to bear his seed and his daughters. All of the young will be treated as one of us, and not as the motherless who search for a home and a tribe. They will be taught our ways and the ones with sky eyes and leaf eyes who wish to go and live among the farmers will be allowed to do so. Thus will our seed and our wombs live on. This ends the revelation of the Vision Moon."

The sound of outrage rose on the air. Old Mother looked at Sees into Darkness. He stood and addressed the Hunters and the Warriors.

"When we fight, once each battle is ended and our enemies sacrifice their blood into the land, their women will be brought to the Womb Circle. To these *Farmers*, we will teach our language. Each Farmer woman will be allowed to choose a mate from the tribe that defeated her people. We will raise her children, the children of the *Farmers*, with our children of the Womb, mixing our seed with their wombs, and their Moon-Blood with our tribes. When they have three sky-eye or leaf-eye children, they will be allowed to return to the Farmers, taking the sky-eyes and the leaf-eyes with them. We will keep and raise their dark-eyed sons to fight the *Farmers*, their own families, the people from the east. We will keep their dark-eyed daughters as our own. Their dark-eyed sons and daughters will grow up with and will and mate with our Women and our Hunters and they will learn our ways…" He went silent, his eye of the world and his eye of the darkness closed in pain.

Old Mother took up the commands, Wise with Herbs again calling out. "The sky-eye and the leaf-eye will carry *us* in their blood. Thus, we will leave our mark and our blood and our way of life upon the *Farmers* who come and kill our trees. And we will become one people."

A voice shouted from the smoke filled dark someone shouted, "Then shall we become farmers? Shall we kill our own trees?"

Sees into Darkness shouted, "We have no other path! Go! Make the weapons of war! At the First Gather, each woman will choose a mate and many babes will be born. This will bind us all together in the Circles of Trees and when the babes are safe in the womb, the Hunters and Warriors will take battle to the Farmers. Our wombs and our seed will survive into the future. We…" He looked at Old Woman.

She crawled slowly to her feet, her back hunched, her body tired, her spirit broken. She found her own breath and waved Wise with Herbs away. Old Mother took the hand of Sees into Darkness. Together, they spoke the words of their vision.

"We go forward into the future. Our circles will endure. And we will reappear many and many and many hands of years in the future, and our trees will live again."

The Hunters and Warriors talked, their words about weapons and the long coast they must defend. They created new words for a new clan: Sentries and Runners. And words of war: walls, ditches with sharp sticks, shields, throwing spears, throwing axes. The best sizes and kinds of throwing rocks. They discussed ways that they might carry word from village and tribe to village and tribe, and ways to hide the paths through the trees, ways to ambush the invaders, these *Farmers*.

The Old Mothers of each tribe talked together, making plans for supplies for the Hunters to make war. They discussed ways to hide their most sacred herbs and foodstuffs from the invaders. Their places of power from the Killers of Trees.

As the Hunters and Women of the Womb talked, the power in the land began to alter. Despite the visions of their leaders, no one could believe that they might lose the war with *Farmers*.

No one but Old Mother and Sees in Darkness had seen the visions. They would fight until the last Warrior. The two grieved as only leaders who have seen visions can grieve. And Old Mother grew weaker. Her heart pounded and skipped beats. Her breath was labored.

At last the moon was two hands-width above the horizon. Knowing her time was near, Old Mother of Winter Trees beat her singing stones again. Silence fell over the hillside and down through the People. Wise with Herbs called out her words, "My staff must be passed. My tree calls."

Grief and excitement rolled across the land.

"The staff will choose," she repeated.

Old Mother pulled the small obsidian blade from the leather bag at her neck. The blade came from their first lands far to the east, over two seas, over many lands, to this isle at the west end of the world. "Old Mothers from every tribe," Wise with Herbs shouted. "Come forth and be presented to the staff of the People of the Trees."

Old Mother of Salt Tribe stood and walked to her. She took the small blade and pricked her finger. She touched her blood to the staff, but it did not move. Her mouth tight with disappointment, she walked on. Old Mother of Works Flint Tribe was next. Again, the staff did not move. The blood of each of the Old Mothers around her fire were rejected by the staff, and they moved off to the side, waiting and bearing witness.

Each member of the next generation, according to rank and according to how many daughters they had given to the People, came next, the blade and the staff growing slick with the blood of the women. And the staff did not move.

The next generation came. And the next.

Woman after woman among the Women of the Womb who suckled young came, their blood on the staff until it was sticky. The blood of the People trickled and ran across the back of her hand where Old Mother of Winters Trees gripped her staff.

And Old Mother of Winter Trees despaired. Her staff accepted no one. Which meant the trees accepted no one. And the Moon was near to setting, only a quarter of the orb still above the horizon.

In desperation, Old Mother of Winter Trees called for the women who had not yet chosen a man, those old enough to have experienced their Moon-Blood, but too young to have mated. One by one, many hands of unmated women passed by her. And the staff remained still. Silence fell upon the land. In all the oral tales, this had never happened. Except for once. So long ago. In the most ancient oral tales. And then Old Mother understood.

Softly, she said, "In the oldest tales, when the People of the Trees were still searching for the westernmost lands, there was change. The Staff chose a special woman. One who had been… warrior and hunter and birther. A woman who had lived as both. The women of the Hunters will pass by now, all those who still experience Moon-Blood."

"No." Old Mother of the Eastern Sea Tribe said, her face creased with worry and fear. "We have been here, on our island, for many and many tens of years. The Hunter women have made their oaths to the Earth. They will not carry young unless they become oath breakers, and such a one may not become the Old Mother of the People of the Trees. Their oaths prevent this."

"Our ways are changing," Old Mother of Winter Trees murmured. "Death of the trees is upon us. Perhaps the Staff of my Tree is telling us that the Hunter women and the Women of the Womb must be in harmony."

There was murmuring and much discontent. As they talked, Old Mother of Winter Trees bowed her head. One of her women gave her warm bone broth and then wiped bear fat on her lips where the cold had chapped the flesh. The tribes' Old Mothers' argument subsided and they fell silent. Fortified, Old Mother of Winter Trees said, "Let each of the Hunter women bleed upon the staff. The staff will decide. And if new oaths are to be taken, we will consult the oldest stories to tell us the way forward. But we must hurry. The Moon is almost gone."

The Old Mothers of the tribes faced her and Old Mother of Salt Tribe said, "Let it be as you have said."

Uncertain, apprehensive, the Hunter women crossed from the Hunter's side of the hill to the Womb side and gathered in a line. They were agitated, but it was an internal distress, clear on their faces and in the set of their shoulders, leaving them silent and still, as only Hunters can be. One by one, they pricked their fingers with their own blades, and added their blood to the staff. Her own daughter was first among them, leading the way, as she had always done. Warrior Woman of Blood and Battle was not chosen. Woman Who Left Her Children to Make War was not chosen. Woman after woman followed, and the staff still did not move.

But… as the hard edge of Cold Wolf Howls Moon slipped behind the horizon, a woman limped to the staff. Her left knee was stiff and swollen beneath the hides that covered her. Her hair of vines and leaves was woven with the white feathers of mourning. Her belly was bare and marked with the wrinkles of childbirth, her breasts long and hanging from suckling children. Her hands and her face were etched with lines grooved into the chalk that marked the Ceremony of Change of Status. She was not young, but was not old. Her face wore grief and wisdom and hard-won peace. And round her waist she wore the garment for Moon-Blood. She was still fertile. This woman spanned all the women who now lived and who were to come.

She pricked her finger. Touched it to the staff.

The staff *moved*. It slammed into her hand, ripping itself from the hand of Old Mother of Winter Trees. The full moon dipped below the horizon in a final flash of silver light.

All that witnessed the Choosing of the Staff drew shocked breaths.

When the sound quieted, Old Mother of Winter Trees said, "You wear the Moon-Blood garment. And you wear the white of change and grief. Tell your story."

"I was Blossom of the Crocus. I bore two daughters with my mate, Kills the Great Seal. He died of a fever and I gave my daughters to my sister to raise and turned from the life of the Womb to the life of the Hunt."

Shouts came from down the hill to speak louder. The woman shook her head. She had no great voice. Wise with Herbs shouted her words to the dawn winds, sharing her story.

The woman continued. "I became She Who Loves the Moon. For two hands of years, I hunted with my new partner, Moon Hunter, at my side.

She died in the hunt at the last gather, when the great boar attacked her and tore her open. Her life blood was sacrificed to the land and all my soul bled onto the ground with her. And she died."

The new Old Mother of the Womb raised her head, tears leaving trails in the chalk on her face, carving through the hematite like trails of blood. "I killed the boar with my own spear. As it died, it gored my leg and the wounds are now forever with me—the wound of my heart and the wound of my leg and the end of my time as Hunter. I may not Hunt…" She took a breath that shuddered with tears. "The Hunters tell of the Hunt of the Great Boar and the Death of Moon Hunter. It is a great tale of valor and blood.

"Now I am nameless." She raised her face to the moonless sky and howled, "I can no longer hunt. I do not desire to lie with another and birth more daughters." She looked at the staff in her hand, bloody and sticky with the blood of all the tribes. Her face drew down hard as the import steeped into her. "My Ceremony of Change showed no new path. But tonight I understand. My path is the path of war. My previous oaths no longer bind me."

"The staff has chosen you," the former Old Mother of Winter Trees said. "You will carry me to my tree and place me there among the roots. You will bury my staff in the outermost parts of the Womb Passage. Each morning after I am beneath my tree, you will walk among the trees. The trees will give a staff to you. The tree that speaks its gift will be your tree from that day forward. Upon that day, you will enter the Passage of the Womb Circle and take your place there. You will lead the People of the Trees."

"She will lead the People of the Trees," the Women of the Womb murmured.

"What will your name be?" Old Mother asked.

"I will be Old Mother of the Blood Women and the Blood of War."

"It is a name fitting to your story. Take my staff now. Bury it at the opening, so that it is the first staff seen when any enter the most sacred place. Then carry me to my tree, for I am old and worn and my heart beats its last. My tree calls me." She fell to her knees. Her breath was short and harsh. She coughed and blood came once more to her lips.

Old Mother of Blood and Change turned to the women who served. "Take me to the Passage."

Silent, grieving, the three of them led the way to the opening of the Passage. The sounds of digging and grunting followed. No one among the gathered moved. No one spoke. All waited.

Old Mother, once called Old Mother of Winter Trees, coughed and gagged and spilled her blood upon the earth. Leaves unfurled in her hair, rustled, took on the brightness of autumn, wrinkled, went brown, and fell upon the ground.

When dawn was bright, the sky lit with the rising sun, Old Mother of the Blood Women and the Blood of War approached her. "I will take you to your tree." She held out her hand. Old Mother of Winter Trees placed her cold hand into the warm palm of her successor. The women who served removed all her furs. Pulled all her hides away, leaving her bony, frail body exposed to the icy wind. She shivered hard and then that passed and she breathed out.

The rising sun was a misty haze as the Women of the Womb Circle lifted her in their hands and carried her away from the hill, into the forest, following her whispered directions until the bare branches of her tree appeared. It was a massive tree, ancient and wise.

"Clear away the snow just there," she whispered, pointing. "And place me among the roots. Then stand back and bear witness."

The women who served moved quickly and broke the snow with small axes and hand knives. The roots were exposed, close by the trunk of the tree. They placed Old Mother among the roots, naked, wearing only her jewelry and her small bag. She pulled it from her neck and placed in the hands of Old Mother of the Blood Women and the Blood of War. "The blade is within. The treasures of faraway lands are within. Listen to the old stories, learn their wisdom. Remember my last vision."

Old Mother of Winter Trees pulled away and curled into a ball, like a babe in the womb. Vines pushed through the ground and twined around her, twisting up her legs and arms, tightening. Shoving inside her. There was no pain. Old Mother of Winter Trees looked up and saw the winter sun bright through the bare branches. It was golden and lovely. And it was not the end. It was only the beginning.

Old Mother of the Blood Women and the Blood of War watched as the hawthorn tree pulled the frail body inside itself, and took her home. Hours passed as the transformation took place, as the truth of the name she had chosen long ago proved itself true. The shape of Old Mother of Winter Trees was still visible, woody and covered with bark.

Old Mother of the Blood Women and the Blood of War turned and walked back through the forest, the Women Who Served behind her. As she walked, a great crack sounded from the oak above them. The old oak spoke. "I am your tree." It dropped a branch. It fell and landed at the feet of Old Mother of the Blood Women and the Blood of War. No one moved. No one spoke.

Old Mother of Blood and Change bent and picked up the staff. "This is my staff. This is my tree. I will lead the People of the Trees forward into time."

The End

We hope that you enjoyed this title and look forward to many more to come. Please, leave us a review! Reviews matter to all of our authors.

And don't forget to check out the latest edition of *Car Wars*

http://www.sjgames.com/car-wars/

Or the other amazing titles from
Steve Jackson Games

http://www.sjgames.com

…or the latest in the Car Warriors: Autoduel Chronicle fiction series.
https://threeravenspublishing.com/car-warriors-autoduel-chronicles/

Take a look at some of our other award-winning series at
https://threeravenspublishing.com/series-universes/

Visit us at https://www.threeravenspublishing.com and sign up for our
newsletter for the latest and greatest news on upcoming titles and events.

Other series and titles you might enjoy.

DECLAN FINN
DECLAN FINN
DECLAN FINN
DECLAN FINN
Demons are Forever
Honor at Stake
Live and Let Bite
Good to the Last Drop
The Dragon Award Nominated Series
FREE on Kindle Unlimited!

AVAILABLE ON
AMAZON
JOINT TASK FORCE
13
HOLDING THE LINE
BETWEEN HEAVEN AND HELL

MYSTERY, MAGIC & MAYHEM
WITH A TWIST OF ROMANCE
J.F. POSTHUMUS
ON AMAZON
FIND ME
B.E.N.T.
BIOLOGIC   ENHANCED   NASCENT   TALENT

THE RAVEN AND THE CROW
MICHAEL K. FALCIANI
FIND ME
ON AMAZON

STARFLIGHT

IT CAME FROM THE
TRAILER PARK

Three Ravens Publishing
Are you looking for fun, new fiction?
The Written Word Will Never Be The Same…
https://www.threeravenspublishing.com
Veteran Owned and Operated

You can also keep up to date with our latest release announcements on Scifi.radio and get some of the best fandom programing on the planet.

Scifi for your Wifi

And don't forget to check out our other Sponsors and Affiliates

A southern Appalachian jewel for craft beer lovers, Buck Bald Brewing offers something for everyone. With delicious, locally brewed beverages from across the spectrum, Buck Bald Brewing offers craft brews that are consistently amazing.

From the dark and smooth Shesquatch Scottish ale, to the intense hops of Hippibilly IPA, to the puckering sour of the blackberry and cinnamon in Berry My Heart at the Trailer Park, and more than 60+ rotating brews, you'll find what you're looking for and more.

With smiling faces behind the bar ready to help you find your next favorite brew, a constantly rotating selection of delicious craft beverages, toe-tapping tunes always playing, and the biggest games on TV, you can kick your feet up in either Copperhill, Tennessee or Murphy, North Carolina and immerse yourself in the Buck Bald Brewing experience. So, come out, fill a pint, fill a growler, and fill your mind at your new favorite family-owned craft brewery.

To discover more visit us at buckbaldbrewing.com or follow us on Facebook @buckbaldbrewing and @buckbaldbrewingmurphy.

Vesper Wren's
TRAILER PARK
PIXIE
PUNCH
· A PEACH STRAWBERRY SELTZER ·
BUCK BALD BREWING

BRAXTON
HICKS
MIDNIGHT MOCHA MILK
STOUT
BUCK BALD BREWING